Lewis W. Cave.

38

December 1950

THE SHADOW

&

THE PEAK

By the Author of
THE WIND CANNOT READ

RICHARD MASON

THE SHADOW
&
THE PEAK

THE BOOK CLUB
121 CHARING CROSS ROAD
LONDON, W.C.2

First Printed . . *September* 1949

PRINTED IN GREAT BRITAIN FOR
THE BOOK CLUB BY ARRANGEMENT
WITH HODDER AND STOUGHTON
LTD., LONDON, BY MORRISON & GIBB
LTD., EDINBURGH.

For
FELICITY

AUTHOR'S NOTE

THE site of the school in this book could be roughly identified; but Jamaicans will need no reassurance that the school itself does not exist—not at any rate in Jamaica. I have not heard of any "progressive" boarding-school on the island, nor of any attempt to start one, although there is a day-school in Kingston which is particularly notable for the advanced outlook of its headmaster—a young Jamaica-born Rhodes Scholar of great sensibility and imagination. I am happy to say that, unlike my fictitious school, it has had a splendid success.

R. M.

CHAPTER ONE

You could always count on some exciting distraction during a class in the open air, and on Monday afternoon there was the crash. Until then nothing untoward had occurred —nothing untoward for a school that called itself progressive. There had been no tropical insects causing exaggerated screams of alarm, no open rebellion from Silvia, not even a new ship sailing round the end of the reef four thousand feet below—nothing until five minutes to four when the air-liner came into sight, drifting listlessly up the valley in the fierce Jamaican sun.

"Mr. Lockwood—look!"

Douglas was sitting with his back against the trunk of a juniper, reading a book to them. During the last class in the afternoon it was useless trying to do anything but play games or read : half the children were asleep, the other half wondering how to spend their free time after the bell went at four. He was used to interruptions, although aircraft generally went by unnoticed. They came over a dozen times a day, British and Dutch and American, flying up from the airport on the reef and heading north across the Blue Mountains to Nassau and Miami and Camaguey in Cuba. You could set your watch by them.

He laid the book on his knee and said :

"Sit down, Alan. I want to finish this chapter. I'm getting quite interested, even if you aren't."

"You must look at this aircraft—there's something wrong with it."

He had paid no attention to the aircraft while he was reading, but now he heard the uneven note of the engines. They were spluttering and shutting off and spluttering into life again. He closed the book.

"We'll go on with this tomorrow."

All the children were standing up. There were six in the class, four girls and two boys.

"Quick, Mr. Lockwood!"

He rose to his feet. They were out on the grass slope just below the Great House, which stood by itself, massive and grey, on the outer ridge of the Blue Mountains. On one side of them, far below, a thin line of surf like an edging of lace divided the rocky coast from the sea. On the other side, across a deep jungle-choked valley, rose the precipitous wall of another ridge.

"I can't see anything," Douglas said.

"Look there! You must be blind!" The boy was jumping up and down with excitement. Then he exclaimed all at once: "It's on fire!"

A moment later Douglas caught sight of it, lower than he had expected, drifting up the valley below them, close to the steep wall of the ridge. It was a huge machine with four engines. From the inside engine on the near wing a short flame fluttered stiffly backwards like a flag.

"It's the Bahamas plane," one of the boys said.

"It isn't," a girl said. "It's the one that takes off at a quarter to four. It goes to Cuba."

"It goes to the Bahamas after that."

"No it doesn't; it goes to Florida."

Douglas said, "What a time to start quarrelling!"

"We're not quarrelling. I know it's the Bahamas plane." This was Alan—Alan always knew everything.

A mile beyond the Great House the ridge fell gradually to a saddle, and then rose again in a broad shoulder to join the higher mountains. The air-liner was nosing round the contours of the mountainside, trying to gain height. If it passed over the saddle it could probably glide back to the airport or come down in the sea. The fire was still isolated to one engine, and it looked for a minute as if it might succeed.

Rosemary said in a small frightened voice, "Couldn't they jump out with parachutes, Mr. Lockwood?" She had turned white. She was a nervous child, who always went into a trance of speechless terror during thunderstorms.

"I don't think they carry parachutes in civil air-liners."

"They'd be too low to use them, anyhow." This was Alan again.

One of the girls said, with intense interest, "I wonder if all the people on board know they might be killed at any minute."

"They probably won't be killed," Alan said. "They'll probably get over the saddle all right." He was afraid he might have sounded disappointed, and added, "I hope so, at any rate."

A moment later the air-liner went out of sight behind

8

the curve of the slope. The two boys bolted off at once, without asking permission, but one of the girls said :

"Is it all right to go, Mr. Lockwood?"

"Yes, if you want."

"I'm not going," Rosemary said. "I shall wait here." She was trembling. One of the other girls, Silvia, had sat down again and opened a book, pretending to take no interest. She was sulking.

"I'll wave to you if it gets over safely," Douglas told Rosemary.

He followed the others slowly up the grass slope. He could still hear the engines of the air-liner, more distant now, choking fitfully. Two months ago he had come out from England in an air-liner of the same type; and he remembered thinking, in one moment of anguished depression on the journey, that he would have welcomed the quick extinction of a crash. Now, listening to the failing engines, he knew he wouldn't have welcomed it at all. . . .

All at once he heard the explosion. It was a long boom that resounded in the valley like a distant bomb.

He paused for a moment, and then hurried forward. The children were standing at the top of the slope, quite motionless, looking along the ridge. As he reached them the saddle came into view, a little over a mile away. Flames were springing briskly out of the jungle just below it. The breeze blowing from the Caribbean carried the smoke over the valley and across the face of Blue Mountain Peak.

They all stood watching in silence. Then a bell began to jangle unevenly in the Great House. It was four o'clock.

It wasn't until after Joe had found the tail of the aircraft that the disaster became real. At first Douglas had stood there, in the blackened circle of jungle, feeling guilty that he wasn't more upset : that he should have found time to wonder, amongst the scattered and smouldering debris, if his own mail for England had been on board. His last letter to Caroline. . . .

It had taken him nearly an hour to reach the wreckage, hacking his way through the undergrowth. He had brought along a first-aid kit and a couple of stretchers, but his lingering hopes that they might be needed had vanished at once. The exploding petrol tanks had blown the machine to bits. There was nothing left to recognize except the engines. By that time the flames had died down and the smoke was rising quietly from amongst the charred and broken tree-trunks and the shrivelled leaves. He had the sense that the crash had occurred years ago : the sense of arriving at a dead city.

Three or four Negro peasants, who had arrived before him, were poking about with sticks, walking on bare feet over the hot white ashes. They had made a pile of objects that had somehow escaped complete destruction : a small charred suitcase, a cup, a portable typewriter, the remnants of a mackintosh. They had also dragged out one body—the body of a woman. The fire had scorched off her hair and most of her clothing and blackened her skin. She looked like a Negress. Only one leg had been untouched by the flames. It was still perfectly white.

After a time Douglas had found another body under a twisted mass of pipes and wires. There was no point in trying to drag it out. Then he saw a shrivelled, dismembered, surrealistic hand. Nothing else. He had retired from the heat again, wiping the greasy perspiration from his face with the sleeve of his shirt. Already the sense of reality had left him. The hand wasn't real, and nor was the woman with the stark white leg. He couldn't really grasp that two hours ago this wreckage had been an intricate assemblage of ten thousand delicately fashioned parts, an infinitely complex and beautiful monster shining silver in the sun. He was in the midst of death, and yet couldn't feel it—couldn't feel that around him lay the ashes of thirty men and women who had climbed into the aircraft with handbags and novels and brief-cases, thirty separate minds, each with its own structure of memories and hopes. Now the ten thousand polished parts and the memories and hopes lay in this charred and smouldering confusion, and he stood there wondering about his letter to Caroline. . . . If only there had been something he could have done—someone he could have saved.

Just then he heard Joe shouting.

"You come now, please, sir. I done find something."

Joe was the school handyman and chauffeur, who had accompanied Douglas to the crash. Now he was standing over on the other side of the wreckage grinning with excitement. Douglas went round to him.

"I done find something, Mr. Lockwood, sir."

He led the way into the jungle. Twenty or thirty yards

through the undergrowth they suddenly came upon the whole tail section of the aircraft. The tail-plane and fin were caught in the branches of a tree, and the fuselage rested vertically on the ground. The windows weren't even cracked.

Joe was down on his haunches by the lowest window. "Listen here now, please, sir."

Douglas went down beside him. It was too dark inside to see through the window, but when he put his ear against it he could hear someone moaning.

Joe grinned. He was a strong, well-built Negro of twenty-five.

"Please, him no duppy, sir." Duppies were spirits of the dead. Most coloured people were scared of them, but not Joe.

Douglas knocked on the glass and called out, but the moaning continued in the same dull way. He told Joe to fetch the stretchers and call the peasants. Then he walked round the upturned fuselage, looking for the best place to break in. It was impossible to climb in from underneath because the broken jagged edges had crumpled against the ground. The windows were too small to climb through. The only way was to break a panel of the fuselage. He started hacking at the aluminium with Joe's machete, close to the spot where he had heard the moaning. The aluminium was strengthened by metal ribs, and it took him ten minutes to open up a hole large enough for his head and shoulders. He looked through and saw that it was the toilet. At this angle the seat looked as if it was sticking out of one of the walls. A man was lying crumpled in the corner below, still moaning faintly. His face was badly cut and bleeding, and there was blood all over his white tropical suit.

Douglas crawled into the compartment, straightened the man's limbs, and began to manœuvre him out through the hole. Joe and the others took hold of him and laid him on the ground. The door of the compartment was buckled and jammed, so Douglas climbed out of the hole again. He told Joe to make a second hole round the other side of the fuselage. Then he had a look at the man on the ground. He was about fifty. He had stopped moaning, and was now breathing rather stertorously. His pulse was thin but steady. There was one nasty gash on his cheek, but otherwise the cuts were clean and superficial. Douglas wiped them over with disinfectant from the first-aid kit and bandaged him up. By that time Joe had finished making his hole, and was already inside the fuselage. As Douglas went round to climb in, he heard his muffled voice from inside :

"I done find somebody else, sir."

"Alive?"

"I don't know as yet, sir." There was silence for a moment, and then he said, "She got breath all right, sir."

Douglas crawled through the jagged hole in the aluminium. There wasn't much light inside, and with the fuselage at this cockeyed angle it took him a moment or two to get his bearings. Then he realized that he was on his hands and knees on the partition that divided the rear and central compartments of the aircraft. The door of the partition was hanging open beneath him, with the ground a few feet below. There was a heap of stuff about the place : broken crockery, cardboard trays, thermos bottles, cutlery, packets of biscuits, sandwiches, and all the other contents of the canteen. Joe had climbed up somewhere above. Douglas followed him, finding footholds in the cupboards of the galley. Above the cupboards there was a recess, forming a broad level shelf, on which Joe was crouching. The body he had discovered had been flung into a contorted position in the corner. It was a girl of about twenty-five. He saw by her white uniform skirt and blouse that she was a stewardess. The red swallow symbol of the air-line was stitched on her shoulders. Her face was a dead white, giving her red lips the incongruous look of lips painted for a joke on a marble statue.

Joe said, grinning, "She pretty for true, Mr. Lockwood, sir."

"That won't help her much unless we can bring her round," Douglas said. "And, anyhow, don't forget you're a married man."

"You marry too, please, sir?"

Douglas began to straighten out the girl's arms, which were twisted under her body.

"I used to be married," he said.

The trek back to the school just about finished him. He had sent Joe on ahead with a message to fetch the doctor up to the Great House, in case nobody had thought of doing so in anticipation. Two of the peasants were carrying the man on the stretcher, and the third was helping Douglas with the girl. The other peasant had mumbled some objection to coming along, and Douglas hadn't stopped to argue. Probably he had his eye on the few bits of loot from the wreckage.

After the first few hundred yards they lost the track that Douglas and Joe had made on the way down. They had to hack a new path through the undergrowth. Every time they stopped to use the machete, it was necessary to lay down the stretchers. They changed direction several times, trying to hit the path that ran somewhere near the top of the ridge. Even the peasants, the direct descendants of tough slave stock, began to weary perceptibly. Douglas's hands were breaking out in blisters. The dull pain in his back sharpened to agony. Presently he told himself that if they didn't hit the path in the next five minutes, he would leave the men with the stretchers and go ahead for reinforcements. When five minutes had expired, he gave himself another three. Then he added a further two to make a total of ten. He then thought he could see the line of the path through the trees, so he kept on. He was surprised to find it really was the path. As they broke through to it, Joe appeared with a party of three men who had come up from the air-port. One of them was a pilot. He said :

"I say, by Jove, it's honestly marvellous of you chaps to have organized all this. I hear it's almost a complete burn-out."

"Except for the tail," Douglas said. "It looked as if it had been amputated with a razor-blade."

"They do that. I saw one like it in the war. They're converted bombers, you know."

"They'd better stop converting them if this is what happens."

"Too true they ought." He was looking at the girl. "She's only been with us three weeks. I forget her name. She's a gay kid." He suddenly gave a queer laugh. "There were two of them on board. I didn't know which one it was when this chap told me you'd rescued a stewardess. I was engaged to the other one."

Douglas forgot about the pain in his back.

"I'm awfully sorry," he said.

The pilot turned away. "That's all right. I'd better get on down and have a look at it."

Douglas said, "I don't think it's worth your while. Couldn't you leave it until tomorrow?"

"Better not. You don't mind your chap showing us the way, do you?"

"Of course not." They all went off. Douglas followed the path with the stretchers. After a while he had to call a halt for another rest. He gave the men cigarettes and lit one for himself, and sat down on the bank. Neither the man nor the girl had regained consciousness, although the girl had moved her hands and spoken a few incomprehensible words in a sleep-talking sort of way. She had received quite a nasty knock on the back of her head and was a mass of bruises, but otherwise there wasn't much wrong with her. He wondered whether she'd retreated to the back of the aircraft out of wisdom, or whether it was one of those absurd little chances that afterwards take on such portentous significance, like the unaccustomed pause at a shop window that causes someone to miss an ill-starred train.

He was just finishing his cigarette and thinking they'd soon have to move on again when he noticed the girl open her eyes. She looked at him in sleepy bewilderment, and then closed them again.

"I know it sounds crazy," she said presently in a drugged kind of voice, "but I can't remember where I am."

"You're in Jamaica," he said. "You were in a smash. You're all right now, though."

There was no change in her expression, and he thought she must have passed out again. But after a while she said in the same slurred, drugged way:

"It was just after we'd taken off. The engines were cutting. I thought we'd all be killed."

"You were lucky," he said. "It was a miracle."

"My life must be charmed," she said. "That's the second time."

"Your second accident?"

She opened her eyes and looked at him.

"Oh no," she said. She saw he was smoking. "Can I have a cigarette?"

He felt for his packet. The girl smiled faintly and said, "I tried to commit suicide last time. In Mexico. I messed it up."

He supposed she was talking nonsense. She was still only semi-conscious. He put down his own cigarette, and took

14

another from the packet and lit it for her. As he held it out, he saw that her eyes had shut again.

"Do you want it?" he said.

She didn't answer. She was breathing heavily. She was probably dreaming that she'd hit herself on the back of the head with an axe. Joe was right, she was pretty. She also had nice legs. He put the cigarette back between his lips and trod out the old one. Then he signalled to the men. They started off on the last lap with the stretchers. He felt about to collapse at any moment with the weight. Then he pretended to himself that the stretcher was really on pneumatic wheels and he was only pushing it along. It was a silly idea, but it seemed to help quite a lot.

CHAPTER TWO

"Yes, please, Mr. Lockwood."

He opened his eyes and saw Ivy's chubby black knees beneath the hem of her apron. She was giggling. She always giggled when she spoke, and the giggles suited her fat, comfortable little face.

"Yes, please, Mr. Lockwood." She went on repeating this until she was sure he was awake. She was holding a cup of tea.

He told her to put the cup down on the bedside table. "And leave the door open as you go out," he said. It was necessary to give these precise instructions daily.

She went off, quivering with merriment. He pulled his hands from under the bedclothes. The blisters were not so bad as he'd expected, and he could even close his fingers over his palms without much pain. He hoisted himself on to his elbow. Ivy had knocked over the elephant with the cup of tea. He stood it up again with the trunk pointing towards the window, and then began to sip his tea, gazing through the door at the view.

The door opened directly on to the verandah. Without moving from his bed he could see practically the whole of Kingston and the harbour four thousand feet below. At this time of the morning there were usually shreds of mist still hanging over the town, although they were rapidly disappearing in the heat of the sun. Every day at twenty past seven an aircraft from Curaçao came into sight, crawling across the sky like a tiny silver insect. He used to watch it lose height and come in to land on the Palisadoes. The airport was at the elbow of the reef, which stretched a seven-mile arm across the harbour. He would make himself get out of bed the moment the aircraft came to a standstill in front of a hangar. This morning it was on time. It was evidently no more upset by last night's crash than a fly by the death of another fly on an adjacent window-pane.

Before it touched down the view was obscured by John, who came running up the verandah steps. John was nine and the darkest pupil in the school. He looked completely negroid, although he was of mixed blood. He flung himself on to the bed and started pounding Douglas, shouting with laughter, "Why aren't you up, Mr. Lockwood?"

Douglas said, "Go away, you little brute!"

"Why?"

"I'm not in a condition for that sort of thing this morning." John went on pounding, so he said, "How long can you keep that up without getting tired?"

"For ever if I want, but I don't want." He stopped and sat on the side of the bed. "Mrs. Morgan won't let us go in and see the two people you rescued—but they're still all right. I wish I'd gone with you to the smash. How many people were killed?" He was excited, but he evidently didn't think of the deaths as a tragedy.

"I don't know," Douglas said.

"Were the bodies all messed up?"

"They weren't very pleasant. Now go away, because I've got to get up."

"What were they like?"

"It doesn't matter now, does it?" Douglas said.

"Did you see the pilot's body?"

"I don't know."

"Robin says he wouldn't be a pilot now he's seen a crash. I wouldn't mind, though. I wouldn't mind getting killed like that. It'd be much better than drowning. I'd hate to drown."

"Run away before I drown you in my bath."

"I bet you wouldn't do that, even if I stayed."

"I'd do something just as horrid."

"What?"

Douglas pushed him off the bed with his knees.

"Go on, run off," he said.

"All right. I've got time to go down to my tree-house before breakfast. Do you know what Mr. Morgan's given me?"

"No."

"A rope." His brown eyes shone. He had forgotten the crash. He had been craving for a rope as later he might crave for a white skin or a woman. "I'm going to hang it from the trap-door, so that I can pull it up when I'm inside, and only let it down for people I want to come up. I shan't let it down for Silvia."

"Why not?"

John grinned. "Because she's a bitch."

"What sort of language is that?"

"I thought we could use any sort of language we liked here."

"I shouldn't let Silvia hear you, or you'll get a black eye. Now you'd better hurry if you're going to your tree-house. And don't gorge too many mangoes in your solitude up there."

"They don't do me any harm, anyhow."

He bolted off, and Douglas got up. After he had shaved and dressed he walked up towards the Great House. His bungalow had once been some sort of servant's cottage and was surrounded by undergrowth, but just above it he came out on the grass slope dotted with junipers. The junipers were festooned with Old Man's Beard, a fungus which was supposed to be slowly destroying them, but which gave them the enchanting appearance of tinselled Christmas trees. The Great House stood at the top of the slope. It was a massive grey building, only saved from being hideous by its magnificence and maturity, and by the flowering creepers that broke the starkness of its stones. The stones still carried memories of the perspiring Negro slaves who had lifted them into position. Douglas went through the long, panelled hall into the dining-room. Most of the twenty-five children were still at breakfast, sitting at small tables in groups of four or five. It was the custom for the staff to sit with them at lunch but to take breakfast at a table of their own. The staff table was now empty except for Duffield.

Duffield wished Douglas quite a cheerful good morning.

"Must have been a sweat, carrying those stretchers yesterday," he said. He spoke with a Lancashire accent. He was a small man of about forty. His face gave the impression of hardness because of his rather starved-looking cheeks and the tightness of the skin over his cheek-bones. His sandy hair was closely cropped. If any duty caused him to miss the barber's weekly visit, he became touchy and disagreeable for the next seven days.

"I'd have come along to give you a hand," he said. "Only I didn't think there was a blighted chance of any survivors."

"It was a chance in a million," Douglas said.

"What's going to happen to that pair upstairs?"

"They'll probably go down to the hospital when they're fit enough for the journey."

"I hope that's soon," Duffield said. "It'll upset the children having them here. They're still excited about the crash. Ruddy noise they've been making this morning. We're going to have a job getting any work out of them today."

"Isn't it your day off?"

Duffield shook his head. "Nothing I want to go down to Kingston for. I don't know what you see in the place. It's a sweat getting down, and there's ruddy-all to do when you're there."

"Except sit in the Carib Cinema and keep cool."

"If you're interested in pictures, that is."

Duffield hadn't been down to Kingston once in the six weeks that Douglas had been at the school. Occasionally he admitted that the place held no attraction for him, but more often he would imply that he was only prevented from going down because his presence at the school was indispensable. This was nonsense, but he had come to believe it himself, and never made use of his days off.

They ate in silence for a bit, and then Duffield said :

"I hear the latest idea's to send up ice-cream every day for the children who've misbehaved—and twice on Sundays."

Douglas recognized this as a joke, not a statement of fact. When Duffield was in a good humour he always made jokes commencing with "I hear that . . ." followed by some improbable fact. They usually reflected his views on Pawley's so-called progressive education.

"I wouldn't mind them having it sent up for us," Douglas said lightly. He had learnt to avoid being drawn into an argument with Duffield.

"Catch them doing that."

At this point Mr. and Mrs. Morgan came into the dining-room. Duffield pretended not to notice them. There had been a feud going on between himself and the Morgans for over a month. It had been started by a remark of Duffield's, in which he was alleged to have spoken of Morgan as a nigger in front of the children. Duffield now liked the Morgans to think that he simply ignored them, and that their presence made no other difference to his movements or behaviour. He had been ready to leave the table, but he now remained in his seat in case the Morgans should think he was leaving because of their arrival.

The Morgans came across the room as if they hadn't noticed Duffield, said good morning to Douglas and sat down side by side. Morgan was about Duffield's height, but swarthier and looking better fed. His African blood might have passed unnoticed, at any rate outside Jamaica, except for his tiny black curls which resembled a rather moth-eaten wig of astrakhan. He taught geography and physical training, but his chief function was running the school farm. The farm covered a few acres on the side of the hill. Practically every crop known to the Jamaican cultivator was grown there, including pineapples, grapefruit, oranges (sweet and sour), limes, papaya, coffee, and about fifty different sorts of vegetables. The only important absentees were sugar and coconuts—there was not enough water for sugar, and coconut-palms wouldn't yield at an altitude of more than five hundred feet. The farm was the school's favourite show-piece but one of its least popular pursuits. As farm-work was voluntary Morgan had only managed to persuade two boys and one girl to help him. His energetic propaganda for more recruits was counteracted by Duffield, who assiduously discouraged any inclination towards farming that came to his notice.

Morgan knew a great deal about agricultural science, and could talk about it inexhaustibly. He had told Douglas the history of Panama Disease at least three times, giving detailed statistics of its devastations to the banana industry. He could also talk inexhaustibly about matters with which he was less well acquainted. If other listeners wearied and disappeared he was happy to carry on talking to his wife. Mrs. Morgan also had a dash of African blood. She was said to be thirty-two, but she looked about forty-five, with a red pock-marked face and an amiable soul hidden in rolls of fat. She thought her husband was a brilliant man who

19

ought to be in politics, and was an excellent wife to him, although her fondness for rum bothered and often humiliated him. He had instituted some system of rationing, but her appearance sometimes gave grounds for suspicion that she had found an even more efficient system for circumventing it. Morgan himself was strictly and evangelically teetotal.

"As I was saying," Duffield said across the table to Douglas, "I can't afford to take my day off today. Too much to do. If you ask me, it's about time Pawley got some more staff. We're carrying too much weight on our shoulders." The "we" gratuitously included Douglas but not the Morgans, who were presumably part of the weight. He wiped his mouth on his napkin a second time, and said, "Well, I reckon I'll be getting along. I've a special maths class first thing." He left the table and went out.

Douglas asked Mrs. Morgan about the two survivors of the crash.

"It's a real wonder," Mrs. Morgan said in her Jamaican-Welsh accent. "It really is. You'd never know what they've been through. It's all I can do to keep the girl in bed. I'll be glad when the doctor comes up again this morning and talks some sense into her."

"The human body's an amazing thing," Morgan said didactically. "I'm sorry I wasn't with you yesterday, Lockwood. I'd have liked to study the effects of the crash, and write up a few notes for the *Gleaner*. But I didn't know anything about it—I must have been in one of the farm sheds at the time."

"There weren't many effects left to study," Douglas said.

"I wish I'd been there, all the same. I'd go over and see it this morning, but the *Gleaner* will probably be sending up its own reporters."

"I'm sure they'd be glad of anything you sent them, too," Mrs. Morgan said. "You know how highly the editor thinks of you. He told me it was a pity you weren't a journalist yourself."

"I might send them a letter," Morgan said. "I shan't write an article, though. I don't want to profit out of a tragic event like that."

"After all, it wasn't your fault."

"That isn't the point," Morgan said impatiently. "You understand what I mean, don't you, Lockwood? I'm only interested in making an analysis of what happened. There may be some important conclusions to be drawn. I don't know whether it's struck you, but all the previous crashes in Jamaica have occurred within a few minutes of take-off. . . ." He went on to list all the other crashes in Jamaica since the first airfield had been built in nineteen something or other. Douglas couldn't be bothered to point out that in view of Jamaica's inconsiderable size, an aircraft that didn't crash in the first few minutes wouldn't crash on the island at all. Morgan's ponderous analyses drove him to exasperated boredom. Shortly he rose from his chair. Morgan went on talking to him, so that out of politeness he had to stand listening for another minute. Then he made his escape, leaving Mrs. Morgan to be enlightened alone by her husband's catalogue of all possible disasters by which an aircraft might be overtaken in flight.

The Great House had only been a school for two years. It had been built at the end of the eighteenth century, and according to tradition, which there was no reason to doubt, Nelson himself had often sat in the garden, as a guest of the house, enjoying an aerial view of his fleet in the harbour and receiving signals, with the help of a powerful telescope, from the commanders of his vessels. At that time the building had been the Great House of a wealthy coffee estate, the home of slave-owning Englishmen. The property had prospered for more than another century, until after the First World War. Then the business had fallen into a decline, the factory had been given up, and the English family had departed. The building had later been run as a guest-house, but no roads came within two or three miles and it had been necessary for the guests to ride up on horses and mules. By that time most people who could afford holidays preferred to stay at places where they could run their motor-cars right up to the front door. After a few years the guest-house had been abandoned, and throughout the Second World War the house had stood empty except for an old Negro caretaker who had lived in the kitchen. Then Pawley and his wife had taken it for their school. They had bought it for a song, but it had cost them a great deal of money to extend the road. The money had been inherited from Mrs. Pawley's father, who had made it in sugar, and didn't seem to matter to them very much except where salaries were concerned, and they were still running the school at a loss. Sometimes Douglas felt that if they were to run it at a profit, Pawley would lose a great deal of satisfaction. There would no longer be the same tangible proof of his selfless love of children.

Pawley called the school progressive, but the progressiveness had only been dispensed in a timid half-measure. As a teacher, you never quite knew where you stood—at what point your gentle guiding hand should become the stern iron hand of authority. Probably Pawley didn't know either—but to do him justice he hadn't much chance of running anything really progressive with the sort of teachers he had to make do with. He had engaged Douglas, and evidently been glad to do so, not only without a personal interview, but knowing that he had never tried to teach a child in his life. The only other applicant for the position, according to the scholastic agency in London, had been a neat little man with a carnation in his buttonhole whose last employer, the headmaster of a boys' preparatory school, had refused to furnish a reference. Duffield and the Morgans were the survivors of half a dozen teachers who had come and gone during the two years since the school was founded. The shortage of good teachers in Jamaica, as well as Pawley's nominal salaries, made replacements difficult to find. The shortage of good teachers couldn't be helped. The salaries might easily have been increased—if not from profits, then from Mrs. Pawley's ample inheritance. But Pawley justified the present low scale on the grounds that its acceptance was proof of idealism.

The subjects that Douglas taught were English and French, and he was also in charge of the library. The library was the best room in the Great House. The walls were lined with mahogany shelves, and at one end there was a huge fireplace, built nostalgically in the English country-house style by the first English coffee planter. At the opposite end Douglas had his desk. He sat there when he wasn't taking a class, available to any of the children who wanted to discuss their work. The children themselves had only two or three classes a day. The rest of the time they spent working by themselves on the assignments which were given them weekly in each subject.

There was a pile of assignments in Douglas's tray when he sat down this morning—French exercises and English essays. He enjoyed the essays and hated the exercises, and, judging by the results, the children felt the same. He started on the exercises first.

Soon after nine there was a knock on the door. He guessed it was Rosemary. Rosemary was the only girl who bothered to knock before coming into the library. She was an English girl of eleven.

"Can you help me, please, Mr. Lockwood?"

She sat down by his desk.

"What's the difficulty?"

"I can't do this." She opened an exercise-book and slid it in front of him a bit diffidently. He at once saw the reason for the diffidence. The page was covered with mathematical workings.

"Aren't you doing this for Mr. Duffield?" he said.

"Yes."

"Then you'll have to take it to him."

She was silent for a moment. Then she said :

"You're my tutor, though."

"That's for looking after you generally. I can't help you with work you're doing for another master."

"But Mr. Duffield's taking a class this period."

"You could see him after break."

"I want to get my maths assignment finished." She paused, and then said nervously, "I've asked Mr. Duffield how to do this once already. I've forgotten what he said. He'd be furious if I asked him again."

Most of the children were pretty afraid of Duffield, and Rosemary was a particularly nervous child. She owed that to her dear devoted parents. She had been tutored by them until the previous year, when she had come to the Great House. They had tried to make up for lack of school discipline by an iron regime at home, never relaxed for a minute. Her father had come up to visit her one week-end and given Douglas a sample of what the child must have been through. He wanted to show how attentive he was to his daughter's good breeding, and Douglas counted twelve "dont's" in a little less than five minutes. "Rosemary, don't walk in front of Mr. Lockwood like that. Square your shoulders and don't slouch, Rosemary. Rosemary dear, stop fidgeting." He doted on Rosemary. He told Douglas that his child came first in his life, and his wife second. That was lucky for his wife but unlucky for Rosemary.

"What are you stuck over, anyhow?"

"Long division of pounds, shillings and pence by pounds, shillings and pence."

He had to rack his brains before he could remember how

to do it properly. He showed her, and then said:

"You'd better not tell Mr. Duffield you asked me, or we'll both be in trouble."

"I won't." She looked at the pile of assignments on his desk. "Have you read my essay yet, Mr. Lockwood?"

"Yes." It was one she had done last week.

"Was it any good?"

"It wasn't bad." He fished it out. It was an essay on *Christmas*. He handed it to her and said, "Read me the first few sentences."

She began to read: *"On Christmas Eve Ann walked over to her friend Joan's house to deliver a present. The snow lay on the ground like a white blanket and the pond was a mirror of ice. Ann——"*

"Stop," Douglas said. "You haven't been out of Jamaica yet, have you, Rosemary?"

"Daddy once took me to the Cayman Islands."

"I don't suppose there's any snow or ice there, either. You've never seen any?" It was curious that at least half the children who'd written about Christmas had pictured a white one with all the Christmas symbols of a northern clime.

"I've seen ice in the refrigerator."

"Could you use it as a mirror to do your hair?"

She thought for a moment. "No, I couldn't."

"I've never seen my reflection in the ice of a pond, either," Douglas said. "In fact, if the ground was covered with snow, the ice would probably be covered too. It sounds as if 'a mirror of ice' is a phrase you've picked up somewhere and used without thinking. I don't like your description of the snow, for the same reason. It 'lay on the ground like a white blanket.' That's somebody else's phrase. Now read this paragraph down here."

"As Ann entered Joan's bedroom, Joan dropped her mending with a guilty look. She did not want Ann to know she was so poor that she had to spend Christmas Eve mending her clothes."

"Now that's a different kettle of fish," Douglas said. "It reads as though you'd really thought about what you were writing down. It shows that you really understand how poor people sometimes feel. Now go through the rest of the story yourself and underline all the phrases like 'a mirror of ice' which wou didn't invent yourself. Then try and replace them with something original."

"Thank you, Mr. Lockwood." She slipped the essay into her file. Then she said, "Mr. Lockwood——" She blushed and faltered.

"Well?"

"I—I wondered if I could move into another dormitory."

"Oh dear. Why do you want to do that?" She hesitated, so he went on, "Can I have one guess? You don't get on with Silvia."

She nodded. "I can't stand her."

"She hasn't been bullying you?"

"She hasn't hit me or anything like that. But she's always being nasty and bossing everybody about. I don't see that she's got any right to. She's only twelve."

"Don't the others object to being bossed about?"

"Yes, but there's nothing they can do." She paused. "Nobody likes her, but some people say they do because they're afraid of her. She once told everyone who liked her to put up their hands. We all did except one."

"What did she do about that?"

"She told the girl who didn't that she'd give her three sweets if she'd put up her hand, and the girl did."

"It's a pity any of you put up your hands."

"None of us can ever talk if she wants to. She's always boasting. I don't believe half what she says. She says she doesn't mind if she's expelled from this school, like she was from her last."

"She won't want to be expelled if we can make her happy here," Douglas said.

Rosemary looked doubtful.

"I don't see what use it is, if she makes everyone else unhappy."

"She wouldn't make other people unhappy if she was happy herself."

"I don't think she's the sort of person who'll ever be really happy," Rosemary said. "Anyhow, I'd much rather be in a dormitory full of people I like."

Douglas said, "It would be nice if we could all live in a world full of people we like. Unfortunately we're always knocking up against people we don't like. If we're going to have any peace of mind we must try and tolerate them. They've probably got some good points somewhere if we're patient enough to look for them. I wish you'd stick it out a bit longer in Silvia's dormitory. After all, somebody's got to. We can't keep her shut up in a room by herself all the time."

He hated having to sermonize like that—he knew what he'd feel like if he had to live in a dormitory with Duffield and Morgan—but there wasn't much else he could do. Rosemary just looked miserable, and said :

"All right, Mr. Lockwood. I'll try and get to like her if I can."

After Rosemary had gone he started worrying about what he was going to do with Silvia, and he was still sitting there worrying when Mrs. Pawley came into the library.

"Oh, hullo, Douglas," she said. "My husband wants you to go down and have a word with him."

Mrs. Pawley's dogs had rushed past her into the room. They were two large, irresponsible Dalmatians. They followed her, or at least pranced about in her vicinity, wherever she went in the school grounds. Douglas hated their invasion of the library, because they were capable of overturning chairs, nosing trays off his desk, and even dragging books from the shelves in their friendly, tail-wagging fashion. Dogs were supposed to grow like their owners, or vice versa, but Mrs. Pawley had nothing in common with her black-spotted Dalmatians—certainly not the black spots. Although she was Jamaican, in the sense that she was born in Jamaica, she was thoroughly English —sometimes rather too thoroughly, Douglas thought.

She was thirty-five. She paid only fitful attention to her appearance, and the dull yellow of her hair was faintly suspicious. She gave the impression of being a discontented woman. Like so many women in the colonies, she yearned for England, and although she paid lip-service to her husband's shaky convictions on the equal rights of Negroes, she secretly despised everything colonial. She had always made herself agreeable to Douglas, presumably because he was English and spoke without a marked provincial accent. She usually called him by his Christian name, a favouritism spared to Duffield.

"I've no idea what it's about," she said. Her manner was rather offhanded in a neurotic way.

"I'll go down now."

The dogs were scampering about the library, full of infinite jest. Mrs. Pawley called to them harshly. "Come

26

here, Rex! Here, Queenie!" They bounced out of the room with uncustomary obedience.

Mrs. Pawley accompanied Douglas out to the garden. She was wearing her navy-blue slacks. She was not very tall, and she walked with a kind of impatient swagger.

"I'm sorry you had such an appalling time yesterday, Douglas." Her voice was also impatient, as if she had no interest in what she was talking about. "I don't know why that thing had to crash near us. My husband's always writing to ask them not to fly over the school. If they'd taken any notice there probably wouldn't have been an accident at all."

"Perhaps not." Her arguments were never very logical, but it wasn't worth-while contradicting her.

They strolled through the garden, amongst the sprawling bushes of Japanese Hat and white, red, and purple bougainvillæa. The small orange flowers of the Japanese Hat attracted humming-birds, and two or three were hovering there now, their wings almost invisible witfi the speed of their vibration, but the feathers on their bodies a radiant, liquid green in the sun.

Mrs. Pawley picked impatiently at a red bougainvillæa as they passed.

"By the way," she said, "did you find some flowers in your room the other afternoon?"

"After I'd been down in Kingston? Yes, I didn't know who'd put them there."

"I told my servant to cut you some from the garden. I thought you might like to have them. It's rather dreary coming back to that bungalow after a day in town."

"I'm always delighted to get back," he said. "It's far too hot in Kingston now."

She picked at the bark of a tree with her nails.

"I expect you're beginning to make friends in Kingston, aren't you?"

"I don't know anyone there," he said.

"Really? How extraordinary." She gave a short laugh. "I'd imagined you had an awfully gay time. You must find us so appallingly dull up here after living in London."

"Not in the least."

"Of course you must. There's no need to be polite. You must find us hopelessly unsophisticated." He protested again, and she said, "We are, I'm afraid. My husband is, at any rate. Of course when I met him I'd been living in

27

London for years. I only lived in Jamaica until I was five, you know."

"I know." She had made a point of telling him two or three times before.

"I should never have believed that I'd come back here one day as a schoolmistress."

"Hardly a schoolmistress," he said. She was supposed to be in charge of the girls and do the catering with Mrs. Morgan, but she took no classes.

"Isn't that how you think of me?" She looked at him quickly, and then as if to show that she didn't care about the answer, she turned and called abruptly to the dogs, "Rex! Queenie! Come here!" She turned back to him and said quite snappily, "I expect my husband will be waiting for you. Don't let me keep you."

He left her and went on down the slope towards Pawley's bungalow, which was two or three hundred yards below the Great House. He was a little apprehensive about the purpose of this summons. Two or three days ago, on his day off in Kingston, he had entered into conversation in the bar of the Myrtle Bank with a man who owned fifteen thousand acres of sugar, bananas, and coconuts in St. Thomas. He was rather a loud-mouthed, back-slapping sort who over-compensated for his few drops of Negro blood by talking about "we white fellows" and boasting of his wealth, but Douglas had found him quite interesting. He joined the man for dinner, and then let himself be talked into going on to a night-club. The night-club was called *The Glass Bucket*. The man knew plenty of girls there, and they danced until eleven. Then Douglas said he had to go. He was driving the station-wagon from the school, and he told the man that he would drop him anywhere he liked. As they started off, the chap said:

"You're not stuck up, are you, man? I mean, you like to see a bit of life?" He talked with the Jamaican accent that sounded like Welsh.

Douglas laughed. "Lord, yes. I've got to get back now, though."

"Why not come along for half an hour? I know plenty of places."

"I ought to have been back hours ago," Douglas said. "But I'll put you down where you like."

"Then take the next turning to the right, man."

They turned into a road of small bungalows with little

28

front gardens, like a poorer suburb of an English seaside resort. Two half-caste girls in cotton dresses were hanging over one of the gates. They stood up expectantly as the station-wagon stopped. The chap got out, and said good night and went to the gate, where they awaited him with frozen grins.

It struck Douglas afterwards that he'd been a fool to run the man right up to the brothel in the school car; and for that matter dancing at the night-club wasn't the sort of pursuit that a schoolmaster in Jamaica was expected to follow. Some of the girls the chap had dug up were not exactly from the tennis-playing top set. Probably someone had seen him or heard that he was there, and had written to Pawley threatening to remove their child unless the master who went the rounds of night-clubs and brothels wasn't promptly dismissed. Scandal travelled fast in Jamaica. Anyhow, it wasn't as though teaching was his career, or as though he had to depend on this job for a living. He could afford to knock around for a year or two before he settled down to serious work again.

As he went up the steps of the verandah he saw that the french windows of Pawley's study were open. He knocked on the glass and went in. Pawley was sitting at his desk. He went on writing for a moment, and then looked up as if he had only just noticed Douglas.

"Ah, Lockwood! You got my message?" He beamed and goggled through his horn-rimmed spectacles, and waved Douglas to a chair. "I'm afraid you'll find that one a bit rickety, but I don't think there's any real fear that it's going to collapse. If you've any doubts about it, though, I should draw up the one from over there."

Pawley always opened an interview with a few chatty remarks—he'd probably read somewhere about how to put people at their ease. The chattiness was no indication that he wasn't going to talk about the brothel, but as it turned out he wasn't—he was going to talk about Silvia.

You couldn't help feeling about Pawley that there was something missing—something like gin from a cocktail or seasoning from the soup. Probably Pawley felt it too, and that was why he wore a beard. He must have hoped the beard would make up for what wasn't there.

He was a lank and tallish man, dressed in a badly fitting tropical suit. The beard was certainly the most impressive thing about him, but even so it failed to give him a positive and commanding presence. It somehow didn't match his features; and until you had spotted the incongruity and imagined him clean-shaven, you had an uncomfortable feeling about him as you might about some woman wearing an unsuitable wig. Even then you went on feeling a bit uneasy. There was something fish-like about the way his eyes goggled from behind the horn-rimmed spectacles.

"You're prepared to risk it, then?" He was still talking about the chair.

"This'll be all right," Douglas said. He sat down. There was nothing wrong with the chair at all.

"It's on your own head, then," Pawley beamed. "I only like to warn you, so that if the worst should happen you can't hold me responsible." He leant back and put the tips of his bony fingers together. His eyes looked shapeless and indistinct behind the lenses. "I suppose you've never forgiven me, have you?"

"What for?" Douglas asked. Pawley always liked to introduce his subject cryptically.

"For picking on you to bear our heaviest cross. I'm sure you know what I mean now." He beamed. "I thought it was time we had a little chat about the lady—I haven't had much chance to watch what was going on lately. All this administration, you know. . . ." He indicated the papers on his desk with a martyred smile. "I expect you picture me sitting here twiddling my thumbs, don't you? I only wish I could give you some idea of what a vast amount of paper work is necessary to keep this place running."

"I'd handle half of it in exchange for Silvia," Douglas said.

"That sounds ominous," Pawley said. "I hope you haven't decided we were unwise to take her on?"

"I haven't decided that yet." Silvia had only been at the Blue Mountain School for a fortnight. She had come in the middle of term, after being expelled from her last school for incorrigibly bad behaviour. Pawley had accepted her in the hope of improving her and demonstrating the superiority of his progressive system.

"Rather a puzzling incident occurred yesterday afternoon," Pawley said. "It was while you were at the crash." He put on a smile that looked suspiciously reproachful. "As a matter of fact, I looked for you at the time. I didn't know where you were."

"I'm sorry," Douglas said. "There wasn't time to let you know. I thought I'd better get to the aircraft as quickly as possible."

"Very right of you," Pawley said. "I'm not finding fault with you, of course." He still managed to sound a bit pained about it, all the same. He was good at that sort of thing. "And I hear you were able to make yourself useful."

"Joe was the hero," Douglas said. "He discovered the survivors first."

"Good—I'm delighted to hear it," Pawley said vaguely, obviously not interested in the crash. He returned to the puzzling incident. "Anyhow, I don't think your absence was the cause of Silvia's behaviour."

"She's usually on her best behaviour when I'm away," Douglas said. "So far most of her misdeeds have been to demonstrate her contempt for my authority as her tutor."

"She was apparently making use of Joe's absence," Pawley said. "After he'd gone off with you, there was nobody to keep an eye on the lighting plant. Silvia took the opportunity of nipping down there."

"To smash it up?"

"Fortunately she stopped short of that," Pawley said. "She seemed satisfied with putting water into the petrol in the spare cans."

Douglas laughed. "I'm glad you caught her before we had to spend a night in the dark."

"We didn't catch her—that's the extraordinary thing." He paused, stroking his beard. He always left significant pauses when he was talking. He found them rather effective, and was too busy appreciating them to notice that other people found them irritating. His eyes goggled at you in what was meant to be a tantalizing way. Presently he went on, "Alice came down to tell me about it." He paused again. "I suppose you find that rather extraordinary, too?"

"Most extraordinary," Douglas said. "I thought Alice was much too timid to tell tales about anybody. Least of all about Silvia."

"Exactly. That was what I thought. I naturally asked her why she was doing it. She was in a highly nervous state, and I had some difficulty in making her talk." His eyes tantalized again. "Then she explained that Silvia herself had told her what she'd been up to—and forced her to come down and report it."

"I suppose Silvia had told her to pretend she was reporting it off her own bat?"

"Yes, she had," Pawley said. "And not only that. After I'd seen Silvia about it, she accused Alice in front of the other children of sneaking to the headmaster about her practical joke. She started hitting Alice. There was quite a scrap. Fortunately the other children stood up for Alice. I heard about it later." He spread out his hands and beamed. "Well, Lockwood, she's your pupil. What do you make of it?"

"I find it all rather typical," Douglas said. "She's spent a fortnight trying to get me to punish her, and hasn't succeeded. Now I suppose she's hoping for better luck with you. I take it you didn't punish her?"

"My dear chap . . . !" He looked rather hurt. Then he decided to make a joke of it, and grinned. "Naturally I gave her a thousand lines to do before supper." In case Douglas had taken this seriously, he added, "No, Lockwood, I only told her I'd speak to you about it. I didn't make this an occasion to break our record." The record, of course, was that nobody had been punished in the two years of the school's existence.

"A thousand lines would have delighted her," Douglas said.

"I should have hardly said that. . . ."

"I think it would. She's dying to be punished."

"In that case she must have been extraordinarily happy at her last school," Pawley grinned. "I understand they expelled her because they couldn't devise any more punishments to give her." He always liked joking about the barbarism of other schools.

"I've no doubt she derived a great deal of satisfaction from it," Douglas said. "It gave her the nice cosy feeling of being a martyr." Pawley ought to have known all about that nice cosy feeling, if only he'd been able to recognize it.

"She's not going to feel like that here," Pawley said. "She's bound to get a much more healthy outlook."

"I can't see her being done out of her martyrdom without a fight," Douglas said. "Ever since she's been here she's been working overtime to make it perfectly clear that she's a rebel. She can't make out why we're not exchanging hostilities. She'd regard it as a terrific triumph if she could make us lose our tempers and punish her. It would do her pride no end of good. Personally I think that before she gets the healthy outlook, she'll redouble her efforts at rebellion and try to make things jolly uncomfortable for us!"

Pawley looked thoughtful for a minute. He removed his glasses and started to polish them with his handkerchief. His eyes were even queerer when they were deprived of the lenses. They looked out of their element, like fishes on a slab. Presently he said :

"Look here, Lockwood, I want your honest opinion. Do you think we'd be unwise to keep Silvia at the school? It wouldn't be too difficult at this early stage to say we can't handle her. We could point out that we ought to have started with her when she was younger."

"Why shouldn't we keep her?" Douglas said. He hadn't been expecting this.

Pawley replaced the spectacles slowly.

"We must think of our reputation," he said. "An incident like yesterday's doesn't seem awfully important to us, but the parents may feel differently about it. We don't censor the children's letters—as you know, that sort of thing runs entirely against the grain with me—and Alice is certainly going to write home and say what Silvia did to her. It'll be talked about widely. We don't want to give the impression that we're prepared to tolerate behaviour of that sort."

Douglas said, "Presumably if we accept a girl who's been expelled from another school, we must be prepared to tolerate a good deal more than that. In any case, I thought that toleration was part of the system."

Pawley goggled patiently.

"I don't think you've quite got my point," he said. "I only want to make sure that our system isn't jeopardized by Silvia. Our position's very delicate, you know."

"In what way?"

He toyed with a pencil, smiling vaguely as if Douglas ought to have known that the position was too delicate to explain. Then he said, "We must still look upon our system as experimental out here. We can't afford any failures. We literally can't afford them, Lockwood. I believe you know we're still losing money on the school?" He looked at Douglas to make sure that he did know.

"Yes, I do."

"Not that we aren't glad to do it," he smiled quickly. "Both my wife and I feel that we oughtn't to bother how

33

much we're out of pocket—not while there's a single child in Jamaica that we can help."

"I should have thought Silvia was the one child we *could* help," Douglas said.

Pawley looked as though he was going to be frank, and said, "Frankly—I'm disappointed she isn't making better progress."

"I don't see how we can expect to see any progress in a fortnight," Douglas said.

"You mustn't think I'm making any criticism of the way you're handling her." He beamed. "Veiled or otherwise."

"I know," Douglas said. "But I still think we'll be lucky if we see any signs of improvement this term at all."

"You do feel that?" Pawley said.

"Yes, I do. You don't tame an animal overnight. You've got to go on holding the sugar out and getting your hand bitten off for weeks before it really believes that you haven't got a whip hidden behind your back. But I'm sure we can do something with Silvia eventually."

Pawley looked as though he was allowing himself to be humoured. He spread out his hands.

"Very well, if you feel you have the patience. . . ."

"It's not only a question of my patience," Douglas said. "I can manage that. I don't mind watching her chop up school desks all day, if that's how she feels like expressing herself. I don't have to pay for the desks. But it's no use if you're worrying what the parents are thinking."

"You're rather inclined to exaggerate everything, Lockwood," Pawley said good-naturedly. "I'm not worrying—but it's just as well to bear these things in mind."

"All the same, if you think it's too much of a responsibility to keep Silvia on. . . ."

"I didn't say that," Pawley said. He smiled disarmingly. "I only raised it as a point of discussion. I'm delighted to hear that you feel we can help Silvia. Well, let's both do our best, shall we?"

It was always like that. Pawley put up an objection and you knocked it down, and then he behaved as though he'd never made it. The trouble was that he left you feeling that so far as he was concerned you hadn't knocked it down at all, you were merely being allowed to have your own way.

Douglas rose. As he did so, Pawley felt in his pocket and pulled out his pipe and tobacco pouch.

"By the way, Lockwood——" He leant his elbows on the

34

desk and started filling the pipe, goggling rather awkwardly. Then he looked up and said chattily, "Sit down a minute, won't you?"

Douglas sat down. Perhaps there'd been a letter about the brothel after all.

Pawley took about a minute to stuff the tobacco into his pipe. The pipe had an S-shaped stem. Probably he felt this gave him character, like the beard. He started lighting it, looking at Douglas over the match flame. Then he puffed out a lot of smoke, and blew out the match and said cheerfully :

"Don't look so gloomy, old chap. It's nothing serious. I only wanted to tell you that I think you're doing a very fine job of work here."

He was rotten at this sort of thing. The cheeriness always sounded so put-on.

"Thank you," Douglas said.

Pawley made a movement of settling himself comfortably.

"I sometimes feel, after our little discussions, that you think I'm pulling you to bits. I'm not, you know. I start you arguing on purpose." He beamed complicitly. He was the conjurer letting the audience into the secret of his tricks. "I find it's the best way of getting you to express your opinions."

"I'm afraid I'm inclined to do that a bit dogmatically," Douglas said.

"I like people to hold strong opinions." He was like that himself. "I don't think you've any need to worry that you're not going to make a good teacher. I've been most impressed by the quality of your work."

Douglas fidgeted a bit. Pawley sucked contemplatively at his pipe, and then went on :

"I don't mind telling you that when I first considered your application for the vacancy, I was in two minds about accepting it. There were two things against you—your lack of experience and your divorce." He took the pipe out of his mouth and looked questioningly at Douglas. "You don't mind my speaking frankly, do you?"

"Of course not."

"I thought you wouldn't." He put the pipe back. "Whatever our own opinions, we must realize that there's a marked prejudice against a divorced man in the scholastic profession. I need hardly mention that my own views are broader than the average"—he smiled modestly at the euphemism

35

—"but of course I had to take that into consideration. After all, you can't run a school without pupils. And you can't get pupils unless you inspire parents with sufficient confidence to entrust you with their children."

"Naturally not."

"Anyhow, I talked it over with my wife, and decided to take the risk." He paused, while you appreciated what a great risk it was. Then he enlightened Douglas about the outcome. "I've not had any cause to regret it. On the contrary."

"I'm very glad," Douglas said fatuously.

"I just thought I'd let you know. I like to give credit where it's due." He leant forward and began to straighten the papers on his desk. "Well, that's all, thanks, Lockwood. The chair seems to have stood up to your weight all right, doesn't it?" He goggled playfully. "I thought it probably would, you know."

There was ten minutes before his French class, so he went upstairs to the surgery. Mrs. Morgan was pottering about in her matron's uniform. Her sleeves were rolled up and her arms looked like sausage balloons. He asked her if he could see the patients.

"You'd better not, Mr. Lockwood. The doctor only left them a quarter of an hour ago. He said they'd both got to rest."

"But they're all right?"

"Oh yes, it's a wonder. I'm awfully sorry about Mr. Taylor, though. That's the name of the gentleman. His wife and daughter were with him on the aeroplane." Her pock-marked face sagged with distress. "They were on their way back to England after a holiday. The daughter was only seven."

"How damn wicked," Douglas said.

"There isn't any justice in it, is there? It makes you wonder what it's all about. It really does."

"And the girl?"

Mrs. Morgan looked non-committal.

"She doesn't seem a bit worried or upset," she said. "She behaves as if she thought the crash was something funny. It's queer, isn't it? You'd think she'd feel it badly, seeing that the friend who worked with her was killed. I can't make her out." She thought for a minute, and then said more charitably, "Still, you never can tell with people,

36

can you, Mr. Lockwood? You can't judge by appearances. It's often the laughing ones who are suffering the most."

He put off seeing Silvia until the afternoon. Throughout his class she had sat in silence, adopting the contemptuous manner that was designed to suggest the lesson was beneath her. When the bell rang at four o'clock, he called her over. He asked her to come down to his bungalow for a chat.

"I don't mind," she said condescendingly. "I want to put my books away first, though."

"Don't be too long if you want any tea," he said.

"I don't care about tea."

She went off with a studied effort to appear unhurried. Douglas walked down to his bungalow and sat on the verandah. Presently Ivy came with the tray, and placed it on the table beside him. He waited five or ten minutes and then poured out a cup. Silvia's delay was typical. It was a point of pride to show her independence—a routine gesture of rebelry. But he was confident she would turn up sooner or later, if only out of curiosity. It was no fun being a rebel unless you knew what people thought of your rebellion.

He was not looking forward to the interview—he still hadn't made up his mind what he was going to say to her—and while he was waiting he suddenly started wishing that all he had to do was to lecture her and administer a punishment selected from a catalogue. He remembered the catalogue of punishments at a school he had been to in England. The punishments were graded according to severity. The mildest was four runs round the cricket field before breakfast; the most severe was a beating from the housemaster. The runs scored one point against you and the beatings ten. If you attained an aggregate of thirty points in a term, the headmaster called you up for a soul-shaking jaw; or if the jaw didn't seem to shake your soul, a briefer and sharper pronouncement on your unprotected behind. Life for the masters must have been free from worry, once they had digested the principles of crime assessment. They must have enjoyed themselves—unless, of course, it had upset them to think they might just as well have been policemen or sergeant-majors.

Twenty minutes later Silvia came. She stood at the bottom of the verandah steps.

37

"Do you want me?" she said. It was as if she couldn't quite remember whether he'd asked her down or not.

"Yes," he said. "If you want some tea, there's a cup on the table inside."

"I don't want any tea."

"Then come and sit down."

She came up the steps, trying to look perfectly at ease. She was only twelve, but she looked much older than most girls of that age in England. She was a white Jamaican. She had dark, bobbed hair, and a pale little face that happiness might have made pretty. But her expression was always strained and unnatural. She liked to give the impression, with her superior airs, that she was already a woman.

She sat down, crossing her arms with careless resignation, inviting Douglas to say his piece and have done with it.

He said, "I'm always hearing from other people how you're getting along, but you never come and tell me yourself. I'd much rather hear from you."

"I suppose Mr. Pawley told you about the petrol," she said, with a thin, supercilious smile. "I don't care—he can believe Alice if he wants." She stared at him flatly, as if she was not looking at him at all, but only presenting the surface of her eyes to him to make what she said more convincing. "It doesn't interest me in the least. The other girls can do what they like. I don't care about any of them."

"You can't have much fun here if you feel like that," he said.

She shrugged. "They're all jealous of me, like they were at my last school."

"Were you happy at your last school?"

"I hate school," she said.

"So do heaps of people. I did myself. At least, I hated my first school, and then I went to one that I liked."

"I hate all schools," she said airily.

"What do you like, then? Being at home?"

"Sometimes."

"What do you like most of all?"

"Doing what I want."

"What's that?"

She gave another shrug. "Oh . . . going to the cinema. Going out. I hate Jamaica, though. I want to live in America."

"Have you ever been to America?"

She turned the flat stare on him.

38

"Of course I have."

"Where did you go?"

"All over the place," she said vaguely. "I've been to Washington and New York."

"New York's a fine city, isn't it?" he said. "Where did you stay?"

She shifted her arms uncomfortably. "Oh, I've masses of friends there. I can't remember all the places I've stayed at." She had moved her eyes away, but she turned them back towards him again and said, "I've stayed in people's apartments." She must have been told that you couldn't look someone straight in the face if you were lying, and had trained herself to do it. He didn't want her to know that he thought she was lying, it would give her another reason for hostility, so he turned away casually and said :

"Well, you're one up on me there. I've always wanted to visit the States. I haven't got round to it yet."

"It's glorious," she said more easily. "That's one of the reasons why they couldn't stand me at my last school. I knew much more than all the others did."

"What were the other reasons?"

"I used to do things that nobody else dared."

"What sort of things?"

She put on the supercilious smile to show she wasn't afraid of telling him.

"I used to write letters to men, for one thing," she said. "We weren't allowed to, but I didn't care."

"And what happened when you did what you weren't allowed to?"

"They punished me," she said. "They used to shut me up in my room. It just made me laugh. I got out of the window if I felt like it. I sat in the bushes and smoked." She evidently thought the boasting impressed him, and she went on, "I've brought some cigarettes here, if you want to know."

"You needn't have bothered," he said. "I've any amount." He pushed a packet across the table. "Help yourself."

She stared at him uncertainly.

"Don't you mind me smoking?"

"If you've smoked before, it evidently doesn't bring you out in spots," he said. "You can come down here and have one whenever you want."

She hesitated and then said, "I don't want one now." She was probably afraid of choking in front of him.

He said, "They say it stops you growing if you smoke cigarettes when you're young, but I doubt if it's true. It would be rather interesting to see."

"You don't seem to care what anyone does here," she said. It sounded as if she was putting out a feeler.

"We've got to draw the line somewhere. We can't let you go round killing off the other girls, or their parents would have something to say. And we're not particularly keen for you to burn down buildings or do anything destructive of that sort."

"I don't see the point in a school where you can do practically anything," she said.

Douglas said, "As you've probably discovered, we've got funny ideas here, Silvia. At least, they're funny to some people, though not to us. We believe that you can only work properly if you enjoy what you're doing. You've probably got hold of the notion that schools exist for the purpose of making children unhappy. This school exists to try and make you happy, so that you can enjoy learning. And it's not a bad idea to learn a few things before you go off and tackle life by yourself."

Silvia sat still with her arms crossed, looking supercilious and unimpressed. After a minute she said challengingly:

"Aren't you going to punish me?"

"What for?"

"For all the things people have told you about me."

"No, we're not."

"I don't care what you do to me, anyhow."

"In that case it certainly wouldn't be any use punishing you," he said. "It would be much more useful if we could find some way to make you happy. You know what I once read? 'No happy man ever disturbed a meeting, or preached a war, or committed a murder.' I have an idea that if you were really happy here, people would stop complaining about you."

"I'm perfectly happy," Silvia said.

"All right," he said. "But if you ever decide you aren't, I wish you'd come down and tell me about it."

Silvia stood up. There was still nothing in her expression that resembled friendship or trust.

"Is that all you want me for?" she said.

"Yes, you can go when you want."

She went off down the steps. He watched her turn up the path, feeling absurdly hurt by her sudden departure, and angry with himself for handling the business so badly. All that pep talk about happiness. You didn't make people happy by telling them it was what they ought to be. You didn't gain their confidence by shoving cigarettes at them, either. It was all so easy in theory; you were nice to a child, and the child responded by being nice in return. It stopped being naughty, and everyone lived happily ever after. Rubbish! What happened was that the child despised you for being weak and a fool, took advantage of you and behaved far worse than before. All the same, what else could he have done? The catalogue of punishments and the policeman's baton weren't any solution. They might have kept peace for the pedagogues, but they wouldn't have helped Silvia. The pedagogues were for Silvia, not Silvia for the pedagogues. Perhaps he was just being too impatient. He'd told Pawley you couldn't expect immediate results. You couldn't.

He saw Silvia coming back. He felt hopeful for a moment; then he saw that her manner had in no way softened. She stopped at the foot of the steps.

"It's perfectly true that I've been to America," she said.

He laughed. "Why shouldn't it be?"

"My father will tell you that I haven't, but I have."

"How did you manage it without letting him know?"

"I expect they told you that I ran away from my last school for a week, didn't they?"

"They didn't mention it."

"They probably daren't admit it. But I did. I never told them where I'd been."

"And you'd been to America?"

"Yes." She seemed to be looking at him properly now. "One of my American friends had a private aeroplane. He came and picked me up. We flew to New York. Then he flew me back again. We landed in a special field at night. Do you believe me?"

"Why not?"

"It's quite true. I thought I'd tell you, in case you spoke to my father and thought I was a liar."

"I'm glad you did," he said.

She watched him for a moment, then turned and walked away again. It was curious with what conviction she'd told that little story, as if she believed it herself. Perhaps she did believe it. An adolescent mind was rich in phantasy, and the line it drew between daydreams and reality was often indistinct.

41

He thought over the nature of Silvia's phantasy, the great feat performed for her in the spirit of pure love; and then he remembered a boyhood phantasy of his own, in which he had seen himself at some point in the future, loved purely by a beautiful woman whom he had rescued from a sinking ship, and then he thought of Caroline and the unsatisfactory messy way that love had turned out. If only you could live in phantasy always! But only lunatics could do that, while poor sane creatures had to accept the shoddy substitute of reality. Perhaps training children to accept the shoddy substitute was roughly what you might call a good education.

He sat for another few minutes, and then got up and went inside the bungalow. The wooden elephant stood on the bedside table with its trunk pointing towards the door. Ivy had moved it again while she was dusting.

He went over and turned it, with an automatic movement, to face the window.

He hadn't told Ivy about the peculiar properties of the elephant because one of two things would have happened. Either she would have gone off into a record-breaking bout of giggles, or else she would have been so overawed, on account of her superstitious peasant nature, that she would have refused to enter his bungalow again. There was also another reason why he didn't tell her—in fact, why he didn't tell anyone. It might sound as if he took it seriously.

The elephant was about three inches long. It had been given him in India during the war, in return for alms, by a fakir with long black matted hair and a facility for sticking six-inch nails into his flesh without apparent material damage. The fakir had probably known more about Occidentals and what they expected of him than he had known about the Infinite. He had explained that to bring good fortune the trunk of the elephant should be pointed towards a window. Pointed towards a door, it would bring the reverse—or at any rate it would lose its power to avert evil. There had been an imminence of danger in Douglas's life at the time; and danger made you superstitious. He had kept the elephant as an insurance, in the same way that the agnostic said his prayers: "Oh, please, God—if there *is* a God . . ." During the following months he had been in a dilemma: he had been living mainly in tents, where the window and the door were a single aperture. He had not known where to point the trunk. But his difficulty must have been appreciated, for he had been rewarded with an uninterrupted succession of lucky breaks, and the protection of his life beyond reasonable expectation. After the war the power of the elephant had noticeably declined—but this only went to prove that the supernatural was not immune from war-weariness. He had benefited from its dispensations for so long that he would have been an ingrate to abandon it. He had hung on to it and pointed it to the window all through that awful business with Caroline, and finally packed it in his suit-case and brought it to Jamaica. In his bungalow he corrected its position daily after the disarrangement of Ivy's dusting, with the same confirmed habit that he dried his razor after use.

Now, as he twisted it through the all-important ninety degrees, a trivial but amusing thought occurred to him. It was probably nothing to do with the elephant that the thought occurred at that moment, although afterwards he sometimes liked to wonder. He had still had in mind the boyhood phantasy in which he rescued a girl from a sinking ship; and the thought was simply that he had never come nearer to the boyhood phantasy than yesterday when he had rescued the girl from the crashed aircraft.

He told himself that he found this amusing because it would have been too absurd to admit that he found it significant. He stood there for a minute, amusing himself by supposing that he lived out the rest of the phantasy and fell in love with her, and that she fell in love with him, and that their love was the pure love of dreams and not the messy thing that in reality it always turned out to be. He had a vivid pictorial imagination, and almost at once a string of pictures presented itself to his mind, representing the smooth evolution of their idyllic affair, and culminating in a scene in which he was lying by her side on the sands of a Caribbean beach. Behind them, amongst the palms, was the bungalow where they were living, and on the verandah of the bungalow (his mind tracked up to it like a motion-camera) was a table on which stood a bowl of ice cubes and two Old-fashioned Cocktails, looking rather like a coloured advertisement in an American magazine. And here he laughed to himself to show how much this banal similarity amused him, and turned away from the elephant and looked at his watch. It was after five. He ought to be up helping the children with their hobbies.

43

The hobbies were voluntary, and most of the children preferred playing about in the grounds. There was a ball-game in progress amongst the junipers as he climbed the hill. He declined an invitation to join in and went up to the modelling shed. It was empty—not even Rosemary. In that case he would go and see the patients. He turned into the garden. As he entered the Great House he met Duffield coming out. Duffield said testily:

"That sort of thing wouldn't happen if I was running the place."

"What sort of thing?" Duffield had an irritating habit of making a statement about something that had just happened to him as if you already knew all about it.

"I've just caught Alan relieving himself out of a window. Said he couldn't be bothered to go upstairs."

"It was thoughtful of him to go to the window," Douglas said.

"I shouldn't wonder if some of the girls didn't see him from the garden, either. And there's not a blighted thing I can do about it."

"There isn't much.

"I'd go to Pawley—but you know the kind of tommy-rot he'd start talking, don't you?"

"He'd probably put it down to natural high spirits," Douglas said; "if he wasn't too worried about what parents would think."

"Likely as not he'd tell Alan to relieve himself out of the window every day for a week until he got tired of it." He jerked his head incredulously. "If I had my own way, he'd get tired of it sooner than that. He'd get tired of it in the time it took me to whack him. When Pawley's had as much experience of boys as I have, he'll want less high spirits and more sore bottoms." This thought seemed to humour him a bit, and he added more lightly, "It's a good thing I didn't take my day off, anyhow. I might have got back to find the whole school lined up watering the flowers." He managed a dry smile. "Well, see you at supper." He went off.

Douglas went upstairs. There was only one sick-room in the school; there were no children there at present, and it had been used for the girl. The man who had lost his wife and daughter had been put in one of the boys' dormitories, and the boys moved out.

Douglas went to the dormitory and knocked lightly on

44

the door. There was no reply, so he looked in. The man was asleep. He closed the door again with guilty relief : he had dreaded the duty of commiseration. He went down the corridor to the sick-room. He had not dreaded this visit, but as he approached the door an unexpected reluctance came over him. He had almost forgotten the girl's appearance—it had been displaced in his imagination by the girl who went with the Jamaican beach and the Old-fashioned Cocktail—and to see her now must bind his thoughts to reality and forbid the amusement of the dream. Nevertheless, he knocked on the door.

The girl was standing by the window.

"Oh!" she said. "I thought it was Mrs. Morgan."

"I'm sorry," he said.

"I'm not," she said. "I mean, not that I don't like her—but she'd have been absolutely wild at catching me out of bed."

She was wearing a nightgown that was far too large for her. It must have been one of Mrs. Morgan's. Its surplus folds were wrapped round her waist and tied with a pyjama cord. Her hair was fair and hung loosely on to her shoulders. She had a slightly tilted nose and a quick, friendly smile. The sort of smile that dispensed with all the formalities of introduction.

"I can sympathize with Mrs. Morgan," he said. "I can see she's been having difficulty with you."

"But there's absolutely nothing the matter with me."

"Except that you were concussed."

"Oh, rubbish," she said. "I only had two stitches. Isn't it unbelievable, after what happened? The scar's not even going to show. Look, you can see if you like. Are you interested in that sort of thing?" She spun round without waiting for him to answer, and parted her hair with her hands. Then she turned back and said, "Aren't you the person who rescued me?"

"I gave a hand."

"I wish I knew what to say. I'm rotten at thanking people. I ought to give you a box of cigars, or a gold cigarette-case or something. Would you like a gold cigarette-case?"

"No," he said. "But I'd like you to get into bed."

"You sound like a schoolmaster," she said. "Is that what you are? Anyhow, I don't mind being in bed if I have

45

someone to talk to. You're not rushing off again, are you?"

She jumped into bed with an eagerness and energy that were astonishing for someone who had just been knocked out in a crash. She had the young energy of a child, yet she was not a child, and she had the freshness of a virgin, yet she probably wasn't that either. He noticed that her finger-nails had been painted, and the paint was wearing off unevenly. She saw him looking, and said :

"I know, isn't it hideous? I've nothing to take it off with—and no more to put on. I suppose it's no use asking anyone here?"

"Only Mrs. Pawley—the headmaster's wife."

"Does she paint her nails?"

"Cyclamen."

"Oh, that would just do." She forgot about the nails and said, "I can just remember coming up on the stretcher. Wasn't I gabbling a lot of rubbish?"

"Yes, you were."

"I thought I was. What did I say?"

"That you tried to commit suicide in Mexico." He smiled. He knew it was rubbish now. She wasn't the sort of girl who committed suicide.

"Oh, that was perfectly true," she said with the quick, frank smile.

"I can't believe it."

"Yes, I did!" She was indignant at being doubted. "I took thirty-five sleeping tablets."

"That should have done the job all right."

"It should, shouldn't it? I cut my wrist at the same time, as a matter of fact, but I fainted before I'd cut the vein. Do you want to see?"

She held out her arm. There was a thin scar an inch long on the inside of the wrist. Across it were the marks of three stitches.

"Isn't it wonderful the way they can darn you up? I once knew someone who had seventeen stitches after an operation."

"You'll soon have more than that, if you go on in this way," he said. "What did you do it for? Were you broke?"

"Oh, no," she said. "At least, that wasn't the reason. It was the other obvious one."

"A man?"

"Yes; wasn't it silly of me?"

46

"What happened to him?" Douglas said. "Did he know about it?"

"Good Lord, no," she said. Her eyes looked quite untroubled and amused. They were green eyes, and their loveliness disturbed him. "He'd already gone back to his wife."

CHAPTER THREE

THE name of the girl was Judy Waring. She was twenty-seven, although she seemed no more than twenty-three or four. She didn't look at all a suicidal type, and she was not depressive or neurotic; in fact she seemed to have the sort of innocence that no experience of life could sully. It astonished Douglas that she could have tried to kill herself even under the exactions of love. Her nature was so gay and easy-going. She told him all about the suicide in a casual way; not boastfully, or shamefully, or even as a joke, but as a fairly natural episode in what she considered quite an uneventful life.

The man who had caused her to try and commit suicide was called Louis. He was a Hungarian, and she had met him in Paris nearly two years before. She was living in Paris with a young French law student at the time. The student had been in the Free French Air Force, and she had fallen in love with him in London during the war. They had often talked of getting married. But Judy had a passion for fair-grounds—for the curiosities of sideshows and the exhilaration of scenic railways. It was a passion which the student didn't happen to share; and that was why he hadn't been with her in the tent of the Hairy Man from Indo-China, on the Place Pigalle, when she first met Louis. It was also why he hadn't been there the next day, when she met Louis again at the Wall of Death.

She met Louis several times after that; and one day he took her back to his room. It then occurred to her that her love for the law student must be waning, if she could so easily commit an infidelity. A fortnight later—there had been one or two quite unpleasant scenes in the meantime—she had ceased to live in the student's elegant flat and was installed in Louis' shabby lodgings. She had discovered that she loved Louis very much indeed.

Louis had no money; but Judy had done some modelling in London, and she took a job with a couturier. Louis was making arrangements to emigrate to the New World, and not doing any work at all. He was married. His wife, who was Swiss, had a great deal of money and lived in Zurich. He had left her after a quarrel in which she had stated categorically that she never wished to set eyes on him again.

One day, when Judy had been living with him for nearly six months, his wife turned up in Paris. She had changed her mind about renouncing him. Louis told Judy that his wife's reappearance left him cold. On the other hand, it would be inexpedient to offend her, now that the only barrier to his emigration was shortage of cash. Shortly afterwards he announced, with a breaking heart, that he was going to Venezuela, and that his wife was accompanying him. They sailed from Cherbourg three days later.

Judy resisted the law student's anguished and forgiving pleas to return to him, and went on working at the couturier's. Another six months passed, during which she received only two picture post-cards of Caracas, the capital of Venezuela. Then a cable arrived, followed by an airmail letter, in which Louis explained that his wife had left him and gone to New York. She had no intention of returning. Unfortunately she had departed in a tantrum, thoughtlessly leaving him without enough money to provide Judy with a passage across the Atlantic. Nevertheless, he hoped she would find some means of joining him, by which time he would have found a job sufficiently remunerative to keep them both in the style to which Europeans were accustomed in Venezuela. Judy could just afford the passage, and as Louis still occupied her heart, she booked it at once. The day before she was due to sail another cable arrived from him. It stated briefly that he was now in Mexico, a more promising land in which to build their future. She switched her passage and sailed. When she arrived in Mexico City she found Louis living in a sordid room reminiscent of his room in Paris, not yet employed but fertile with ideas. He proposed to start a business exporting stuff to Europe.

Judy didn't mind the squalor, she was overjoyed at being with Louis again, and ready to find some employment in order to keep him as she had done in Paris. After a fortnight, with her ability to write letters in French and English, she found a job as a stenographer. She was due to commence this job on the following Monday when Louis' wife turned up, unannounced, from New York.

Louis' wife, who was called Greta and who was six years older than Louis, had decided to forgive him everything. She had also decided to forget all her own indulgences in New York. She had not expected to find Louis with Judy; but when she did so she was prepared to overlook that too, provided Louis promised not to see Judy again in his life, except for the length of time it took to advise her to return to Europe forthwith.

Louis came back from the hotel where his wife was staying, which was the most expensive in Mexico City, and kept the taxi waiting outside while he went up to the sordid little room to collect his belongings and deliver the ultimatum to Judy. He delivered the ultimatum regretfully, since his love for Judy far exceeded his love for his wife; but he had now perceived that Mexico was not a suitable country for a beautiful and cultivated European girl such as herself. Moreover, he had come to the conclusion that the competition in the export business gave a newcomer little chance of success. He was really angry with himself for so thoughtlessly allowing her to come over. However, his wife had very generously (in view of the circumstances) forked out enough money for Judy's return fare to England or France. He had the notes in his pocket.

Judy laughed and told him that he had better keep the money against the day when he quarrelled with his wife again. She didn't want to leave Mexico—the Latin type quite appealed to her, and she might even marry a Mexican and settle down. Louis thought this quite a good idea, if she didn't mind him telling his wife that she was actually proposing to leave. This would not only satisfy his wife, who had rather a jealous disposition, but—since he perfectly understood why Judy didn't want to accept the money—would also enable him to pay off one or two small debts about which he preferred not to trouble Greta.

After Louis had gone, Judy left the room almost at once and inquired where she might find a doctor. She was quite calm. She told the doctor that she was sleeping badly, and he wrote her out a prescription for ten sleeping tablets. She thought these might not be fatal even if taken at a single dose; and while she was in the dispensary, which adjoined the doctor's surgery, she managed to grab and conceal a bottle of tablets similar to the one from which

49

the dispenser was making up her prescription. She returned to her room, packed her bags, and went in search of another room where she wasn't known, so that what became of her wouldn't reach the ears of Louis. When she had found a room, she told the landlady that she was tired and didn't wish to be disturbed before the next morning. Then she took a glass of water, sat down on the bed, and swallowed the ten tablets that had been prescribed her and the twenty-five from the bottle.

Since setting out to find the doctor, she hadn't had much time to think about Louis; but she had known that life without him would be unbearably empty. She was appalled at the thought of returning to Europe, which she had left with such great expectations. The stenographer's job, if she wasn't doing it for Louis, would be meaningless drudgery. Killing herself was the obvious solution, and she had no horror of death. Now that she had taken the tablets her only fear was that they might not work. She could still feel nothing happening to her, so she got up from the bed to find a razor-blade in her bag. She stood with the blade in her hand for a moment before she could gather enough courage to cut her wrist. Then she dragged it across the skin, and as she did so she fainted and fell on the floor with a crash that was loud enough to arouse the curiosity of the landlady.

She remembered nothing else until she awoke in hospital. But then all the unpleasant business with the stomach-pump was over, and there was a little Mexican nurse sitting by her bedside, embroidering a tablecloth. She remembered quite clearly what she had done and why she had done it, and was neither pleased nor sorry that she hadn't succeeded. It didn't occur to her to try again. She set about thinking what she was going to do, but before she had reached a conclusion the doctor informed her, on official instructions, that Mexico's warmth of hospitality didn't extend to suicides. He advised her, since she hadn't enough money to return to Europe, to go to the British West Indies. A week later she was in Jamaica.

Two days after landing in the island a rich Jamaican, whom she had met within a few hours of her arrival, asked her to marry him. He was lonely, and Judy felt sorry for him. He had once been in love with another English girl. The girl's parents had objected to their marriage because he was a half-caste. The girl was going to marry him all the same; but it was then discovered that he had been keeping a coloured mistress at his estate. This was a shock to the girl's idealism. She returned the ring to him through the post.

Judy toyed with the idea of accepting the Jamaican's proposal. She had suddenly felt, after the suicide, that her life was absolutely pointless. She wanted a purpose. She could never love the Jamaican, but she saw that in many ways she could be a great help to him. She decided with typically impulsive enthusiasm that this was her mission. She was going to tell him the next day, and she spent the whole night thinking what a wonderful thing a mission was. But the next morning she began to doubt her capacity for saintliness. She would be unfaithful to the Jamaican by the end of a week. She would make him unhappy. She decided to look for a job instead.

She went to one or two shipping companies without success, and then to the offices of the air-line. Usually the air-line only engaged staff in England, but they happened to be short of a stewardess, and so they cabled to London for authority to take her on. They gave her an air test, an allowance for uniform, and sent her off on a trip, under the tuition of another stewardess, to Trinidad. On her return she worked for a week in the Kingston office. It was on her second flight that the crash occurred.

The aircraft was going to Cuba and Miami, and was supposed to return the next morning. Immediately after take-off from the Kingston airport Judy and her fellow-stewardess had set about serving tea. The aircraft circled Kingston to gain height and then set course for Camaguey. Soon after they had crossed the foothills of the Blue Mountains the alarm signal was given. Judy and the other stewardess went forward to make the passengers fasten their safety-belts. Half of them didn't want to do it; they had realized something was wrong with the engines, and although the air-liners didn't carry parachutes, they wanted to be free to jump out. By this time the aircraft was in the valley, which afforded no possible place to land.

While Judy was still urging the passengers into their safety-belts, a woman told her that her husband had gone back to the toilet. Judy went to the rear and knocked on the toilet door. At that moment there was a tremendous jolt, which was probably the aircraft hitting the top of a tree, and she remembered clinging on to some shelves, and then there was just the same painless blank that had followed the cutting of her wrist with the razor.

Judy looked serious as she told this, but it wasn't in her nature to look serious for long. Presently she gave a little shrug and said :

"Oh, well. I suppose for the others it was just a painless blank without waking up at all." She smiled briefly. "I'm getting awfully used to thinking I'm dead. I must have a charmed life or something, musn't I? As I wasn't killed, I suppose I wasn't meant to be. I'm rather a fatalist like that. Are you?"

They sat in silence for a minute or two. Douglas pulled out a cigarette and gave it to her, and lit one for himself. He watched her as she sat curled up on the bed in Mrs. Morgan's nightgown, looking wistfully at her chipped nails. After a time he said :

"Are you still in love with Louis?"

"I still have tremors every time I think of him, if that's what you mean." She looked up at him quite brightly.

"He must be a pretty fascinating person if he could make you go through all that for him."

She tossed the hair away from one eye and laughed.

"Oh Lord, no," she said. "I always had a queer taste in men. He's about half your height, and terribly Jewish-looking, and he's got T.B."

CHAPTER FOUR

As if there hadn't already been enough excitement for one week, a couple of days after the crash there was the anonymous letter about John.

That afternoon Douglas had been taking a class under one of the junipers on the grass slope. He had never found outdoor teaching very satisfactory, and always held his most important classes in the Great House in the morning —for the children's capacity for concentration, like his own, had a steady downward graph from approximately half an hour before the sounding of the lunch bell. In the open air attention wandered easily from the subject of the lesson. It was not surprising. The view from the slope was one of the most spectacular in all Jamaica. The whole of Kingston was spread out below, sometimes indistinct beneath a shimmering haze, sometimes so sharp and clear that you could pick out individual buildings—the Government offices, the Myrtle Bank Hotel, the new telephone exchange, the huge white Carib Cinema. Some of the children could identify their own homes.

The arrivals and departures of ships always attracted the children's attention, but even more fascinating were the endless activities at the airport. The main runway was built out into the bay, and the aircraft, coming in to land, often looked as though they had misjudged their distance and were dropping into the water. The take-off was still more exciting. When the sun was shining you could see the machine parting from its shadow as it lifted from the runway; but on dull days there was nothing to show it had lifted, and you waited for a breathless second, half expecting it to plunge off the end of the runway into the sea.

During outdoor classes it was a test of pedagogic ingenuity to compete for the children's interest with the ships and the aircraft—and even with the variety of insects that inhabited the grass. Douglas didn't often try, but gave up his afternoon classes to play-reading, story-telling, or topical discussions. If some visual distraction came along he simply stopped and talked about it.

This afternoon his class had hardly begun when someone spotted a fully rigged schooner sailing into the harbour round the end of the Palisadoes. They watched for a time, and then began to make up stories about it and about the people on board. It was a good imaginative exercise, involving geography and history, and nobody was bored or went to sleep.

John, who was amongst the pupils in the class, knew how to make up stories as well as he knew how to build tree-houses. His schooner story was up to standard. It was about a vain old captain who prided himself on possessing the fastest and most beautiful schooner in the Caribbean. A young man in the crew hated the captain, and one day jumped ship and started building a schooner of his own. When it was ready he sailed it close to the captain's schooner. The captain knew that no ship was faster than his, and proudly unfurled his sails. The young man in the new schooner raced alongside him neck and neck—and then suddenly unfurled another sail and left the other ship behind. The captain was so enraged that he tried to sink the new schooner at night. In the fight his own schooner was sunk and he was taken on board the rival vessel, where he became one of the young man's crew.

Obviously John saw himself as the young renegade of this story, and it was probably not too far-fetched to suppose that subconsciously he identified his own father with the captain of the vessel. By beating the captain and making him a member of his own crew, he had won the victory over his father that he desired. Douglas had always suspected John's resentment of his father from the reserve with which he spoke of him. Now he felt quite certain of it. The children's stories often gave you hints about them like that, telling you what they were unable or unwilling to explain in more direct terms.

Soon everybody grew tired of the schooner, and Douglas took out a book to read to them for the last twenty minutes of class. Just then Pawley's coloured maid came up the slope and handed him a note. It was written in Pawley's neat and painstaking hand.

Mr. Lockwood.
Would you kindly come and see me at your convenience?
Leonard Pawley.

He told the maid that he would go down after the class, and went on reading to the children. Five minutes later Pawley himself turned up. He hovered about in rather an agitated, apologetic way until he had attracted Douglas's attention. In front of the children he usually adopted a self-effacing manner, designed to show them that although he was headmaster and wore a beard he was really quite approachable and a boy at heart.

He goggled round at them. "I hope I haven't chosen a bad moment to interrupt?" There were a few murmurs, and he said, "You don't mind if I take Mr. Lockwood away from you for a minute? I expect one of you can go on reading for him." Douglas gave the book to one of the boys. Pawley beamed at them. "You'll forgive me, won't you?"

They walked off along the slope. Pawley was holding a letter in his hand. When they were out of earshot of the class he said:

"Let me see, Lockwood, how long have you been in Jamaica now?"

54

"Two months."

"Two months, of course." He nodded. "Naturally you can't learn much about a new country in that time. Even with a sharp eye, it's surprising how long it takes to get to know a small island like this. I've been here more than two years myself and I confess there are still large gaps in my knowledge." He smiled at Douglas to emphasize the frankness of this admission. "I've heard my wife say that although she was born here, hardly a day passes without her learning something new about Jamaican life."

This time it sounded definitely as if Pawley was leading up to a homily on improper night-life—although he was capable of prefacing practically anything with this sort of preamble. Douglas glanced at the letter in Pawley's hand again. It had a Jamaican stamp. The postmark was Kingston.

"If you were to draw a comparison," Pawley went on, "you might compare Jamaica with a small English provincial town, where everybody is aware of one another's business. In fact," he warmed to the analogy, "you might compare the class differences in the English town with the colour differences out here. We can't ignore the fact that a man's employment and income usually bear a direct relationship to the colour of his skin. However, that's beside the point. I'm only trying to stress that owing to Jamaica's provincial nature, you're bound to get a great deal of gossip. Backchat is probably one of this country's worst enemies."

Decidedly the brothel. He only wished Pawley would get on with it.

"Even worse than disease," Pawley said. "And that brings us to this disagreeable letter that I've just received." He took the letter out of the envelope, but kept it folded. "I apologize for having to pass on anything so unpleasant. But I've tried to prepare the ground. I think you'd better read it yourself."

Douglas took it. He saw at once that it had nothing to do with his night-life in Kingston. It was an anonymous letter written on cheap lined paper in an uneducated hand. He read it over carefully.

I feel it a duty to tell you, Sir, that John Cooper who is at your school is not fit to mix with other human beings. His grandfather died in the Spanish Town leper colony, also his aunts, facts which you may prove for your good

55

*self. It is well known that leprosy is passed through to
children, and therefore, Sir, you must send John Cooper
away from your school, otherwise when the facts get about
you may confidently expect other children to be withdrawn.
In writing this letter to you only your Personal Interest is at
heart, Sir, since you do not wish other children to become
lepers or to lose your school.*

Douglas handed back the letter with disgust. Pawley
said with some satisfaction :

"Now you see the sort of thing we're up against in this
country, Lockwood."

"Yes, I do."

"But from one point of view, I'm not sorry to have
received this." He watched for Douglas's surprise at the
paradox, but Douglas was still feeling too disgusted to look
surprised, and he went on, "There are plenty of people who
opposed my wife and myself when we started this school.
They told us there were already too many schools here,
and that in any case it was no use trying anything experimental—it wouldn't suit the island character." He flapped
the letter. "I think this proves them wrong in both res-
pects. Nobody who read it could claim that Jamaicans were
well educated."

Douglas couldn't follow that argument. It seemed to him
that the writer of the letter wasn't the sort of person who
would have gone to one of the more expensive schools
anyway, but he wasn't interested in it as a justification of
Pawley's system. He only wanted to know what Pawley
intended to do.

Douglas said, "Well, there's only one place for anonymous letters. The waste-paper basket." He was a bit
annoyed about all the palaver Pawley was making—why
hadn't he torn up the letter straightaway instead of waving
it in front of the staff? For all he knew, Douglas would
start talking about it to Morgan, and Morgan would pass
it on to someone else, and by the end of the day the
rumour would be round the whole school, doing exactly
the sort of damage that the writer intended.

"Quite," Pawley said, nodding his beard. "But on the
other hand we can't afford to ignore it altogether."

"We can send it to the police," Douglas said. "But I
doubt if they've any chance of finding out who wrote it—
and investigations are bound to start people gossiping."

"I agree with you," Pawley said. "It would be a great mistake to drag in the police at this point." He sounded as if he had come to that conclusion pretty regretfully—no doubt he would have enjoyed demonstrating to the police that the letter was a complete justification for the existence of Blue Mountain School. "But in fairness to the other children I feel we ought to investigate the accusations."

Douglas said, "I don't see that it matters if the entire Spanish Town leper colony is composed of John's grandparents and aunts. We know that John's fingers and toes aren't dropping off in the bath."

Pawley's eyes goggled patiently through their lenses.

"Unfortunately—or perhaps I ought to say fortunately —the disease doesn't always show itself at first in quite such a hideous form. A child might have it without any of the outward signs of a leper."

"It wouldn't be contagious at that stage, would it?" Douglas said, climbing down a bit.

"It's far less contagious at any time than most people believe," Pawley said. "The popular fear of it is largely due to superstition." Douglas couldn't help feeling that he had just been reading it all up in the encyclopædia. But Pawley put on a modest smile and said, "You see, Lockward, my two years in Jamaica haven't been entirely wasted."

Douglas said, "Then what do you propose to do?"

"I'd rather ask, what do *you* propose to do? As you know, my policy is to leave as much as possible in the hands of individual tutors. I don't like to think of myself as your superior officer. Only as your guide."

"Then I suppose we'd better ask the doctor to give John a medical examination," Douglas said.

"Exactly." Pawley looked gratified. "I thought you'd agree about that. In fact I've already telephoned Dr. Knowles and asked him to come up to the school this evening. You might warn John that he'll be wanted about half-past five."

"John's going to think it pretty funny," Douglas said.

"We can't help that."

"Some of the others might be examined at the same time," Douglas suggested. "Otherwise all the children will be trying to guess what's the matter with John—and if any of them have heard rumours about leprosy in his family, they'll start gossiping wildly. We might ask Knowles to examine the whole dormitory. It would avert suspicion."

57

Pawley looked pleased. "I always said we could achieve the best results by putting our heads together." He put on a smile of modest humour. "Whatever my faults, Lockwood, I don't think you've ever found me too proud to accept ideas simply because they aren't my own."

John didn't have leprosy, of course—at least not in any recognizable or contagious form.

The doctor came up half an hour early, and the boys had to be fetched from all over the grounds. They assembled in the surgery. The only difficulty was what to tell Mrs. Morgan, who was touchy about her authority as O.C. medicine and medical inspections. Douglas knew that if he told her about the letter it would reach the ears of Morgan in a matter of minutes, and the least they would have to put up with thereafter would be a discourse on leprosy, including its history, causes, cures, and the statistics of its incidence. Douglas consulted Dr. Knowles downstairs.

"Don't worry," Knowles said. "I'll tell her I'm writing a special report on the improved health of boys at school in the hills. I'm just taking this as a representative bunch." He winked. He was a nice little chap with a nut-brown face and white hair. He was used to dealing with the credulous Mrs. Morgan.

Half an hour later he came downstairs again. Douglas walked into the garden with him.

"All poppycock," he said. "The little chap's as sound as you or I."

"Thank God for that."

"Tell Pawley for me, will you? I've got to get off."

Douglas found Pawley in his bungalow and passed on the news.

"I'm very pleased to hear it, Lockwood," he said, as though there was a possibility that he might not have been. "Very pleased indeed."

"I hope it's the last we hear of it."

Pawley smiled ruefully.

"I hope so. But malice is a bad thing to be up against. I should describe it as one of the most dangerous and primitive of the passions."

That sounded a bit second-hand, coming from a man so unpassionate as Pawley. But then Pawley wasn't too proud to use other people's ideas—and in any case it was decidedly true.

CHAPTER FIVE

THE crash had been on a Monday, and on the following Thursday Douglas had a day off. It had been arranged for him to take Taylor down to a nursing-home in Kingston in the station-wagon. Taylor's physical injuries were not very serious, but the shock over his wife and girl had almost paralysed him. He had been lying in bed, looking stunned and not touching any food, and clearly requiring the sort of attention that was not available at the school. Judy, on the other hand, had continued her recovery. There was no point in sending her to a nursing-home, but the doctor had recommended her to rest for at least a week in the cool of the hills. Before Douglas set off with Taylor, he called in to ask her if there was anything she wanted from Kingston.

"I should think there is! Will you ransack my room? Shove practically everything you can see into a suit-case. And for heaven's sake don't forget lipstick and stuff. I feel like a nun without it—and I don't honestly think it suits me being nunnish, do you?"

Douglas and Mrs. Morgan helped Taylor down to the station-wagon. Going through the hall he said, "It's all right, I can manage by myself." But the moment they relaxed the pressure under his arms he began to fold up, so they held on to him tight for the rest of the way. They put him in the front seat. Douglas said little for the first part of the journey—he was feeling embarrassed, not wanting to mention the man's loss, and at the same time afraid of bothering him with small-talk. He was a chap of over fifty, a prosperous businessman from the Midlands, with a smooth round face like a baby's. His usual manner was probably crude and jovial. He was the kind that invite fun to be poked at them and enjoy it, but underneath the boyish jollity are as shrewd as foxes.

After they had been going for a while, Taylor said:

"Difficult road for you to drive on."

Douglas told him there were nearly a hundred hairpin bends in five miles.

"You don't mean it?" he said.

"You have to watch what you're doing. You can't afford to look at the view."

"I'll wager you can't." They went on in silence for half

a mile, and then he said, "Lot of corners on this road."

"Yes, aren't there?" Douglas said. "The deuce of a lot."

"No time to look at the view."

"No; you've got to go carefully."

Taylor said suddenly, his voice trembling, "My wife didn't want to fly, you know."

"She didn't?"

"No. She was thinking of the girl. I told her it was nonsense to worry. She let me have my own way in the end. She always did."

Douglas could think of nothing to say.

"She was a marvellous little woman," Taylor said. "She was interested in pictures. Paintings, you know. I laughed at her. She wanted to buy a painting just before we came away. Thirty-five pounds. I wouldn't let her have it." His voice stuck in his throat. He tried two or three times, and then managed, "I'll never forgive myself for that. I wouldn't let her have it."

"It wouldn't have made any difference to what happened," Douglas said.

"It would have made her happy. And you know what I gave her last Christmas?" He gave a series of gasping laughs, as if he was fighting for breath. "A fountain-pen, thirty-two and six." He squeezed out the last words in a tiny pinched voice, as if forcing them through a hole in a dam he had built against his grief. But the next moment the dam broke and be began to sob. Douglas drove on slowly. There were few things more affecting than the tears of a grown man.

After a time Taylor pulled out a handkerchief and wiped his face.

"I'm sorry, old man. First time I've done that. Damn selfish to bother others. I'm not the first person who's lost someone."

"There's nothing I can do for you?" Douglas said. "Write letters or anything?"

"No, thanks. I don't know what I'm going to do yet. It's going home that worries me. Going into the house, you know. The wife's stuff all over the place. Peggy's room just as she left it. I don't think I can face it."

"I expect you've relations who'll help."

"Yes. I'll probably go to my sister's for a bit. Might get her to close up the house. I'm wondering if my wife would have liked me to handle her things myself, though. I wish I knew."

"I'd get someone else to do it," Douglas said.

They went on in silence for a good way. He thought Taylor had recovered, but when he glanced at him he saw that his baby-face had crumpled up again and he was silently crying. Taylor noticed him look, and said with difficulty:

"The trouble is, I don't know where my wife saw that picture. I can't buy it, even now."

After he had seen Taylor into the nursing-home, he drove on into the town. Down here it was like a sweat-bath, and what with the heat and Taylor's tragedy he was already feeling thoroughly wretched and exhausted. Taylor's absurd guilt about the picture, and the tears rolling down his white fleshy cheeks, had upset him more than all the other aspects of the crash put together, including the sight of the charred woman with the one white leg. That was how you always reacted: you could see fifty butchered bodies laid out in a row with only a momentary turning of the stomach, but the frills of a personal tragedy shook you to the core. He supposed it was only the frills that brought home to you that "but for the grace of God . . ." Well, but for the grace of God there were a million other people he might have been apart from Taylor, people he would rather have been than himself.

There was something about coming into Kingston that always affected him like this—gone was the shimmering enchantment that called him down from the school. Never had a town so lacked distinction, never had there been such unalleviated mediocrity. The mediocrity seeped into him and settled on his soul—settled like a shabby vulture and waited for the pickings as his spirit bled away. Mediocrity calling uncomfortably to his own. He began to see himself, down here, in a new and convincingly real perspective, as he might have appeared to some stranger to whom he gave the main facts of his life—a refugee from a bad marriage and a dull career, now a teacher in a crank colonial school, a man of over thirty with no achievements, no attachments, no fundamental happiness. As he walked through the mediocre streets, they mocked his well-remembered adolescent dreams. Fame, perfect happiness, pure love . . . all the things that had always been just around the corner, that were round the corner even now—not consciously admitted but unconsciously hoped for—until Kingston, like

61

a shabby shop-window, reflected the true image and filled him with despair.

Today he had meant to buy another tropical suit, but instead he drove straight to the Myrtle Bank—the largest hotel in Kingston, and the best refuge from shop-windows and mediocrity. There was a swimming-pool in the gardens. He took off his damp clothes in the changing-room, then had a shower and dived into the pool. In the cool water he felt better at once. He floated about, looking at the fronds of the palm-trees, motionless in the heavy tropical air. Then he climbed out, and sat under an orange parasol and ordered a drink and some lunch. The wretchedness came back to him slowly, sitting there alone. When he was in England and the divorce was over and Caroline had gone, he thought that all he had to do to escape from himself was to cross the Atlantic, to surround himself with bamboos and palm-trees instead of the familiar London streets. Well, it didn't work, you didn't change yourself by changing your position on the face of the earth. He remembered the chap in the office in London who'd warned him, "Keep out of the colonies if you've anything to forget—they're all full of memorial stones to fellows who've already tried." It was the same chap who'd said, when he'd told him he was going to teach in a progressive school, "Aren't those the places where they're proving the wicked old methods must be right?" He used to think that the chap only made cracks for effect as he made up advertising slogans, but perhaps he had wisdom, after all. When Douglas was down here and thought of Silvia and all her superciliousness and lies, he could have gladly wrung her neck.

The waiter brought his lunch on a tray and placed it on the low table by his chair. He was an elderly Negro, with grizzled hair like grey Persian lamb's-wool. Caroline had once had a swagger-coat of Persian lamb, and he began to think of Caroline and wonder what she was doing now. He visualized her, with a pang of envy, lying on a rock in the kinder Italian sunshine, or sitting beneath another parasol on a Paris boulevard, or even in London again, dressing extravagantly for Ascot. Or was Ascot over? He couldn't remember. The days were all gone when he cared about Ascot, about private art shows and dinners by candlelight, about knowing the right people and being seen in the right places. They'd hardly lasted a year. Their novelty had ended with the war, and one after another the discoveries of new realities had dealt successive death-blows. In Malaya, when the war had ended, he had believed that his love for Caroline had died with his love for the life she represented; he had returned home uneasily from the arms of a Chinese whore in Penang. When he found that her own love had expired more certainly, he was overcome with a fresh desire for her. Vanity! Vanity! He had tried to recapture the detachment from her that he had felt in Malaya; but now there was only the pain of not being loved, the humiliation of her open infidelity. The smarting memories of the next six months still stuck to him like open sores, and he tortured himself by examining them with his finger one by one. Sometimes he tried to spread an ointment across them, telling himself, I don't love Caroline, we could have found no happiness together. But the ointment of reason seldom cured a wound.

He brooded and prodded his sores all the time he was eating lunch, and when he had finished he decided that it wasn't any use going on like that, he would return to the cool of the hills as soon as he could. He changed into his clothes again and went out to the station-wagon. It wasn't until he was almost out of Kingston that he remembered the things he had promised to collect for Judy. It was funny he should have forgotten. He turned the station-wagon round and went in search of her address. It was a boarding-house that called itself a guest-house, situated on the out-skirts of the town where incomes were beginning to rise and skins become lighter. The landlady was the colour of coffee, with a girth like Mrs. Morgan's. When she had read about the crash in the newspaper, she hadn't known whether to weep with sorrow over the tragedy or laugh with happiness over Judy's escape. She was still on the verge of both laughter and tears. In the shabby little room she helped him pack Judy's clothes, while a sound of heavy snoring came monotonously through the thin partition. He carried the bag out to the station-wagon. Twenty minutes later he had left Kingston behind and was beginning to climb. Almost at once he felt the air grow fresher and cooler and he took deep breaths of it into his lungs, and the vulture sitting on his soul ruffled its feathers and flapped disconsolately away. In the distance he could see the lofty summit of Blue Mountain Peak. In some people the great wild mountains induced a sense of their own insignificance or triviality. For Douglas they were an antidote to the town's mediocrity,

63

their greatness and their wildness called to his spirit. He felt reborn.

It took a little over an hour to reach the school. He drove the station-wagon between the two tall, smooth-trunked eucalyptus-trees that stood like sentinels at the gate. In the garage he nearly ran over Joe.

"You like me for carry your bag, sir?"

"No, I'll manage it myself."

He walked up to the Great House. Pawley was taking a history class under one of the junipers, and goggled at Douglas as he passed. He went straight up to the sick-room. Judy, for once, was lying in bed. She sat up.

"I was absolutely certain you were going to forget!"

"I hope I've brought what you want."

"I'd feel marvellous in anything after this. I can go out now—it's all right, the doctor said I could. Will you take me somewhere? Will you take me round the school?"

He looked at his watch. "In half an hour. It's free time then. You can see the hobbies if you want."

"That'll give me time to dress. Will you come back and collect me?"

He went to his bungalow. There was a letter on his desk from Caroline. It had an Austrian stamp. He left it while he washed and put on a fresh shirt. Leaving it unopened for a few minutes was an idiotic pretence to himself that he didn't care. Not that he took himself in. It was a sort of discipline, anyhow—an exercise in emotional control. He even opened it in a controlled way, pretending he had no more interest in it than in a circular. She wrote telegraphically. "Hoping to God they don't ask us how we've managed two months on thirty-five pounds. But *divine* here. (Sorry, too 1920s, you'd say.) Had to flee Switzerland owing influx Southend crowds. Alec met ex-wife in Lucerne and danced with her. Rather *chic* dancing with ex-wife. You should come back and try it, dear; very fashionable. Why *Jamaica,* for God's sake? Alec says your only trouble is Midland morals." Nice of Alec. He tore the stamp off the envelope to give to John, threw the letter in a drawer, and walked up to the Great House. Judy was making up in the wall-mirror.

"Heavens, I'm not ready. Do you mind this?" She waved the lipstick.

"Not in the least."

64

"I look rather a tart when I'm made up. You've probably had quite the wrong impression of me up to now."

"You had lipstick on when we picked you up."

"I bet it was smudged."

"It wasn't—it must be crash-proof."

She laughed. "Crash-proof and kiss-proof. It would do as a slogan if you go back to advertising."

"Wonderfully." She went on doing up her face. After a while he told her, "You're the only person up at the school that I've ever been able to talk rubbish with. It's a terrific relief."

"I can't talk anything but rubbish," she said. "I never was any use at intellectual conversation."

"That isn't the trouble up here," he said. "It's treading on people's toes and offending sensibilities."

"Awful," she said. "I'd be in the cart the whole time. I'm rotten with other people's sensibilities."

She came across the room on her bare feet, and sat down to put on her shoes. She was wearing a gay summer dress, her figure was as slender as a boy's. You could see what a good model she must have made. But she had none of the poses that many mannequins develop; she moved with the young eagerness of a foal. It was queer to think she'd tried to commit suicide. He supposed she had done it with the same eagerness and innocence and irresponsibility.

He smiled.

"Why are you smiling?" she said.

"So that you'd ask me why." She looked perplexed. "I hadn't enough courage to tell you unless you asked."

"Tell me what?"

"I used to have a day-dream as a boy. I rescued a beautiful girl from a torpedoed ship. Finding you in the aircraft is the nearest I've ever come to it. My heroics weren't quite up to the phantasy, though."

She brushed the hair away from her eyes and looked at him, amused.

"What else happened?"

"I fell in love with her, of course."

He felt foolish after he'd said that, it was like reaching out under the table and pinching a pretty girl's knee. But a girl with Judy's looks, who'd knocked about the world as she had, knew how to take knee-pinching and innuendoes in her stride. She just laughed pleasantly and said without any self-consciousness :

65

"Don't for heaven's sake fall in love with me, Douglas, will you? It'd go to my head at first—and then I'd start behaving like a first-class bitch, and you'd be wishing like hell that I'd never walked out of your day-dream, or that you'd left me to drown."

When he went in to supper at half-past seven the Morgans were on the point of leaving, but Duffield had only just started. Duffield was delighted to see him, because he hated being alone at the table with Morgan and his wife. It was a strain for him to pretend to ignore their conversation, and he had no opportunity of addressing remarks to a neutral party which were intended in a thinly veiled way to cause offence to the Morgans. It might have been thought that in the stir caused by the aircraft crash they would have started talking to one another and ended the feud—but evidently they hadn't.

Duffield was in an unusually good temper. His hair had been cut down almost to the roots again.

"I hear you're making good headway with our young friend upstairs," he said after the Morgans had gone. Of course he hadn't heard it at all—he had happened to see Douglas showing her round the school.

"Magnificent headway," Douglas said. "I took her down to eat guavas off the trees. She liked those. It sent my stock up a mile."

"Want to take her down to eat some of Morgan's oranges next time," Duffield said. That amused him enormously. He practically smiled. Morgan allowed no one within fifty yards of his orange-trees.

"Or the grapefruit," Douglas said. Morgan's grapefruit always won prizes. But he was sorry he'd said that. It sounded as if he was taking sides with Duffield, and he never took sides. However, Duffield was delighted with the remark. He glowed.

"Don't care for a woman with painted nails myself," he said reasonably, as though he conceded that it was no more than a trifling personal prejudice. "But I grant you she's a good-looker."

"For these parts, anyhow."

"You want to watch out, though." He was the man with infinite experience of women. "Don't want to burn your fingers, or we'll be hearing wedding-bells before we know where we are." He spoke waggishly.

66

"We didn't get as far as discussing anything like that this afternoon."

"You looked as though you were getting on all right." He was still joking. "I don't miss much, you know. I've had plenty of experience myself. You don't stay a bachelor to the age of forty without knowing how to look after yourself. You'll grant that."

Douglas granted it. It sounded as though Duffield was leading up to his reminiscences. He was. He went on to tell Douglas about a girl in Bolton whom he'd courted, until he'd come to the conclusion that marriage would interfere with his career. He had broken the girl's heart, but think of all the children who had thereafter benefited from his singleness of purpose. Then there'd been the girl in the Middle East during the war. He'd been an education officer out there in the R.A.F. The girl was a sergeant. She'd wanted to go to bed with him, and so that was that. Not that he objected to a spot of fun, he'd been a "bit of a lad" himself in his time, but with a girl it was different. Douglas remembered Morgan once hinting that Duffield slept with one of the coloured servants. He doubted if it was true.

The reminiscences put Duffield in an even better humour. After supper he asked Douglas down to his bungalow for a tot of rum. Douglas went in order not to offend him. The tots lived down to their name, you could hardly taste the rum after adding water. Duffield never drank much himself, probably out of parsimony, although he had long since turned it into a matter of principle. Douglas suspected that he had remained a bachelor for the same reason. He had made that into a virtue, too. He was an adept in the art of justification, always convincing himself first. Well, there were others who were pretty good hands at that game.

From romantic biography Duffield passed on to education. A discussion about education with Duffield rarely touched on anything more subtle than the question of corporal punishment. He trotted out a few old stories about boys he'd licked and then shaken hands with, and ten years later they'd come back as successful men and thanked him for the lickings. One of them had become a Member of Parliament at thirty. The Member of Parliament had told Duffield that he might not have been a Member of Parliament but for Duffield's conscientious attention to his behind. Douglas asked Duffield if he was a good M.P., and Duffield said, "He doesn't stand for any of this bolshie

67

nonsense, anyhow." That didn't seem to answer the question, but it was left at that. Douglas tried to lead him off corporal punishment before he trotted out that in his days at school you got the sort of whacking that stopped you sitting down for a week, and it hadn't done him any harm, had it? But Duffield wouldn't be headed off, and so Douglas just gripped his glass and resisted the observation that if it hadn't been for that sort of whacking, he might not be so obsessed with the idea of whacking now. Soon afterwards he said he ought to be getting along. Duffield said what about one for the road, and poured out a rather more generous tot. He was damn lonely, and liked talking once he got warmed up. He quite liked Douglas, thinking him misguided and inexperienced, but open to conversion to his own points of view. He also liked Douglas because of his feud with the Morgans—he hadn't quite enough nerve to dislike everyone at once. While Douglas drank the tot for the road, Duffield told him why he hadn't gone back to teach at the same grammar-school after the war. It was because of the new headmaster. He'd taken one look at the new headmaster, and that was enough. The new headmaster was only thirty-two and a blighted bolshie. Douglas thought that things in the grammar-school must be looking up, and finished the drink. Duffield said, "I was offered the headmastership myself in nineteen-thirty-nine, and I turned it down to join up. That's how they thank you for doing your bit." Douglas took this with reservation, but thought he now understood why Duffield had come to Jamaica. He'd often wondered. He got up.

"Might as well finish the bottle," Duffield said.

"I'll leave that to you."

"Hurrying off to call on our friend?" he said, getting waggish again.

"That would cause a scandal, wouldn't it?"

He left Duffield and walked back towards his bungalow. The moon was nearly full, and he could see his way as if it was daylight. He hadn't thought of going up to call on our friend, but now he did think of it, and the idea threw him into a state of perturbation. He might have been a schoolboy contemplating a daring prank. He stopped at the fork where one path led on to his bungalow and the other up the grass slope to the Great House. He was actually trembling, and his stomach was leaden with apprehension. He didn't know whether he was apprehensive about what Judy would think or about what anyone else might think who found out. He was sure to run into Mr. or Mrs. Morgan, who lived in the Great House on the same floor as the sick-room. He looked at his watch. It was just after nine. He couldn't stay in the sick-room, but he could ask Judy if she would like to come to his bungalow and have a drink. She was bored, he felt sure she would come. If she came he would make love to her. He saw himself making love to her, and he was stroking away the hair from her forehead and he was saying, Judy darling, darling Judy, you came to me out of the sky . . . and then he again thought of running into Mrs. Morgan in the corridor and feeling a fool and not knowing what to say, and Mrs. Morgan going back to talk scandal with her husband. And then he thought Judy didn't want to be made love to, and then he remembered her saying it would go to her head and he thought that she did, and then he didn't know what to think and he stood there in the moonlight at the fork of the path perspiring with indecision. God, one never grew up. He had stood like this long before the war, and before Caroline, at the fork of a road in Notting Hill Gate trying to find courage to call on a girl in a boarding-house and seduce her. On that occasion he'd called and he had been paralysed with nerves, and the girl, who was nineteen and probably a virgin, had said she would give him the benefit of the doubt and assume he was mad. He had learnt something since then, though, and he had lost his spots. He hoped nobody was watching him standing there in the moonlight, and he pretended to be examining the leaves of a shrub. He hadn't learnt all that much. He hadn't learnt expedience, it appeared; he hadn't learnt that as a school-master you didn't start making love right in the middle of the school to a girl you scarcely knew. He let this argument of expedience impress him, and he left the bush and started walking down the path through the undergrowth towards his own bungalow. The weight of apprehension left his stomach. God save expedience; what a bloody fool he'd nearly been.

When he reached the bungalow he felt exhausted after all that indecision, and he fetched a glass and a bottle of rum and a bottle of ginger from inside and sat down in a chair on the verandah. He knew it hadn't been expedience at all, it had been plain funk. Calling it expedience was a Duffield trick, making a virtue of a shortcoming. All the same, he was glad he hadn't gone up to Judy now. He had stopped wanting her so much, and it didn't seem so likely that she wanted him. She wouldn't have assumed he must be mad, she wasn't that sort; but she might have laughed and said no. She might have told him she was still in love with Louis. Not that he thought that would stop her. Or would it? You never knew.

He poured himself out a small rum, and then he made it a large one just to show Duffield. It was a warm night; the moon increased in brilliance as it rose. The harbour and plain lay below him, bathed in the flat white light. The spidery line of surf on the Palisadoes was like a streak of forked lightning on a photograph. The lights of Kingston radiated like yellow stars into the bony whiteness of the plain. He remembered what he had felt like in Kingston that morning. He remembered it so well that it was as though he still existed down there, and had been permitted at the same time to step up to heaven and take a look at himself from the viewpoint of a god—or that he was an actor who had left his shell on the stage while he went up to see what he looked like from a box. It was queer how you could look at yourself in different ways. Not that it meant much. In the end you were just yourself; you were the person who did or didn't like figs, the person who did or didn't believe in beatings, the person who had or hadn't been divorced. You might sometimes cover your mediocrity with a cloak of yellow stars, but came the dawn and you had to throw it off.

He remembered he had a cigar in the bungalow, and went in to fetch it. He sat down again and lit it, and wondered what he ought to do about Judy. He thought about her long, slender legs and her quick, frank smile. Probably she was very promiscuous and would let him make love to her, and afterwards he would regret it because she would go away. He was not good at making love to people and not falling in love with them; he was more like a woman in that way. He had even got upset over that Chinese girl in Penang, who had loved him so much on account of his nice red tins of Craven "A" cigarettes which could be sold for eight dollars a tin, and he hadn't even been able to talk to her except in mime. He could fall in love in a brothel; though unfortunately he couldn't fall out of love with Caroline in one or he'd have tried it long ago. Perhaps Judy would help him fall out of love with Caroline a bit. It was a good excuse, anyhow.

The cigar was a good one. In England it would have cost five-and-six, but in Jamaica it only cost a shilling. Its aroma gave him a sense of well-being, and he thought of stroking the hair out of Judy's eye again, instead of her having to do it for herself, and the pleasure of saying Judy darling, darling Judy; and he decided that he would see her tomorrow and ask her if she would like to come down after dinner; and she would know what he meant and would say yes or no. Thank God, she wasn't the sort who would say yes, if you promise not to take advantage of me, and would come down and arrange her skirt so that you saw her thighs and then say, now don't spoil it all, you remember you promised.

It was only half-past nine, and he gave himself another rum. As he put the cork back in the bottle he wondered if tomorrow morning he would be feeling expedient again—he was nearly always expedient in the mornings—and would decide to leave Judy alone, and in a few days she would go away and that would be that. It was funny not to know whether he would ever make love to Judy or not. If it wasn't Judy, he wondered who would be the next person he'd make love to. He was still wondering this when he was startled by the sound of an animal crashing through the undergrowth, and a moment later one of Mrs. Pawley's Dalmatians bounded out on to the path in front of the bungalow. It was immediately joined by the second. They both stood there, panting in the moonlight. Their coats might have been designed as a moonlight camouflage, for the black spots were like the speckled shadows of leaves.

A minute later Mrs. Pawley herself appeared on the path. She stopped, looking at the bungalow, evidently unable to see him in the darkness of the verandah. Then she came forward abruptly and mounted the steps. He stood up.

"Oh, I didn't see you, Douglas," she said, impatient and casual. "I was just taking the dogs for a walk. I thought I'd drop in this book you wanted." She handed him the book as if she was passing on something in which she had completely lost interest. He couldn't remember ever having wanted a book of hers. He looked at the title. It was a novel she had once asked him if he'd read, and he had told her that he hadn't. He thanked her. "I'd no idea you were in," she said. "Am I disturbing you?"

"Of course not." He glanced at the table, wondering if he could avoid offering her a drink. She saw his glance and gave a short, impatient laugh.

71

"It's all right, you don't have to invite me."

"I'd have liked to——" he said a bit awkwardly.

"But you're afraid of what my husband would think? Really, Douglas, it's not as late as all that, you know." She was trying to sound teasing, but she didn't quite carry it off. "We're not so conventional as you imagine."

It looked as though he was caught.

"I've only got rum," he said.

"I always drink rum. But I'd better leave you. I don't want to make you feel embarrassed." She laughed again.

"I'll get another glass," he said. He hated this sort of thing.

"Are you sure it won't hurt your conscience, entertaining the headmaster's wife after nine o'clock?"

"Not at all." He went into the bungalow for the glass, and when he came out he switched on the verandah light.

"You don't want that, do you?" Mrs. Pawley said.

"I can see better to pour out."

"And it makes it all look so much more above-board," she said, joking badly.

"That, too."

She sat down in one of the basket-work chairs. She was wearing slacks. He had not seen her in a dress more than twice in a couple of months. Probably she preferred the slacks because they hid her ankles, which were on the thick side. Otherwise her figure wasn't bad for a woman of thirty-five. If it hadn't been for her bearing and her neurotic manner, she might have been quite attractive.

He filled the glass with rum and ginger and handed it to her. As he was sitting down, she said with casual petulance:

"Thank heavens, we're going to have the place to ourselves again tomorrow."

He didn't understand what she meant.

"That girl will be going," she said.

"You mean the stewardess?"

She only answered by saying impatiently, "Is that what she calls herself?"

"I thought she was staying another few days," Douglas said. "Dr. Knowles said she ought to."

"Dr. Knowles has no right to say anything of the sort," Mrs. Pawley said. "He doesn't own the school—he's just employed by my husband."

Douglas said reasonably, "He only put it forward as a suggestion. He told me he'd spoken to Mr. Pawley, and Mr. Pawley had agreed."

"Perhaps he did." She picked with her nails at the wicker arm of the chair. "But presumably my husband has the right to change his mind. He doesn't want the school to become a public hospital."

"Naturally not," he said. "But that hasn't quite happened yet."

"In any case, we may need the sick-room for one of the children."

"Can't she stay until we do?"

Mrs. Pawley waved the question away with a gesture to show that the whole matter was outside her interest.

"Really, Douglas, it's nothing to do with me. I don't see why you should bother about it, either."

"I thought it might be my fault for taking her round the school this afternoon. It was stupid of me not to ask your husband's permission first."

"Oh, I don't suppose you could help that," she said off-handedly. "She's rather been attaching herself to you, hasn't she? I don't think she's a very good type to have about near the children."

"She probably isn't as fast as she looks," he said, passing this off lightly. He was trying not to sound too concerned about Judy; but he was pretty indignant. He guessed that it was Mrs. Pawley herself, and not her husband, who objected to Judy staying on at the school; and it occurred to him that she might have come to his bungalow this evening to find out if Judy was with him.

"Please let's talk about something else, Douglas," Mrs. Pawley said. "Personally I'm quite indifferent about whether the girl stays here or not. I don't think she's likely to interest anybody, except perhaps Duffield." She said that scornfully—her opinion of Duffield had always been low; but before he had time to make any comment she said with an emphatic change of subject, "I'd forgotten you had such a marvellous view from your verandah. It's even better than ours."

"It's delightful," he said without much enthusiasm. He was wondering what Mrs. Pawley would have done if she had found him with Judy. Now it looked as though he wouldn't be able to ask Judy down tomorrow night either. She'd have gone.

"I wish you'd turn the light off again, Douglas. You can see the view much better without it."

He got up and turned off the light.

"That's much nicer. You don't mind, do you?"

"No," he said.

"I love talking in the moonlight." She gave her quick laugh. "I shan't stay long, though."

"Stay as long as you like." He made his voice toneless.

"You do sound pressing." She changed her tactics, and said in a laying-the-cards-on-the-table sort of way, "I'm sometimes awfully glad to talk to someone besides my husband, you know. I'm afraid I often get bored with him. He's terribly dull."

"Perhaps in some ways."

"He is if you have to live with him. Of course he's much older than me. You probably guessed that, didn't you?"

He said yes, he had suspected there might be a slight difference in their ages, although he was sure it wasn't half what she intended to imply. He could see exactly what was coming. She was going to tell him why she'd married him, and how there had been another man in love with her, and what she would have been like if she had made a different choice. He wondered how many times he'd heard that sort of story, introduced with "Of course my husband's much older than me." He wasn't far out. She said :

"Everyone discouraged me from marrying him, you know. He was only a master at a preparatory school in England at the time. My family wanted me to marry someone with their own social background, but I never cared about that sort of thing. You'd be surprised how many proposals I'd turned down. When I became engaged to Leonard, one of the men who'd proposed to me sent a cable from India begging me to reconsider. He was A.D.C. to the Governor of Bombay, and the first in line for a very good title. Of course I laughed. I always was tremendously full of ideals. So was Leonard. That's what I liked about him. I hadn't discovered that he was too weak to carry them out."

"Aren't you rather hard on him?" Douglas said. "It isn't everybody who can start a school."

"He couldn't have done it without me. I've always had to make decisions for him. He wanted to start a school in England first. He'd never have succeeded there. There were far too many experimental schools already. That was why I made him come to Jamaica. I knew he'd have a much better chance here. Of course it meant making many sacrifices. But we both wanted to have a school. You know why, don't you?"

"No."

"I thought my husband might have told you. We're both so fond of children. We couldn't have any of our own."

"I didn't know," he said. "I'm sorry."

"It doesn't matter," she said, brushing it aside impatiently. "I just thought you might be interested. Probably you don't care at all." She looked at him and smiled. "I'd much rather hear something about you."

"You know all about me."

"I only know you were divorced," she said. "I share my husband's views about that kind of thing. It doesn't prejudice me in the least. I'm sorry for what you must have suffered."

"I hope I don't look as if I've suffered."

"You look lonely," she said. "I've noticed it so often."

"Surely not."

"Yes, you do." She still wore the fixed smile. "That's why I think we can help each other."

"In what way?" He didn't want to know, but there wasn't much else to say.

She didn't answer. He supposed the smile was meant to do the answering. To avoid it he took another drink. Presently she said with one of her hard, nervous laughs:

"In some ways you're only a boy still, aren't you, Douglas?"

"Really?"

"You're terrified of doing anything incorrect. I find it rather charming. You mustn't let it stop you having fun, though."

"I have all the fun I want," he said. The conversation was becoming too banal, and he wondered how he could bring it to an end not too impolitely. Fortunately Mrs. Pawley stood up.

"Do you?" she said, in what was meant, he supposed, to be a shocked-girlish way. "In that case perhaps I'd better go before you start wanting any fun tonight. You mustn't let it go to your head because the headmaster's wife visits you so late."

"I'll try not to."

"Otherwise I shan't be able to visit you again."

"That would be most unfortunate." He stood up, pushing the chair back first so that he wasn't too near her.

"I'll let you kiss my hand, that's all," she said. She held out her hand towards him. He took it, feeling ridiculous, and kissed it quickly. She was in no hurry to remove it. She laughed. "You're so absurdly bashful, Douglas. I love to tease you."

"I'm very easy to tease."

The dogs had seen her get up and were scampering about expectantly outside the bungalow. She went to the top of the steps. He had thought it wiser not to mention Judy again, but now he changed his mind.

"Mrs. Pawley . . ."

She stopped and turned round expectantly, smiling in the full moonlight.

"Are you too shy to use my Christian name?"

He couldn't remember her Christian name. He believed it was Joan—but anyhow he wouldn't have used it.

He said, "Don't you think we might persuade your husband to let the stewardess stay a few more days? Dr. Knowles was quite definite about the need for it."

Her smile went.

"You seem very interested in that girl," she said angrily, and turned and went down the steps. "You'd better ask my husband about it yourself. I've told you I've no interest myself in whether she stays or not."

He said, "All right, I'll ask him. Good night."

She didn't say good night, but called to the dogs, "Here, Rex. Here, Queenie!" and went off impatiently down the path without looking back, her hair brassy in the brilliant white light of the moon.

CHAPTER SIX

Usually he calmed down about things overnight, but when Ivy woke him with the tea the next morning his indignation came back with a rush. It wasn't only that he liked Judy and wanted her to stay. He would have felt equally angry if it had been Taylor they were turning out. The sickroom wasn't needed at the moment for any of the children, and there were eight coloured maids in the kitchen to help carry up the meals. Judy's presence wasn't causing the slightest inconvenience.

Mrs. Morgan was at the staff table when he arrived for breakfast. Pawley had just sent her up a note. It said that "owing to the lack of facilities at the school" he regretted he would have to ask Miss Waring "to make other arrangements." The sort of note Pawley would write.

"It's really a shame," Mrs. Morgan said. "It really is."

She had come to like Judy, whom she described as having a heart of "really sterling gold."

Douglas said, "Well, can't you tell Pawley that you've got all the facilities Miss Waring needs?" It seemed much better that the representation should come from her. Strictly speaking, it wasn't any of his business.

"Oh, I couldn't do that," Mrs. Morgan said. She shook her head so that her cheeks wobbled. "Mr. Pawley must have his reasons." She was frightened of offending Pawley because he might dismiss her for drinking, which would mean her husband would also have to leave the school.

"When is Knowles coming up next?" Douglas asked.

"Not till this evening."

"Then I'll see Pawley myself."

Mrs. Morgan looked nervous.

"I'd rather you didn't mention anything I said, Mr. Lockwood."

Pawley was taking a class in the Great House at nine. Douglas caught him as he came into the garden.

He said, "I know I'm interfering in something that hasn't got much to do with me, but I wanted to have a word about Miss Waring."

Pawley said, "Oh yes, Lockwood, of course." It was one of his principles that there were two sides to every question, and everyone had a divine right to a hearing. He tilted his beard on one side and lent his impartial ear.

"Dr. Knowles felt she ought not to go down into the heat for another two or three days," he said. "She hasn't had the stitches out of her wound yet."

Pawley nodded understandingly.

"Yes, he told me that."

"She's not much of a nuisance here. If you don't like her in the sick-room, she could have my bungalow and I could stick up a bed with Duffield. I don't suppose he'd mind."

Pawley pondered this carefully, goggling through his horn-rimmed spectacles at the Japanese Hat. Then he said :

"I appreciate your offer very much, Lockwood. But it doesn't solve our problem. My wife feels we're creating a precedent by letting her stay. We don't want to give people the idea that we're running a public hospital."

Douglas recognized that one. It struck him as just about the limit of absurdity.

He said, "As far as I know, this is the first crash in these hills for at least five years. There probably won't be another for the next five years, and even then there may not be any survivors."

"Quite," Pawley said reasonably. "Quite. But once people realize the advantages of recuperating up at this height, we shall be flooded with requests to find room for patients. There are no other large buildings at the same altitude, you know."

"It's easy enough to turn down requests," Douglas said. "But it's quite a different matter throwing out someone who's already here."

Pawley looked a bit pained.

"I don't think we need use the expression 'throwing out.' You must remember we've already been looking after Miss Waring for several days."

"Well, it's about what it amounts to," Douglas said. Pawley's arguments seemed so darned stupid that he was finding it hard not to sound angry.

"In any case, it's nothing we need get worked up about." Pawley smiled tolerantly.

"I'm sorry," Douglas said. "But after a damned awful accident like that I feel we ought to do all we can, if only to give the school a good name." That gave him an idea, and he added, "And one of the things we've always wanted to advertise about the school is the advantage of the healthy air up here. If people talk about Miss Waring, it'll be good publicity."

Pawley looked quite impressed. He gave it several moments' thought, and then said :

"I wonder if that's occurred to my wife. It's a most interesting point."

"It's a vital point," Douglas said, driving it home. "And if anything happened to Miss Waring because she left here too soon, you know what sort of rumours would get around. They might do us a lot of harm."

"We might reconsider it in that light," Pawley said. He chewed it over a bit longer, and Douglas was afraid he was going to say he would have to talk it over with his wife, but presently he said, "I'll speak to Mrs. Morgan and ask her if she can let Miss Waring stay in the sick-room a few more days."

"Mrs. Morgan won't mind."

"Yes, I'll do that, Lockwood," Pawley said. Then his expression clouded. He stared at the toe that he was twisting on the path. Perhaps he had decided after all that he had better consult his wife. After a minute he said awkwardly, "This is rather difficult to explain, Lockwood. I hope you won't take it personally. But my wife had another reason for suggesting Miss Waring should leave. She felt her presence up here might give rise to unpleasant gossip."

"The presence of any woman might, for that matter," Douglas said, indignant again.

"Yes, of course. But an unmarried woman . . ." He appealed for an understanding with an embarrassed smile. "We've both had examples of how easily scandal can be started in Jamaica. One of the children has only to write a word to his parents—of course it might be quite unfounded. . . . You know what I mean, I'm sure."

"I'm sorry," Douglas said. "I ought not to have taken Miss Waring round the school yesterday afternoon. I expect that's what bothered your wife."

Pawley held up an apologetic hand.

"Please don't think we have any personal objection, Lockwood. But we must consider what other people are likely to say. And in your case we should be wise to exercise particular caution . . ." He beamed awkwardly. Douglas was meant to guess the rest of that sentence. He did.

"Naturally," he said. "On account of my divorce."

His quickness of uptake pleased Pawley.

"You understand it's only a question of safety-first."

Douglas said, "Well, you're not going to send Miss Waring down just because I've been divorced and because I showed her round the estate yesterday afternoon?"

"No; in view of the other point you mentioned, we might find an alternative. That is to say, if you wouldn't take it as a personal criticism . . ."

"You mean you'll let her stay, but you don't want me to see her?"

Pawley smiled apologetically.

"I'm afraid it's imposing rather an unwarranted restriction on you."

"Very well," Douglas said. He was feeling pretty rattled, but after the way he'd nearly gone to Judy last night it was

79

only what he deserved. "But you don't mind if I see Miss Waring to explain? Otherwise she's going to think it rather odd."

"Oh, of course, of course," Pawley said readily. He had evidently been expecting much more of a fuss. "And I'd like to say that I'm delighted you approached me about this —there's nothing like a personal discussion to clear the air."

At first he thought he would just send up a note to Judy, and then he thought he wouldn't, he would at least make his one rationed visit to her, and he put it off until after tea. He went about feeling pretty rattled all day, and then in the afternoon he had trouble with Silvia, which rattled him more than ever.

During the last few days a much more positive attitude towards Silvia had developed amongst the other children. At a meeting of their own, convened to discuss her anti-social behaviour, they had come to a unanimous agreement to ostracize her for a week. They were putting this agreement into effect conscientiously. In class and at table they ignored Silvia with the same inflexible purpose that Duffield ignored the Morgans. Silvia had reacted with a show of lofty indifference. At the same time she had probably been plotting how to attract their attention again—she missed it badly.

She was present that afternoon in one of Douglas's outdoor classes. He had started off the class with twenty minutes of *Situations,* which the children thought of as a game, but which was no less an exercise than making a précis or writing an essay. The idea was to start a discussion about how they would act in some hypothetical predicament. "You hear that five pounds has been stolen from the village post-office. You know it was stolen by a nice peasant whose mother is starving. Would you report him to the police?"

When the children had expressed their opinions and the majority had decided against reporting the peasant, he would complicate the issue : "Then supposing the peasant hadn't stolen the money from the post-office, but from another peasant whose own mother would starve unless he got the money back?" If they now agreed that the thief must be handed over, he would make it more difficult still : "But if the starving mother of the robbed man was cruel to her grandchildren, while the mother of the thief had once sold her only hat to buy her grandchildren bags of toffee for Christmas. . . ?" The final conclusion was seldom unanimous, but it helped to teach the children clarity of thought and expression.

This afternoon he had no real poser ready, so he just turned them loose with a hundred thousand pounds. One of the girls, who was eleven, thought she would buy the whole of Jamaica and make herself Queen. He asked her what she would do then. "I'd execute all the other women," she said. The two boys had more modest ideas. One wanted to spend all the money at once on a firework display. The other decided altruistically that he would buy a huge house with lifts instead of stairs for all the people in the world who had only one leg. He asked Silvia what she would do with it, and she said superciliously, "I don't want a hundred thousand pounds." The other children looked away from her and kept silent as if she hadn't spoken. Douglas said she was probably the most sensible of them all, and left it at that. A short while later Silvia stood up.

"Please may I go?"

He asked her why.

"I want to go to the lavatory." She spoke in a sing-song way, still smiling superciliously, presumably to underline that this was only an excuse. He hesitated a moment, and then said :

"All right, you can go."

She gathered up her books and went off purposefully in the direction of the Great House. He went on with the class. A quarter of an hour later Silvia came down the slope again. She had changed into her best dress and was carrying a small fancy handbag. She passed along the path which ran twenty or thirty yards from the class. The path led to the main entrance of the school. She didn't look at the class as she went by, but she must have come this way to enable them to see her. The direct path from the Great House to the entrance lay out of sight.

The children's resolution to ignore her died in the face of this new development. So did their interest in the class. They all stared after her.

Douglas asked, "Nobody knows where she's going?"

Nobody did know. They only knew that she hadn't got permission to leave the school. They began to chatter excitedly. She must be running away. No—if she had been running away she would have taken more of her clothes.

81

No, she wouldn't—if she had taken more of her clothes, it would have made it too obvious. . . .

Someone said, "Aren't you going to stop her, Mr. Lockwood?"

He didn't know what he was going to do. He didn't want to run after her. He wondered if he ought to send someone down to tell Pawley.

"Suppose she is running away, Mr. Lockwood?"

She was just disappearing round the corner of the hill. He was damned if he was going to call Pawley.

"Norah," he said. Norah was the girl who had wanted to be Queen of All the Male Jamaicans. "Run after her and ask her what she's doing."

"Shall I tell her to come back?"

"No," he said. "Just find out where she's going."

She ran off. He said to the others :

"I thought you were all supposed to be ignoring her. It looks as if she'll win the game yet."

"I don't believe she's going anywhere," one of the boys said. "She's just trying to make everyone look at her."

Douglas said, "I should forget about her if I were you. What were we talking about just now?"

After five minutes Norah came back.

"She says she's got a friend coming up in a car to meet her, Mr. Lockwood. She says she had a letter this morning. He's going to take her down to Kingston. She says she'll probably be back this evening."

There was a moment's awed silence; then an outburst.

"She did have a letter this morning."

"I didn't see it."

"She did, I saw it."

"It's probably her father."

"I think it's colossal cheek."

"She'd have asked permission if it was her father."

"You're not going to let her go, are you, Mr. Lockwood?"

He said, "Well, I'm not going to start a fight in the road and carry her back on my shoulder."

"Supposing everybody went off like that without permission?"

"That would be most unfortunate," he said. "The only way to run the school would be to keep policemen hidden behind all the bushes. But luckily most people have more sense. It's worth losing Silvia for an evening to save the rest of us the bother of a police force."

"I don't see why she should be allowed to do it, all the same." This was the fireworks boy.

Douglas said, "If you kept stealing my pocket-handkerchiefs, Alan, I might stop you with a spanking. But the spanking wouldn't tell me why you wanted to do something silly that Michael didn't. I couldn't help you unless I knew why you wanted to do it. I can't help Silvia either unless I find out why she's always doing silly things that the rest of you aren't."

"I don't think Silvia deserves to be helped."

"Whether she deserves it or not, it happens to be why she's here. Her father pays fees like your father. But if you don't like her, you can leave the helping to me. Just go on ignoring her."

He could see that this explanation didn't satisfy the children, but they were silent and he went on with the class. He was trying not to show that he wasn't satisfied either. It was a fairly safe bet that Silvia wasn't meeting anyone and would be back in time for supper, but he couldn't absolutely count on it. In any case something might happen to her in the meantime, something she didn't intend. If she was knocked down on the road or fell over a cliff or got herself raped, he wasn't going to have a leg to stand on. He began to see what a fool he had been to let her go off.

As soon as the bell went at four o'clock he packed up the class and walked down towards the school entrance. Joe was washing down the station-wagon outside the garage. He hadn't stopped Silvia because Norah had told him not to.

"She done walk off down the road, sir," he said.

"All right, Joe."

He went out of the gate, between the eucalyptus trees. When he reached the first corner he could see most of the road for the next two miles, winding in and out of the ravines on the hillside. He stood and watched for five or ten minutes, but there was no sign of either Silvia or a car. It wasn't surprising. She had already been gone for half an hour.

He turned and walked slowly back towards the gate. It looked as if he would have to tell Pawley what had happened, but he was very reluctant to do so. Probably Pawley would fly into a panic and send out search parties and telephone the police. On the other hand, if he didn't tell Pawley and then some harm came to Silvia, he was going to find himself in a worse mess than ever. It was taking too big a risk. He walked slowly down the path to Pawley's bungalow, wondering if it was better to defend himself for letting Silvia go off or just admit that he had made a stupid mistake.

He didn't have to do either as it happened, because Pawley wasn't there. The maid said he had set off for a walk with his wife a few minutes before. Douglas might have followed them—he knew the direction in which they always went for their afternoon walks—but he was damned if he was going to explain about Silvia in front of Mrs. Pawley. After his efforts over Judy this morning, she would have been only too delighted to see him in a mess. He decided to leave it and catch Pawley alone. By that time Silvia might be back. You could soon get tired of sitting in the undergrowth sucking your thumbs.

His tea was standing on the verandah table. It was nearly cold. He drank a cup and went inside to do some work. At half-past five he went up to the Great House. Silvia still hadn't turned up. He had already left it so long without telling Pawley that he now thought he would leave it until after the children's supper-time at half-past six.

He was beginning to feel calmer. The more he thought of it, the more improbable it seemed that Silvia had been met by a friend or that she would come to any harm by herself. She was twelve. She had often been out in Kingston alone, and up here in the hills she was a great deal safer than amongst the traffic of a city street. She could recognize a cliff when she saw one, and the local peasants were not in the habit of committing rape. Curiosity alone would bring her back quickly. She must have been dying to know what sort of impression she had made.

He left the Great House and went down the garden to the modelling shed. It was empty, except for Rosemary. Douglas himself knew little enough about modelling in clay, but he had been put in charge because none of the other staff knew anything at all. Several of the children had shown great enthusiasm at first, they had spent every spare minute digging clay—the clay in the neighbourhood was ideal for the purpose—and moulding it into animals and heads. Douglas had hoped to discover some real creative talent, but the results were disappointing and the craze had died quickly. He suspected that Rosemary only kept it up because she was afraid of losing his favour if she didn't.

She had less talent than most, and it wasn't easy to discourage her without hurting her feelings. Her present effort was meant to represent a bird. It might just as well have been a lion or a whale. There was nothing interestingly surrealistic about it either; it was simply bad observation and no sense of form. He told her she'd be better off trying to copy something in front of her, and sent her out for a pear. While she was copying the pear he tried to do a bird himself, but it didn't go very well.

At half-past six Rosemary left her pear, which hadn't gone very well either, and went up to supper. He waited another ten minutes and then followed her up to the Great House. All the children were in the dining-room—all except Silvia. Mrs. Morgan, who was supervising the supper, had just heard what had happened. She accompanied Douglas into the hall. He told her not to worry, Silvia would be back in a minute, and in any case it was his responsibility. She looked very upset, and said she had always known that Silvia would come to a really bad end. He left her and walked down to the entrance again, and then to the corner of the road. Still no sign of Silvia. As he returned to the grounds, he met Duffield coming away from Pawley's bungalow.

"Just been having a row," he said. The row had been about a boy whom Pawley had allowed to give up maths because he didn't like it—which probably meant he didn't like Duffield. Pawley had stuck to his guns. He had told Duffield that the boy's difficulties over maths had been upsetting his other work, not to mention his digestion, and that it wouldn't do him any harm to go without it for a term. Duffield was profoundly fed up. "It's a lot of damn nonsense," he said. "I've a mind not to turn up for my own maths class one day. If Pawley says anything, I'll tell him they're upsetting my digestion. See what he says about that."

Something made Douglas tell him about Silvia. Duffield was less outraged than might have been expected.

"Won't be any loss if she doesn't come back," he said. "Should tell Pawley you didn't see her go off, if I were you."

"I can't do that. All the children saw what happened."

Duffield shrugged.

"I expect you were afraid of making a scene, weren't you? If you ask me, half these new ideas are only because the masters are dead scared of the kids."

"There may me something in that."

"It's all wrong," Duffield said, almost paternally. "Unless they're afraid of you, you might as well try and educate a herd of wild pigs. That's why you've got to have proper punishments. Needn't necessarily use them—but you must have 'em handy to create the fear of God. They're only animals, you know."

"Quite." It was no time to start an argument.

"That's your trouble, Lockwood—you're too easy with them. They take advantage of you. I've often heard your classes making the devil of a row if you arrive a bit late. Know what I do, if I catch anyone chattering after the bell's gone? Make them all sit for five minutes in silence. Anyone who fidgets has to sit for another five minutes after the class."

He might have risen to that one, but he was still too worried over Silvia. Duffield noticed it and said comfortingly :

"Shouldn't worry, if I were you. I expect she'll be back. Then you'll have to give her something to think about. Scare the daylights out of her. Why not ask Pawley if you can shut her up in her dormitory after class every afternoon for a fortnight? That'll stop her bolting off again."

"That's what they tried at her last school."

"Can't have given her enough of it, that's all."

As Duffield went off, John came running down the juniper slope.

"Mr. Lockwood, you promised to come and see my tree-house."

"I've seen it dozens of times."

"Not since I fixed up the rope."

"I've got something else to do now." He had to go and see Pawley.

"Can't you come just for a minute?"

"All right—for a minute."

John's tree-house was in one of the mango-trees above the farm. As the trees were not part of the farm, the building activity was tolerated by Morgan, who even dispensed the necessary wood and nails. John spent most of his free time playing there. He had built a platform three or four feet square between two horizontal branches, and then added sides and a roof, making a rather oddly shaped hut. There had once been pieces of wood nailed to the trunk, making it easy to climb. Now these had been removed and the only access was up the rope which hung over the side. The rope was fortunately knotted.

"You've got to go up," John said imperiously.

"I hope it's safe."

"It is. Mr. Morgan tried it."

He began to climb the rope. The platform of the hut wasn't more than ten feet from the ground. As he put his head through the opening he saw that three children were already squashed into the corners—two boys, and Norah, Queen of Jamaica. He registered suitable surprise. John screamed with delight from below.

"You didn't know anyone was up there, did you?"

"I didn't."

"Get right in, I'm coming up too."

He squeezed into the small space. John scaled up quickly after him, and then pulled up the rope.

"Nobody else can get up now."

"There wouldn't be much room for them if they could."

"It's like having a castle with a moat and pulling up the drawbridge. I wish I had some enemies. I'd pour boiling oil on to them."

"Wouldn't it be fun to pour boiling oil on to Silvia?" said the Queen of Jamaica. Everyone agreed.

Douglas said, "Will you let the drawbridge down again, please, John. I've got to go."

"Supposing I threw the rope away? Then you couldn't get down."

"I'd throw you down first and then jump on top of you."

"Why've you got to go?"

"I've got to see Mr. Pawley."

"About Silvia?"

"About all kinds of things."

"I bet you're going to see him about Silvia."

He lowered the rope. Douglas squeezed through the hole and began to climb down. As he was doing so, one of the boys said:

"Look, here she is."

All the children became excited.

"Yes, it's Silvia."

"I wish we'd got some boiling oil."

"Don't let's take any notice of her."

"No, don't let's."

Douglas dropped to the ground. Silvia was coming along the path. She was holding her handbag and walking with an assumed dignity. He tried not to show his intense relief. He had not felt more relieved at the return of a friend from a dangerous mission in the war.

"Hullo, Silvia," he said.

"Hullo." She had never looked more strained in her effort to be supercilious.

"Did you have a good time?"

"Yes, thank you."

"What did you do?"

"Oh," she shrugged carelessly, "I went to the cinema."

She was careful to speak loudly enough for the children in the tree-house to hear, although she was pretending not to notice them. There was powder and lipstick on her face. She had but it on badly and looked pretty comic.

"I hope you had something to eat," he said. "You've missed supper."

"Oh, I've had lots. I had dinner at a restaurant."

"Good—we'd hate you to starve. What's happened to your friend?"

"He dropped me outside the gate. I didn't want him to come in."

She walked on towards the Great House. The back of her dress was crumpled and there was a thorny leaf stuck to it where she had been sitting down. None of the children in the tree-house seemed to have noticed, and it hadn't yet occurred to them that it would have been a pretty tight squeeze to get down to Kingston and go to a cinema and have a meal and come back again in the time that Silvia had been away. It might be better if it didn't occur to them. So long as the phantasy boy-friend existed for them, he existed for Silvia. She needed him just now. If Douglas managed her all right, one day she wouldn't.

The children watched her out of sight. They were obviously awed.

"I wonder who it was."

"She'd put on lipstick."

"I know; she kept it in her bag. She showed us once."

"It can't have been her father, then. She wouldn't have dared."

"How do you know?"

Then one of the boys said:

"I don't believe she's been to Kingston at all. She's only showing off. Do you believe she's been down, Mr. Lock-wood?"

They were all silent, wondering what he was going to say. He laughed.

"Why not? She must be jolly hungry if she hasn't."

He had been far too worried after tea to go and see Judy, but now that Silvia had come home all right he went up and knocked on the sick-room door. Judy was dressed and lying on her bed, reading a book that he had brought her from the school library. She looked a bit bored.

"Oh, hullo, Douglas."

"You've heard what's happened? I've been forbidden to see you. A ukase from the headmaster."

"Oh, Lord." She laid down her book.

"It would give the colonial scandal-mongers the chance of their lives—immoral goings-on in the next room to a girls' dormitory, and all that sort of thing."

"I say, I'm sorry. I'd no idea. It was my fault. It was so marvellous having someone to talk to." She didn't sound as if it had meant much more to her than that.

"It was my fault," he said. "I wanted someone to talk to as well."

She leant on her elbow and pushed the hair from her eye.

"I'm going tomorrow, anyhow."

"Pawley said you could stay."

"I know. But I hate causing a fuss like this."

"It's all settled now."

"I'd decided to go, anyway. The doctor's coming up in the morning. He's taking me down with him."

He felt miserable. He didn't know why; he wouldn't have been able to see her, anyhow. Perhaps it was because this evening she seemed a complete stranger. He remembered how he had nearly come up to see her last night, and with what intent. The memory embarrassed him. He must have been out of his mind.

"I'm awfully sorry."

"You've been marvellous, anyhow," she said. "I wish I'd thought of some way to thank you."

"You don't have to thank me." There was an awkward silence. There hadn't been any awkward silences before. "You're not going back to the air-line again?"

"Good Lord, yes. Why not?"

"It'll take a lot of courage."

"I don't think so. They only have crashes once in a blue moon."

He said, "You won't have started again by next Wednesday? I'll be down in Kingston then. We might meet if you're free."

"I'd love to." She didn't say it with much enthusiasm.

"Only if you want to."

"Of course I do. I was only thinking your headmaster might object."

"It's none of his business."

"I know I don't look awfully respectable." She smiled. There was nothing particularly intimate about the smile, the way he had remembered her smiling.

"Nonsense. Do you honestly want to meet?"

"Honestly."

He was miserable all that night. He drank several glasses of rum on the verandah. There were clouds and Kingston was out of sight. He thought he might drop Judy a note before Wednesday and tell her he couldn't meet her. She obviously didn't care about it, so what was the point? His life seemed empty. He thought of Caroline, and pushed his finger into one or two sores. Then he thought of Judy again. He had needed someone like Judy—as badly as Silvia needed her boy-friend with the car. He had scarcely got her into the sick-room before he had seized on her as a prop. Like a prop used in a coal mine to stop the roof falling down. Now the prop had been kicked out of the way. His roof had collapsed. Hence the rum. God, he could understand how people went to pieces in the colonies.

In the morning he felt a bit better. He thought he would catch Judy as she went off, and say good-bye. He looked forward to this. Probably he had only imagined her coldness. She had just been upset over the trouble with Pawley. At breakfast he asked Mrs. Morgan when Dr. Knowles was coming up. She said eleven o'clock. At eleven he went upstairs. Mrs. Morgan said that Knowles had come at ten, and had already left with Judy. Judy had gone.

"She was really a nice girl," Mrs. Morgan said.

She didn't say that Judy had told her to say good-bye to him. Why should she have done? They'd said good-bye last night. All the same, he thought he would cancel Wednesday. He began to think how he would word the note to her.

He ran into Mrs. Pawley as she came up to lunch. He hadn't seen her since her visit to his bungalow. He had expected to find her triumphant about Judy's departure. She wasn't.

90

"The girl's gone, hasn't she?" she said, without much interest. "I'm sorry if you felt my husband was making an unnecessary fuss. It was probably the best thing, though."

"It probably was."

She smiled impatiently. She was as distant as Judy.

"You were most amusing the other night, Douglas. You didn't mind my teasing you?"

"Why should I?"

"You looked as though you were afraid I was going to seduce you." She laughed quickly. "Don't worry."

"I won't."

She called the dogs. At lunch the dogs roamed the dining-room. It was Douglas's turn to sit at Silvia's table. The children were still not speaking to her. Douglas spoke to her once and she was damned supercilious and rude, so he didn't speak to her again. She looked more sure of herself than before, as though the boy-friend who fought her battles and who loved her was sitting right by her side.

CHAPTER SEVEN

THERE was no more trouble with Silvia that day, she took a book out of the library after tea and sat reading by herself under one of the junipers, but the next evening she went off again.

In the morning she had come of her own accord to see Douglas in the library. She had invented some difficulty over her work, but probably the purpose of her visit was to give him an opportunity to comment on her behaviour. He would have been wise to say nothing—lack of comment left her in a vacuum, made her rebelry pointless—but he asked her, on some impulse, if her friend was coming to take her out again.

She looked straight at him.

"He's coming this evening." She was obviously delighted he had asked.

"What a pity," he said. "Couldn't you put him off?"

"Are you going to try and stop me meeting him?"

"No, I'm not," he said. "But I thought you might like to listen to some music."

"In your bungalow?"

"Yes."

She considered this. Then she said :

"It's too late to stop him coming."

"If you didn't turn up, he would guess you were doing something else. I'm sure he wouldn't mind."

"I'll see," she said.

"In any case, you don't have to go off before school ends, do you?"

She had it all worked out. She said without hesitation :

"No, I'm not meeting him until half-past four today."

"Well, put it off if you can."

He gave these gramophone recitals at his bungalow once a week. Pawley had provided enough money for a machine and a small library of records, and often came along himself. Usually eight or nine of the children attended, half of them because they genuinely liked music, the rest because they hated to miss an occasion. Last week Silvia had been amongst them, sitting away from the others on the verandah in an attitude of studied entrancement. She affected a superior knowledge of classical music—it was an adult virtue that enhanced her prestige—and it was reasonable to hope that she might use the recital this afternoon as an excuse to put off her outing without loss of face. It can't have been much fun sitting for hours alone in the jungle.

She was not amongst the first arrivals at half-past four, but Douglas didn't lose hope. She had a calculating mind —she wanted her performance to be convincing. Probably she would turn up in twenty minutes, pretending to have met her friend and told him she had another engagement. Douglas handed round the bag of chocolate biscuits that had become a recognized introduction to the recitals, and put on the first record.

At a quarter to five Silvia still wasn't there, nor at five o'clock. Shortly after five Pawley turned up to join the group on the verandah. It was in the middle of a symphony. The children began to rise. Pawley goggled and flapped his hands, as though he was shaking out dusters, to indicate that no one was to move. Then he tip-toed up the verandah steps in an exaggerated sort of way, his finger to his lips. One of the boys had vacated a chair for him. He waved the boy back and sat down between two of the children on the floor. Music was a democratic pleasure—a good opportunity for self-effacement. He took out his pipe and began to stuff it with tobacco.

The gramophone had a clockwork motor. Between records two of the children collaborated in re-winding and inserting new needles. The others sat in sacred silence, or vindictively hushed an unmusical offender who thought the symphony had come to an end. This evening they didn't reach the end, because in the middle of a pianissimo passage in the third movement there was a sudden outburst of shrieks from the juniper slope behind the bungalow. These were ignored, the music swelled; but a minute later a boy called Roger came racing wildly down the path. He stopped on the verandah steps, looking as scared as a rabbit. He hadn't noticed Pawley. He said urgently to Douglas:

"Can you come, Mr. Lockwood? Silvia's gone mad."

Douglas rose at once, and followed Roger back along the path that led up by the side of the bungalow. As they came out into the open he saw Silvia half-way up the grass slope. She was lashing about in hysterical fury with a length of bamboo. Alan, the boy whose ambition was a mammoth firework display, was dodging her blows and making ineffectual attempts to stop her. Silvia was not only keeping him at bay, but also managing to land an occasional whack on a girl who had fallen over on the grass. The girl was Norah, the Queen of Jamaica. She was crying exhaustedly and making no attempt to rise. Douglas ran forward quickly. As Silvia saw him coming she increased the violence of her attack. Then she turned on him. She only had time to strike him once before he caught hold of the bamboo and wrenched it out of her hands. She stood there panting, her face distorted with fury. Norah lay on the ground, gasping and sobbing. There were red weals across her arms and legs. Douglas helped her to her feet, and told Roger to take her up to the house. She went off on his arm, her hobble looking rather overdone. As Douglas turned back to the others he saw that Pawley had followed him up the slope. He was standing some yards away, watching with an expression of pained but impartial concern, as though a spectator at a particularly gruelling boxing-match. He was still sucking his pipe. He apparently didn't intend to take on the job of referee.

"What happened?" Douglas said to the children.

Neither of them spoke. Silvia put on an expression of haughty indifference to show she didn't care about the revelations of an inquest. Then Alan said:

"She said she was meeting a friend and going down to

93

Kingston again. We didn't believe it, so we followed her. We found her hiding in the jungle. She chased us back with the stick."

"You're a lot of cowards," Silvia said. "It was three against one."

"We didn't use sticks."

Pawley interrupted and said rather diffidently:

"Lockwood, I'll leave this to you to sort out. Perhaps I'd better have a word with you afterwards. Would you mind coming down to my bungalow?" He shambled off.

Silvia said, "I was meeting someone, anyhow. If you don't believe it, I can show you the letters." In spite of her haughty manner, she was pretty nearly crying.

"You're a liar," Alan said. "Everyone's had about enough of you. It was time you were found out."

"Mr. Lockwood knows I was meeting someone," Silvia said. "He gave me permission. If you'd waited a bit longer you'd have seen for yourself."

"Oh, shut up," Alan said.

Silvia opened her mouth, and then realized she couldn't stop herself crying. She turned and walked off. Alan said in a superior tone:

"We're not such fools as she thinks. That'll teach her to show off. Will you expel her?"

"What for?"

"She'd have killed Norah if I hadn't been there."

"I'm sorry any of you were there," Douglas said. "Why did it matter whether she was meeting anyone or not?"

"She was only doing it to make us think she'd got someone in love with her who took her to the cinema. She thought she was being clever."

"She wasn't doing you any harm. You should gave gone on ignoring her. It would have saved Norah a nasty beating."

Alan looked at him suspiciously.

"You're not going to let Silvia get away with it, are you?"

"Punishing Silvia won't help Norah. You were all asking for something like that to happen. Didn't you expect Silvia to be furious when you found her out?"

"I suppose so," Alan said. "But somebody'd got to do something. No one else seems interested in making her behave."

He said this rather pointedly, and Douglas didn't like it. He said:

"They're more interested than you think, Alan. Now you'd better get up to the Great House and see what you can do for Norah."

Alan went off in silence. Douglas saw that Silvia was standing under one of the junipers, and he went over to her. She tried to look as if she hadn't been crying.

"That wasn't a very dignified performance," he said.

She suddenly screwed up her face again. He waited. After a time she said through her sobs:

"He'll think I didn't want to meet him because I wasn't there. He won't come again now."

Pawley, of course, was reasonable—portentously reasonable and patient. He goggled in silence from behind his desk while Douglas explained the whole thing, and then after a pause to ensure against over-hasty comment, he said:

"I only wish you'd thought it worth-while to speak to me the first time she went off, Lockwood. I feel perhaps you should have done."

"I probably should," Douglas said. "But after she'd come back, it didn't seem to matter."

"I might have been able to give you some advice." He was afraid this had sounded presumptuous, and qualified it at once. "Or at any rate it might have helped if we'd put our heads together."

"I don't see how we could have stopped her going off a second time."

"I think if we'd spoken to her a little more firmly. . . ."

"Short of locking her up, she would probably have gone anyway," Douglas said. "In any case I thought it was best to let her. If the others hadn't followed her it would have been all right."

Pawley shook his head slowly.

"We can't have children wandering off all over the countryside like that. It's not a question of what we think is best ourselves. It's a question of what other people are going to think."

"In that case we might as well start running this place on the same lines as all the other schools in Jamaica."

"We need hardly go quite so far as that," Pawley said moderately.

"If we're going to be progressive at all, we've got to stick to our ideas and show people they work."

Pawley smiled.

"I'm afraid Norah's plight isn't going to help convince them."

"We couldn't tell that was going to happen, though," Douglas said rather lamely.

"If we'd stopped Silvia leaving the grounds this afternoon, it wouldn't have happened at all."

"But you agree that from Silvia's point of view it was best to let her go."

"Yes, but not from the point of view of people outside." They were going round in a vicious circle.

"Well, I'm sorry," Douglas said. "I thought I was only putting your ideas into practice. I share them—and I don't share the ideas of people outside."

Pawley spread out his hands regretfully. "I'm afraid we can't afford to be extremists, Lockwood. The world being what it is, we must learn how to compromise. We must learn to apply our ideas where and as best we can."

"I'm no good at that sort of thing," Douglas said. "I'm not sufficiently in touch with local feeling to know when we can apply our ideas and when we can't."

"I think I can rely on your judgment," Pawley said patiently.

"I don't know that you can." He knew he had no right to be annoyed, in Pawley's position you couldn't afford to overlook public opinion entirely; but the trouble was that Pawley lacked the personality to make compromise seem a virtue. "I can see the same thing is going to crop up over and over again with Silvia. Unless I have a free hand, I'd rather not be in charge of her. I'd rather you gave her to someone who can handle her according to outside opinion with a clear conscience. Why not give her to Duffield?"

Pawley looked rather hurt. "I wasn't suggesting I wanted to take her away from you."

"I know," Douglas said. "But why not? Duffield won't let her wander about all over the countryside. He'll flog her and keep her in after school."

"I don't think that's the solution," Pawley said.

"Well, then, what is?"

Pawley considered this carefully. After a time he said, "I tell you what, Lockwood. I'd like you to go on treating Silvia exactly as you have done up to now. Only perhaps"— he waved his hand unimportantly—"perhaps we could put our heads together if any particularly awkward situations arise."

"Life with Silvia is one long awkward situation," Douglas said.

"I feel quite confident that you'll be able to decide when you need my help," Pawley said. Then as if he was asking a favour, "Would you mind awfully if I didn't give her to someone else? You'd be doing me a great service if you persevered."

Finally Douglas agreed.

"Thank you, Lockwood," Pawley said. "I've every reason to feel extremely grateful to you." Douglas got up to go, but Pawley held out a hand to detain him.

"There was just one other thing I was going to ask you."

There was always one other thing with Pawley. Douglas sat down.

"A less serious matter, this time," Pawley said. "I wonder if you enjoy cocktail parties?"

Douglas looked non-committal.

"I hope you do," Pawley said. "Because I've been invited to one next week, and I shall be too busy to attend. All this paper work. . . . I wondered if you'd like to represent me? You could take my wife down—it's her brother who's giving the party, on Wednesday."

"That's my day off," Douglas said. "I've made arrangements to go down to Kingston." He had written the note to Judy to say he couldn't meet her, and then torn it up.

"What a pity," Pawley said. "I was particularly hoping you could make it."

Douglas laughed. "I should have thought if anything was going to cause scandal in Jamaica, it would be my appearance at a cocktail party with your wife."

"You sometimes take me rather too literally," Pawley said. "We musn't make the mistake of underestimating people's intelligence. And of course I should ring up my brother-in-law to explain."

"I'm sorry it isn't some other day," Douglas said.

"I'd be delighted to let you have Thursday off instead," Pawley said generously. "You couldn't manage to alter your engagement?" He goggled hopefully. Then he gave an apologetic laugh and said awkwardly, "To be perfectly honest, Lockwood, I hoped you might manage it for my wife's sake. It's not very exciting for a woman up here, you know. Mind you, she hasn't said anything—but I expect she gets a bit bored at times." He grinned frankly. "She probably gets a bit bored with me. It would make a change for her if you could take her out once. I can't insist on it, of course. But it would be doing me a great favour."

He wasn't particularly anxious to do Pawley a favour, not this sort of favour anyhow, but he could see that difficulties were going to arise over the station-wagon—he wouldn't have it to himself all day if Mrs. Pawley wanted it too—so he said he would take her.

Pawley leaned back in his chair with a gratified smile. His tact had triumphed again.

"Thank you, Lockwood. I hope you won't find it too much of an imposition." And then in case Douglas had got hold of the wrong idea, he added, "By the way, it's entirely my own suggestion. I thought it might be worth-while to mention it.... My wife had no idea I was going to ask you."

Mrs. Pawley also thought it might be worth-while to mention it, and she mentioned it within five minutes of setting off in the station-wagon on Wednesday afternoon. She said :

"I was so surprised when my husband told me he'd asked you to take me down. You didn't think it was my idea, did you ?"

He told her he had no reason to think it was her idea. He had no reason to bother whose idea it was; he was only cross with himself for being so easily persuaded. He was particularly cross because there had been no answer to the letter he had written Judy. He had asked her if she could meet him on Thursday instead. Either she had already left Kingston, or else writing a letter had been too much effort. Or else his letter had got lost—or hers had. In any case, he was afraid that on account of Mrs. Pawley's brother's cocktail party he was going to miss her altogether. It upset him to contemplate missing her, which showed that he was still making use of her as a pit-prop. He wished he hadn't been so short of pit-props. He wished he really cared about playing the violin or studying the habits of ants. Or even about being a successful teacher.

"You're very silent," Mrs. Pawley said.

"I'm concentrating on the road."

"You're not in a bad temper?"

"Not at all."

"That's a good thing," she said. "You might as well enjoy yourself, even if you're doing this as a duty."

"It's not a duty."

"Isn't it?" She gave a short, impatient laugh. "How charming of you to say so."

Mrs. Pawley's brother lived in a house on the lower slopes of the hills behind Kingston. It was half-past six when they arrived. The drive was already filled with cars. As they got out of the station-wagon Mrs. Pawley said:

"Oh, for heaven's sake remember not to call me Mrs. Pawley—unless you want to give the impression that we're hardly on speaking terms. People here aren't half so conventional as you seem to imagine."

Her name was Joan, he remembered now, but he still couldn't bring himself to call her by it. He wouldn't call her anything.

The party was on the lawn. There were a couple of hundred people there, and a dozen white-coated Negro servants carrying round trays of drinks and canapés. None of the guests were coloured. It must have been quite difficult in Kingston to rustle up two hundred guests of positively guaranteed Caucasian extraction. You could only do it if you didn't mind admitting Jews. Mrs. Pawley's brother evidently didn't—broad-mindedness ran in the family.

Douglas had not met Mrs. Pawley's brother before. He ran a large sugar property that had belonged to their father, and he never came up to the school. Mrs. Pawley seldom went down to see him; she said she disliked his wife. She led Douglas over to her brother, and the wife was with him. The brother was tough and good-looking in a rather brutal and insolent way. His name was Findlay. His wife was plump and good-natured and over-painted. According to Mrs. Pawley she had married her brother for his money, and tricked him into transferring half his property to her name. If it was true, she was brighter than she looked.

Findlay had one of those bone-crushing handshakes.

"Are you from that mental home, too, man? How d'you stick it? I'd shoot myself if I had to spend a week up there. Still, I suppose you're one of these brainy chaps." He said to Mrs. Pawley, "He's one of these brainy chaps, is he?"

"I don't know what we'd do without Douglas," Mrs. Pawley said.

"I don't mind admitting I'm not a brainy chap," Findlay told Douglas. "I only know how to run a property. If you asked me what five times seven were, I shouldn't know. I can't say it bothers me. I pay a clerk to do my arithmetic for me. Come on, man, let's find you a drink."

99

Douglas followed him through the crowd. There were whisky and gin drinks on the trays, but no rum. Douglas took whisky. Findlay said, "How do you get on with that bearded monster up there? He gets my goat, you know. I was damn relieved to hear he couldn't make it this evening. He's no good at a party like this. He's no idea how to mix."

Douglas said something about Pawley having other qualities—at a distance he always felt quite loyal.

"I never could make out what my sister saw in him," Findlay said. "Still, she's a bit of a crank herself."

Douglas said something about Mrs. Pawley having qualities too.

"Do you get on with her?" Findlay said. "Wouldn't have surprised me if you didn't. She can be difficult if she wants. Always had the deuce of a temperament. Perhaps you're doing her some good, though. She needs someone to knock her about."

"I haven't got round to that," Douglas said.

"I wish you'd teach them both some sense," he said. "They're wasting their time up there. All this modern stuff might be all right for us at home. But the people out here aren't ready for it. They've got to be prepared slowly."

"I don't think it's anything they've got to be prepared for," Douglas said. "It's supposed to be a way of preparing them."

Findlay didn't look as if he registered that. He said, "Of course I'm all for progress myself. I'm not one of these chaps who's prejudiced against colour. But it's no good pretending the nigger's the same as ourselves. He's bone lazy, and if you want to get any work out of him you've got to show him who's boss. That's what I don't think you chaps just out from England realize. Now excuse me, old chap, I've got to mix around a bit. I'll introduce you to someone."

He picked on a middle-aged man and pulled him out of a group. It was another estate owner, called Higgins. He said to Higgins :

"Lockwood's one of these brainy chaps. He's got hold of the idea that we're a lot of nincompoops out here. Rough colonials, you know. Tell him about those nuts of yours, and see if that changes his mind."

Higgins was dry and taciturn. Douglas had to press him to talk about the nuts. In 1938 there had been twenty-five thousand coconut palms on his property. They were insured for ten shillings a palm. He reckoned that every year there wasn't a hurricane, there was more likely to be one the next, so in 1939 he stepped-up the insurance. He stepped it up higher every year after that, and by 1944 they were the most heavily insured palms in Jamaica at four pounds a palm. That year there was a terrific hurricane. Its centre passed right over his property. The next morning there were only five thousand palms left standing. The rest had been snapped in half like match-sticks. The insurance company had to pay up eighty thousand pounds. Douglas was going to ask him more about the hurricane, but just then someone else came up and started talking to Higgins, so he faded away and pushed amongst the crowd. Presently he found himself near an elderly Jewish-looking man with a stoop and a monocle hanging on a black ribbon round his neck, and he was just thinking of something to say to start up a conversation when the Jew gave him an amiable smile and fingered his monocle and said :

"I never know how to start conversations at cocktail parties, do you? I remember reading a story of a brilliant professor of science who had the same difficulty. It worried him. He wanted to be a success at parties to please his wife. After a time he thought of preparing some topics of conversation and witticisms, and jotting down key-words to remind him on his cuff. He became one of the most sought-after men in the town. His wife was delighted. Then one day he muddled up all the key-words and started talking gibberish. Nobody could stop him. He was carried off to a lunatic asylum." He gave Douglas a twinkling smile. "The only note on my own cuff is a reminder of that story. The trouble is that I never know what to say when I've told it. Unless I satisfy my curiosity and ask you point-blank what you do."

Douglas told him what he did, and he told him a bit about the school, and then the Jew said :

"I had a niece who went to a school of that kind in England. Before she went she was a nasty, irresponsible little child. When she left it she was even more nasty and irresponsible. Five years later she killed herself." He fingered his monocle and smiled charmingly. "Of course, if she'd been to a different type of school she might have killed herself a few years earlier. It's so difficult to tell, isn't it?"

Douglas asked him what sort of school he had been to himself.

"An inexpensive and inferior private school in the Midlands," he said. "I find it difficult to remember who were the most sadistic—the masters or the boys. I was persecuted by them all for being a Jew."

"It didn't embitter you?"

"On the contrary, it taught me an extremely valuable lesson. It taught me that human behaviour was never rational, and consequently saved me a lifetime of disappointments. Three years of great misery was a modest fee for such convincing instruction."

"We'll have to include persecution in the curriculum at the Blue Mountain School," Douglas said.

"Certainly you should. May I suggest that you adopt a system of allowing naughtiness to go unpunished, whilst inflicting the most hideous punishments on innocent children by lottery? It should be most interesting to study the results."

Douglas thought the Jew was rather a find. He liked the twinkle in his eye and the same twinkle in everything he said, and he would have stuck to him all evening, but cocktail parties being what they are all over the world from Shanghai to Valparaiso, he lost him after a time and found himself with a woman who asked if he had been over to Montego Bay to watch the polo. He said he hadn't, and so she said that polo bored her too. She then asked if he had been to the Governor's last reception at King's House. He said he hadn't, and she said that she could never understand why people set such store on being asked to receptions at King's House, especially in view of the fact that you never knew who you were going to meet there. She herself could remember the days when black men only served at the Governor's table. Now they sat there. She was only wondering how long it would be before white men actually waited on the black men. Douglas was just marvelling at the accuracy and eye for detail with which English women in the colonies lived up to novelists' conception of them, when she reclaimed his attention by saying that she had been sorry to hear about his divorce. She explained that she knew who he was because his photograph had appeared in the *Gleaner*. (Nearly everybody who landed in Jamaica, whether for a "restful holiday in Montego Bay" or to "look into the possibilities of Jamaica as a field of investment," was photographed by the *Gleaner*. His own likeness had been modestly captioned, "Mr. Douglas Lockwood, who has forsaken a brilliant career as one of London's advertising élite to assist Mr. Leonard Pawley in his educational experiment in the Blue Mountains. Welcome to Jamaica, Mr. Douglas Lockwood!") But since the *Gleaner* had tactfully omitted to mention his divorce, he presumed that the lady had gleaned this information elsewhere. She hastened to explain that she herself did not regard divorce as an adverse reflection on a person's character.

He felt very gratified by this, and allowed himself to exchange his empty glass for a full one that was being held out on a tray. She then asked him in a lowered and confidential voice how he could tolerate living in such close proximity to Mr. and Mrs. Pawley. Before he had had time to sketch any of Mr. or Mrs. Pawley's qualities, she quickly pointed out that she had nothing against them personally, except that they were both such bores, that Mr. Pawley's beard was probably to conceal some blemish on his chin, and that Mrs. Pawley was notoriously a snob. She had also heard, though it was probably only one of those rumours that circulated with such scandalous ease in Jamaica, that Mrs. Pawley was not indifferent to the opposite sex. It was puzzling, was it not, that such a couple should have appointed themselves to the education of children? After that she forgot she had asked him how he could tolerate living with them, and invited him to tell her whether or not it was true that one of the boys at the school had leprosy.

"It is not true," he said.

She smiled knowingly. She was a woman of thirty or thirty-five with the superiority of someone who thinks herself a *femme fatale* because junior officers in the colonial garrison have no one better to make passes at.

"You'd naturally want to keep it a secret," she said. "I'm sorry, I shouldn't have asked." Nevertheless she looked as though she had faith in her flapping eyelashes to elicit the truth.

"If one of the boys had leprosy, he presumably wouldn't be kept at the school," Douglas said.

"Oh, the Pawleys have such weird ideas."

"They're not so weird as all that," he said, and then he said he would be interested to know where she had heard the story about the leprosy.

She shrugged and flapped her eyes. Her eyes were too close together.

"It must have been gossip. It's extraordinary what stories

get around. It reminds me of a boy I once knew—he was a friend of my husband's—who told someone in Port Antonio that the King of Sweden was coming to Jamaica for a holiday. He only said it as a joke. A month later he was being fitted for a suit in Kingston and the tailor told him that he'd been asked to prepare six suits for the King of Sweden on his arrival. Of course my friend told him he'd started the rumour. The tailor didn't know where to look. He was so ashamed that he let my friend have his suit at half price."

Douglas detached himself from the flapping eyes as soon as he could. The leprosy story had made him furious. It was the first he had heard about it since Pawley had received the anonymous letter, and he had almost forgotten about it. Anyhow, gossip couldn't turn John into a leper. If the worst came to the worst they could publish a denial.

He found himself another whisky, and then entered into a dull conversation with a group of people about the rising cost of everything since the war. Rum, that used to cost two shillings a bottle, now cost six. He wandered away and discovered the Jew again, and the Jew's eyes twinkled and he looked at his cuff and said :

"Dear me, I've used up this story on you already, haven't I? Never mind—let me tell you about a little success I've had this evening. I believe I'm the only male resident on the island who isn't a member of the secret brotherhood. I've been trying for some while to discover the brotherhood's handshake. I think I've cracked it at last. I tried it out on a man who's disliked me for a long time, and he became quite amiable for a moment or two. Unfortunately I haven't mastered the confirmatory passwords, and he became rather hostile again. You see what I mean about human behaviour never being based on reason?"

Douglas spent the rest of the evening with the Jew. He was still twinkling very brightly and fingering the monocle when Mrs. Pawley came and said :

"Oh, here you are, Douglas dear! I wondered what had happened to you. We ought to go."

The lawn had been brightly lit by electric lamps, and he had hardly noticed it growing dark. The moon wasn't up yet, but the headlights of the car threw a powerful beam along the road, making a tunnel of light under the trees.

Presently Mrs. Pawley said :

"I'm starving. Aren't you, Douglas?"

"Not after all those snacks." He had only eaten a couple of olives.

"You must have a proper meal. We'll be much too late for anything at the Great House."

"I could manage without."

"I can't let you. I've got to look after you properly. Let's go to Mount Mansfield."

"Its rather late," he said. "It's after nine."

She said in her awkward, teasing way, "Is it after your bedtime?"

"I was thinking of your husband."

"Oh, heavens! Do you think he's afraid of you leading me astray?"

They went to Mount Mansfield. It was a restaurant on the road back to the Great House, a few hundred feet up in the foothills. There were tables and a gaily lit bar in an arbour outside. The bougainvillæa tumbled all round. It was the kind of place you would call romantic. He had another whisky, and Mrs. Pawley had some gin. They ate cold ham.

"You seemed to enjoy the party," Mrs. Pawley said.

"I met an interesting man."

"That Jew?"

"He was most amusing."

"Didn't you meet any girls?"

"A very dull one."

"I should have thought you'd want to meet some girls. You must be getting so bored."

"Not at all."

"You're not getting drunk, are you, Douglas? I don't think I'd trust you if you were drunk."

"You could do—but I'm not."

"What a pity!"

He recognized this sort of conversation. He tried to change it, and told her about the leprosy gossip.

"Oh," she said impatiently, "you get that kind of thing."

"It might do the school a lot of harm."

"It might do. You can't help it, though." She waved it away. "We don't want to bother about the school tonight, do we? Say something nice to me, Douglas."

He could think of nothing nice to say. He said something about the bougainvillæa.

"You're hopeless at paying compliments, aren't you?" she said. "You're so shy. It's sweet. I'll say something nice to you instead. You were by far the most handsome man at the party. I felt quite proud of you."

"Having such a handsome teacher at the school?"

"Yes." She laughed quickly. "And having him to escort me."

"You teased me enough the other night," he said.

"You needn't be so modest. I'm not teasing."

"Why do you say it, then?"

"Can't you imagine?"

"No."

"You're so amusing, Douglas. You're so loyal."

"Loyal?"

"You can never forget that I'm the headmaster's wife."

The moon was rising as they drove up the mountain road. It rose exactly behind the Peak. There was a white cloud over the Peak like a bonnet, and the moon shone from behind and turned the edges of the cloud into a fabulous glory of silvery-gold. You expected the voice of God to come ringing out of it.

"Let's stop and look at it, Douglas," Mrs. Pawley said.

"There's not much room on the road."

"You can stop under the cotton-tree farther up."

The cotton tree was an ancient monster whose trunk rose for thirty feet before sending out gigantic branches. The coloured inhabitants of the locality believed that it was the assembly place of duppies—the spirits of the dead —and they never paused on the road if they passed at night. He stopped the station-wagon. The moon had risen above the Peak and shone through the windscreen.

"Do you want to get out?" he said.

"No, let's sit and talk."

"I've done a lot of talking since six o'clock."

"There's no need to talk, then."

They sat in silence. He felt uncomfortable, and he wished he had drunk more and been able to make love to her: it would have been easier. He hated this. He would have preferred the discomfort of remembering what had happened next morning. He looked sideways at her. She smiled. She looked no prettier in the moonlight. Her face had the brittle hardness of a china doll's. The white light made her red lips black; and he could see the little white spots in the shadows under her eyes.

"You remember I told you that my husband and I couldn't have any children, Douglas?"

"Yes."

"I expect you wondered why. It isn't my fault. It's my husband's."

"I'm awfully sorry," he said.

"Because it isn't my fault?"

"No. I'm sorry that anything should be the matter with your husband."

She laughed awkwardly. "You'll probably think this funny. But we've never consummated our marriage."

"I don't think it funny in the least." It explained a good deal about Pawley, though.

"Of course I could have had the marriage annulled if I'd wanted; only it didn't seem fair to him. It's been difficult for both of us. He's always felt so guilty about it."

"I imagine so," he said. "But the school was a good idea. You've always had heaps of children to take an interest in."

She laughed again. "That doesn't make up for everything."

"Perhaps not."

"I haven't always been faithful to him. He's been glad in a way. It's made it easier for him."

"It's lucky he's so broad-minded." He tried not to sound ironical.

"Isn't it?"

They were silent. He looked away from her.

"So you see there's no need to be afraid of him," she said.

"I'm not."

"Of course you are." She said this in her teasing way, and to show that she was teasing she put her hand on his knee. She left it there. He didn't touch it.

"Was your wife very attractive?"

"Too attractive."

"She's made you so unhappy."

"I shall get over it."

"Of course you will."

She moved closer to him. He felt in his pocket for a packet of cigarettes. As he did so he leaned unintentionally against her, and she responded at once with a yielding pressure; and then she saw that he had only been taking out the cigarettes and she withdrew herself with a sudden angry movement. He offered her the packet.

"Will you have one?"

"No."

He drew one out for himself and lit it.

"You like smoking," she said. Then all at once she got out of the car, slammed the door, and walked briskly forward for twenty yards and then stopped and stood still, looking towards the Peak. She stood like that for several minutes. He had almost finished the cigarette when she came back. She got into the car in a business-like way, sitting as far as possible from him on the seat.

"Aren't you going to start the engine?" she said, as if she had been talking to a chauffeur.

He started the engine, switched on the headlights, and drove on. He said presently, to test her mood:

"This car's splendid on hills."

She didn't speak. He could sense her fury. Another five minutes passed before she said suddenly:

"My husband tells me you've an engagement in town tomorrow." She said it as if it was something she hadn't wanted to say—something that had only been forced out by the mounting pressure of her anger.

"Yes, I have."

"I'd better tell you that he doesn't approve of that sort of thing."

He laughed. "But he approves of me taking out his wife."

"Are you trying to be insulting?"

"I don't mean to be."

She couldn't speak for a minute; then all her bitterness exploded.

"That's what comes of being sorry for people! I've only been nice to you because I was sorry for you. You don't think I'd bother about you otherwise, do you?"

He said nothing.

"If you want to know the truth," she said, "you absolutely repulse me."

CHAPTER EIGHT

IT took them another twenty minutes to reach the school. Neither of them spoke. He stopped the station-wagon outside the garage.

"Will you get out here?" he said.

She got out without a word. He let in the clutch to drive

the car into the garage. At the same moment he saw that she was trying to open the door again. Her arm was dragged forward before he could put on the brake.

"I'm sorry," he said, although it couldn't have hurt her. "I didn't notice what you were doing."

She flung open the door. She was almost crying with anger.

"Where's my bag?"

It had fallen to the floor. She snatched it out of his hands.

"If you wait a minute," he said, "I'll see you down to your bungalow."

She slammed the door viciously, without answering, and walked off. He watched her disappear along the path. Then he put the station-wagon into the garage and closed the doors. He walked back to his bungalow. He thought a letter might have come from Judy, saying she could meet him tomorrow. Or couldn't meet him. He went straight to his desk. Ivy had cleaned up the desk, the papers were all placed neatly in the trays, and there was no letter. He looked through the papers to make sure it hadn't been put amongst them by mistake, and then sat down on the bed. As he did so he noticed a vase of roses on the bedside table. They were roses from Mrs. Pawley's garden. She must have told her servant to put them there before leaving for the cock-tail party. He looked at them and laughed. He didn't know why he was laughing, because he was not very much amused.

The next morning at breakfast Duffield chaffed him dryly about taking out Mrs. Pawley, and then about his proposed trip to Kingston that day. He said that he had heard Douglas was meeting Judy, which meant he hadn't heard at all. Douglas didn't satisfy his curiosity. The Morgans came, and Duffield said to Douglas, "Well, I'm going to have a busy day by myself," and left. Morgan said that he was expecting rain and a blow before sunset. He gave details of the meteorological data, as recorded by his instruments on the farm, which had led him to this belief. His prognostications were seldom correct, and Douglas looked forward to a fine day. He left the Great House, and went down towards Pawley's bungalow. He thought he had better remind Pawley that he was having the day off.

Pawley was already in his study.

"Good morning, Lockwood. You probably want to see me before your first class?"

Douglas reminded him that he wasn't going to have a first class. Pawley looked rather hurt.

"Yes, you're quite right," he said justly. "I did say you could take a day off, didn't I? But I was rather hoping you might postpone it until next week."

"I shall have a day off next week, anyhow."

"Yes, naturally." He goggled awkwardly. "It's only that these alterations tend to upset our timetable. . . ."

"I quite agree," Douglas said indignantly. "But it wasn't my suggestion in the first place. It was you that wanted me to take Mrs. Pawley to the cocktail party."

Pawley calmed him with two outstretched hands, as if he was about to strike chords on the piano.

"That's all right, Lockwood. If that's how you feel about it, of course you must go. You're quite right."

He got up from his desk and came with Douglas to the french window. His sagging beard showed there was something else on his mind.

He said after a minute, "I'm afraid that something must have rather upset my wife last night. . . ."

"Yes, I thought so."

"I can't understand it. It's such a pity. I'd hoped you two might get on very well. I hate dissension in the camp, you know, Lockwood."

"So do I."

"Never mind," he said, cheering up. "You're both intelligent people. I'm sure you'll settle your differences, whatever they are."

"I'm sure we will."

He left Pawley on the verandah. As he went through the garden he ran into Mrs. Pawley. She was coming down the path with the dogs. He thought he would make some casual remark about last night and try to pass it off. He said good morning. Mrs. Pawley kept her eyes turned away as if she hadn't seen him. Then she walked right past him, cutting him dead.

It was only half-past eleven when he reached Myrtle Bank. He parked the station-wagon and went through to the pool. He hadn't asked Judy to meet him until half-past three. He bathed, and then ordered lunch. The lunch came, but he didn't feel much like eating. Kingston had never been muggier. The mugginess was held in by the leaden blanket of the sky. He thought that Judy wouldn't come, and the Kingston mood settled over him heavily and the shadow of the heavy black vulture fell darkly on his soul. The waiter who served him was the waiter with the hair like Persian lamb. That made him think of Caroline again, and he spent half an hour masochistically prodding sores. After lunch he dressed again and walked round Kingston. He went into the public library and started looking at books; then he nearly fell asleep with the heat, so he went out and had an ice-cream soda in a bar on King Street. While he was having the ice-cream soda he talked to a mulatto with an unshaven chin at the bar. The chap called him Mr. Lockwood. Douglas asked him how he knew his name was Lockwood, and the chap said that although he was a poor nigger he knew all the illustrious white men in Jamaica. It was the first time Douglas had heard a mulatto call himself a poor nigger. As he went off, the chap grinned obsequiously and said he had fallen on hard times. Douglas gave him sixpence and went back to the Myrtle Bank. He was quite sure that Judy wasn't going to be there, and he tried to prepare himself against a tidal wave of disappointment. He looked round the pool and she wasn't there, and the tidal wave broke and he might just as well not have prepared himself at all. He sat down under a parasol. A minute later he saw her coming out of the changing-room, and another tidal wave broke over him, a tidal wave of joy.

She was already wearing her bathing-costume. Her body was brown and slim.

"I didn't think you'd come," he said.

"Why on earth not?"

"You didn't write."

"Was I meant to? I never thought of it. I'm rotten at letters."

After they had bathed they had tea, and it was the waiter with the Persian-lamb hair, but he didn't think about Caroline. He had never liked her in the Persian lamb, anyhow.

"I don't know anything about you," he told Judy.

"Except that I rush about after men and commit suicide."

"I mean before that. Where were you born? I can't fit you into a background."

"I'm one of those people without backgrounds." She smiled and pushed away her hair. "Cities throw us up. We end in brothels in China."

"You had a family, didn't you?"

"After a fashion."

"I'm sorry," he said. "I'm too inquisitive."

"I'll tell you if you like—I never mind telling people in the least. I'm illegitimate." She laughed. "Don't you know you're supposed to look shocked?"

"I'm terribly shocked," he said lightly. "I don't know what to say."

"You're supposed to say, 'Well, nobody cares about that sort of thing nowadays, do they?' and then you talk about the weather."

"I'd rather hear more about it. Who were your parents?"

"My mother was my father's secretary or something—mainly something, I think. She died when I was born, which gave him rather a bad conscience. He already had a delightful family. At least they looked delightful. I saw him with them in a theatre once by mistake. He had to pretend he hadn't seen me. He felt awful about that, and the next time we met he gave me a fur coat."

He asked who had brought her up.

"A childless couple in Ealing," she said. "My father gave them a marvellous allowance, and came to visit me once a month. He was supposed to be an uncle. They told me the truth when I was sixteen. They were afraid I'd die of mortification, but I thought it rather a joke. The next time my father came he gave me a hideous evening bag. I asked if I could change it. He gave me five pounds to do it with. I couldn't think why everyone wasn't illegitimate."

"You were lucky," Douglas said.

"Yes, wasn't I? My father's rather nice. He makes ball-bearings or something, and he's handy on the Stock Exchange. I wanted to act, so he sent me to the R.A.D.A. I was rotten at that. I started living with someone who wasn't rotten at it, to try and make up, and then he got killed in the war. I nearly got killed, too, messing about in an ambulance. I could never understand why I didn't. I didn't know my life was charmed then. Funny, isn't it?" She shrugged and smiled. "Anyhow, to finish the story, as I wasn't any use on the stage I had a shot at being a mannequin. Then I met the Frenchman at a party. You know the rest. I met Louis in Paris, and let the Frenchman down. I'm rotten about letting people down."

"You didn't let Louis down."

"I probably would have done, but he thought of it first. There's nothing like being let down to stop you doing it yourself."

"I learnt that from Caroline," he said.

"We're a marvellous couple, aren't we?" she said. "But I hate people who sit round licking their wounds."

"So do I," he said. "I hate myself when I do it."

"I never noticed you did."

Later they drove up to Judy's boarding-house, which was called the Haven Guest House. The little room looked more cheerful now, with all the signs that she was living there again, but the sound of a man snoring still came monotonously through the thin partition.

"He does that all day," she said. "He never eats. He gets up at seven in the evening, and puts on a beautiful khaki-drill suit and his sun helmet and goes out and gets drunk. He comes back at one o'clock, and wakes me by making a noise on the verandah. Then he makes an improper suggestion, and I say no, and he goes to bed and sleeps until seven the next night. He sleeps in his sun helmet. Go and have a look."

Douglas went along the verandah and looked through the wire-netting that covered the open window of the next room. The man lay on the bed, naked except for a pair of pants, looking like a huge grey fleshy grub that you might have turned up with a spade. The sun helmet was tilted over his forehead. His whole body swelled up with each snore.

When Douglas was back in Judy's room he asked her, "Can't you find somewhere better to live?"

"Yes—didn't I tell you? I've found a flat. A tiny one—but there's a fridge. I'm moving on Monday."

"You're really going back to the air-line?"

"Yes, of course. I suppose my father would send me some money if I asked him—but I've never asked since I left the R.A.D.A. I feel I've rather let him down since. And taxes are such hell in England now."

"I hate you flying again," Douglas said.

"But I love it. Honestly, I'd pay to do it if I had any money. I'd pay just to see all the new places. And I haven't seen Rio yet. They've promised to send me there soon."

"But you'd come back?"

"Oh yes, it would only be a trip—I should have to come back."

He went out of the room for her to change, and while he was waiting in the hall the landlady came waddling from the back regions to talk to him. She said she liked having Judy at the Haven Guest House, she was a brave girl, and couldn't he persuade her to stay instead of taking a flat? He said no, he doubted if he could. The woman asked if Judy was leaving on account of the snorer; she greatly regretted the snoring, but unfortunately could do nothing about it because it was the brother of her husband. If Judy liked, she would remove the snorer to a remoter room. Or more easily, in order not to offend family relationships, she would remove Judy to a remoter room—a cooler and more delectable room. He said he was sure it was not on account of the snorer that Judy was leaving. Then Judy called him back, and she had drawn her hair up on to the top of her head, and she looked curiously sophisticated and out-of-place in the cheap little room, with the sound of the snorer snoring beneath his sun helmet on the other side of the partition.

"Do you like it like this, Douglas?"

"I shall have to get used to you all over again."

"Do you like it, though? I'll put it down again if you don't."

"No, leave it," he said. "It's nice for the evening."

"Louis made me have it like this all the time. He liked me to look sophisticated. He was that sort—especially when he hadn't a sou."

"Caroline wore hers like that."

"Stop licking sores," she said.

"You started it."

"I wasn't licking sores."

"We're quarrelling," he said. "What a good sign. We must be getting to know each other."

They had dinner at a Chinese place. The food was poor and wasn't Chinese at all, and there weren't even chopsticks to show off with. It was served by a girl of nine who was mixed Negro and Chinese, with probably some Indian thrown in. It was an interesting mixture.

"I'd be afraid of losing you if that girl was six years older," Judy said.

"I was wishing we had a mixture like that at the school." She asked him what had been happening at the school, and he told her about Silvia's latest escapade, and then said, "Anyhow, let's stop talking shop. You're the only person I know that I don't have to talk shop with—except a nice old Jew I met last night."

"What did the Jew say?"

"He said that human behaviour was never based on reason."

"Isn't it?"

"No," he said. "If it was, I shouldn't be having dinner with you now."

She smiled.

"Do you want me to go home?"

"No," he said. "When we've finished dinner, I want you to come and dance."

They drove over to the Colony Club. The tables were outside, round a palm-tree strung with coloured lights. The evening air palpitated with jazz. He led Judy into the crush on the dance floor and held her, and the jazz faded and the crowd disappeared, and Pawley and Mrs. Pawley and the school disappeared, everything disappeared except Judy's smile and the nearness of her eyes and her hair.

"You remember the evening I took you round the school?"

"Yes."

"I nearly came up to you again that night. After dinner."

"Did you?"

"I'd have asked you to come down to my bungalow." She smiled and said nothing. "Would you have come?"

"I've told you how easily things go to my head."

"It was a good thing you didn't come," he said. "Mrs. Pawley turned up to bring a book."

"It might not have been a good thing, anyway."

"Don't you think so?"

"I don't know."

Her eyes were green and amused. The soft fragrance of her hair mingled with her scent.

Presently he said, "I can't stand this. I'm too close to you. Let's sit down."

As they went off the floor a man called from one of the tables, "Hey, Judy, girl!" He was a Jamaican, with a dark olive skin and a boisterous manner.

"Excuse me," Judy said. She went over and talked to him. Douglas sat down. Two or three minutes later she rejoined him.

"That was the man I nearly married."

"Don't you want to dance with him?"

She shook her head. "I decided I wasn't any use at having a mission." She was suddenly looking rather wretched. "I wish I was. He's a darling when he isn't showing off. I could have helped him quite a lot."

"I expect you could."

"But I'm not good enough to do it. I'm a rotten sort of person, Douglas. Why don't you see it?"

"You didn't live with him, did you?"

She shook her head. "I was rotten to him, though. I let him down."

"Because you didn't marry him?"

"Because I let him think I might."

"It was only for two days," Douglas said.

They danced two or three times more. The last time she held him very tight and said:

"Douglas, send me home."

"Take you home," he said.

"Drop me home," she said. "Douglas, darling, I'm rotten. Just drop me."

They went out to the station-wagon. Her boarding-house wasn't far from the Colony Club. He stopped a little way beyond the entrance.

"Send? Take? Drop?" he said.

"Douglas, I've been leading you on dreadfully."

"I didn't need much leading."

"We ought not to have danced."

"Drop?" he said.

"Douglas, I'm not fit," she said. She was still wretched. "I'm not fit. You can come if you want, but it won't be any use. This place is no use. Why don't you forget me altogether?"

"I'll be down next week," he said. "You won't have flown away by then?"

"I don't think so."

"We could have all day. We could go out on the harbour."

"I shan't feel hurt if you've changed your mind," she said.

"I shall feel hurt if you've changed yours—but I'll try not to show it."

"All right, darling. Good-bye."

He sat there feeling tremendously happy, but at the same time there was a weight of lead in him, because a week seemed like an eternity, and he wasn't sure what to believe: whether Judy wanted to meet him again, whether she had wanted him tonight or not.

Suddenly an old Negro stuck his head through the open

window of the car, close to his own. He had pink gums and decayed teeth.

"You like an interesting place, Mister?"

"No," he said.

The Negro pushed his head nearer.

"Listen, Mister, please——"

"Go to hell," he said.

He felt sick all that night. He thought of the snorer calling on Judy, and he thought of the man she had nearly married, and he wondered if it was true that there had been nothing more between them—she was the sort of person who would give herself out of kindness of heart. Then he wondered if it was only out of kindness of heart that she had shown warmth to himself, and he tried to remember her words as they parted, her exact words and her intonation, and one moment they sounded sincere, the next moment they rang with the cracked pitch of an excuse. That night he didn't sleep much, or at least didn't seem to.

The next morning he was in the library when Pawley's maid came in.

"There's a telephone call for you in Mr. Pawley's bungalow, Mr. Lockwood."

He hurried down. It was the first time he had been rung up at the school, and he was certain that it must be Judy ringing to cancel the meeting next week. Fortunately neither Pawley nor his wife was in the study. He picked up the receiver from the desk.

"I know I oughtn't to have 'phoned, ought I?" Judy said. "Are there people there?"

"Nobody."

"Oh, darling," she said. "I was so bloody ashamed about last night. I don't know what you thought. Don't you hate me? You don't honestly want to meet me again next week, do you?" He made his answer quite clear, and she said, "Honestly! I didn't know. I didn't know if you were just being kind to me because of all I told you, the illegitimacy and suicide and all that."

He was laughing as he put down the receiver, and when he stepped outside the bungalow all Jamaica was quivering with laughter in the sun.

CHAPTER NINE

THE service in the library on Sunday morning was supposed to begin at eleven, and by five-past eleven the Minister still hadn't turned up. Pawley looked at his watch.

"All right, Lockwood. You'd better go down and see what's happened."

Everybody already knew what had happened, because it happened about once in every three Sundays. The Minister's ancient Austin Seven, despite the divine nature of its mission, had again been defeated by the steep gradient of the road. Its capricious behaviour defied scientific explanation. Morgan had advanced various theories from time to time, based on the co-relation of weather, road condition, and atmospheric pressure, but each had subsequently been disproved. He now admitted himself baffled.

Douglas set off in the station-wagon with six of the children, who took it in turns to accompany him on these occasions. Three or four miles down the hill they came upon the Minister standing, with the patience of true religion, by the side of his car. The Austin's radiator was steaming mournfully. They hitched up the rope and towed it slowly back to the Great House. Three-quarters of an hour late, the service began.

The service was voluntary, because in the matter of religion Pawley still adhered to the principles of the advanced schools in England that he aspired to emulate. On wet days there had always been a good attendance; but on fine days the great out-of-doors offered too many counter-attractions, and there had often been only a scanty audience of girls to reward the Minister's epic struggles with his Austin. However, the matter had been remedied by an inspiration of Pawley's. He now invited the children who attended the service to foregather on his verandah afterwards, to partake of bars of chocolate and glasses of lemonade. This had meant deviating slightly from progressive principles concerning bribery; but it had ensured the Minister an audience of at least half a dozen gourmands, and also a glass of lemonade for himself.

After the service parents would start arriving in cars to take their children out for the day. This was a custom which Douglas deplored. He would have liked to forbid visits except at half-term. The renewed contact, quickly broken again, often created an emotional disturbance in the children. Moreover, the children who were not visited, because their parents were unable to afford cars, were placed at a disadvantage and made to feel inferior.

He also deplored the custom because some of the parents, such as Rosemary's father, made their visit an occasion to discuss their children with the staff, and expected a weekly report on behaviour and progress. Rosemary's father was even in the habit of giving his loved one a weekly verbal examination in front of Douglas. "Have you learnt to spell *government* yet, Rosemary?" "What's the capital of China, Rosemary?" "Rosemary—think, now—what were the dates of Queen Elizabeth?" If Rosemary answered correctly he gave Douglas a jolly wink—he was a jolly sort of man—to express his satisfaction. If she couldn't answer he told her, "Find out from someone, dear. You won't remember if I tell you. I'll ask you again next week." He then said to Douglas out of Rosemary's hearing, "She's a bright girl—but we must keep her up to the mark. Watch her carefully, won't you? She's all I've got." He would then take her out to lunch, and undo all the good which the school was doing her. His shadow would hang over her until Tuesday or Wednesday, before she started being herself again.

Douglas usually tried to avoid the parents on Sunday, but he liked to meet any he had not met before, to find out what they were like. It made it easier to understand their children; and it was interesting to compare them with preconceived ideas based on the children themselves.

This Sunday Silvia's father came up to the school for the first time. Douglas had formed a picture of a hard colonial type with the sensual and brutal face of Mrs. Pawley's brother. He turned out to be nothing of the sort. He was a small, shrunken man with sad eyes and a pale face, and but for his tropical suit you might have expected to find him, bowler-hatted, catching an electric train to business from a London suburb.

He had arrived after lunch and taken Silvia for a walk. Afterwards he came to see Douglas. He stayed only five minutes. He looked worried and apologetic about the trouble Silvia was causing.

"Mr. Pawley tells me you're being very patient with her," he said. "I'm awfully grateful to you. I know she's not giving you an easy time."

Douglas said that he thought Silvia had started off with the idea that everyone was hostile and bore her a grudge. He hoped they could eventually show her that this wasn't true.

"I don't know why she ever felt like that," her father said. "I've always been decent to her—all the more decent because her mother died when she was a baby. She's had a good home. Everything she wanted within reason. I sometimes wonder if I've spoilt her."

"I doubt if it's that," Douglas said. He asked who had brought her up.

"I had two or three different nurses looking after her before she went to school. They all treated her well, but she never showed them any affection."

"Doesn't she show you any?"

"I'm afraid she often gives the impression that she hates me." He shook his head. "I can't make it out. I'm fond of her, you know."

"You've never thought of re-marrying?"

"I did once, as a matter of fact. Silvia hated the girl. I hardly dared ask her to the house because of the way Silvia behaved. That was partly why I didn't go through with it."

"She sounds pretty jealous of you," Douglas said.

"Other children don't behave like that, though. I know a man who re-married, and his girl was nicer to his second wife than she was to her own mother." He pondered a minute. "I suppose if a child is born bad, you can't do anything about it. I believe she has a bad streak in her, you know—inherited. Her uncle on her mother's side was a bad lot. He was in prison in England once or twice."

"Heredity may have a lot to do with it," Douglas said. "Still, we must make the most of what we've got."

"You think there's a chance of straightening her out a bit?" he asked hopefully.

"I'd say a good chance, given time."

He rose and shook Douglas's hand.

"I've a great deal of confidence in you, Mr. Lockwood." He was embarrassingly sincere. "I'd like to make a success of the girl for her mother's sake. I feel I can count on you."

Douglas walked back with him to his car. The same evening he met Silvia going in to supper. She had been making herself inconspicuous since the incident with Norah on the juniper slope, but she still showed no sign of friendliness. He asked her if she had been glad to see her father.

"He can come up here if he wants," she said, shrugging her shoulders. "It doesn't bother me."

Every Monday morning at nine o'clock there was a staff meeting. It was held in the Common Room next to the library. Mr. and Mrs. Morgan sat on one side of the table and Duffield and Douglas on the other. The Pawleys sat facing each other at the ends. For some weeks the proceedings had been complicated by the Morgan-Duffield feud, which prevented a matter raised by one party from being discussed by the other. It was now further complicated by Mrs. Pawley's feud with Douglas. He had met her several times since Thursday. On each occasion she had cut him dead. This morning he made another attempt to restore their relationship to normal. When she came into the room he wished her good morning. She ignored him. They were a very happy party.

Luckily this morning there wasn't much to discuss. Pawley himself had only one point. He wondered if his staff would find it too great a burden to participate more actively in the children's hobbies. His wife, for her part, was intending to encourage fresh interest in piano-playing, which it was one of her functions to teach. Morgan then expressed a public regret at the falling-off of interest in butterfly collecting. Pawley suggested tactfully that this might be due to the children's aversion to memorizing a list of Latin names, which was a necessary qualification for membership of Morgan's Butterfly Society. This set Morgan off on a lengthy speech about the international nature of entomology and the importance of using labels that were equally comprehensible to collectors in Omsk and Timbuctoo. When Pawley managed to interrupt after five or six minutes, the original question had been forgotten.

Mrs. Pawley then voiced an impatient opinion that Joe was becoming too familiar with the girls. She had caught him lifting one of the girls up the bank where they went to dig clay—quite unnecessarily, since all the girls could scramble up it themselves. As clay digging was under Douglas's jurisdiction, he took this to be aimed indirectly at himself, although Mrs. Pawley spoke without looking at him.

Pawley referred the matter to Douglas, and Douglas said that he would instruct Joe not to lift children up the bank, although he suspected it to be his helpful nature rather than a prurient interest in little girls. Pawley then referred the matter back to Mrs. Pawley, who shrugged as if she hadn't been listening and had anyhow lost interest.

After that Morgan, who had been silent for at least five minutes, put forward a plea for compulsory work on the farm by all the boys. He put this forward at nearly every meeting, supporting it with a compelling discourse on the importance of scientific agricultural knowledge to every Jamaican. Pawley retaliated with another time-honoured speech on the detrimental effects of compulsion, and finally, after having considered the question from all angles, rejected the proposition. Duffield smiled with discreet satisfaction. Pawley then asked if there was any other business for today's meeting. He goggled at each of the staff in turn.

"Duffield? Lockwood? Mrs. Morgan?" None of them had anything, so he placed his hands on the table and beamed and ended up with his customary speech, "Thank you all for attending, then. I hope we can look forward to another satisfactory week." He then said to Douglas, "I'd be glad if you could spare me one more moment, Lockwood."

When the others had gone, he put on rather a martyred smile, handed Douglas a folded letter, and said :

"I'm afraid we haven't got rid of our anonymous correspondent yet."

The letter was in the same uneducated hand as the first. It said :

I regretfully note, Sir, that you have not taken action upon my friendly warning and John Cooper is still at your school infecting innocent companions with the terrible disease which he is known to have contracted from his ancestors. I have informed you that this disease is leprosy. The matter is already being discussed by many concerned people all over Jamaica, and it is only in the spirit of friendly help that I advise you to send John Cooper away from your school before any unfortunate consequences arise.

Douglas put down the letter.

"I suppose we'll have to do something this time," he said, and he told Pawley what he had heard at the cocktail party.

Pawley looked troubled—more troubled about the gossip at the cocktail party than he had been about the note.

"Yes," he said. "That's something we can't afford to ignore. I'd like to make a suggestion. Of course you may have a better idea—in which case we shall certainly discuss it—but in my opinion the first step is to consult John's parents. We should do so in common fairness. They may know who's writing the letters. Personally I believe it's someone who objects to a coloured boy being at the school."

"It sounds from the language as if a coloured person had written it," Douglas said. "Or at any rate a mulatto."

"Probably a mulatto," Pawley said. "They'd be the first to find fault with John—for being blacker than themselves."

"Anyhow, I agree we ought to see John's parents," Douglas said. "If we don't tell them what's going on, they're bound to hear about it from someone else."

"I'd like you to see them as soon as possible," Pawley said. "What about tomorrow morning? You'll have to put off your classes, of course."

"I could take my day off tomorrow instead of Wednesday," Douglas suggested. "It would mean losing less time at the school." And it would mean he would be with Judy a day sooner.

"You don't mind? I hadn't liked to ask you after switching you about last week."

The post-runner took the post down in the afternoon. Douglas wrote out a telegram and sealed it in an envelope with some money, and put it with the letters after lunch. He was in an excellent mood all the rest of that day. Tuesday had seemed like a long desert of time, without an oasis, that he would have to trek wearily across before seeing Judy again; and now all at once she was standing this side of it.

He left the school immediately after breakfast and was in Kingston before ten. He had not met John's parents; they did not own a car, and never visited the school on Sundays. He went straight to their address. It was a bungalow in a small garden, amongst many other bungalows exactly like it. They all had an air of respectability maintained on small incomes.

As he opened the gate a woman came on to the porch, wearing an apron and holding a broom. She was middle-aged, with negroid features and coffee-coloured skin. It was John's mother.

After Douglas had introduced himself she took off her apron apologetically and showed him into the little room which she called the lounge. She wouldn't let him refuse a drink, and she went to the cupboard for a bottle of whisky. It was right at the back, evidently kept there for special occasions. On a side-table there was a photograph of Mrs. Cooper with John and her husband. Her husband worked in a Government office. He looked much less negroid than his wife, and John looked the darkest and most negroid of them all.

Mrs. Cooper sat down with the hopeful look of someone not giving way to fears of bad news. He told her why he had come, and reassured her that there was nothing the matter with John; they had no intention of sending him away, and their only concern was to kill the gossip.

As he spoke her face subsided into an expression of hopeless misery. Her plump hands were shaking.

"I knew people were talking," she said. "I didn't know anyone had written letters, though."

"You've no idea who might have done it?"

She shook her head uncertainly.

"We've got to find out somehow," Douglas said.

"I can't think who it could be." She said this very unconvincingly. She was shaking more than ever.

Douglas said, "We've got to find out for John's sake, Mrs. Cooper."

She suddenly began to cry. She took a handkerchief from the short sleeve of her cotton dress. When she had recovered a bit, she said:

"I think I know. But I daren't tell you. I daren't."

He pressed her and promised discretion, and presently she said, "I think it's a woman who's trying to get my husband. She hates me. She knows I've given up everything to send John to a good school, and it would break my heart if he had to leave. She'd like to break my heart, that's what she wants."

"We could prosecute her for writing the letters," Douglas said.

"No." She shook her head. "I daren't. Because of my husband."

"Your husband would want to stop her writing the letters, wouldn't he?"

"He wouldn't want to get her into trouble."

"But if he knew about this?"

She started crying again.

"It's been going on for ages. She's been trying to get him. He likes her—she's fairer than me. She's younger, too. She'd never make him happy though. She's a hussy."

"Writing libellous letters is a curious way of trying to win someone's affection," Douglas said.

"He doesn't care about John. He wants a fair child. He was terribly angry that John wasn't fairer."

"Does he know what people have been saying about the leprosy?"

"Yes. It only makes him more angry with me. It's quite true that my father and sister died of leprosy. I never had it, though. I didn't tell him when we were married, because people don't like it. They seem to think it's a crime. Then he found out afterwards. He nearly left me then. I expect he told the girl himself."

"I'd like to talk to your husband about it, if you're agreeable," Douglas said.

"No," she said. "Please don't do that."

"I might be able to make him understand what a frightful thing these letters are."

She shook her head.

"I know what he's like. It would only turn him more against me. It would turn him more against John. He'll say we're the cause of it. That's what the girl hopes. She hopes he'll feel so ashamed of us that he'll leave us."

"Would you mind if I gave the letters to the police?"

She looked terrified.

"Oh no," she said. "You mustn't do that."

"I could do it without bringing you in. I won't say I've been to see you."

"People in the road will have seen. My husband will find out. He'll blame me if anything happens. He'll make me take John away from the school. I'd much rather you didn't do anything."

"And you won't let me speak to your husband?"

"No, please don't," she said. "It would only make everything worse. It wouldn't take much to make him go away with the girl altogether. He only stays because of his Government job and what people would think."

"Very well," Douglas said. "We shan't do anything unless you agree. Perhaps it'll all die down."

She came with him to the door. At the door she said:

"Mr. Lockwood—John doesn't know about it, does he? You haven't told him anything?"

"Of course not. We've been very careful about it."

"Oh, thank you," she said with great relief. "Thank you, Mr. Lockwood. I suppose he'll have to know about it one day, but I don't want to tell him yet. It's been such a terrible blight on me."

"Don't worry," he said. "John's a wonderful little chap. Everyone likes him at school. He'll go a long way."

As he said this, her whole face filled with pleasure and pride. Her damp eyes shone.

"I don't mind what happens if he goes on like that," she said. "I don't mind what."

Judy's new flat was two miles from the centre of the town, on the first floor of a house that had been converted into apartments. He had been worried that she might not have received his telegram; but when he arrived he found her waiting, with lunch already prepared to take out to the bay. She was wearing a dressing-gown.

"I thought I'd find out what you wanted me to wear," she said. "These pink slacks—or this playsuit."

"The slacks would remind me too much of Mrs. Pawley," he said.

"All right, the playsuit. We shan't be walking through Kingston, shall we? The air-line would sack me if I appeared in Harbour Street like that. You can look at the flat while I change. Not that there's much to look at."

There was only one living-room, quite plainly furnished, but it was high and airy, and a neat little kitchen led off it, with a refrigerator and an electric cooker. A wide balcony to the living-room overlooked the garden. The bushes of bougainvillæa were neatly paraded and manicured, the lawn freshly striped by a mower. In the centre of the lawn grew a tree with knotty, twisted branches. It was a mass of tiny blue flowers that reminded him of flowers springing up on the heels of melting Alpine snow.

"You know what that is, don't you?" Judy said, coming out on to the balcony.

"I've seen dozens of them down here. But they don't grow up at the school."

"It's my favourite tree. It was my favourite before I found out what it was called. I laughed when I heard." She laughed now.

"What is it?"

"The *Lignum Vitæ*—the Tree of Life. I wonder if I was born under one? Perhaps that's what put a charm on me."

"It's a good emblem for you, anyhow," he said. It was a wonderful emblem—she had so much vitality that he could feel himself drawing from it, sharing it, so that even down here in the town, where usually he felt jaded and sick at heart, he was for once completely alive.

"Shall we go?" she said. "We can't afford to waste a minute of today."

They drove down to the docks in the station-wagon, and found a boatman to take them out in a launch. The oil and scum of the docks slipped away at the sides of the launch, and soon the water became quite clear and blue, and above their heads was the blue-grey haze of tropical heat. They followed the marking posts across the harbour. There were pelicans standing on many of the posts. At the approach of the launch they flapped patiently away across the water, as if turning their backs with faint disgust but without reproach. They flapped round in a circle, and came back again to their posts after the launch had passed. It was several miles across the bay. On one side stretched the low, deserted walls of an old fortress. Then the coast became rocky, and behind the rocks lay stony, uninhabited hills. It was strange, this trick that nature played with Jamaica. A few miles away, beyond Kingston, were jungles of orchids and bamboo and fat tropical plants, and the broad wet acres of sugar-cane, but here nothing grew except cactus. The cactuses stood on the ridges, silhouetted against the sky like a grotesque army of soldiers in the stark landscape of the moon.

They came to a point where they could land. There was a small jetty built on the rocks, and a bare stone building with gaping doors and windows. Some rusting metal rails led steeply up the hillside between the cactuses. They followed these to the top, and found themselves at an old gun-site, with concrete pill-boxes and a huge circular concrete pit. The place was littered with yellowed and torn bits of newspaper and rusting tins, the rubbish of departed humanity that flies had long since discovered and abandoned.

"I rather like places like this," Judy laughed. "I love things that are grotesque and twisted and stark. The cactus is my favourite plant after the *Lignum Vitæ*."

"Much less appropriately," he said.

"We'll have to eat under a cactus. Do you mind?"

Some of the cactuses were enormous, they gesticulated with long prickly arms and flat green hands. Here and there a few blades of grass pushed weakly through the sand. There was no wind. The air burnt against the skin. Down below, the sea toyed with the rocks, idly and intermittently breaking into froth.

"Do you like salad and pâté?" Judy said. "I'm rotten at this sort of thing. I've brought practically nothing."

She had brought plenty, a huge salad wrapped in a damp cloth, and cream cheese and oranges and bottles of beer. The beer tasted less like beer than like some cheap kind of perfume, but Douglas was delighted with it none the less; and some time later, at the school, when Duffield gave him a bottle of the same brand, it brought back to him in a sudden overwhelming flood the whole mood and atmosphere of that lunch, with the heat and the cactuses and his happiness and Judy's long, smooth, bronzed legs stretched out on the sand.

"Did Caroline divorce you?" Judy said. "Or vice versa?"

"No prodding today."

"No, but I'd like to know."

"She divorced me," he said. "She'd have liked it better the other way round—more *chic*—but I was damned if I'd let her have the fun of making confessions in court."

"She sounds a nice sort of person."

"Awfuly nice—except that she came off the assembly-line without a heart."

"Why were you in love with her?" Judy asked.

"She was rather a catch. It was good for my ego. And it was bad for my ego to be fallen out of love with. All vanity. Nobody bothers half enough about vanity, and it crops up all over the shop. Look at Silvia. She must always be a heroine, even if it's a suffering one. That's what's behind all her pathological lying and her romantic love stories."

"Doesn't she believe them herself?"

"Yes, she's the age when she can—and she's out to impress herself first. Vanity, you see—and the sense of being inferior on the other side of the coin. I can understand all that, but I doubt if you can."

"Why not?"

"You've no experience of buried conflicts and feeling

128

inferior. As an illegitimate child you ought to be monstrously problematical—but you're not, you're completely natural."

"But I'm vain," she said.

"What about?"

"I can spend hours doing myself up in a mirror. I'm sometimes rather vain about my ankles as well. That's why I was glad you chose the playsuit and I didn't have to hide them."

"Aren't you vain about your legs, too?"

"I've never been so sure about my legs."

"You could be."

"What about you?" she said. "Aren't you vain about your hands?"

"The last thing I'm vain about," he said, looking at them. "They've no good points at all."

"They've hair on the backs," she said. "That's one of the things I'm queer about, like cactuses and starkness. I suppose that partly explains why I went mad over Louis."

"You're going to start prodding," he said.

"I'm not," she said. "Honestly, I'm not. I've nothing to prod. I know I had awful sores at first, but they healed right up. I would never have thought of Louis' hands if you hadn't mentioned them."

"That's got rid of Louis and Caroline, then," he said. "Consider them impaled on a cactus."

"They might be safer at the bottom of the bay."

"All right," he said. "If only the gun was still here, we could fire a salute. That leaves only us."

"And the boatman," she said. "I suppose he's coming up to ask for a cigarette."

The boatman was young and brawny and coal black. He wore a multi-coloured American shirt and a pair of expensive-looking sandals. He said he had come to tell them about the gun-site, from which not a shot had been fired throughout the war. He then told them that his brother had been in the war; he had been in the navy, and had been sunk and saved. He would have been in the war himself, only he had been disqualified for service by a pernicious croup. He forced a strange croak out of his broad chest to demonstrate how pernicious this croup was. It seemed a curious way of asking for a cigarette, but Douglas gave him one and he looked pleased and put it behind his ear. He then told them about another brother who had been a stoker on a banana boat. After a time, he ambled off down the hill. Judy was lying with her head on the haversack, and Douglas lay close to her.

"Douglas, I warned you."

"You didn't hide your ankles."

"I was rotten to you the other night. I hate girls who do that."

"It was true, wasn't it?"

"It would have been all right," she said. "I was just delaying. I was giving you a chance to be put off. I'm no good, you know. I've told you where I'll end."

"The brothel in Shanghai?"

"I'm the sort that does. I just drift. You're not a drifter —that's the trouble."

"It would be fun to drift a little way with you."

"It would for me. I'm not much use at drifting alone."

"Nor am I."

Her eyes were closed, her mouth open a little.

"You must have learnt to kiss in France," she said.

"I'm only just learning," he said.

"Don't you mind, amongst the cactus?"

"I shall forget them."

"I shall always remember them," she said.

"Oh, Lord," he said. "Listen."

The boatman was walking up the hillside just below. He appeared through a screen of cactuses, ambling up to them genially.

"He wants a cigarette for the other ear," Judy said.

He had remembered another brother he had quite forgotten about, and who would have resented the omission. This third brother had excelled in civic virtues and become a prison warder—and very possibly they had seen him in his khaki uniform, with a rifle on his shoulder, guarding the convicts who quarried the chalk cliff on the road to the Palisadoes airport. He had only used his rifle once and he had missed the target. The malefactor had escaped, but had been recaptured on the following day in the house of a light woman.

Judy said, "Douglas, shall we go back and have tea in my flat?"

"It might be more civilized."

"And less prickly. Look at this thorn in my leg."

"Could we buy something for supper, too?"

"I've already got enough to stand a siege for weeks."

He told the boatman, "Let's hear about the rest of your family on the launch. You've surely some sisters?"

"Yessir—me sisters them fat an' nice."

A wind had sprung up and the bay was choppy. The water plup-plupped against the lifted nose of the launch. Patiently, without reproach, the pelicans flapped off their posts in front of them, and made their circles and converged again behind.

"Louis and Caroline must be somewhere about here," Douglas said.

"I can't see them, can you?"

"No, the water's deep." He watched her smiling into the wind with half-closed eyes. "Perhaps we ought to have brought along a cactus—to keep the mood."

"I don't need a cactus," she said. "Do you need anything?"

"I never did," he said.

At the dock they paid off the boatman and climbed back into the station-wagon. It took twenty minutes to reach Judy's flat, going through the town. He stopped outside the gate.

"We've nothing to celebrate with," he said. "It's quite an occasion—living out a day-dream."

"There's some more scented beer in the fridge."

"Couldn't we do with something else? I could run back to town and get some gin."

"Let's have rum. You can buy it from the grocery just up the road. I'll go in and tidy up." She got out, and said through the window, "But don't be long, darling, will you? Please don't be long."

"Five minutes," he said.

"I'll be waiting."

He drove a quarter of a mile up the road to the grocery. Like all the Chinese groceries, it was as clean as a hospital surgery. There were American comics strung out with clothes-pegs on a wire above the counter, and a prodigious stock of tins and bottles and cartons stacked symmetrically on the shelves. The proprietor had a lean and wrinkled face, and wore a traditional Chinese wispy beard. He rolled up the rum in a piece of brown paper, twisting the top. Then he asked Douglas if he required aspirins, fruit salts, toothpaste, chocolate . . . ? Douglas said no, nothing, and he climbed back into the station-wagon, and he looked with especial care in each direction before he swung round in the road because an accident at this juncture was the sort of trick that fate delighted to play. He turned with the same care into the drive of the house, and parked the wagon round the back and pocketed the ignition-key. He took the bottle of rum and went in. As he reached the top of the stairs Judy came out of her flat. He thought at first, from her expression, that the place must be on fire.

"Douglas," she said.

"What's the matter?"

"Louis is here."

He stopped on the stair. He couldn't take it in. He wondered if she was playing a joke.

"Louis?"

She was still wearing the playsuit, and her legs were long and smooth. She was looking utterly wretched.

"He was waiting on the stairs when I came in."

"But he didn't know you were in Jamaica," Douglas said.

"He found out what happened to me in Mexico City. The hospital told him I'd come here. He flew in this morning and the post-office gave him my address."

"I suppose his wife's left him again?"

"No; he told her he was coming to Jamaica on business." They were both silent.

After a minute he said, "Can't you throw him out?"

She looked at him wretchedly and didn't speak, and presently he said, "No, of course you can't."

"Douglas, please come in."

He followed her into the flat. There was a suitcase standing in the hall. It was made of expensive leather and was plastered with labels. They went into the living-room. At the same time Louis came out of the bedroom. He was in his shirt-sleeves and carrying a towel over his hands as if he had just been drying his face. He was small and swarthy, and had black greasy hair and the sunken chest of a consumptive. His ears were very large and his nose grotesque.

He smiled at Douglas amiably.

"Hullo, old chap." The "old chap" sounded rather peculiar, because he spoke with a foreign accent. "I hope I'm not upsetting anything?" He was very concerned and sincere.

"Not at all," Douglas said. "Except that we thought you were at the bottom of the bay."

Louis didn't bother to inquire what this meant, but

grinned all the same. Judy went on looking wretched. Douglas felt quite sorry for her; she wasn't enjoying herself a bit.

"How long are you staying?" he asked Louis.

"A fortnight, I hope. Depending." He was really being very friendly.

"I may run into you again later."

"You're not going, Douglas?" Judy said.

"I'd better be getting along."

"Douglas, please . . ."

"I might as well leave you this." He put the bottle of rum down on the table, and went to the door. Judy followed him outside and shut the door behind her. She was nearly crying.

"Oh, Lord, I'm sorry."

"It's not your fault."

"It is."

Then she suddenly said, almost angrily, "Well, I told you, didn't I? I told you I was a rotten sort of person. I told you to leave me alone."

"Yes," he said. "I didn't have to choose the playsuit."

She stared at him. He turned and went downstairs. He paused downstairs, and after a minute heard her go back slowly to the flat. The door slammed. He went out and started up the station-wagon and drove out on to the road, only this time he did not bother so much about looking out for other traffic. It was four o'clock. He didn't feel like going back to the school just yet, so he drove to the Carib Cinema. It was cool in there, anyhow. He entered in the middle of a news-reel. Then there was an American film about a man who went out to New Zealand and wrote home for the girl he loved; but he was drunk when he wrote the letter and he wrote the sister's name by mistake. The sister went out, and he had to marry her; they had a baby and an earthquake, and he became very prosperous; and then they all went home. By that time the sister he had loved had become a nun and wore a beatific smile; but luckily he had now decided that he loved Lana Turner after all in a pure proven way, and Lana Turner showed by the tears in her eyes that she loved him. It was all very beautiful, and everybody except Douglas seemed to end up feeling fine.

CHAPTER TEN

HE had hoped that the leprosy gossip could be kept from the children at the school, but two days after his interview with Mrs. Cooper Rosemary came to him in the library.

"Is it true that John's got leprosy, Mr. Lockwood?"

He said emphatically, "No, Rosemary, it is *not* true"; and he asked her where she had heard about it.

"I can't remember," she said.

"Well, you've got to remember," he said. "I want to know."

She thought.

"I heard two people talking about it."

"Who."

"It was Alan and someone."

"Go and fetch Alan," he said.

Alan was a little bit surly.

"I just heard it," he said. "I'd not the slightest idea whether it was true or not."

Douglas had to talk to him firmly before he would say any more. Eventually he said:

"Well, Joe told me, if you want to know."

"How long ago?"

"Yesterday."

"Has anyone said anything to John?"

"No; I'm certain he doesn't know about it. I'd never dream of telling him."

"You might not, but someone else might," Douglas said. "John hasn't got leprosy, but if he hears what people are saying, he could be badly hurt. You can tell all the people you've spoken to that it isn't true. You can also tell them to shut up about it."

He promised to do so. Later in the day Douglas went down to the garage and found Joe.

"Please, Mr. Lockwood, I hear it from the man at the garage, and him plenty liar. I only tell Mas' Alan what I hear, please. I don't say it for true."

"You shouldn't repeat things you don't know for true," Douglas said. "You can cause a lot of damage."

"Yessir, Mr. Lockwood, I never say it again at all."

But he had already said it once too often, as it turned out the next day.

The next day was Thursday, and it was Expedition Day, which occurred once a year. The expedition was always to the same place : a coffee factory in the bottom of the valley five miles from the school. Last year it had been conducted by Duffield, but this year Douglas was to be in charge. The arrangements had been made before his outing with Mrs. Pawley, and Pawley had hinted that his wife would be delighted to accompany the expedition, although he would probably be too busy to go along himself. Now it appeared that owing to certain unspecified duties Mrs. Pawley would not be able to go along either. Douglas was to conduct the expedition alone. There would only be eighteen children, because seven of the younger ones were not up to the ten-mile walk.

They assembled at ten o'clock, with sandwiches, outside the Great House. It was a fine morning, and Morgan prognosticated a whole day of fair weather. The departure was photographed by Pawley, who was accustomed to record such events for the school album with a dilapidated folding camera. They set off down the hill past the farm.

Silvia was one of the children on the expedition. During the last few days she had not committed any acts of sabotage, she had attended classes on time and worked at her assignments, but there was no reason to suppose from her demeanour that the fire of her rebelry had gone out. It was probably just smouldering. Since the affair with Norah, the other children's efforts at ostracism had collapsed. They now spoke to her when necessary, and one or two of the weaker ones showed an expedient friendship. They professed to believe, and possibly did believe, that there was a man in love with her, and that the recent event had somehow prevented him from coming up again.

She had two of these children with her as they started out on the expedition. They walked just behind Douglas, and he heard her telling them, as a matter of course, that she already knew all there was to know about a coffee factory. She had once been taken round one by "her friend," who owned several as a side-line. She had been a guest of honour, and had sat drinking rum on the verandah of the manager's bungalow.

Douglas was walking with John and Rosemary, who liked to show, as his pupils, that they had a certain proprietary right in him. They had only gone about half a mile when John said over his shoulder to Silvia :

"Stop kicking stones at me."

"I wasn't kicking stones at you," Silvia said.

"You were."

Probably Silvia hadn't been kicking stones at him purposely, but now she felt she must live up to the accusation. A moment later a stone hit John in the calf of his leg.

"I told you to stop it," John said. He was being particularly bold in front of Douglas.

"Walk somewhere else, if you don't like it," Silvia said.

"Walk somewhere else yourself."

"I shall walk where I like."

Douglas told them to stop squabbling, and they walked on. Then another stone must have hit John, because he suddenly dropped behind. Douglas went on talking to Rosemary; but presently he heard a row and looked back and saw John and Silvia scrapping on the path. Neither of them stopped when he called to them, so he went back and parted them, and told them to behave or he would send them both home. This started them bickering about who had been responsible. He shut them up. They looked at each other angrily. Then Silvia said with venom:

"I don't know why I touched you, anyhow. You're a filthy little leper. I suppose I'll catch it now."

This may not have signified much to John, he had heard Silvia's violent invective before, but it signified a great deal to Douglas. He told John and the other children to go on. Then he ordered Silvia to return to the school.

"It was a most disgusting thing to say—you're not fit to mix with the other children." He was extremely angry. He had seldom lost his temper at the school, and even more seldom shown it; but now it must have been quite evident. "You can tell Mrs. Morgan I sent you back. Ask her to give you some lunch."

"I don't want to go back," Silvia said. She put her head in the air and started walking off down the path.

Douglas overtook her and stood in her way.

"You're not coming on this expedition," he said. "If necessary I'll have you taken back by the others."

Her eyes were bright with hatred, and at the same time there was something like triumph in them—perhaps the triumph of arousing his anger. He thought she would refuse to go, and he would have the discomfort of carrying out his threat; but she smiled in a way that was dangerously undefeated, and said:

136

"All right, I'm not interested in your stupid expedition, anyway." She turned and walked off up the path.

When he caught up with the other children again, John came to his side.

"It was partly my fault, Mr. Lockwood," he said meekly. "I pretended to hit her, and she thought I really meant to, so she started the fight."

"It was silly of you both," he said.

"Why did you send her back? Because she called me a leper?"

"It was a disgraceful thing to say to anybody."

"You don't think she could have really thought——?"

"Don't be absurd, John," Douglas said. "You're used to Silvia by now, aren't you?"

The coffee factory was on a stream. Part of the stream was directed through the building, where it washed the berries, and then the berries were spread out on the flat concrete barbecues to dry in the sun. A rain-cloud drifted overhead. The manager blew his whistle, and half a dozen Negroes jumped into action and brushed the berries into sheds. The rain-cloud passed without giving rain. The manager blew his whistle twice. The workmen brushed out the berries again, coating the concrete with an even layer.

The manager was a Jamaican, with bushy white hair and a kind brown face that matched the newly sun-tanned berries. He led the children into the factory to demonstrate the machines—one that sorted the berries into sizes, and one that picked out the misshapen offenders which might displease the connoisseurs of Blue Mountain coffee. Then they all trooped into the shed where plump and jolly coloured girls were making the final inspection, dribbling the berries through their fingers—and after that they sat by the stream and ate their sandwiches, and the manager sent down a tray of lime-juice, freshly made. They had only just finished lunch when the manager's whistle blew. A cloud obscured the sun and it began to rain. After Morgan's forecast of fine weather, they might have expected it.

They sheltered in the factory. The first deluge settled down into a steady drizzle, and the sky became a dull uniform grey. They waited half an hour, and then decided to step out into the drizzle and start home. It was a steep track up the hillside, but the children were in a good humour and still very lively.

Douglas was not in such a good humour : he was upset about John and worried about Silvia. It occurred to him that Silvia might have taken it into her head to run away. He recalled the expression in her eyes of hatred and triumph. He should have sent her back with an escort— sent her straight to Pawley and transferred the responsibility to him. He wished he had thought of it at the time. But it was no use wishing. . . . He decided to think of something else, and he thought of Judy and wondered what she was doing at this precise moment with Louis. It was probably raining in Kingston as well, and they would be in the flat, and he thought of the intimate little flat with the kitchen and the fridge and the stock of food to withstand a siege for a month, and the bedroom and the golden smoothness of Judy's legs. . . .

"What are you thinking about, Mr. Lockwood?"

"I'm hoping nobody will catch pneumonia."

"I shan't. I adore the rain."

"Your hair's dripping," he said. "You look like a mermaid."

"I don't believe in mermaids."

"You ought to. It's good to believe in things."

When they reached the farm they found Morgan working amongst the grapefruit trees. He was enveloped in a black sou'wester and an immense black mackintosh cape.

"Sorry I didn't catch you again before you went off," he said. "I had another look at the barometer. I could tell this was coming. I'm glad for the farm."

They were all soaked through to the skin by now. They dripped all over the hall of the Great House. He hurried the children upstairs to have baths, and went into the kitchen to arrange for a brew of tea. Then he went upstairs and found Mrs. Morgan. He asked her if she had seen Silvia.

"Yes, she came back, Mr. Lockwood. She wouldn't say why. I thought she must be ill, because she didn't eat any lunch. She's been sitting in the library all day."

"She's still there?"

"I think so."

He went downstairs and looked into the library. Silvia was sitting at a table, reading a book. She glanced up and saw it was Douglas, and immediately looked down at her book again. He felt most relieved. Perhaps her need for revenge would be satisfied by the rain and the fact that they had all got wet. He closed the door and went into the kitchen for a cup of tea. Ivy saw his wet clothes and started giggling, and the pain of restraint drove her into retreat in the pantry. When she eventually returned, he asked her to run down to his bungalow and fetch his towel and a change of clothes, so that he could take a hot bath up at the Great House. She put on her mackintosh and went off, her plump little body still quivering with mirth. He took his tea into the dining-room, and began to wonder what would have happened if Louis hadn't turned up the day before yesterday. How long would the happiness with Judy have lasted? A long time, perhaps—until Louis turned up somewhere else. Louis would always turn up. . . . He was just finishing the tea when Ivy returned. She had none of the things he had asked her to fetch. She was no longer giggling. She looked as frightened as if she had run into a whole battalion of duppies.

"What's the matter, Ivy?"

She could hardly speak.

"Somebody is bin in your bungalow, sir."

"What do you mean?"

"Yes, please, sir. Somebody is bin in."

It was all she could say. He left her and walked out of the Great House and down the grass slope. It was slippery and he had to go carefully. The door of the bungalow was standing open—there were no thefts up here, and he was not in the habit of keeping it locked. He went in, and stopped at once.

It was necessary to stop, because there was no room to walk. He had never seen a room in such incredible confusion. It looked as if a hurricane had passed through. Everything possible had been overturned. The floor was a chaos of torn papers, bedclothes, and broken glass. The drawers had been dragged from the chest and emptied out. The gramophone lay open and upside down amidst fragments of records. The bedside table had been smashed. Everything had been swept off the top of the desk. A bottle of rum had been shattered in the stone fireplace.

He stood for a minute staring in bewilderment. Then he stepped across the bed. The mattress had been thrown off, so he sat on the bare springs. He had cooled down after the climb, and he began to shiver in his wet clothes.

Soon he noticed something scribbled in red pencil on the

opposite wall. It was in large lettering, but he had to get up and go across before he could read it. It said :

Dear Mr. Lockwood,
* I hope you had a nice expedition.*
*   With love from,*

*   Silvia.*

Underneath this she had written, in capital letters and followed by an exclamation mark, the worst obscenity she knew. Douglas could have thought of no worse one himself.

After a hot bath he accepted a stiff glass of rum from Mrs. Morgan, and then went down to Pawley's bungalow. Pawley left his wife in the drawing-room and accompanied Douglas to the study. He listened to the story with his customary patience.

"And now," Douglas said, when he had reached the end, "you'd better ask Silvia's father to take her away." This was obviously what Pawley would want to do, so he might as well suggest it first.

It was not what Pawley wanted to do at all. After a long pause for considering every angle, he pushed himself back in his chair and said :

"I'm disappointed you should suggest that, Lockwood. I should have thought it was rather an admission of defeat."

This was also what Douglas would have thought, but it was a point of view he had not felt up to defending. He wasn't sure that he wanted to defend it either—just then he would happily have given Silvia away with a crate of rum.

"I'm sorry," he said. "I imagined that by now you must have lost faith in her—or at any rate in me."

Pawley beamed reassuringly.

"I don't ask you to work miracles. But perhaps it's too much to expect you to have more patience. You must have suffered a substantial loss. Of course I shall ask her father to reimburse you—and meanwhile we can help you from school funds—but it's naturally caused you a great deal of inconvenience."

"I don't mind about that," Douglas said. "Most of the stuff belonged to the school. I've nothing except the few clothes I flew out with."

"All the same——" Pawley said condolingly. This was one of his psychological gambits, straight from the book about how to influence people. He was influencing Douglas very well.

Douglas said, "I'd be perfectly happy to keep on trying with Silvia. But I want your support. If her next move is to murder Mrs. Morgan, I don't want to feel it's all my responsibility."

"I don't think you've ever found me unwilling to accept responsibility, have you?" Pawley asked in a plaintive sort of way.

"Not at all," Douglas said. "But I want your advice on what to do with Silvia. Are we going to punish her?"

Pawley knitted his brows.

"We must put our heads together," he said. "What are your own ideas?"

"Well, I know all the arguments for punishing her," Douglas said. "Let her get away with it, and she'll do it again. Don't punish her and she'll despise you. I can hear the whole chorus shouting out that all she needs is an almighty thrashing that will stop her sitting down for a week. There's probably a lot in it."

"You think it's the solution?" he said, goggling non-committally.

"I've no doubt it would save a great deal of further expense in broken gramophone records."

"And it would help Silvia?"

"Perhaps it would," Douglas said. "Perhaps her last school wasn't ruthless enough. They shut her up in her room, but forgot to bar the windows. Perhaps she ought to go to a reformatory. Some place where they're tough enough to break her."

"Shall we recommend it to her father?" Pawley said, looking humorous. "Shall we close down the Great House and admit we're barking up the wrong tree?"

"Why not?" Douglas said. "Because if we don't, I'd like to know what I'm going to say to Silvia, and in what way."

Pawley smiled and looked confident, and said helpfully :

"It's no use my giving you advice about that. It's a matter of individual touch. But I know I can rely on you absolutely, Lockwood—absolutely."

He had seldom felt less like relying on himself absolutely. He would have sacrificed a great many principles to have the cowardly catalogue of penalties at his elbow—but now he was committed to the progressive way of treatment, so he sent a message up for Silvia. He still didn't know what he was going to say to her. He had got over being angry and now he was only nervous about messing up the interview. He had hardly been more nervous as a boy when it had been the other way round, and his name had been read out after Prayers to attend outside the housemaster's door.

He reminded himself that Silvia must be nervous, too, but she was working desperately hard not to show it. She came down at once in response to his message, to demonstrate her boldness and lack of guilt or concern. He was beginning to tidy up. She stood insolently in the doorway, and he went on tidying, trying not to look concerned either.

"Now you've got an excuse for expelling me," she said.

"You didn't make a very good job of it," he said. "I thought you might like to finish it off." He picked an unbroken gramophone record from the pile, and held it out to her. She didn't take it, so he said, "Go on. I want to see what you look like in the throes of your destructive passion."

She took the record with a smile and tossed it lightly on the floor. It broke into several pieces.

"That's fine," he said. "Only there wasn't much passion. Try something else." He lifted an upturned chair and put it in front of her.

"I've done all I want," she said.

"Have you lost your spirit?" he said. "I'm disappointed in you. Look, you even forgot to tear up my clothes. I'd have been furious if I'd got back wet and found nothing to change into. What on earth made you overlook them?"

"I couldn't be bothered," she said with a shrug.

"Well, why did you do it at all?" he said. "Have you the faintest idea?"

She smiled contemptuously, without answering.

"It evidently wasn't because you missed the coffee factory," he said. "You said you didn't care about that."

"It was because you made me go back and not John. It wasn't fair."

"How would you like to be called a leper?"

"John is one."

"He isn't," Douglas said. "And you might have done a great deal of harm by calling him one."

"I don't care."

"Perhaps you don't care," Douglas said. "But I do, because I'm here to look after the interests of all the children, not only yours. What would you have done if you'd been in my shoes?" She shrugged again, and he said, "But if you ask me, that's not why you smashed up my room. You did it to show you hated me."

"I don't hate you," she said indifferently.

"Yes, you do. You hate me because you can't succeed in making me punish you. You're going to hate me more than ever after this, because I'm still not going to punish you. I'm a rotten spoil-sport, aren't I? I don't give you anything to get your teeth into. I stop you feeling important."

"I don't know what you mean," she said.

"You'll know if you think about it," he said. "Now for heaven's sake stop trying to look so damned superior. Go and sit on the bed."

She hesitated. Then she went haughtily across the room and sat down.

"Don't you ever relax?" he said.

"I'm quite all right, thank you."

"You're not posing for a photograph. Relax. Lie down if you want."

"I don't want to."

"Well, let yourself go. Just look at your fingers!" She looked at them involuntarily and looked away again at once. "They're as taut as violin strings. So are the muscles in your face. How in the world can you be yourself when you're all tensed up like that?" She said nothing. "Or don't you want to be yourself?" He picked a drawer off the floor and fitted it back into the desk.

After a minute he said, "You know, it must have taken a lot of energy to muck up this room. Has it ever struck you that you've only a certain amount of energy to spend in the whole of your life? It's worth wondering what's the best way to spend it. Some people spend theirs building ships or painting beautiful pictures or making films or simply being happy—and here you go squandering yours on trying to make an impression on a handful of schoolchildren and teachers. Trying to show them all how clever you are—and leaving yourself no time for being clever."

"How silly!" Silvia said. She had glanced covertly at her fingers once or twice to see if they looked relaxed.

"You must admit that other girls don't run after boy-friends and smash up rooms. How do you explain that?"

"They daren't."

"They don't want to dare. They don't have to boost themselves up all the time like you. Perhaps one day they'll be drawing attention to themselves by being successful or interesting, and you'll still be offering round sweets to make people say they like you."

She flushed.

"Who said I did that? It's a filthy lie."

"Is it? Well, that doesn't matter much. You've done lots of other things to make people take notice of you. It puzzles me why you haven't been still more daring. Why didn't you set fire to this place instead of emptying the drawers? It would have been far more impressive."

"I would, if I'd thought of it."

"Would you like to try now?" He threw a box of matches on to the bed.

"What's the use when you're here to stop me?"

"I won't stop you."

He turned away and went on clearing up the floor. Silvia sat motionless on the bed, ignoring the matches. He had been quite confident about that : her pride would stop her doing anything he suggested.

Presently he said, "Hullo, look what's here." He had spotted the elephant on the floor amongst some pieces of smashed crockery. "What a stroke of luck. It isn't broken —not even the tusks." He showed it to her. "Did you spare it on purpose?"

She stared at it sullenly. "Why should I?"

"I'm delighted it isn't a casualty, anyhow." He put it down on the desk, looking towards the window and aiming it. "I'll have to get this right."

"What are you doing?" She tried to drain her voice of interest.

"He's my mascot. He's supposed to bring me luck if I point his trunk to the window. Isn't it nonsense? I expect you grew out of that sort of thing years ago." She was silent. "It must be nonsense, anyhow. He was pointing to the window today—and now look what's happened."

"Did you ever believe in it?" She meant to sound scornful.

"I might have done. I kept him to be on the safe side."

"How childish," she said. He could see that in some way she was rather impressed. Perhaps for the first time he seemed human to her.

He laughed and said, "Even at my age people go on

144

wishing things could be better than they are." He picked a propelling-pencil off the floor and examined it. "You must have stamped on this. Do you think there's any hope of mending it?"

He gave it to her. She held it in her hands for a minute, looking at it; and then as if she had realized all at once what she was doing, she put it down quickly on the bed.

"Don't imagine you can make me sorry for what I've done," she said.

"Why on earth should you be sorry? You smashed up the room for a reason. You should only be sorry that you didn't do more."

He went down on his haunches and started sorting out the papers. From the corner of his eye he saw her glance at the scribbling on the wall. When he looked up at her she turned her eyes away quickly. After a minute, crossing the room to dump the papers in the basket, he nodded casually to the wall and said :

"By the way, your writing's rotten. I wish you'd read that out to me."

"Why should I?"

"You wrote it for my benefit, didn't you?"

"I don't mind reading it, if you want," she said, with something like bravado.

"Go ahead, then."

She read the message, but left out the word at the bottom.

"There you are," she said. She sounded uncomfortable.

"There's something else underneath," he said, squinting at the wall. She said nothing, so he went across to the wall and looked closely at the word and laughed and said, "Good Lord, what's the matter? Don't you know how to pronounce it?"

She sat there dumbly.

"Have a shot at it," he said.

She shook her head.

"I'll pronounce it for you, then," he said, and pronounced it. As he did so she turned suddenly scarlet. He was quite surprised by her confusion—he had never seen her like that before. He laughed. "Bless my soul! That word's as old as the hills."

Presently she said in a rather shaky voice, "Don't you know why I was expelled from my last school?"

"I thought it was because you were always getting into mischief."

"That wasn't what made them do it. It was because I said that word."

"It's funny the way some people don't like it," he said. "I suppose you know what it means?"

"I think I do." She didn't sound sure.

"You know what men and women do to have babies, don't you?" She nodded, blushing again. "That's all it is. That's why it's so odd; thousands of people have babies every day, and yet you're not supposed to use it. But nobody's going to bother you about it here. You can go on to my verandah and shout it at the top of your voice if you want. I'd much rather you did that than smash my propelling pencil." He looked at his watch. "Now you'd better run along." She didn't move from the bed, so he said, "Go on, off with you. You're getting in my way."

She went off; but less than five minutes later he heard steps on the verandah again. She reappeared in the doorway.

"Now what?" Douglas said.

"I want to help you clear up," she said.

"I don't need any help. You'd better hurry up or you'll miss your supper."

"I'm sorry I did it," she said.

"Think it over until tomorrow. You might have changed your mind again by then."

"I won't. It was a filthy thing to do."

"I suppose you want to be punished now," he said. "Well, go away and write an essay on intelligent expenditure of energy. But, anyhow, go away."

She remained in the doorway.

"If anybody did this to me I'd never forgive them," she said.

"What do you mean by 'forgive'?"

"I'd never be friends with them again."

"We weren't friends to start off with," he said. "So what does it matter?"

"You must hate me," she said.

He laughed and said, "I think you're a confounded nuisance, and I've had quite enough of you for one day. Now run away and think up some new way of making trouble." She stood motionless. "Go on, pop off."

She still didn't move, and he had to start closing the door before she made a reluctant retreat.

146

The next morning John came to see Douglas in the library. He looked worried.

"Mr. Lockwood, I haven't got leprosy, have I?"

"Of course you haven't. You're not still upset about what Silvia said, are you?"

"A lot of people knew about it. I heard them talking in the bathroom."

"Don't take any notice," Douglas said. "It's a lot of rubbish."

John didn't seem satisfied. He said with diffidence :

"Do you remember when all my dormitory had a special medical examination? I wondered if that was anything to do with it."

"Yes, it was," Douglas said. "Somebody had said there was leprosy about. We didn't believe them, but we wanted to make sure. It was nonsense."

"You don't think my family could have it, either, do you?"

"They wouldn't be wandering about in public if they had. Don't let it worry you, John. The talk will all die down."

Douglas told Pawley about it, and Pawley spoke a piece to the children after lunch about the gossip being quite unfounded. He was not much of a speaker, and didn't sound awfully convincing; but the children were not without tact, and if any of them still believed the gossip and avoided contact with John thereafter, they were careful not to let it appear too obvious.

CHAPTER ELEVEN

It was his day off on Wednesday, and he went down to Kingston intending to keep away from Judy's flat. He hung round the shops all morning and then had lunch, and after lunch it occurred to him that if he didn't call at the flat it would look as if he was behaving like a sulking child, so he decided to do so. Probably in the back of his mind he had known that he would all along.

The door was opened by Louis. He was in his braces. He showed a very fine spirit of camaraderie, and put his arm round Douglas's shoulder and called him "old chap" and invited him to have a drink and wait for Judy. Judy had started work again, but for the time being was only employed in the office. She was due at any minute. Louis went into the kitchen to fetch some ice, looking as if he had lived in the flat all his life. When he came back he pointed to the *Lignum Vitæ* and said :

"That's Judy's favourite tree, old chap. The Tree of Life."

"She told me," Douglas said.

"I expect she did." He grinned amiably. "You know I'm glad she's found a friend like you here. She's been telling me all you've done. I'm damned grateful to you." He was so sincere about it that his eyes watered. He was squatting on the sofa with his legs crossed, looking like a little Jewish tailor. He said, as if he was imparting some esoteric knowledge, "She's a damned nice girl, you know. I'm exceptionally fond of her." His eyes watered more freely. "I say, I'm afraid my English isn't up to much. I hope you understand me ?"

"Perfectly."

"I've tried to get hold of it colloquially. I've asked Judy to correct me more, but she doesn't bother. Would you mind pulling me up if I make a mistake?"

"You make so few," Douglas said.

"Really? That's awfully nice of you to say so." He began to cough painfully. "Excuse me—that's my bad chest. I expect Judy's told you, hasn't she?"

"She's talked a lot about you."

"You probably heard what happened in Mexico. I was damned distressed about it—I felt I was responsible, in a way. I only wish she'd got in touch with me before doing anything so drastic."

"It hardly seemed wise under the circumstances," Douglas said.

"No; I see what you mean. My wife has certainly made things awfully difficult for us. She's not at all a sympathetic type. Luckily she thinks that Judy's back in England now." His smile took for granted that Douglas also thought this lucky. "I say, can I fill up your glass?"

Presently Judy returned. Louis went out into the hall when he heard her. She burst into high-spirited and affectionate greetings, and then there was silence. They were presumably embracing. Douglas wondered what they looked like when they embraced : Louis was so much shorter than Judy. Then Louis said :

"That chap's here—Douglas."

"Why didn't you tell me?"

She came through into the living-room, looking rather embarrassed. She was also looking very fresh and slim in her plain white uniform dress. He hadn't seen her in a dress like that since the crash.

"I never expected you, Douglas," she said. She was smiling tentatively, uncertain of his mood.

"I needn't ask how you are."

He managed to sound quite cheerful, and her embarrassment quickly passed and her happiness took possession of her again. She found it difficult to keep her eyes off Louis, and every glance she gave him was a tender caress. When she went into the bedroom to change, Louis said generously :

"Go and talk to her if you want, old chap. I expect you've a lot to say to one another."

"It'll wait."

"As you like. But I don't mind, you know."

Douglas was persuaded into joining them for dinner, and they went to an hotel just out of town. After dinner Louis suggested going to the Colony Club.

"I don't know about the Colony . . ." Judy said doubtfully. She was thinking of Douglas's feelings. She was afraid he might feel sentimental about the Colony.

"Why not?" Douglas said. "It's as good as anywhere, isn't it?"

They found a good table at the Colony, and Louis ordered a bottle of whisky. Douglas drank most of it, watching them dancing. Louis danced in an exaggerated way like an acrobatic monkey; he had a very white grin, and his oily black hair shone under the spotlights. Douglas knew he ought to have had the guts and the good sense not to come. But perhaps he was getting some sort of kick out of it. He had always loved prodding sores. . . .

He danced with Judy himself, and that was like adding salt to the sores as well.

"You haven't forgiven me, Douglas?" she said.

"Of course I have."

"You are a fool," she said. "You are, honestly—you're a fool to be so nice."

"I know what I'd feel like if I got back to my bungalow and found Caroline. Or would have done. I don't know that I should now."

"Why not?"

"Now I'd rather get back and find you."

"You'd hate me to keep on saying I'm sorry, wouldn't you?"

"Yes—just keep on looking happy."

"I can't help looking happy," she said. "I know it's dreadfully tactless, but I honestly can't."

They danced in silence for a while, and then he said:

"Can't you make Louis stay?"

"Oh no, he's going." She smiled. "I'm not thinking about it."

"You're not thinking about taking sleeping tablets again?"

"I swear I'm not."

"Will you let me know when he's going, so that I can stop you? You're not awfully good at dropping post-cards —you could 'phone if it's easier."

"I shan't take any sleeping tablets," she said. "Not again."

"I'd like to hear from you, all the same."

"All right," she said. "But honestly, darling, you oughtn't to be such a fool. You oughtn't to be so nice to women—they don't appreciate it. Look what Louis did to me, and look how I'm behaving. You're too nice."

"I'm just progressive," he said.

"Yes, that's the trouble; you're just too damned nice."

The music stopped and they went back to the table. Louis stood up.

"Jolly handsome couple you make," he said. "I've enjoyed watching you." His grin was as white as a toothpaste advertisement.

They sat down, and presently a man came over from a neighbouring table. It was the Jamaican whom Judy had nearly married. He asked Douglas if he'd mind if he danced with her. Douglas said he had better ask Louis. Louis said not at all, old chap, and so they went off and danced. Louis said to Douglas:

"Can't be much fun being a schoolmaster. Poor pay, isn't it? I could probably do something for you, once I've set up my business. You're a decent chap, you know."

"Oh, yes, awfully."

"I'm hoping to go down to the Argentine soon. I've been wasting my time in Mexico. Everybody in Mexico is either lazy or crooked—a chap hasn't a chance of turning an honest penny. But my plans are all worked out for South

America. They're go-ahead down there. There's room for expansion. I'm going to set up a little import-export firm. It would help to have a decent chap like you with me. I could fix you up with a first-rate job."

"I'm quite happy at the school," Douglas said.

"Don't think I'm offering to do you a favour. You'd be doing me a favour if you joined."

"I'm going to stick to teaching for the time being."

"That's all right, then." He grinned. He was very conscientious about showing that he didn't take offence. "I was just letting you know I'd be glad to do something for you. I knew you were decent the first time we met. You had a weak spot for Judy, and that was enough for me. Some chaps in my place might have taken it the wrong way—but I take you for what you are, a damn decent fellow."

Douglas said, "Look here, Louis. Are you in love with Judy?"

"What do you think?"

"Then why don't you hang on to her?"

Louis made a gesture of helplessness. A large gold ring flashed on his finger.

"There's nothing I'd like better—but I'm not a free agent. My wife would never divorce me."

"To hell with divorce," Douglas said. "Why don't you just go off with Judy?"

"You think I ought to?"

"I damn well do."

He liked being told this, but he shook his head regretfully.

"I couldn't do it. I'm not established yet. Of course, it'll be different when my business is running properly."

"Judy wouldn't mind roughing it. She's done it with you before."

"No," he said. "I might have asked her to do it if I was in decent health. But I'm an old crock, you know. I was in a sanatorium in Switzerland all through the war. I ought to be there now, but I'd rather enjoy a short life than spin it out in hospital. I might crack up at any time. It wouldn't be fair on Judy to have her with me. It simply wouldn't be fair to ask her." The pathos was positively dripping off him.

"It's what Judy wants," Douglas said. "Whether you're at your last gasp or not."

Louis shook his head.

151

"I like her too much. And then there's another thing." He turned his eyes towards Douglas. They were watering so much that he must have been almost blind. "I'm a Jew."

"What's that to do with it? I haven't noticed it bothering Judy."

He shook his head lugubriously. "No, it wouldn't. She's too fine a person. But I know what it means to other people. I like her too much to ask her to share the burden."

"It didn't stop you coming to have a nice holiday with her in Jamaica."

"That's different," Louis said, shaking his head. "You don't understand, old chap—quite different."

Douglas said, "Personally, Louis, I think Judy's a marvellous girl, and I think you're a bloody fool."

Louis was wonderful at not taking offence. That even seemed to cheer him up. He said bravely:

"I won't let that alter my opinion of you. I still think you're a damn decent fellow, Douglas. Damn decent."

"Everybody appears to think that tonight," Douglas said. "Oughtn't I to feel happy?"

They left the Colony Club at eleven. The waiter brought the bill and gave it to Louis. Louis looked embarrassed, so Douglas took out his wallet.

Judy exclaimed, "No, Douglas, you're absolutely not to. Not tonight." She opened her bag quickly and handed some notes to Louis, but Douglas had already paid.

"Make him take the money, Louis," Judy said.

Louis tried half-heartedly as they went out, and Douglas refused, so Louis held on to the notes and said:

"That's damned good of you. I'm a bit stuck for money here—there's been a misunderstanding at the bank. But don't forget about the job in the Argentine. I'd be glad to do you a good turn."

Douglas drove them back to the flat. He wouldn't go in for a drink. He waited until he saw their lights come on, and then he started back for the school. There was no moon, and it was a very dark night. He couldn't see the mountains even in silhouette; but there was a small forest fire burning on one of the hilltops, and it looked like an aircraft that had burst into flames in the sky, and had stopped in its flight but forgotten to drop.

He was passing John's tree-house a few evenings later when he heard voices from within. He called out, and

John's black little face appeared at the trap-door. John lowered the rope, and he climbed up. There were two girls sitting inside. One of them was Silvia, and the other was Norah, the girl on whom Silvia had once inflicted quite painful injuries. They had brought tea in a tin from the Great House and were having a party. Silvia was the first to offer Douglas her mug.

Silvia's recent change of heart had been obvious to everyone. Even Duffield had grudgingly admitted, "I don't know what you've done to her, but she's been going round looking like a ruddy little angel." He went on to say that he mistrusted this appearance, since devils could only be driven out with sticks. Douglas was not without mistrust himself. He doubted if the friendship of the other children went very deep either; but they had all been afraid of Silvia and were glad to call a truce. It was interesting that John and Norah, whom she had most offended, were the first to do so.

Pawley was delighted when he heard about the scene in the tree-house. He congratulated Douglas on the way he had handled Silvia, and then congratulated himself on his own perspicacity—he had always recognized that Douglas had the makings of a first-rate pedagogue (although it had taken courage, of course, to overlook certain aspects of his personal history). You could almost hear him purring.

Mrs. Pawley, however, resented the apparent success with Silvia, and was not delighted at all. She was still not speaking to Douglas. He had even detected her hand behind the delay in reimbursing him after the bungalow disaster. Pawley had explained that this was due to certain technical difficulties that prevented the payment being made from school funds; but his embarrassed manner suggested that technical was not strictly the right word. Douglas's late return to the school the other night probably hadn't helped matters with Mrs. Pawley. She was bound to have heard the station-wagon coming up the hill, and drawn her own conclusions about how he had spent the evening. The conclusions would have been the kind that made her angry. Now the news about Silvia made her more angry still.

At the staff meeting on Monday she raised the matter of the tea-party. She objected to it on the grounds that tea was supposed to be drunk in the Great House and not taken outside, and that it was improper for John to entertain girls in his tree-house. It had also come to her notice that a member of the staff had been present at the party, thus implicitly condoning it.

Pawley had evidently not been briefed about this protest, and he seemed rather put out. He called for Douglas's observations. Douglas observed that there could be no objection to tea being taken outside except the fear of broken crockery; and on this occasion the children had carried the tea in a tin and drunk from enamel mugs. As for the question of impropriety, if John was prevented from entertaining girls in his tree-house there should logically be a complete segregation of sexes during all free time, because there was nothing you could do in a tree-house that you couldn't do better in the jungle, where there was more room. In which case the idea of co-education might just as well be abandoned. Pawley wagged his beard in tentative approval of these arguments, and referred the matter back to Mrs. Pawley. As Mrs. Pawley was not prepared to recognize anything that Douglas said as having been said at all, she shrugged impatiently and said, "I still think that no member of the staff should have condoned it without your authority."

Pawley looked awkward about this, and shuffled the papers in front of him. Then he goggled at both sides of the table and said, "Shall we leave it, then, that there will be no objection to such proceedings in the future, provided that school crockery isn't used?" There were no dissentients, and he passed on to another item on the agenda, which concerned a complaint from the children that salt fish and acki appeared too often on the menu. Salt fish and acki was the Jamaican national dish, but Douglas would have been quite happy if it had not appeared on the menu at all. Duffield didn't like it either, and was obviously torn between a desire to support the motion, and a natural instinct to condemn it on the grounds that children should eat what they were given and be made to like it. He finally allowed the interests of gastronomy to outweigh the interests of discipline, and gave a guilty vote. The guilt passed from his face when he saw that Morgan was voting in favour of retaining the present diet. Morgan was the only defender of salt fish and acki, and the motion was therefore carried, and Mrs. Morgan was requested to modify the menu.

On Tuesday Silvia came to Douglas in the library.

"I've written a story," she said.

154

She laid a pile of manuscript in front of him. There were fifty or sixty pages.

"What gave you the idea of doing that?" he asked.

"I just felt like it. I did it all in free time."

He sent her away and started to read it at once. He knew it would be interesting, because he had never read a story by a boy or girl that didn't give away a great deal about the writer. Whether the plot was worked out against a background of their own environment or against the imaginary background of Mars, it inevitably betrayed the child's hopes and fears and ambitions and hates. Characters and stories were not created from a vacuum. They were conjured from hidden sources of the mind.

The background of Silvia's story was drawn from the films, it was about grown-ups, and the principal character was a man—but nevertheless it remained, quite unintentionally, a story about herself.

The hero was called Julian. He worked in a department store in New York, where he loved one of the girl assistants and hated the manager. The manager was extremely ugly, as befitted a bully. One evening, after the manager had gone home, something cropped up that had to be reported to him at once. Julian went to his apartment and found the girl there. They were surrounded by bottles of champagne and all the other adjuncts of film debauchery. Julian threw himself at the manager to kill him, but the manager fought free and locked himself in a room, from the safety of which he taunted Julian with diabolical laughter. To avenge himself, Julian went back to the department store and set it on fire. Silvia, as the story teller, obviously felt this quite justified. Meanwhile the manager came out of his room, tripped over the carpet, hit his head on the fender, and was killed. It looked as if he had been murdered by Julian, who had been seen to enter the apartment. Julian was arrested, but managed to escape. He bolted from New York, and in due course found himself in Hollywood. He was spotted in a Hollywood restaurant by a film producer, and on account of his good looks was invited to play a leading rôle. He became a film star, adored by the whole world. Soon he fell in love with another film star. She was very beautiful, and their love was idyllic. The idyll continued despite their marriage. Then one of the employees of the department store recognized Julian on the screen. He was arrested, tried for the murder of the manager, and sentenced to life imprisonment. He was taken from the court amidst the hostile yells of the crowd that had formerly idolized him. The story ended up with him breaking stones on an island gaol, under the eye of a brutal, whip-yielding guard. The title of this saga was *The Road to Fate*.

Silvia had probably chosen to make the hero a man in order to deceive herself that she was not writing subjectively; but it was obvious that she had vividly imagined herself in the rôle of Julian In the first part of the story Julian's relationship with the manager of the department store interested Silvia far more than Julian's love for the girl assistant—the love was only put in to satisfy the assault on the manager, and was rapidly forgotten. There could hardly be any doubt that the manager represented her father.

Julian had tried to kill the manager, but without success —because if Silvia had allowed him to succeed she would, in effect, have been killing her own father. This was an evil from which she shrank. However, she had achieved the same end without guilt by causing him to die by accident.

Julian's career in Hollywood was Silvia's dream of happiness in very thin disguise. The adoration of the world represented her idea of success and her deepest wish : to be loved by everyone. The purity of Julian's love also belonged naturally to her adolescent fancy. But just as Silvia was haunted by the fear of injustice and hostility, so Julian was haunted by the fear of exposure. Then came the arrest and the ultimate victory of injustice. The crowds did not understand the truth, and victimized Julian; and finally all the hostile forces—the crowds and the manager and Silvia's father—were embodied in the single figure of the guard with the whip. It was surely Silvia's perpetual fear of this unjust and brutal figure that had found expression in her rebelry. If Douglas had psycho-analysed her or had had access to her dreams, he could hardly have elicited a clearer statement.

Even so, it didn't go deep enough. It was only a confirmation of what he had already guessed, and didn't explain why she hated her father, who had been good to her, or feared injustice. He was half afraid to delve further, for he was not a psychologist and he suddenly felt himself getting out of his depth. He held an instrument in his hand which fascinated him, but which he had not been trained how to use. He wished there was someone in Jamaica to whom he

156

could turn for advice; but he knew no one, and it was wiser to leave the instrument alone.

Yet it was not only the content of Silvia's story that interested him. He was also interested in the writing, which for a girl of twelve seemed a considerable achievement. The background lacked verisimilitude and the plot was full of improbabilities; but she showed a facility for self-expression that had never been apparent in her careless essays or her speech. Her descriptions were vivid and original, and her analyses of emotions, although reflecting her immaturity, were carefully detailed. It was not difficult to tell when she had been writing directly from experience. When Julian first fell in love with the beautiful film actress, he didn't know whether or not his love was returned. He took an old book and began tearing out the pages, saying, "She loves me, she love me not," as children do when blowing fluff from dandelions. The last page informed him that she loved him not. He was not prepared to accept this, and concluded that he must have torn out two pages together by mistake, thus reversing the final verdict. This description was so human, and the behaviour so closely observed, that Douglas felt quite sure Silvia had done something of the kind herself. The passages in which she excelled were all of this nature. Her courtroom scene, from some half-remembered film, was absurd; but her account of Julian's reaction to the derisive crowd—his determination to look scornful and keep his head in the air—was written excellently. It would have interested Douglas to know if Silvia had been aware that she was describing her own feelings during the period of her ostracism. Probably she had not.

When Silvia came to him to hear his opinion of the story he was tempted to explain some of her unconscious reasons for writing that particular plot : it might have helped her to understand herself. But now he funked the use of the instrument in hand, and he only discussed the work in its literary aspects. He gave her a modicum of praise.

She was eager for more, and for reassurances about her future.

"Do you think I could be a writer?" she said.

He told her it was entirely up to her—she probably could if she worked hard enough to that end. She wasn't satisfied. She wanted to know that she was going to be a success.

"But is the story really good? Do you think I've got talent?"

"It shows a tremendous amount of promise," he said. "But you've a lot to learn. Talent isn't any use unless you train it."

She went away, and the next day brought a poem. It was imitation Wordsworth, scanned badly, was about the English countryside which she had never seen, and contained no original thought. He gave her a modicum of adverse criticism. She resented it, flushed, and became angry. He told her that if Wordsworth had tried to write about Jamaica in the style of Milton, he would probably have made a mess of it. She must find a style that suited her, and write about what she knew; and in doing so she would inevitably turn out a mass of bad stuff. She still sulked rather, and went off to try her hand at another story. It was a short one, because she was impatient for opinion, and it lacked many of the merits of the first; but it was still better than average. He praised her again and she cheered up. He was not yet satisfied that all her devils had been exorcized, it could hardly be expected in a month, but he was confident that sympathetic treatment was working where harsher methods would have failed. And once or twice he allowed himself to day-dream : in some house in England, where he was enjoying a comfortable old age, he was entertaining Silvia to lunch. She was now an eminent novelist, but she still retained an affection for the master from whom she had received her first literary lesson. They reminisced in amusement about the smashing of the bunga-low and her other escapades. There was someone else at the table, joining in the amusement; but he had refused him-self a licence to include Judy in this day-dream, so he tried to ignore her, and turning back to Silvia began to discuss her latest book.

There was a note from Judy at the beginning of the following week. It ran to four lines, and said that Louis was leaving on Thursday, and she was feeling quite resigned and not a bit suicidal. Nevertheless Douglas went down to Pawley to alter his day off. Pawley agreed at once. He would have probably agreed to a week off on double salary if he'd been asked. He had heard about Silvia's burst of literary activity, and been so delighted that it was only a wonder he hadn't written to the Governor to recommend Douglas for a knighthood.

On Thursday morning he drove down to Kingston and

158

went straight to the flat. Louis was still there—he was catching a plane for Mexico in the early afternoon. Douglas arranged to meet Judy afterwards at the Myrtle Bank. He then set about saying good-bye to Louis. He found this an agreeable duty, but Louis showed convincing signs that it was breaking his heart. He wrung Douglas's hand, and then accompanied him downstairs with an arm round his shoulder. On the way he told Douglas what a decent chap he was, and how happy he felt to be leaving Judy in his care. He then apologized for his behaviour at the Colony Club. Douglas said he saw no reason for an apology, but Louis wouldn't be done out of it.

"I must have given you the idea that I'm ashamed of being a Jew. I'm not—I'm proud of it." His eyes were watering already. "The trouble is that I'm too sensitive. I always have been. I feel things too deeply. It's an awful drawback."

"It must make life hell."

Louis looked grateful for such profound understanding of his handicap.

"You should be thankful you're not like that. You can't imagine what I'm going to suffer, leaving Judy this afternoon."

"Don't leave her, then," Douglas said.

He shook his head.

"No—I've thought over what you said, but I know I was right." He coughed weakly and put his hand to his chest. "It wouldn't be fair to her." He wrung Douglas's hand again. "But look after her, old chap. It's all I ask you—look after her for me."

He had a few purchases to make in Kingston, so he stopped at the shops. While he was in the stationer's the mulatto from the milk-bar, who called himself a nigger, materialized out of space. He called Douglas Mr. Lockwood, and inquired after his health with the ingratiating concern that Louis might have shown. Douglas told him that his health was excellent and said good-bye and left the shop. The man was still with him at the tobacconist's, where he informed Douglas that his own health had shown a marked deterioration of late owing to lack of food, which was due to the difficulty of finding employment, which was due to the economic state of Jamaica. There were certain people who blamed this sad state on England's exploitation of her little colony, but he himself considered this a traitorous attitude towards the mother-country. He was amongst the few who realized what England had suffered in the war, and how lightly Jamaica had escaped. He supposed that Mr. Lockwood must be particularly nauseated by those Jamaicans who did not understand what war meant, since he had obviously played a valiant front-line rôle. At this point Douglas gave him the ninepence change that he had received from the tobacconist, and the man vanished as mysteriously as he had come.

Douglas went into a bookshop and bought a novel and an American magazine, and then went to the Myrtle Bank. He bathed, had lunch, started to read the novel, then gave it up and started on a story in the magazine. He soon gave that up, too, and turned over the pages of the magazine, looking at the pictures and reading the advertisements. Louis' plane was due to depart at three-fifteen. At exactly three-twenty a plane came over the harbour. It circled the town, gaining height, and flew off over the hills in the direction of Cuba. It showed no likelihood of crashing. Less than half an hour later, Judy appeared.

"Now," she said, "what about helping me break into a dispensary for some sleeping tablets? Or shall we have tea first! I'm really too exhausted to bother about killing myself for the moment. I may not bother at all. It might inflate his ego too much if I succeeded."

"And he's so sensitive about that sort of thing."

She laughed. "Has he been telling you how sensitive he is, too? He told me about it this morning. I think he was reading a book about a sensitive person last night."

"Was he reading a book last night?"

"Oh, he loves books. He's so cultured. Didn't he tell you about his culture, as well?"

"He forgot that."

"He must have thought you took it for granted." She laughed again, and said unconvincingly, "Isn't he a horror? Can you imagine what I see in him?"

"The backs of his hands are fabulously hairy."

"Yes, isn't it funny? Because his chest isn't at all."

"Perhaps he sticks it on with gum-arabic."

After tea they went to the Carib. It was an absurd American film, with up-to-date slapstick behind the scenes of a television studio, but Douglas found it very funny and laughed a great deal, and Judy laughed too. If it had been the Marx Brothers fooling around with the television cameras, it would have been funnier still. They came out of the cinema in a good mood, and had supper at the Chinese place with the Chinese-Indian-Negress waitress.

"Perhaps she isn't too young for you, after all," Judy said. "You know what girls are in the tropics. And she obviously wants some white blood for the family collection."

"I'd like to see her have a baby with a Russian-Eskimo-Javanese."

"Have you ever met one of those?"

"Yes—except it wasn't Eskimo, it was Icelandic. He was a man who lived in a boarding-house in London and studied law. He kept feeling nostalgic, only it was rather confusing because he never quite knew where he was nostalgic for. He died."

"Of nostalgia?"

"No; he caught pneumonia in the English winter. It was probably the Javanese part of him that let him down."

Judy laughed and said, "How wonderful to be talking rubbish again! Louis never talks rubbish. I'm so glad he's gone."

"He must be in Cuba by now."

"I wonder what a Jewish-Hungarian-Cuban would be like," she said.

"A Jewish-Hungarian-Hairy-Ainu-of-Japan would be better," Douglas said. "Then there'd be no need for gum-arabic."

"What a splendid idea—shall we send him a cable about it?"

"He might take it seriously," Douglas said. "Think of all the hair there'd be in the next generation. People would be committing suicide all over the shop."

Judy ate very little supper. She left the food on the side of her plate without saying anything. After supper they drove back to her flat, and Douglas went up for coffee. Judy said she would only be a short time making the coffee, and disappeared into the kitchen. Presently he followed her, but she kept her back towards him, arranging the cups. He told her the kettle was boiling. She turned round.

"It's no good, you'll have to see. I've made an awful mess of my face." She had been crying, but now she was smiling through the tears which were still in her eyes. "I was perfectly all right until we got up here. Then I saw a cigarette that he'd squashed out in the ash-tray. Isn't it silly? I was only crying about the cigarette."

"He'll pop up one day and squash out some more."

"No, he won't."

"Louis will always pop up."

"No." She shook her head positively. "I've told him I won't see him again. He knows I mean it."

"Do you mean it?"

"Yes; it's stupid to go on like this. I've absolutely made up my mind. He's not even going to write. I shall tear up his letters if he does." The tears were still coming up in her eyes. She brushed them away, laughing. "I'll make the coffee now."

"I don't really want any coffee."

"Don't you? It's an awful nuisance—and I can't see properly."

"I'll go," he said.

"You'd better. Otherwise I shall keep on doing that. You've been so damned nice—that's partly what makes me cry. I don't know what I'd have done today if you hadn't been here."

"To talk rubbish with."

"The rubbish saved me. I'll be all right now when you've gone."

"Shall I take away the cigarette?"

"No; just let me have it for tonight. I'll throw it away in the morning."

"We could embalm it."

"We're not going to embalm anything," she said. "It's all finished in the morning. I've got to be at the airport at eight. I'm going to the Bahamas."

"For long?"

"Oh, I'll be back in the evening."

"I'll wave to you as you go over the school," he said.

"I'll be waving, too."

That night when he arrived back at his bungalow there was a letter on his desk from Caroline. It was no strain to delay opening it, he even felt reluctant to do so, but he opened it eventually, and it said that she was back in London and was going to marry Alec. Alec was the man he had once caught in his own dressing-gown, in a scene straight from a French farce, and who had described him as having Midland morals—whatever they were. He forgot about the letter at once.

As he got into bed, he noticed some flowers on the table. He knew they were not from Mrs. Pawley, not only because

Mrs. Pawley's flower-giving period was over, but also because they were wild flowers and arranged in a jam-jar instead of a vase. He thought that perhaps Ivy had put them there, as a gesture of apology for her often misplaced mirth.

In the morning, when she woke him with her "Yes, please, Mr. Lockwood," he asked her about them, and she began to giggle helplessly. In anyone else the giggles might have expressed some knowledge or complicity, but in Ivy they meant only that she didn't know. It then occurred to him that it might be Silvia. He met Silvia coming out of breakfast, and some half-embarrassed expectancy in her manner made him sure he was right. But she didn't mention the flowers, and he didn't either. He had no wish to encourage her to do it again, and it seemed safest to pretend that he hadn't guessed.

CHAPTER TWELVE

THE Morgan-Duffield feud had now continued without interruption for over two months. That week there was a reconciliation, brought about by the agency of rum. The reconciliation was brief, and rum was also the agency of its collapse.

The idea for the reconciliation was Pawley's. He had hoped at the same time to create an opportunity for his wife and Douglas to settle their differences, over the nature of which he professed himself puzzled. Pawley liked to picture himself as the benign patriarch of a happy and co-operative team, and he was deeply sorrowed by the simultaneous existence of two feuds in a staff of only six. He wondered self-effacingly if they didn't reflect in some way on his own leadership.

His idea was to throw a jolly little staff party at his own bungalow. He explained to Douglas rather nervously that he had not yet put the suggestion to his wife, but that he felt sure he could count on her support. The party took place, but judging by Mrs. Pawley's sullen and brief attendance, her support had not been readily forthcoming.

It was on Saturday night after supper. Douglas walked down from the Great House with Duffield, and the

Morgans turned up ten minutes later. They sat out on the verandah. The wicker chairs were arranged in a semicircle round a small table, on which stood three bottles of rum. Pawley was behaving in a jolly manner that gave the impression of long practice in front of a mirror. He himself was teetotal like Morgan, but he dispensed generous portions of rum to Mrs. Morgan and Douglas.

When Mrs. Pawley came out there was only one vacant chair. It was next to Douglas. She hesitated, and then sat down decidedly and turned her head away from him as if she was unaware of his presence. Douglas would have welcomed a reconciliation even more than Pawley, and it seemed up to him to make the first move. He made some comment about the rum being a particularly excellent brand.

"Really?" Mrs. Pawley said frigidly. She only turned her head a fraction of an inch to say it.

He said, "I'm afraid you're still annoyed with me about that night, Mrs. Pawley."

"What night?" she snapped.

"The night at your brother's. I behaved rather badly."

"Did you?" she said.

"I should have taken more care when you were getting out of the car. But it was entirely an accident—I let in the clutch before I saw you were opening the door again."

"I didn't notice anything," she said, still snapping.

"I imagined that was why you hadn't talked to me since."

She turned to him and said, "You're very conceited, aren't you?" He didn't quite see the point of that remark, but before he had time to make any comment she turned to her husband on the other side and said, "Leonard, would you put some more ginger in my rum?" A short while later, leaving her glass half full, she announced that she had a headache and left the jolly little staff party to be jolly without her. That was as far as the reconciliation went.

The other reconciliation had been faring much better. Douglas now saw that Mrs. Morgan was not only listening to a joke that Duffield was telling her, but was actually giggling at it. She was giggling in a way in which she only giggled after she had drunk a good deal of rum—she had probably treated herself to two or three thimblefuls before coming down to the party. Mrs. Morgan was a good-natured person, deep animosities found no place in her abundant rolls of fat, and it was only out of loyal respect for her husband's animosities that she had managed to keep up her end of the feud at all. Now her loyalty had evidently been weakened by the alcohol. When Duffield reached the climax of his joke, she shook in her chair with so much amusement that the rum spilt over the sides of her glass on to her lap.

"Oh, that's a good one," she said. "That's really a good one, Mr. Duffield. Do tell us another."

Duffield had also drunk more rum than he was accustomed to drink, and was looking extremely pleased with himself. He liked an appreciative audience at any time, and now he regarded the capture of Mrs. Morgan's attention as a victory over Morgan. He told another one. It was the old music-hall joke about the man who was asked about the lady he had been out with, and he said that was no lady, that was his wife. Mrs. Morgan spilt some more rum on to her lap.

"Oh dear, you're a scream, Mr. Duffield, you really are —a scream!" She had forgotten that a feud had ever existed. She turned merrily to her husband, "Did you hear that one? It was a scream, wasn't it? You ought to tell Mr. Duffield that joke about the nigger cutting down bananas."

Morgan looked embarrassed. The use of the word "nigger" reminded him of the origin of his feud with Duffield, of which he needed no reminding. He said sulkily :

"I don't know any jokes."

"Oh, you do," Mrs. Morgan encouraged. She turned to them all. "He does. He knows a screaming story about a nigger who—but he's got to tell it himself."

Pawley beamed and said in a jolly way, "Yes, what about it, Morgan? Time we heard your voice."

Morgan looked sulky; but he had more respect for Pawley than all the rest of the staff and children put together. He told the story gloomily. It was about an Englishman who asked a coloured man (he used the term pointedly) to cut him a bunch of bananas. The coloured man couldn't reach the bunch without the effort of stretching, so he cut down the whole banana plant. The Englishman told his friend about this, and added, "You see how lazy the coloured people are. Fancy cutting down a whole banana tree because he couldn't be bothered to reach above his head!" The point of this story was the ignorance of the

Englishman, since all Jamaicans knew that banana plants only yielded once and had to be cut down, anyhow. Pawley guffawed politely, although he must have heard the story several times before, and Mrs. Morgan giggled happily, and would have lost some more rum if she hadn't already lowered the level by other means. Duffield looked condescendingly amused.

"Now it's your turn again, Mr. Duffield," Mrs. Morgan said. She had become the party's entrepreneur.

Duffield allowed himself to be drawn, as though reluctantly, into another story from his repertoire. While he was telling it Pawley crept round on tiptoe, in an exaggerated effort not to interrupt, filling up glasses. When he came to Mrs. Morgan's glass Morgan tried to intervene, and there followed a three-cornered argument in pantomime and whispers. Duffield went on with his story, addressing himself to Douglas. At the end Mrs. Morgan went off into fits of laughter, although she had missed it all. Her glass had been refilled to the brim. Her pock-marked face was growing very red.

Duffield then addressed himself to Morgan. He said with humorous sarcasm:

"Well, Morgan, what's the weather got in store for us?"

Morgan decided to ignore the sarcasm and answer the question. He did so sulkily.

"According to the radio there's an area of low pressure south of Jamaica." He was being purposely obscure.

"Still the same old Morgan!" Duffield said good-humouredly, as if he had just met Morgan for the first time in two months and had found him unchanged. "Always giving you a lecture instead of an answer." He looked at the others for approval. He found it in Mrs. Morgan, who said gaily to her husband:

"Yes; tell us what you mean. We can't all be as clever as you, you know. What is low pressure? It sounds very rude to me."

Morgan said curtly, "It may be going to rain."

His tone brought home to Mrs. Morgan that he was not in the same high spirits as herself. She hadn't realized it before. But now her own spirits were too high to be daunted.

"You do sound cross," she said. She appealed to the others, giggling. "Doesn't he sound cross? You ought to be nice to Mr. Duffield. He's being nice to you. Really nice. And he's such a scream." She looked at Duffield appreciatively.

Morgan was busy hoping that Pawley wouldn't suspect his wife was drunk. The best way to avert suspicion was to look as though he hadn't noticed it himself, so he decided to treat her remarks seriously. He pulled himself up and said pompously :

"Sorry, Duffield. No intention of being offensive. Yes, I'm afraid we may have a little rain. We may also get some high winds soon. But I'm hoping we can get through the season without much damage on the farm."

"You're always talking about your old farm !" Mrs. Morgan said.

Morgan ignored her.

"I lost half my grapefruit and orange-trees last year. You probably remember."

Duffield felt his victory was now complete. He could afford to be magnanimous.

"I remember. Ruddy bad luck. Yes, I hope you don't lose any more grapefruit. Fond of the stuff myself."

"I expect to be growing the finest in Jamaica next year," Morgan said, gratified.

The conversation became agricultural, and Pawley joined in. Presently Mrs. Morgan sighed and giggled regretfully.

"Oh dear, I wish I hadn't started this. Why doesn't someone say something funny again? I don't think we have nearly enough fun up here, do you, Mr. Pawley?"

Morgan was embarrassed by this gambit, his wife's condition was becoming dangerously revealing, and he got up. "We must be going," he said. "It's getting late." He went over to Duffield and patted him on the shoulder. "Glad we've had this talk tonight. It makes things easier." He said good night to Pawley, and then turned to his wife, who was still comfortably settled in her chair with half a glass of rum. "We must be going," he said.

"I'm enjoying myself," Mrs. Morgan giggled. "I don't want to go yet."

An ugly domestic scene might have followed if Pawley hadn't stepped in with some questionable diplomacy.

"That's all right, Morgan," he said. He was still in a party mood, and delighted that at least one reconciliation had been successfully engineered. "It's Saturday night, you know. We'll see your wife home if you want to go off."

Morgan never argued with Pawley, so he went off, wearing the sort of expression that people wear when they carry unexploded bombs. Mr. Morgan then made Duffield tell another joke, which Pawley followed with a modest little anecdote about an American mistaking the National Gallery for St. Paul's. Mrs. Morgan had never heard of either and presumably missed the point, but she accorded Pawley the appreciation due to his position. After this Douglas said good night. He saw no reason for staying to face the consequences of Pawley's diplomatic blunder. He returned to his bungalow.

He read for a time, and it must have been an hour later, when he was on the point of going to bed, that Morgan appeared in the doorway. His face was a uniform grey.

"My wife's with Duffield," he said unsteadily.

"Where?"

"At his bungalow."

Douglas didn't know whether he wanted sympathy or help.

"You'd better go and get her," he said.

"I can't go by myself. You'll have to come with me."

"Are they *in* the bungalow?" Douglas said.

"No, they're on the verandah. They're drinking. I went down and saw them."

Douglas went because he couldn't persuade Morgan to go alone, and he could foresee all kinds of frightful consequences if Mrs. Morgan passed out in Duffield's bungalow, which she was sure to do. They found her bulging over the sides of a narrow deck-chair, giggling hysterically and with her hair wildly disarranged. Douglas explained to Duffield the importance of getting her home. Duffield was also very drunk, but raised no objection. Douglas and Morgan hoisted Mrs. Morgan out of the chair. As soon as they had put her on her feet, she fell forward with her arms round Duffield's neck.

"You're a dear, Mr. Duffield. You really are, you're a dear."

They dragged her away, screaming with laughter. On the way back to the Great House she more or less passed out, which enabled them to make their entrance without waking the children, although it increased the difficulty of getting her upstairs.

In the morning Duffield was at breakfast on time. He said to Douglas:

"You must have had a job with that woman last night.

168

Couldn't stop her coming to my bungalow, you know. But she's not a bad sort. It's hard lines on her, being tied to a man like Morgan."

Presently Morgan arrived. He said good morning to Douglas and ignored Duffield.

"I'm afraid my wife's not very well this morning," he explained. "She's skipping breakfast."

Mrs. Morgan also skipped lunch, but she put in an appearance at supper, when she was very subdued and carefully avoided Duffield's eyes. The feud was on again. It looked as though there was every chance of it outliving the term.

At the beginning of the following week there was a disturbing incident—more disturbing to Douglas than any staff feud.

On Monday morning, when he went down to his bungalow before lunch, the wooden elephant had vanished. This puzzled him, but he did nothing about it until Tuesday morning, when he had an opportunity to question Ivy. Ivy giggled and said that it had been there at ten o'clock on Monday when she had dusted the room and made the bed. He then forgot about it until one of his classes in the afternoon.

In the class they happened to be talking about the fauna of Jamaica, and the reason for the island lacking the larger beasts of other tropical lands. One of the children mentioned elephants, which reminded him of his wooden mascot. He asked if any of them could account for its disappearance.

There was silence—the sort of silence that signified some knowledge shared by them all. He repeated the question, but as no one was willing to speak he dropped the matter until after the class. Then he called over Rosemary, who was the only one of his own pupils present, and asked her to explain. He had to use some persuasion. Then she said reluctantly :

"Silvia's got it. She's been telling everyone you gave it her." After saying this much, she thought she might as well go on, and added, "She's also been telling everyone that you write her notes. She says you leave them for her to collect in one of the bushes in the garden."

"What sort of notes?"

Rosemary looked embarrassed.

"I don't know."

"But nobody believes her?"

She professed not to know this either, but explained, "She let us watch her collect one yesterday. She took it out of the bush—but she tore it up after she'd read it, and wouldn't let us see it. She said it was private."

"I'm not surprised," Douglas said. "You certainly wouldn't have found it was my writing."

The task of speaking to Silvia about this was going to be extremely distasteful, but he would have to face it. He went in search of her after tea. He found her sitting under one of the junipers, writing another story for him.

He said to her point-blank:

"Silvia, have you got my elephant?"

She flushed and said nothing.

He said, "If you must take something that doesn't belong to you, why on earth don't you keep quiet about it? You're obviously going to be found out sooner or later if you go round telling people it was given you."

She stared at him dumbly. He went on:

"You remember what I told you the other day about trying to make an impression on people? I can only think that's why you did it. You see it doesn't work, don't you? You end up by making quite the wrong sort of impression. Perhaps you'll understand what I mean now." This also seemed to cover the notes in the bougainvillæa, so he decided not to mention them. She was still speechless. He said, "Anyhow, you might let me have the elephant back some time. As you know, it's of some sentimental value to me."

He left her and went down to his bungalow. Within half an hour Silvia appeared on the verandah. She had completely regained her composure.

"Please, can I keep the elephant?" she said.

"No," he said. "You can't."

She was silent.

"What's the matter?" he said. "You haven't gone and broken it, have you?"

"No. I just want to keep it."

"Well, you can't. And in future don't take things of mine without asking."

She was not at all upset by his crossness. It was extraordinary how she had pulled herself together in half an hour. She looked at him blandly.

"I know you've heard about the notes as well."

"Yes, I have. I was extremely annoyed about it. You ought to have had more sense. It was obvious that the other children would find out that I hadn't written them."

"You might have done," she said.

"What do you mean?"

"You might have written notes to me, if you hadn't cared about what other people would think."

"I don't understand you at all," he said.

"You care enough about me to have written them."

He said, "My dear girl——"

"I'm not a girl," Silvia said.

"For heaven's sake, what are you?"

"I'm a woman."

"You're on your way to becoming one," he said. "But that's rushing things a bit. Some people are glad to call themselves girls at thirty."

"I have feelings like a woman," Silvia said.

"I don't think any sensible woman would have invented that business about the notes, or taken my elephant."

"I wanted to have something of yours."

"That seems most unnecessary." He was feeling very uneasy about the way the conversation was going.

"No, it isn't," Silvia said. "I'd like you to have something of mine, too. Did you find some flowers in here the other day?"

"Yes, I did."

"You knew I'd put them there, didn't you?"

"I'd not the slightest idea," he said untruthfully.

"You must have done. You knew what I felt."

"I was always under the impression that you hated me."

"I did, until after I'd smashed up your room. I'd always thought you really hated me. But then I knew you didn't, because of the way you behaved. You weren't even angry. Now I don't hate you. I do the opposite."

He could see only two lines to take : either he laughed at her, or else he played a sympathetic, fatherly, you'll-soon-get-over-it rôle. He didn't much care for the idea of laughing—he remembered reading in an authoritative book that children could be badly damaged by having their feelings laughed at—so he took the second and said :

"Feelings have a habit of swinging from one extreme to the other. But if you try not to take too much notice, they finally settle down somewhere about the middle."

"Mine won't," Silvia said. "They'll last for ever."

"In that case, you'll be a very unusual person. Most girls feel strongly about lots of different people before they're twenty."

"I'm very advanced for my age," Silvia said. "I think there might have been some mistake about when I was born. I might be fifteen now. I knew a girl who ran away from home and was married when she was fifteen."

He laughed and said, "The trouble with you, Silvia, is that your imagination's far too vivid. Why not just accept the fact that you're twelve? You'll be fifteen soon enough."

"It isn't imagination if you feel things."

"It can be," he said.

"I know what I feel. I know what you feel, too. You've always bothered about me much more than about the other girls."

"I've bothered about you more because you've been more of a nuisance," he said. "That's my job here."

"It's all right," she said tolerantly. "You don't have to say anything about it. I don't expect you to. I know it's very difficult for you in your position. But I shan't discuss it with anyone else—not now I've talked it over with you."

"You'd better go and explain to the others that it wasn't true about the notes," he said. "And get it out of your head that I think about you in a different way from the other girls."

"I don't see why I should."

"Because I feel exactly the same about you all. Now run away—and don't forget to give me back my elephant."

"I'll go and bring it now," she said.

"I don't want you to bring it now. Give it to me some time when I'm up at the Great House."

"All right," she said. "You needn't worry, anyhow. I'm not going to make things awkward for you."

"Try not to make things awkward for yourself, either," he said.

It was only after she had gone that he began to wonder whether Silvia had been putting on a very clever act, to justify the theft and the fabrication of the notes, and to make up for the humiliation of being found out. He would have preferred this, on the whole, to the disquieting alternative that she had been sincere. He really didn't know what to make of it—and he preferred not to think of what stories she was telling the other children.

He avoided seeing her alone for the rest of that week; but in his classes she wore the knowing and rather superior expression of one who shared a secret with the master. He took good care not to pay her special attention—nor to ignore her, for she might have interpreted that, for the benefit of the others, as an over-played attempt to reveal nothing in public. He supposed the whole situation was one that Pawley would have called unusually significant, meriting a putting together of heads; but he was reluctant to submit it to Pawley's clumsy consideration from all angles, and so he didn't consult him. Pawley was still extremely pleased about Silvia's superficial behaviour, and Douglas half expected to be sent for at any moment and offered the headmastership, whilst Pawley self-effacingly reduced himself to the ranks.

CHAPTER THIRTEEN

On Wednesday Judy was away on a trip to Trinidad, and he spent only twenty minutes in Kingston, buying books and cigarettes, and then drove back to the hills. He went a walk along the top of the ridge and returned to the school in time for supper. As he was going into the dining-room, he met Mrs. Morgan.

"Oh, Mr. Lockwood, I've really bad news for you." Her cheeks sagged with distress. "Really bad."

The bad news was that John had jaundice. After Mrs. Morgan's introductory lamentation, he had expected some much more appalling calamity, and he was quite relieved that it was nothing worse. However, John's jaundice later turned out to be a greater calamity than it had seemed at first.

He went up to the sick-room after supper. John's dark skin was only slightly discoloured, but his eyeballs had turned the conventional yellow. He was looking extremely sorry for himself, which was not surprising in view of the naturally depressive effect of jaundice.

"Cheer up," Douglas said. "You'll be over it in a few days."

John showed no signs of cheering up, and presently he

turned his ochre eyes towards Douglas and said in a shrunk little voice :

"It's all right, you don't have to pretend to me."

"What do you mean?"

"I know I've got leprosy."

Douglas laughed, although he had now recognized the dumb fear that lay in John's eyes.

"That's nonsense. The doctor came up to see you this afternoon, didn't he? He said you had jaundice. He was in no doubt at all."

"That's what he wanted me to think."

"It's what he told Mrs. Morgan."

John stared at him unbelievingly.

"I'm going yellow. I know that's what happens first when you have leprosy."

It appeared that a long time ago somebody had told him this. Of course it was quite untrue, but probably this notion, coupled with his fear of leprosy, had been the cause of the jaundice. He had been worrying himself to death and looking at himself fifty times a day to see if he was turning yellow, and in the end he had turned yellow, although for quite a different reason from the one he supposed. That was the odd sort of way the body behaved —as if it had a mind of its own and liked playing practical jokes. Douglas tried to explain this to John. He said :

"It's just like telling someone you're going to touch them with a red-hot poker, and then touching them with a cold one. They get a blister because they were quite convinced it was going to be hot. You've got jaundice because you were quite convinced you were going to turn yellow. But you certainly haven't got leprosy. I give you my word we're not deceiving you."

Before Douglas left the sick-room John had declared himself reassured, although the fear in his ochre eyes had not completely died out. His fear was not in itself a calamity, because he was bound to recover from the jaundice in time; but there were seeds of calamity in his mere presence in the sick-room.

It was impossible to tell by what agency the news of John's illness was first carried outside the school, but it must have travelled rapidly. They later heard that within twenty-four hours it had been talked about in Montego Bay. Montego Bay was one hundred and thirty miles from the school. In Kingston, which was less than thirty miles away, it had presumably become gossip very much sooner. The gossip was exactly what might have been expected. A few weeks ago it had been rumoured that John had leprosy. He was now ill. It therefore followed logically, to a civilization that had not reached a higher standard in Jamaica than elsewhere, that leprosy was the illness. The corollary of this rumour was equally inevitable. It ran to the effect that Blue Mountain School, being in the habit of accepting throw-outs from other schools and allowing them to mix with other children, was not going to draw the line at retaining a leper and allowing him to circulate freely.

The first hint of these murmurings reached Pawley through his wife, who had been down to Kingston for a morning's shopping. They threw him into a panic. He called Douglas down to his bungalow. They had only just begun to discuss what measures might be taken when the maid brought in the post. There were four letters from parents uttering protests in varying degrees of vehemence. Two of the parents threatened openly to take away their children if the source of infection was not removed from the school; the other two implied the same threat in more veiled terms. As Pawley read them through he could already envisage the complete collapse of the school and "Closed" hung on the gate between the eucalyptus trees.

"It's quite clear what we must do, Lockwood," he said. One of the letters was still shaking in his hand. "We must send John away for the time being. Just until he's better, of course."

"But it's absurd!" Douglas said.

Pawley goggled nervously through his glasses. "I quite agree with you. It seems quite unnecessary to us. But in this case we should be wise to set aside our personal feelings——"

"What about John's personal feelings?" Douglas said.

"Quite, quite," Pawley said quickly. Then he indicated the letters again. "But we must bear in mind the interest of the majority—even if it means temporarily overlooking the individual. . . . It takes a lot of courage to do it, of course."

"The majority haven't the faintest idea what their interest is."

"They think they have—which I'm afraid amounts to the same thing."

Douglas said indignantly, "Do you mean to say we've got to throw John out on his neck, just because people are so damned stupid that they believe a wicked lie?"

Pawley lifted his hands in a helpless gesture.

"I only wish there was an alternative."

"There is an alternative. We can ask a Medical Officer of Health to endorse Dr. Knowles's diagnosis of jaundice, and send a statement to the parents and the Press. After that, anybody who still believes that John has leprosy can be certified insane."

Pawley was not too pleased about this suggestion; he had made up his mind that the only way to placate the parents was to get rid of John, and he said rather uncomfortably :

"We could do that, of course. But it all takes time. We might be wise to safeguard ourselves in the meantime."

"All right, we can send John away," Douglas said. "But I'd like to know what people are going to think of us when they find out that John hasn't got leprosy after all."

This argument impressed Pawley. He thought it over for a minute, and then agreed to let John stay. Douglas called the Public Health Office on the telephone for him, because he was still too harassed to do it himself. He arranged for a Medical Officer to come up the next day. He then left Pawley's study, feeling confident that no fresh snags could arise in the meantime.

He was wrong.

In the middle of the afternoon he was again called down to Pawley's bungalow. As he passed the garage, he saw a taxi standing near the gate. He guessed that it was either the Medical Officer visiting sooner than expected, or else one of the parents come to utter a protest in person. But it was neither. It was John's mother.

She was sitting in Pawley's study, and had evidently been there for some time. Pawley invited Douglas to pull up a chair. He then said :

"I know you'll be sorry to hear this, Lockwood—but Mrs. Cooper feels it might be advisable for her to take John away from the school for the present. I've told her how much we shall regret losing him; but naturally I've no right to stand in her way."

"Why does she feel it advisable?" Douglas asked. He looked at Mrs. Cooper, hoping she would answer, but Pawley said quickly :

"She's naturally very upset about all the gossip. And she feels that while John's ill she can give him much better care at home."

"But he oughtn't to be moved with a temperature like that," Douglas said. "And certainly not down into the heat."

"Nevertheless," Pawley said, "I think that perhaps under the circumstances Mrs. Cooper is taking the wisest course."

Douglas looked at Mrs. Cooper. "What does your husband feel about it?"

"He hasn't said much," Mrs. Cooper said. She was wearing her best cotton dress, and sitting anxiously with her plump hands resting on her lap. "Everything's just the same as when you came to see me."

"Does he want you to take John away?"

"He hasn't said so. I really only came up to visit John because he was ill. I didn't know what a lot of trouble it was causing with the other parents. But now Mr. Pawley's told me, it doesn't seem fair to let him stay. I'd feel dreadful if the school had to suffer because of John."

Pawley looked embarrassed about this. He avoided Douglas's eyes, and said with awkward pomposity:

"It wasn't my intention to make you feel like that, Mrs. Cooper. I understood you to say that you'd be happier looking after John at home—just while he has jaundice, of course."

"No, it isn't that," Mrs. Cooper said self-consciously. "It's just that I don't want to be the cause of any trouble. I'm so ashamed of what's happened already."

"Nobody can blame you for that," Douglas said. "And the Medical Officer's visit tomorrow should put an end to all this nonsense."

It was clear from Mrs. Cooper's expression that she hadn't heard about the Medical Officer.

"I was just going to mention that when you arrived," Pawley said, getting more rattled.

"It would be a pity to take John away before then," Douglas said. "Perhaps Mrs. Cooper wouldn't mind letting him stay until we hear what the Medical Officer's going to say?"

"Oh, no, I wouldn't," Mrs. Cooper said at once. "I'd much rather let him stay, if you really don't mind."

"Very well, if that's how you feel about it," Pawley said, trying to look delighted. "I'm afraid I misunderstood you before."

After Mrs. Cooper had gone, Pawley kept up the pretence of looking pleased, but he knew he had been made to look a fool. He was obviously annoyed with Douglas, although he tried not to show this either. He said :

"Of course, I'm happy John's staying, Lockwood—but I don't think you should have tried to influence Mrs. Cooper like that. She's not a strong character, you know, and she didn't like to press the point about looking after John herself. But there's no doubt she would have preferred to do so. She told me so quite clearly before you came in." He said this as though he was now beginning to believe it. Anyhow, John was staying, so Douglas let it go at that.

The Medical Officer came up the next day. He was a Jamaican who had studied medicine at Cambridge. He said it was absurd to suppose that John had leprosy, and wrote out a strong statement to that effect. He couldn't wait for it to be duplicated, and trustingly signed the bottom of a blank stencil. Afterwards Douglas typed in the statement above. He ran off enough copies for all the parents, and also for the newspapers, ready to dispatch with a covering letter from Pawley. The wording of the covering letter, which Pawley had asked Douglas to write for him, was the cause of another argument. Pawley objected to the leprosy scandal being described as "malicious and detestable gossip." Finally they called it "an unfortunate rumour that had attracted widespread attention," in order not to hurt people's feelings.

The statement appeared in newspapers a day or two later. Letters of protest ceased arriving from parents, and no children were withdrawn. John began to recover from his jaundice. The other children visited him in the sickroom, but there was a reserve in their attitude towards him that had not been there before. It was the sort of reserve that someone who had been on trial for embezzlement might notice amongst his friends—even after his ultimate acquittal.

The next time Douglas met Judy she had just come back from Venezuela. Before that she had been to Santa Dominica and Miami. During the same week Douglas had travelled only sixty miles, down to Kingston and back.

It was somehow disturbing to hear Judy talk lightly of her trips, as in London one might talk of running out to Guildford or down to Bognor, and he remembered the curious sensation that his own flight out from England had given him. They had taken off at night from the Azores, expecting to wake up over the palm-trees and pink sunlit houses of Bermuda. The course had been changed owing to unfavourable Atlantic winds, and in the morning they had looked down instead on the uninhabited northern wastes of Newfoundland. He could have been no more surprised if it had been Tasmania or Peru. During the war, when he had always travelled by aircraft, the Orient had contracted into the size of a pocket-handkerchief; but the New World and the Atlantic, where he had never been, had remained the vast remote areas that he had only known on his Bartholomew's atlas at school. The sudden sense of contraction came as a shock. He would have liked to stay in Newfoundland long enough to re-orientate himself; but a few hours later, in a single hop, they exchanged the northern clime for the tropics. Once in Jamaica, where his air ticket expired, the earth gradually began to expand again to its former dimensions. Newfoundland, which had seemed close enough to pelt with mangoes, retreated to its proper position round the curve of the globe. London became as distant as a star. Now, if the station-wagon was not available, Kingston itself was out of reach. The jungles that lay ten miles away, behind Blue Mountain Peak, were as mysterious and remote as the hinterland of Tibet.

In this reduced world it was strange to hear of Judy's nonchalant trips beyond the limits of the Caribbean. Judy herself took the speed of air travel for granted, but the job delighted her. It was her ideal life : to spend one night in Caracas and the next in Nassau. If it had occurred to her at the time, she would have taken up flying instead of acting or being a mannequin. She had no instinct to own a plot of land or furnish a house, and had never accumulated possessions. She had left in London all that she didn't require for Paris, and in Paris given away all but her needs for Mexico. She saw life only as the present, without a yesterday or tomorrow; and Douglas supposed that it was because of this that she had so lightly tried to commit suicide. If something else had cropped up that evening, if the doctor who prescribed the tablets had asked her out to dinner, or if she had delayed her action an hour and gone to the cinema, her first shock at Louis' ultimatum would have dropped into the past and she probably wouldn't have done it. She made very few demands on the present to sustain her happiness—and least of all the demand of most people, the demand for a rosy future.

This quality of hers enchanted Douglas—for it was always the quality you lacked yourself that you first admired in others. He now saw that he had spent too much of his own life in vague and undefined fear of the future—fear that underlay the absurd dreams of impossible happiness, protracted from adolescence. It was this fear of not living out his dreams that had driven him to make mistakes. He had married Caroline out of fear, though he hadn't known it at the time—leaping at an opportunity lest it shouldn't reoccur. Now, if he fell into a depression and bothered to analyse it, there was the same bogy at the root : not distaste for the present, which he could enjoy, but the fear that his life would be a failure. It had taken Judy to show him that the only failure in life could be the failure of the present, and that the greatest failure of the present was the fear of what was to come. He was aware that many people would call Judy irresponsible; but he was in love with her, and in her carefree spirits saw innocence of heart.

Innocence of heart—he wondered how many others he knew who possessed it. The Jew at the cocktail party, perhaps. . . . He could think of no more, except for the children; but the innocence of their hearts was not yet tested, and one by one they would be corrupted by disappointments and injustice, by jealousy and thwarted desire, and the freshness would fade from their faces with the fading of their dreams. For innocence of heart was a subject that could only be taught by those who had not lost it themselves. There was no formula, no precedent of success, and those in whom it flowered had not learnt it at school—they had been born with it as a vivid and unquenchable talent.

Perhaps one day they would understand how to teach it to the untalented, and the world would lose its distemper. Meanwhile how many of the children, he wondered, would grow up to take what they did not want, to resent what they had not got, to imitate what they could not become? How many would go on looking for their happiness in the future, until all at once they discovered, with bitterness, that the future was past?

They should have had Judy up at Blue Mountain School to teach them, with her wonderfully unembittered smile. But then the letters of protest would soon have buried them alive—because, after all, married Hungarian Jews and suicide were not quite the thing.

That afternoon they drove out to a beach some way from Kingston, and although the sand-flies abounded and the wind was too warm and sticky, it was nevertheless a happy excursion, and as they were returning to Kingston Douglas said :

"I can't help feeling that we're going to find Louis installed in your flat when we get back. This afternoon is waiting for something to spoil it."

"I'll throw him out if he's there," she said.

Louis was not installed in the flat, but there was the next worst thing : a letter from him in the box. It was the first since his departure. It was in a fancy air-mail envelope, and came from the Argentine.

Judy stood staring at it in her hand. Her hand was trembling slightly and she had turned pale. After a moment she gave a rather strained laugh.

"I told him that if he wrote I'd tear up his letters." She said it as if she was trying to remember whether she had meant it or not.

"He probably left his hair-cream here," Douglas said. "Or else his wife's gone off again."

She went slowly through the living-room without taking her eyes off the envelope.

"Why should I let him upset me?" she said. "I'm damned if I'm going to open it." She still wasn't doing much about it.

"It might contain a cheque," Douglas said. "In any case, it's bound to make good reading, just for the culture."

She hesitated another moment, and then suddenly laughed and tore up the envelope and dropped the bits into the waste-paper basket.

"I'm sorry it took so long, but it was such a surprise. I feel marvellous now—as if I'd holed in one or swum the Channel."

"You'll be tearing them up without hesitation at all by the fifth or sixth," he said.

"Well, why on earth should we let him go on messing things up for everybody else?" she said. "He messed us up enough last time."

"In fact, we've never quite got back to where we were interrupted."

"I know." She smiled uncertainly. "I wish I knew whether you wanted to get back or not. I haven't the least idea. I don't know if you've just been bothering about my feelings, or if it makes you sick to look at me after what happened. I wouldn't blame you if it did."

"Do I behave as though I was feeling sick?"

"No—but you wouldn't. You'd just go on being pleasant because you thought I needed you."

"Do you need me?"

She shrugged, smiling. "I was wonderfully happy last night because you were coming down this morning, if you call that needing you. And I tore up the letter. I don't know what you call that."

"Tearing up Louis' letter doesn't stop you wanting him."

"But I don't want him," she said. "I don't, honestly. It just made me feel peculiar for a minute to see his writing again, that's all. I can probably forget him better than you can."

"I could forget him on the beach," Douglas said. "But he seems to hang around this flat. He keeps coming out of that room in his braces."

"Oh, Lord," she said. "And he looks so absolutely hideous in his braces. I suppose it must be his duppy. We'll go out for supper, if you'd rather."

"No; I'll get used to him."

"All right; I'll see what we've got."

While she was in the kitchen Douglas smoked a cigarette on the balcony, and he thought that perhaps Louis wasn't in the flat, after all; but when he went back into the room he saw Louis coming out of the bedroom, grinning in an ingratiating way and drying his hands on a towel. But there hadn't been a duppy on the beach that afternoon, and Judy's legs had been long and golden in the sun; so when they sat down at the table for supper he said:

"There are supposed to be much better beaches in Jamaica—the genuine tropical article."

"And no genuine sand-flies?"

"No sand-flies at all—but a guaranteed moon."

"Can you get to them in a day?"

"No," he said. "Not in a day. You have to rent a bungalow."

Her eyes were green and amused.

"Your holidays don't begin for nearly a month," she said.

"I could take a week-end off. I could have had one before, but I didn't bother."

"But if someone found out?"

"You can get bungalows miles from anywhere, with beaches of their own. We shouldn't take the station-wagon —we'd hire a car."

"It would be awful if you kept remembering Louis," she said. "And feeling sick."

"The duppy won't be with us," he said. "We'll leave it to look after the flat. It might have grown tired of haunting the place by the time we got back."

Her eyes smiled at him across the table.

"It might be so beautiful," she said, "that I wouldn't mind very much if we never got back."

The roads were empty, and he drove fast out of Kingston, exhilarated by the rush of the cool night air, and already living in his thoughts the idyll they had planned. He mused at the same time over possible eventualities that could mar it : he thought of the car going wrong and leaving them stranded, and then, for some reason, there came into his mind a perfectly clear picture of Mrs. Pawley's brother, Findlay, walking along the beach and discovering them together, and this made him wonder what would happen if the news reached Pawley. But in his present state of elation he hardly cared if it did, and his thoughts returned to Judy and her innocence of heart. . . .

He was four or five miles out of Kingston when he remembered he had left a parcel in Judy's flat—a meteorological instrument of Morgan's that he had picked up that morning after repair. He turned the station-wagon round and drove back. When he reached the house he saw that the light in Judy's flat was still on. He climbed the stairs and rang the bell. After a moment Judy came to the door.

"Oh, I couldn't think who it was!" Her manner seemed rather strange, and when he told her what he had come back for, she said, "I'll get it for you, shall I?"

"I'll get it myself if you like." She was obviously reluctant to let him pass through the hall, so he asked her, "What's the matter? You haven't got someone in there, have you?"

She looked grim.

"Oh, well, I suppose you'll have to see."

He went into the living-room. There was nobody there,

but the pieces of Louis' letter were lying on the table. She had been fitting them together.

He laughed without amusement. "I didn't know you liked playing jig-saws. There may be some more letters by the week-end—you can tear them up and play with them all day long on the beach. It'll help pass the time."

"I wish you hadn't come back," she said, looking wretched. "It doesn't mean anything."

"Except that you want to know what's in the letter."

"I'll tear it up again, if you like. I'll burn it."

"No, go on with it now," he said. "You never know, he might be offering me a job. I'd hate to miss anything like that. May I fix myself a drink while you're doing it?"

He found a bottle of rum in the kitchen, and some ice-cubes in the refrigerator. When he returned to the living-room Judy had finished putting the letter together. It had been quite easy because the envelope had only been torn across twice.

"You can read it if you want," she said. "He's hopeless at writing letters, like me."

"What does he want?"

"His wife's gone back to New York. He thinks she might stay. He wants me to arrange a trip down to Buenos Aires."

"Well, why not?" Douglas said. "Your air-line goes to the Argentine, doesn't it? You could fix it up with them."

"I'm not going to fix it up," she said.

"I don't see why not."

She looked at him very miserably, screwing up the pieces of the letter. "I don't want to. I've finished with Louis. I told you before."

"You also told me you'd given up reading his letters."

"I only read it because I'd nothing else to do after you'd gone."

"Nothing except think about the week-end."

She turned away. "I deserve that. I suppose you want to call it off now. I was terrified something would stop it, but I never thought it could happen as soon as this." She sounded as if she would burst into tears; but after a moment she turned back, smiling wryly. "Oh, it's all right, I'm not going to cry. Not until after you've gone, anyhow. No blackmail."

"You always wanted to see the Argentine," he said.

"I always wanted to see Brazil," she said. "I never cared particularly about the Argentine."

"You'd care about it more if you weren't afraid of letting me down again," he said. "I'm much too nice a chap to be let down twice. You're too nice to do it. We're both so nice we can't do what we want."

"I'd go to Buenos Aires if I wanted," she said. "But I don't—I want to go with you."

"You'd better think it over until tomorrow," he said. "There may be another letter from Louis in the morning."

"It wouldn't make any difference. Not if there were fifty more letters. I'll send them to you if there are, and you can burn them yourself."

"You're not tired of playing jig-saws already?"

"Yes, I am." She smiled, still looking pretty wretched. "Can I have a sip of your drink? I'm beginning to need it." She took a drink, and then laughed and said, "I nearly pushed the letter back into the wastepaper-basket when the bell rang. Then I thought it must be the woman from the flat below."

"I hate not reading letters," Douglas said. "I always read Caroline's."

"It's more fun to tear them up first and play jig-saws," she said. "In fact, it's the only way of enjoying Louis' letters —they're so fearfully dull."

Douglas said, "Are you sure the air-line will give you the week-end off?"

"I'll give them notice, if necessary."

"I was probably wrong about the moon," he said. "It might not be full."

"I don't mind if there's no moon at all," she said. "I don't mind if it rains all night. I might not notice."

"You might notice you were not in Buenos Aires."

"Where's Buenos Aires?" she said.

"It's a place you had a letter from today. It was from an Hungarian chap in braces."

"Oh, yes, I remember," she said. "From a duppy. But isn't it lucky?—I'm not hauntable any more."

CHAPTER FOURTEEN

PAWLEY's attitude had never quite recovered its former affability since the interview with Mrs. Cooper, and he boggled for at least twenty minutes. This seemed pretty graceless of him, considering that Douglas was entitled to four week-ends off in the term and so far hadn't taken one. However, when he saw that the threat of his displeasure was not going to make Douglas withdraw his request, he finally gave a grudging consent.

On Tuesday there was a note from Judy. Her office had made no fuss about the week-end, and her anticipatory excitement ran over into two joyful P.S.s. The note appeared to have been written the day after they had last met. Douglas looked at the post-mark. It was Thursday—nearly a week ago. This puzzled him, because the post from Kingston only took two days. It was brought up every day by a runner from the village six miles down the hill and handed to Mrs. Pawley, and private letters for the staff and children were distributed by the Pawleys' maid. Now Douglas wondered if Mrs. Pawley had delayed this letter of his as a haphazard gesture of pique. He even looked at the envelope more closely to see if it had been opened before. There was no evidence that it had. Probably his suspicion was quite unwarrantable—there were many other possible causes of delay.

But whether Mrs. Pawley had delayed the letter or not, she must have heard from her husband that Douglas had asked for the week-end off. She gave every indication that she shared Pawley's displeasure. Douglas noticed the fresh anger in her expression; but there was also a new resolution in her purpose to ignore him, and she vented the anger on Silvia instead.

The incident occurred on Tuesday at lunch. Mrs. Pawley was sitting at Silvia's table, and Douglas at a table on the other side of the room. Half-way through the meal Mrs. Pawley's raised voice was heard above the usual din of chattering and clinking cutlery. It caused a sudden and emphatic silence. All eyes turned towards her. She flushed right down her neck, and then said furiously to Silvia:

"If you can't behave, you can go and sit at a table by yourself." Silvia didn't move, so she went on, "Did you hear me? Go to the table in the corner at once. You can stay there for a week."

Silvia rose in her contemptuous way and walked over to the empty table, where she sat down with her arms folded. The silence continued. Then a girl at Mrs. Pawley's table said shyly:

"Excuse me, Mrs. Pawley, but it was my fault. I took Silvia's fork."

"I didn't ask you to speak," Mrs. Pawley snapped.

The silence was broken by Pawley, who made a clumsy attempt to resume normal conversation.

"Yes, Paul? You were telling me how you were intending to spend your holidays. . . ."

A tentative murmur started up in the room, but it was some while before the noise grew into anything like the usual uninhibited hubbub. Mrs. Pawley had meanwhile instructed one of the servants to take Silvia's plate across to her table. Silvia ignored it. She sat perfectly still with her arms crossed for the rest of the meal.

After lunch it was customary for the staff to take coffee in the common-room, but Douglas felt too angry to face Pawley at once. He went off for a walk round the grounds. Half an hour later he went down to Pawley's bungalow. Mrs. Pawley was on the verandah, but she went inside as soon as she saw him and Pawley came out. Douglas was now feeling calmer. He proceeded to point out that Silvia's banishment to a table by herself was not only a denial of all Pawley's own educational principles—and therefore likely to undo all the good that two months of liberal treatment had done her—but was a punishment that had, in any case, been unjustly dispensed, since another girl had admitted to being at fault.

Pawley might reasonably have excused his wife's action as a momentary error of judgment, of which anyone was capable; but instead he attempted to defend it. He said it would be a mistake to give Silvia the impression that they only knew how to be "soft." There followed an argument on the meaning of " softness," which took them right away from the point. When they finally returned to the point Douglas was feeling so frustrated by Pawley's muddled thought and twisted principles that he was prepared to abandon the discussion and indeed to abandon Silvia. He said that perhaps Mrs. Pawley would like to take charge of her entirely.

Pawley said patiently that he would have accepted this suggestion if it had not been so close to the end of the term; as it was, he would invite Douglas to continue as Silvia's tutor, although it was now apparent that they did not see "eye to eye." He then said :

"I shall trust you, Lockwood, not to use your position

187

with Silvia to prejudice her against my wife or myself—which you may feel tempted to do."

Douglas replied that he had always made an effort not to allow his personal feelings to influence his treatment of the children, and turned and left.

Later in the day Pawley called him down to his bungalow again and offered an olive branch. He said that he put it all down to end-of-term nerves. Douglas allowed himself to agree. Pawley shook his hand, diagnosed "a bit of right and wrong on both sides," and said that he was reducing Silvia's sentence from a week to only three days of solitary meals. He added that he had no objection to her taking a book into the dining-room, if she felt it would mitigate her boredom.

Silvia did not take a book into the dining-room, and at lunch, which was the only meal the Pawleys attended, she continued the protest of the hunger-strike. She sat with her arms folded while each course was put in front of her and taken away uneaten. She made up to some extent by eating ravenously at breakfast and supper, but lunch was the main meal of the day and there must have been a good deal of will-power behind her stubbornness.

On the same day as the incident at lunch she tried to find out from Douglas if he was taking Mrs. Pawley's side against her. He prevaricated, and fell back on the time-honoured defence of erroneous chastisement by exhorting her to remember, if she had really been innocent, how many times she had escaped retribution for undiscovered sins.

This brief interview took place in the library. On the following day she came down unexpectedly to his bungalow while he was having tea. Despite her effort to look casual, there was a handkerchief screwed up tightly in her hand and her knuckles were white. Her hair was freshly brushed. He also suspected a trace of powder and lipstick on her face, although they had been applied much more discreetly than on the last occasion, when she had gone off to meet her phantasy boy-friend.

She stood on the top verandah step.

"Where are you going for your holidays?" she said. It was obviously a rehearsed opening.

"I don't know yet." At the moment he could think of nothing clearly beyond the week-end. "I may fly down to Barbados."

"Will you take me?"

He laughed. "Your father might have something to say about that."

"I'm not going home, anyhow," she said. "I'm leaving home. I'm leaving school this term as well."

"You've been making very big decisions all by yourself," he said.

She ignored this. "So it's all right, you see—you can take me."

"And supposing I did?" he said. "What on earth should I do with you?"

"You could marry me if you wanted."

She spoke perfectly seriously; but he decided to treat it as a joke.

"Do we come back to the school next term as husband and wife?"

"No, we can't come back here," she said. "It might be better if we didn't come back to Jamaica at all. I thought we could go up to America. You'd easily get a job there. Something better than teaching. You're much too good to be a schoolmaster." She pulled a piece of paper out of the pocket of her dress. "You can read this if you want to know what I think of you."

He glanced at the paper. It was a poem called "Ode to Mr. Douglas Lockwood." It showed a marked influence of Shakespearean sonnets, and was not one of her best literary efforts. It began by extolling his wisdom and courage and other virtues, and passed on with a welter of superlatives to his appearance. It described the colour of his eyes as a challenge to the blueness of the Caribbean. He folded up the paper and said to Silvia :

"My eyes aren't blue, you know. They're grey. And nobody could call my teeth perfect. I smoke too much, and six months ago I had seven fillings. This poem isn't about me at all. It's about somebody else."

"It's about you," she said. "I've seen your eyes look blue."

"No," he said. "It's about somebody who only exists in that imaginative little brain of yours. This is what you want me to be like—a wise and handsome chap with blue eyes and shining teeth—so you pretend all these things to yourself, and you pretend to yourself that you care a lot about me. One of these days you'll start caring about somebody who really exists. Then you'll realize this didn't mean anything at all. You'll laugh when you remember asking an old schoolmaster to run away with you."

"You're not laughing, are you?" she said.

"No, I'm not," he said. "I'm taking it just as seriously as all the stories you've written for me. You believed those, too, while you were writing them. It was quite right you should have done, because they really happened—in your imagination. Perhaps this is really happening in your imagination. But that's where we must leave it."

She ignored all this. She had relaxed her grip on the handkerchief, and was looking more at ease.

"I'm quite pretty, aren't I?" she said.

"You may be quite good-looking one day," he said.

"My figure will get much better. And you've no idea what a difference it will make when I have my hair waved. You could be very proud of me."

He said slowly and firmly, "Silvia, I am not taking you away with me."

"Why not? Because you're afraid?"

"Because I don't want to."

"You must want to, if you're in love with me."

"I'm not in love with you," he said. "That's one of the things you've made yourself believe."

"I know you're not in love with your wife any more," she said. "You're divorced. I don't suppose you ever loved her properly. She wasn't meant for you. And you're not in love with anyone else, are you?"

"If I was, it would be with someone of my own age."

"Age doesn't matter—and as I've told you already, I think I'm probably fifteen. But there's nobody else you could be in love with. None of the other girls here are developed enough, and I know you aren't attracted by Mrs. Morgan."

"That only leaves Mrs. Pawley." He said this lightly, but he noticed Silvia flush, and she said in a tense sort of way:

"You're not in love with Mrs. Pawley, are you?"

He laughed. "No, Silvia, I am not. It's quite possible to go a very long time without being in love at all."

"I've sometimes wondered if Mrs. Pawley attracted you," she said. "I wondered it yesterday, when you tried to stand up for her although you knew she was in the wrong. She might attract you in a beastly way. But you couldn't love her properly. She's not good enough for you. She thinks herself so wonderful, and really she's hateful."

"You've no business to say that," he said. "But, in any case, I don't happen to be in love with her."

"Then you must be in love with me. You know how I found out first, don't you? It was after I'd smashed up your bungalow, and you told me about your elephant. There was no one else you would have told about it, because they wouldn't have understood."

"I remember you were rather scornful about it," Douglas said.

"I pretended to be, but I wasn't. I used to have something like that. It was just a stone with a funny pointed end. I had to rub the end with my third finger to make things happen as I wanted."

"Did it work?"

"Sometimes it did. Then I lost it. I was probably meant to, because once I used it to hurt somebody I hated. I should only have used it for good things." She smiled. "You see how alike we are. I believe in people being meant for each other, although I know it's supposed to be silly. Even if you don't really understand what you feel about me now, you will once we've spent some time together."

He stood up.

"Silvia," he said. "It's time you ran away. You can go and write me another story—about a girl of twelve who was far too impatient to grow up and live like someone on the films."

She took no notice of this, and said calmly :

"You've plenty of time to think it over, anyhow. I don't mind if you don't make your decision until the very end of term." She started to go, and then turned back with an afterthought. "I forgot to say you don't *have* to marry me. I'm not in the least conventional about that kind of thing."

On Thursday he was taking a French class in the library when Pawley's maid came in.

"You're wanted on the telephone, Mr. Lockwood."

He hurried down. He had warned Judy that the telephone was in Pawley's study and should only be used in an emergency. He expected the worst.

Pawley looked up from his desk without much enthusiasm.

"Perhaps you'd rather I left?" he said.

"It doesn't matter."

He picked up the receiver, and Judy's voice said :

"Douglas, are you alone?"

"No," he said.

"Oh, Lord," she said. "Can you possibly come down to Kingston this evening?"

"No, I can't. What's happened?"

She was silent for a moment. Then she said:

"Well, actually, it's not so bad as it sounds. One of the girls went down with pneumonia last night, and so they want me for a trip tomorrow. They've been so damned good to me, I can't let them down in a crisis like this. I honestly can't, can I? But it'll be perfectly all right for the following week-end. Would that mess everything up for you?"

"I could probably arrange it," he said.

She sounded terribly relieved.

"Oh, thank heavens," she said. "I'd been feeling so utterly wretched about it—I was terrified you wouldn't be able to. But I'll be back on the Friday morning."

"It's a long trip," he said. "Where are you going?"

She hesitated.

"Douglas, couldn't you possibly get down tonight? Or couldn't I come up and see you or something?"

"It's impossible," he said.

"Or tomorrow morning? I must see you to explain."

"You're going to Buenos Aires," he said.

She said wretchedly and very earnestly, "Listen, Douglas. I swear I didn't arrange it. I didn't even know where they were sending me at first. I know you won't believe me, but you can ask them at the office. The girl's dreadfully ill."

"Very well," he said. Pawley was pretending not to listen, but he was obviously listening for all he was worth and it was damned difficult to talk. It was even more difficult to hide what he was feeling, when he was feeling so sick he could have cried.

"I shall only be in Buenos Aires a few hours," Judy said. "I'm not going to see Louis. Honestly I'm not. I couldn't, anyhow, because I burnt his letter. I burnt his address."

"Good for you," Douglas said.

"Then it's all right about next week-end?"

"Of course."

"Oh, thank God, Douglas," she said. "Thank God, darling."

He knew it was no use pretending to Pawley that the call had had nothing to do with the week-end, so he tackled him at once. Pawley said:

"But that'll be the second last week-end of term."

"That won't matter, will it?" He was feeling extremely awkward.

Pawley spread out his hands helplessly.

"You must do whatever you think best, Lockwood," he said.

"I'd like to go, if you don't mind," Douglas said; and he again reminded Pawley that he had taken no other week-end off during the whole term.

"Yes, you've been most conscientious," Pawley said. "As you know, I've been very gratified by your work. . . ." He said this with more reserve than usual, and began to finger some papers awkwardly. Then he went on, "But I hope you're not going to spoil your good record in the last few weeks of term. I appreciate that we all begin to feel restless about now, but we must try not to lose our discretion. And in your particular case, as I've already pointed out, we should be wise to exercise a little more than ordinary caution." He settled himself back and felt for his pipe. "Not that I would dream of criticizing your conduct, Lockwood—narrow-mindedness is not amongst my many shortcomings. But you've probably learnt by now that there are other points of view which we can't afford to ignore."

"Oh, yes," Douglas said. "I've learnt all about that."

He carried his bag over to the garage after lunch. It was a clear day, and as Morgan had forecast a rainy week-end there was every chance of it remaining fine. Joe was already waiting by the station-wagon to drive him down. They set off between the eucalyptus trees and when he looked round again the school had vanished. The week-end had begun. The point in the future, that at the beginning of the week had seemed incredibly far away, had become the moment he was living now.

He could hardly realize that the long dragging week was over. Last Monday morning it had loomed in front of him like the Alps in front of some traveller from Germany bound for Italy on foot. Each period of twenty-four hours was a separate range to be crossed. In the daytime there was the wearisome upward trek from one calculated stage to another, and at night the speedy descent of sleep—but only to wake up in the bottom of another valley, with the precipice of another morning ahead. Once or twice during the week he had wondered with appalling anguish if Judy had really been deceiving him : if she had engineered her trip to Buenos Aires and gone to see Louis. Then he remembered the frankness of her eyes, the innocence of her heart. How absurd of him to doubt her !

Joe dropped him in the centre of the town, and he took a taxi to Judy's flat. There was no reply when he rang the bell. He looked at his watch. It was nearly three. He thought without dismay that the aircraft had probably been delayed. He went out to the taxi again and drove down to the offices of the air-line in Harbour Street. The clerk told him at once :

"Oh, yes, it was held up at Trinidad. It'll be landing here just after five."

A man who was standing near Douglas at the counter butted in and said :

"Are you asking about the aircraft from Buenos Aires? It was supposed to arrive at ten this morning. It's now expected about five o'clock."

"I've just been told," Douglas said.

"That's all right. I thought you were having difficulty."

Douglas turned back to the clerk, and asked him if Miss Waring was on board.

"Yes, she is," the clerk said. "She made the trip for one of our girls who's got pneumonia. She wasn't too pleased about it."

He was ashamed now that he could ever have doubted her; but at the same time he felt a wonderful sense of happiness and relief. He turned to go. As he left the office the man who had butted in at the counter came up to him again and said :

"Excuse me, old man, but are you going out to the airport?" Douglas said he was, and the man asked, "Would you mind if I joined you? The company haven't a car going out for another hour." He was a bouncing little chap in a Panama hat and khaki shirt and shorts. There was an expensive miniature camera on a strap round his neck.

"I'm hiring a car," Douglas said. "I haven't picked it up yet."

"I don't mind coming along with you—not in the least."

"All right," Douglas said.

The chap grinned. "My name's Burroughs. How do you do?" He shook hands.

"Are you meeting someone at the airport?" Douglas asked. "Or catching a plane?"

"Neither—I'm just taking a few snaps. I do them in colour, you know."

They walked along to the garage together. The car was a large Chevrolet saloon, with a tank to hold thirty gallons. Douglas had it filled right up to the top. As they were driving out into the road, Burroughs said :

"This isn't the way, old chap. You don't mind me telling you, do you?"

"I have to make a call before we go to the airport."

He pulled up in a road just off Harbour Street, and went into the agent's office. He had already arranged by letter about renting the bungalow. Inside the office there were photographs of the bungalow in a showcase : flat-roofed, and gleaming whitely amongst the palms on the edge of a beach near Ocho Rios. There were also photographs of the interior, with wrought-iron standard lamps and ultra-modern easy chairs. The rent was fifteen pounds a week. He paid over the money. The agent counted the notes and said :

"It is a very choice spot, sir. We always let it to Americans in the winter season."

It was now the summer season. He took the keys and went out to the car, where he found Burroughs writing in shorthand in a loose-leaf notebook on his lap. He explained that he had been keeping an hour-by-hour account of his trip ever since he left England—he sent it back to his sister, who typed it out ("She's glad of the bit of extra money") and sent it to his daughter who was at boarding-school. As they drove out towards the airport, he asked Douglas to stop the car. He got out and put the camera to his eye and pointed it at the harbour, and then came back and said :

"It wasn't the shot I wanted, after all. I try to get decent ones to make into slides. They've asked me to give a lantern-lecture at my girl's boarding-school when I get back."

They stopped again a bit later, and afterwards Burroughs said :

"Well, I took it. It may come out all right. But I don't like to print anything that wouldn't look well in the *Geographic*. I use that as my standard."

It was half-past four when they reached the airport.

There were several large hangars built at the elbow of the Palisadoes, with the runway going out to sea. One of the hangars was the customs shed. Douglas parked the car and stood about with Burroughs near the barbed wire that surrounded the field. There were two huge silvery four-engine machines glinting on the tarmac.

"K.L.M. and Pan-American," Burroughs said. "I'll catch the Pan-American as she goes off."

He held up his camera and caught instead a gale of dust as one of the engines started up, slapping out a harsh tattoo in the sultry tropical air. Then another engine started up, and there was more dust.

"I ought to have expected that," Burroughs said. He began cleaning the camera with his handkerchief. "I've lost a good shot now. Don't worry, though—I'll get the next one."

The aircraft had reached the end of the runway. It paused, and then swung round through a semicircle, and paused again, revving its engines. Then it swung back through the semicircle and revved the engines again. It was like an actor making last bows to each section of an audience.

"Boxing its compass," Burroughs said. "I'd need a movie to put that over properly."

The aircraft suddenly pressed forward with a burst of tremendous exertion, as if straining against a leash. A moment later the leash seemed to snap. Its motion became effortless as it passed down the runway and lifted into the air. Beyond the town it turned and began to climb, heading back over the school and the mountain ranges.

"It's a wonder they don't have any crashes up there," Burroughs said.

"Extraordinary." He was not in a mood to give Burroughs his life history.

The noise of the engines melted away as the aircraft disappeared behind the Peak. A minute later, as if it was the same aircraft returning, another came into earshot. It appeared as a fishy black speck like some primitive organism seen in a microscope.

"This isn't yours," Burroughs said. "It's from the wrong direction."

"I'll leave you here," Douglas said. "I'm going into the shed to see what's happening."

"I'll come with you."

Inside the shed Burroughs bounced up to an air-line official and asked about the Buenos Aires plane. The official said it was due at ten-past five.

"It's due at ten-past five," Burroughs said. "Is it a friend you're meeting?"

"Yes, but she may not be on it."

"Don't worry, she's sure to be."

"She may not." As though Burroughs would have known. "Wait a minute."

He disappeared. A Pan-American Constellation man-œuvred up to the shed, making a terrific din. It was going on to Curaçao, and only three or four passengers got out. One was a burly white-haired man with a flashy American tie, who looked like a jovial but dishonest Senator on the films. There were a good many people waiting by the barrier. Douglas mingled with them, hoping Burroughs wouldn't find him. He took out a cigarette. The white paper absorbed the perspiration from his fingers. Presently Burroughs touched his arm. He was holding a sheet of paper.

"I've borrowed a passenger list. What's your friend's name? We can see if she's on it."

"She won't be," Douglas said. "She's one of the crew."

"Really? You ought to have told me."

"I didn't know what you'd gone off for."

"It doesn't matter. I'll let them have this back."

The Senator had only one tiny suitcase. He was a huge man. They let him straight through the customs. He gave the tiny suitcase to a porter. The Constellation taxied off. Douglas dropped his cigarette on the concrete floor. The end had come to pieces in his damp fingers. Burroughs came back and said:

"They're splendid girls, some of these air-hostesses. I've any amount of admiration for them. What do you say to us making up a party tonight?"

"I'm afraid we can't," Douglas said.

"No? Well, let's talk it over when she arrives. I'm glad I've run into you. I like making new friends."

Another aircraft taxied on to the tarmac outside the shed. He hadn't noticed it land. The red swallow was painted on its side.

"This is it," Burroughs said. "It's a minute early."

Douglas went close to the barrier. The engines of the aircraft stopped. A flight of aluminium steps was trundled across. There was a notice on the steps that said "No

Smoking." The door opened and a stewardess came out and Burroughs said :

"You know why I came out for this trip, don't you?"

The stewardess was small and dark. She stood at the bottom of the steps as the passengers began to disembark. Presently he caught sight of the other stewardess standing inside the doorway. It was Judy. She was making the passengers duck as they came through. He pulled out another cigarette and lit it.

"And after the funeral," Burroughs said, "I decided there'd be nothing like travel to help me get over it."

Everyone came to Jamaica to get over things. He wondered how he could shake off Burroughs.

"Of course, I'd my daughter to think of, but I'll be back in time for her holidays."

It was extraordinary how many passengers the aircraft could hold. There might have been a trap-door behind, like the sentry-box in the stage revue from which the entire army of the chorus emerges. One woman came out with two babies. Then a prosperous Negress with a pigskin bag, and then a dark little Jew whom for one awful moment he thought was Louis. Then a bejewelled woman with fox-furs over her arm and then an unhurried Englishman in a city suit. Then the procession ceased and Judy disappeared into the empty bowels of the aircraft, and he stamped out his cigarette again and waited, and then she came to the door again with a handful of papers, and ducked through and came out into the sunlight on the steps, and at the same time he saw that it was not Judy at all—it was a girl who bore no resemblance to Judy beyond the colour of her hair. He waited, and no one else came.

"Excuse me," he said to Burroughs.

He went over to the customs official.

"Is this the Buenos Aires plane?"

"Yes; it's from Trinidad."

"I know it's from Trinidad—but did it come from Buenos Aires before that?"

"Yes, from South America." He was busy.

"From the Argentine?"

The official turned to a passenger : "Have you anything . . .?"

He found a chap with a red swallow on his cap.

"Is there any other aircraft from Buenos Aires today?"

"Not until Monday. Were you expecting someone?"

"I thought a friend might be on it."

"I've the passenger list here."

"No," he said. "It doesn't matter."

He stared at the empty aircraft. He felt for another cigarette, but the packet had fallen to pieces in his pocket. Then he saw the girl he had mistaken for Judy. She was hurrying through the special entrance in the barrier. He stopped her and asked :

"Do you know what's happened to Judy Waring?"

"Yes," she said. "I came up in her place."

"She's still in Buenos Aires?"

"Yes; she's left the company."

"Left the company?" he said. "Why?"

She waved her papers and moved away.

"I say, I'm awfully sorry. I've got to rush. . . ."

"But why's she left the company?" he said.

Burroughs's Panama hat appeared.

"I expect she's ill," he said.

"I don't know," the girl said.

"Look, I must know what's happened to her," he said. "I was expecting her."

"Well, wait here a second, will you . . .?"

She went off.

Burroughs said, "It's winter in the Argentine now. She may have caught something."

The girl had disappeared. The other stewardess had disappeared too. Then the fair one came back. She said :

"All I know about Judy is that she wanted to stay in Buenos Aires. She kicked up an awful fuss with the company. In the end, they let her. I was dragged out of the office at the last moment for this trip."

"You mean she's not coming back?"

"She may come back later," Burroughs said.

"I don't know," the girl said. "The company may bring her back to Jamaica. I don't know."

"She left her stuff here."

"That's her look-out. She may be having it sent down. I know she cabled someone here."

"How long ago?"

"Nearly a week, I should think."

"Well, thanks," he said. "She may have sent me a cable and I didn't get it."

"That sort of thing's happened to me before now," Burroughs said.

They went back to the Chevrolet. The road passed the quarry where the convicts worked. The convicts had all gone home, but Burroughs decided to take a snap of the place where they would have been working otherwise. The quarry reminded Douglas of the boatman whose brother had been a warder, and that reminded him of lunch under the cactus, and he wondered if Burroughs would notice the heat burning behind his cheeks at the memory of what a fool he had been made to look. He began to feel sick.

"We could have a good evening by ourselves," Burroughs said. "I'm quite free tonight."

"I've a lot to do."

He had to elaborate an excuse all the way back to Kingston. He dropped Burroughs at the Myrtle Bank. It was where he was staying.

"Anyhow, you'll know where to find me, won't you?" Burroughs said.

It took him five minutes to close the door of the car. Then Douglas drove to the cable office. He asked the clerk if there had been a cable for him during the last week. The clerk was an elderly Jamaican with gold-rimmed spectacles and grizzled hair. He was anxious to be helpful. He searched through a ledger.

"Yes, there was one four days ago."

"I never received it."

"Please wait," he said.

He went away. When he came back, he was peering at a piece of paper.

"It came on Tuesday," he said. "It was sent to your local post-office. I can't understand why you didn't get it."

"It was probably a mistake at the school," Douglas said. "May I have that copy?"

He took the cable, and put it in his pocket and left the office. He walked across the road to the Chinese grocer's to buy some cigarettes. The Chinese assistant was a long time bringing the change. He looked at the covers of the comics on the clothes-line. This was how he used to delay opening letters from Caroline, to show her he didn't care. The assistant brought the change and he strolled back to the car. He got into the car and lit a cigarette. As he held up the flame he noticed his hand was shaking. He threw the match out of the window, and took the cable from his pocket and laid it on his knee. It had come by the fastest service. It said:

REALIZE YOU WILL NEVER FORGIVE OF UNDERSTAND HOW
MUCH I WANTED YOU BUT LOUIS VERY ILL AND DESPERATELY
NEEDS ME STOP AM THEREFORE STAYING ARGENTINE STOP
OH DARLING IM SORRY

It was unsigned. What a pity, he thought, that she hadn't
signed it "Your ever-loving Innocent-of-Heart." It would
almost have made up for telling him she had burnt Louis'
address.

He took a taxi back to the school.

It had taken him half an hour to come to this decision—
half an hour walking up and down Harbour Street pretending to look at shop windows. It had occurred to him to stay
in Kingston and get drunk and go to a brothel, but only
because in circumstances of this sort it was the conventional
practice. He could work up no enthusiasm for seeking
oblivion in debauchery. Nor could he face a night by himself in the mediocre, suffocating city. The only other
alternative was to take Burroughs to the bungalow; but that
would have been rather overdoing the salt in the wound.

He did not relish the thought of returning to the school
for the week-end, either—he was going to look damned silly
after the fuss he had made about going off; but in one
respect he was glad to get back there at once : to have it
out with Pawley and his wife about the cable. As he thought
about this in the taxi going up, his anger grew hotter. He
had no doubt at all that Mrs. Pawley had withheld the
cable from him maliciously. It was Mrs. Pawley who had
caused him, for almost a week, to live in a state of intense
and excited anticipation. It was Mrs. Pawley who had
allowed him to hire the car, rent the bungalow, and stand
gloating over the showcase of photographs at the agents'.
It was Mrs. Pawley who had been responsible for the last
ordeal at the airport. It was Mrs. Pawley who had let him
go on making a fool of himself when Judy was four
thousand miles away locked in the arms of Louis. He didn't
know whether Pawley had had anything to do with the
cable or not, but now his fury was extending rapidly from
this specific outrage to include all the faults he had ever
found with the school. By the time he reached the school
the anger was burning in him with the heat and thrust of a
blow-lamp.

Douglas got out at the gate and gave the driver the four

pounds that he had agreed to pay, because he hadn't felt like quibbling over this excessive price down in Kingston. The driver counted out the notes as if he was astonished not to find more, and looked at Douglas reproachfully for a tip. Douglas told him to go to hell, and picked up his bag and went straight down to Pawley's bungalow.

Pawley was sitting by himself on the verandah, working on some papers. When he saw Douglas he registered considerable surprise.

"Hullo, Lockwood. What an extraordinary thing! My wife said only half an hour ago that she thought you'd be back before Monday." He goggled inquiringly as Douglas came up the steps. "You look rather upset. Nothing wrong, I hope?"

Douglas said, "Does your wife take in cables that are sent up from the post-office?"

"Yes," he said, puzzled. "She usually does. The runner has instructions to deliver everything to this bungalow."

"There was a cable for me on Tuesday," Douglas said. "Your wife didn't give it me."

Pawley unhooked his spectacles from his ears and began to wipe them, looking at Douglas vaguely with his unfocused eyes. After a while he said moderately, as if prepared to give the benefit of the doubt :

"You're not suggesting, of course, that my wife purposely held back a cable addressed to you?"

"Yes," Douglas said. "That is exactly what I'm suggesting."

"Aren't you being a little hasty?"

"I want to know why the cable wasn't given me."

Pawley replaced the spectacles slowly, looking extremely distressed.

"There must have been a misunderstanding," he said. "My wife has no reason to withhold your private communications."

"Only one reason," Douglas said. And he elucidated, "Spite."

"Come, come, Lockwood," Pawley said, in a hurt way. "We don't want to get offensive."

"As a member of your staff," Douglas said, "I find it offensive to be ignored by your wife for weeks on end. I find it even more offensive when my letters are delayed and my cables not delivered."

"It's a matter we can look into."

"I'd like to look into it now."

Mrs. Pawley had just appeared in the doorway of the verandah. She had evidently heard their voices. Pawley turned round to her and said in his awkward, pompous way:

"Ah, Joan! There appears to be a little misunderstanding. Lockwood's been telling me that a cable of his has gone astray. It was supposed to have arrived last Tuesday."

Mrs. Pawley said impatiently, "Yes, I signed for it. What's the matter?"

"I never got it," Douglas said.

"I sent it across to your bungalow."

"It never arrived at my bungalow," he said.

Pawley took on the rôle of impartial mediator. "If my wife sent it, old chap, it must have been mislaid somewhere. We can't blame her for that."

"I blame her for not sending it at all," Douglas said. "I blame her for opening it. How else do you think she knew I'd be back before Monday?"

Mrs. Pawley went white. After a moment she said to her husband in a tone that was meant to sound like cold disdain:

"I'm not going to be insulted by a member of your staff. I'll leave you to talk to Mr. Lockwood alone." She turned and went.

Pawley said reprovingly, "I'm afraid I must agree with my wife, Lockwood. Those remarks of yours were most uncalled-for. I should take a more serious view if it wasn't so close to the end of term. As I've pointed out to you before, we're all inclined to get over-wrought in the last few weeks. I shall make allowances. By next term I'm sure you'll have both got over your little differences."

"I shan't be here next term," Douglas said. "I'd like to give notice."

This took Pawley by surprise. He looked extremely shaken.

Douglas said, "I know my contract was for a year. But you needn't worry—I'll refund the cost of the air passage." The cost of the air passage was more than a term's salary; but it was worth it, to buy his way free of this place.

Pawley took off his glasses and began to wipe them again.

"Are you doing this because of the cable?" he said.

"Partly," Douglas said. "But I'd thought of it before."

"I hope I've given you no reason to feel dissatisfied with your position?" Pawley said, sounding hurt.

"No," Douglas said. "I'm just generally dissatisfied with the way things are run. I'm dissatisfied with always having to bother about what people think. I'm dissatisfied because we can't afford to have the courage of our convictions." As he said this he knew that he had no right to say it. It wasn't with Pawley and the school that he was dissatisfied, it was with Judy—and himself.

Pawley took it quite mildly.

"I think perhaps you're being a little ungenerous, Lockwood," he said. "However, I don't mind admitting I should be sorry to see you go. We haven't always seen eye to eye, but I felt you were making a real success of the job. The way you've handled Silvia has impressed me most favourably. As you know, our reputation hung on that. We owe you a great deal."

"I'm sorry," Douglas said. "I've quite made up my mind."

"Very well," Pawley said. "But I shan't accept your resignation tonight. You'll be in a less disturbed frame of mind in the morning. I'd like to discuss it again then."

"I'll come down and see you again in the morning," Douglas said. "But there'll be nothing to discuss."

The moon was shining as he walked back to his bungalow with his bag. It was a full moon. It was the moon that should have been shining at this moment on Judy and himself at Ocho Rios. They should have been walking along the sand, and the sand should have been white in the moon, and the moonlight breaking into showers of silver splinters on the sea.

He went into the bungalow and shut the door and shut out the moon. He put the bag on the bed and gave himself a glass of rum. The anger had left him. It had only been a convenience : a clear-cut passion directed at the Pawleys to hide his real pain. It had made Mrs. Pawley responsible for Judy's deception and for the guileless way he had let himself be deceived. Now the anger had gone suddenly, not because of Pawley's blandishments, but because he had resigned. The decision awed him. He had no idea what he was going to do. This afternoon he had left the school without any clear picture of the future, but with the sense of having his feet on some sort of track. In relation to the school and in relation to Judy, he had had a definite existence. One or other or both would lead him down the track far beyond the week-end. Now he existed in relation to nothing—to nobody. The life that he had begun to build up since burning his boats in England, the context into which he had put himself, had vanished. He was alone with a small suitcase, a bit of money, and nowhere to go. He might have been better off without the money. The lack of money would have dictated the future. Perhaps it would have sent him along the track to the doctor's dispensary, if only he'd had Judy's courage. Judy's courage? If he had been mistaken about the frankness in Judy's eyes, he could have been mistaken about her courage as well. How sick it all made him feel! To remember his ludicrous infatuation—to remember how he had seized on Judy to convince himself of his existence, to make her the heroine of his dreams. To remember himself protesting that the lingering dreams of adolescence were not to be realized, and at the same time believing, always inwardly believing, that their realization lay only just ahead. . . . And he set himself up to guide the young!

He gave himself another rum.

He saw now why men took to drink. It was the sense of existing in relation to nothing—which was not existing at all. It was uncomfortable not to exist, so you sought an existence in relation to the bottle. The bottle gave you something to think about and hope for, and finally put you in a state in which not only did your own existence become of great significance, but the whole world existed for you and revolved about your person.

But he lacked the perseverance to attain this condition in solitude tonight, and presently he left the rum and began to unpack the bag. In the bottom of the bag was the wooden elephant. He took it out, remembering how all that week he had kept it pointed to the window. He felt like smashing it on the floor. Then he thought of a better way to show his disillusionment, and he planted it down firmly on the table with its trunk towards the door. At the same moment there was a knock.

"Come in," he said.

It was Mrs. Pawley.

"Douglas," she said, "can I speak to you for a minute?" She wore the sort of expression that she might have worn if she had been breaking the feud to come and tell him that Pawley had just hanged himself from a rafter. However, this did not appear to have happened.

"We must clear this up," she said. "My husband's told me you've given notice because of the cable. I don't know what happened, but I gave it to my maid to bring you. I've just asked her about it. She says she put it on your desk."

"I didn't get it," he said.

"Perhaps it's mixed up with your papers. Ivy might have moved it when she was tidying."

He went to his desk. There was a mass of stuff in his trays because last week he had been too busy climbing Alpine precipices to do much work. He didn't expect to find the cable, all the same. He turned over the papers. Presently he came across a buff envelope amongst some English essays. It was the cable.

"I'm sorry." He felt damned foolish. "I ought to have thought of it. Ivy's done this before. I wasn't expecting a cable, though."

He waited for her righteous indignation. It didn't come. She said without anger :

"I hope you'll tell my husband you're staying now."

"I wasn't going just because of this. I tried to make it clear to Mr. Pawley."

"You're going because of me," she said.

"Not entirely."

"Yes, I know you are. I've been behaving very badly. I want to apologize."

"It's been my fault as well."

"No," she said. "I've been behaving inexcusably. What you told my husband was true. I opened your cable. I read it."

He turned over the envelope. The flap was torn at the edges, but had been stuck down again. He felt no anger about this now. The blow-lamp had gone right out.

"I hope it amused you," he said. "It didn't amuse me much."

"You've been hurt, haven't you?" she said. "I'm sorry."

"You weren't sorry last week," he said.

"No," she said. "But I'm sorry now." Her face was tense. She was standing just inside the doorway. She was wearing her navy slacks and a yellow blouse. Her hands were clutched together in front of her. "I'm sorry because I don't want you to go—for any reason." Her voice shook a bit. "Before you came to the school, I thought I couldn't stand it up here any longer. I don't think I could stand it if you left."

206

He was still sitting at the desk. The world had become very small. The whole world was the bungalow, and beyond there was only darkness. He had the sense of existing again, after a fashion, in relation to Mrs. Pawley.

After a time he said :

"Can I give you a glass of rum?"

She stared at him without answering. He got up and went to the door behind her and closed it.

"What are you doing?" she said. She was trembling.

"Entertaining the headmaster's wife after dark," he said. "Did you bring the dogs?"

She shook her head. He fetched a glass and mixed a rum and ginger, and put it down on the table. Mrs. Pawley gave a queer laugh and tried to sound conversational :

"That girl let you down, didn't she?"

"Yes," he said. "You were right about her the first time you came here. She was worthless."

"I thought she was." She came across to the table. "Douglas, you've given me an enormous drink. Are you trying to make me drunk?"

"Yes," he said.

She picked up the glass. Her hand was trembling so much that she had to put it down again.

"I don't know what's the matter with me." She laughed awkwardly.

"I don't need to make you drunk," he said.

The trembling gradually became worse and she began to shudder. They were long shudders that ran right through her body; and there was an expression on her face that might have been of terrible, unspeakable anguish.

CHAPTER FIFTEEN

THE barber had been up to the school the day before, and Duffield's hair was clipped as close as a convict's. He was in the best of tempers.

"That was a short week-end, wasn't it?" he said as Douglas sat down to breakfast. "What's up? Couldn't you bear being parted from the old Alma Mater?"

"No, I couldn't keep away." Douglas was trying to look

bright, but he felt as though everything that had happened could be read on his face at a glance.

However, Duffield was not bothering to read. He was not even going to demand a further explanation of Douglas's early return. The reason for this lack of interest shortly became clear. He had some news of his own. He was delighted about Douglas's unexpected appearance because it meant he could tell it sooner.

"I suppose you've heard what happened yesterday?"

"No?"

"Alan was disobedient. I took a slipper to him."

He paused to give this full effect. He was smiling. His face rarely stated anything more complicated than the fact that he was in a good or a bad humour, but now there was restrained though unmistakable triumph in his smile. It was the triumph of a man who had won through against heavy odds.

"I gave him a damn sound whacking. I'm surprised you didn't hear it down in Kingston."

Douglas said lightly, because it was obviously expected of him, "So we're back to the evil days of torture."

"I don't know about torture," Duffield said. "I only know it did him a blighted lot of good. If he misbehaves again this term, I'll eat my Midgley and Wade." The Midgley and Wade was his mathematics text-book. "It's made the others sit up, too. This place was as quiet as a cemetery yesterday—all the children creeping about like mice."

"What did Pawley say?"

Duffield radiated the pleasures of victory.

"More to the point if you asked what I said to Pawley."

He recounted the incident in detail. Alan had been talking in class despite a previous ticking-off, and Duffield had told him to come down and see him in his bungalow afterwards. He had given Alan a good lecture, and then asked him which he would rather have : a bad end-of-term report or a beating. The fact that Alan had elected to receive the beating, of his own volition, seemed to Duffield a cunning circumvention of Pawley's ban on corporal punishment. He gave Douglas an intimate account of the manner in which the beating had been administered, and of Alan's manly endurance. After dealing out six of the best on "the place provided by nature," he had shaken Alan's hand and "felt himself respected" for the first time since he had been at Blue Mountain School. The news of his anarchy travelled quickly to Pawley, who called him down to his study. Duffield faced him unrepentant. He pointed out that what had been good enough for the best schools in England for generations was good enough for him— and if it wasn't good enough for Pawley, he was ready to give notice. This put Pawley on the defensive, and being much more frightened of losing his staff than his principles, he told Duffield that he quite saw his point of view about giving Alan an option, but that in future he would feel happier if they put their heads together before resorting to slippers.

"But we'll let the future take care of itself," Duffield told Douglas significantly. "I don't mind betting there'll be a sight more sore bottoms here next term than there were last. And between you and me," he winked, "I don't see why we should wear out our slippers when the whole blighted mountainside is covered with bamboo."

Douglas ran into Pawley in the hall of the Great House later that morning. Neither of them mentioned his resignation. Pawley probably took it for granted that it had been withdrawn. He beamed in his most expansive manner.

"I hear that you sorted out that business with my wife last night. I'm most relieved. These little misunderstandings are bound to arise from time to time—but we always manage to surmount them if we keep our heads."

Douglas had no idea how much Pawley knew. It was too disturbing to think that his air of satisfaction was due to anything more than the settlement of the cable affair—he could do without Pawley's beaming acquiescence; yet at lunch, when Mrs. Pawley came in, he found it hard to believe that anyone, adult or child, could have overlooked the change in her. It was so palpable that he was aware of it even across the room. He was appalled. Instead of her usual impatient, neurotic self, she gave off a positive glow. The discontent had gone from her face. It was the first time he had seen her looking really happy. In her presence the children at her table were usually subdued, but today they were full of gaiety. There was also laughter coming from Pawley's table—and even from Duffield's, where the fear he had created was being held in temporary abeyance by his present exceptional good-humour. The atmosphere in the dining-room had never been more light-hearted. Probably everybody put it down to the approach of the holidays.

Douglas skipped coffee in the common-room and went down to his bungalow. Later in the afternoon he strolled round the grounds. It was Saturday, and the children were free. Rosemary was working in the modelling shed, trying to make a piece of clay look like a cat. John was hammering away contentedly in his tree-house, adding an extension so that he could hold larger parties. Silvia was in the garage, urging Joe to explain the gears of a car, for in the future she had planned she saw herself, amongst other rôles, as Douglas's chauffeuse. Other children were playing amongst the junipers. They stopped when they saw him and invited him to join them. In the attitude of most of them he was aware of confidence and respect, unmixed with fear. If he hadn't messed things up for himself, he might have made a success of this job. . . . But that was absurd, the way he had messed things up was the measure of his incompetence, and the confidence and respect of the children had been as meretriciously achieved as Mrs. Pawley's beatitude. It was not like being an engineer who could build great bridges and yet fail as a man, or a poet who could create beauty out of his own degradation. If you looked after children your function and your character were inseparable, and without integrity there could be no success.

He went back to his bungalow, wondering what to do : whether to stay at the school as a failure, or to set out with his bag again in search of a new existence. He couldn't decide. That night, after supper, Mrs. Pawley came again. Impatience had returned to her manner, but it was impatience of a different kind.

"Were you afraid I wouldn't be able to come?"

"You shouldn't have come," he said. "Someone will find out."

"I'm far too happy to care. . . ." She panted swiftly, and the slow shudders began. They seemed to come from some deep source, like tremors of the earth. "Oh, Douglas, why couldn't this have happened before? How much of the term we've wasted . . . !"

The physical change that had come over her was almost as marked as the change in her manner. Her breasts were fuller and less wrinkled, and the red irritations on her neck had vanished.

Presently he told her she must go.

"I'd stay for ever if you asked me," she said.

"I shan't ask you."

"Ten more minutes." She sighed. "Do you love me, Douglas?"

"No," he said.

"You're afraid to say it," she said. "How funny you are!"

Before she left, she said, "Oh, I forgot, there's a letter for you." She felt in the pocket of her slacks.

He became tense—there had been time now for a letter of explanation to have followed Judy's cable by air. It would only repeat the cable's shallow regrets, but he wanted it: he wanted to know that she had bothered to write, he wanted to read her insincerities. He wanted to begin a new chapter of prodding sores. . . .

Mrs. Pawley handed him the letter. It was not from Judy —it was a circular from a Kingston bookshop. He dropped it into the wastepaper-basket.

"Good night, Douglas." She clung round his neck.

"Good night . . ."

He nearly called her Mrs. Pawley. It was ridiculous: he could bring himself to touch her, and could restrain himself from shrinking beneath her caresses, but he still found the simple name of Joan quite impossible to pronounce.

The next day Silvia came into the library to see him. She had written another story.

"It's babyish," she said. "But you told me to write about what I remembered."

The story was short, and by far the best she had ever written, and also the most honest. It was about a girl called Eve. In the garden of the house where Eve lived there was a bush with foliage that spread across the path. Eve always contorted herself as she passed it, believing that if she allowed it to touch her, or that if it ever came to any harm, it would release a malignant spirit to punish her. One day her father told her that he was going to have the bush removed. He took no notice of her protests. Eve was in a perfect fury with him, and not quite sure that she could rely on the malignant spirit to punish an insensitive adult, she took her own revenge by breaking something inside his radio set. Before her father had found this out, he relented about the bush. He told her he was not going to have it removed after all. Eve now felt guilty about the radio, which she had no idea how to mend; and in order to create a reason for what she had done, she went out secretly into the garden and tore up the bush. Then she accused her father of tearing it up and going back on his word. She worked herself up into a terrible temper, screaming at him and calling him dreadful names. Later, eavesdropping outside the drawing-room when she was meant to be in bed, she heard her father recounting the incident to a friend, and saying in a puzzled tone, "She must have realized that I knew quite well she'd done it herself. I simply don't understand her." And Eve went to bed and cried, "because she didn't understand herself either."

"Isn't it silly?" Silvia said.

"No," he said. "If Eve goes on like this, she'll soon understand herself very well. And if she goes on persevering, she might become a very good writer."

"If you take me away with you, I'll write every day," she said. "I'm going to dedicate my first book to you. I already know what it's going to be about."

"What's that?"

"About the school, and how I was unhappy here, and how you were unhappy, too, until we discovered about each other and ran away together. The only difference is that in the book we run away in the middle of the term. It makes it more dramatic."

"It would be quite dramatic enough, anyhow," he said.

"I've already decided what I'm going to call it, too. I'm going to call it *The Peak*, because all the time we're unhappy we keep looking at Blue Mountain Peak and longing to climb it, in the same sort of way that we're longing for happiness. When we run away, we shall set off towards the Peak, and the book will finish as we reach the top. It'll be the first story I've written with a happy ending."

"We'll leave it as a story, then," he said. "If you try to live something like that, you're always disappointed. You break an ankle as you're climbing, or find the top in clouds when you arrive."

She smiled, unabashed.

"Oh, that part's only put in to be symbolical. We shan't really have to go up the Peak—we'll have to go straight down to the airport and catch the plane to Barbados."

That week passed slowly. It was only enlivened by Morgan, who kept threatening them with destruction by violent storms. He had even invaded the library and erected a blackboard and easel in front of the fireplace. He had drawn a map on the board, and he dashed in from time to time, regardless of classes, to record his latest prognostications in coloured chalk. Soon the Caribbean had become a formidable complexity of red zigzags, green crosses, and circles shaded in blue. By Wednesday morning one of the zigzags had found its way, as if by some inexorable compulsion, to the vicinity of Jamaica. At lunch-time its tip suddenly sprouted a menacing arrowhead. Even without reference to the explanatory legend—which had become confused with the outline of Florida in the top right-hand corner—it was enough to strike alarm. That night they pulled in chairs from verandahs, closed shutters, and generally battened down. Shortly after ten it rained gently for twenty minutes. The rest of the night was calm, and in the morning they awoke to another fine day, to discover that the zigzag had zigged out to sea again. The arrowhead, drawn with rather less flourish, now tentatively menaced Havana. The children were disappointed, but for Douglas the threat had served its purpose. It had kept Mrs. Pawley away.

He was impatient for the term to end, although he still hadn't made up his mind what to do. He amused himself with the day-dream that he really took Silvia away : not as a wife, but as a child, for if she loved him at all, it was in the way that she should have loved her father. He saw her, in this day-dream, as his one success—the rough clay that he had begun to shape, the unfinished creation that, with the possessiveness of the artist, he dreaded losing to the rough-handling of others. He saw her becoming the missing centre of his existence, the purpose of his future, the only pure love of his life. He saw her by his side on the beach at Barbados, scribbling away at another story; then he was introducing her to Europe—to the Opéra in Paris, to the Scala in Milan—and then she was writing again in the window of an English country house; and later, in a scene that was strangely Victorian, he saw her kneeling at his side to tell him that she had fallen in love; and there was a tug at his heart—but he had known this must happen, and he smiled. . . . And he smiled at this day-dream; for as much as Silvia's dreams, it must have derived from some film he had seen or some book he had read. Yet for a few minutes it had been vivid enough to make him forget Judy, and the anguish of waiting for a letter that never came.

On Saturday morning the red zigzag on Morgan's blackboard veered back towards Jamaica. At breakfast he said :

"It looks as though it's really going to hit us this time. The centre may pass to the south, but we'll get some nasty winds on the circumference. Anything up to a hundred miles an hour."

According to the inaccuracy of his previous predictions, they might have expected to be missed again, but on this occasion he was right. The storm started in the evening; but before that, about three o'clock in the afternoon, it began to rain. It began suddenly and rained violently, and Douglas sat just inside his bungalow door watching the cascades that fell from the overflowing gutters and splashed on to the edge of the verandah. In the midst of it Mrs. Pawley appeared. She was wearing Wellington boots and carried an umbrella.

"I shan't be able to come tonight," she said. "I've come this afternoon instead."

"You're mad," he said.

"Douglas—we've only four days left."

"You can't stay now," he said.

"Can't I?" She laughed. Her eyes were bright. She took off her Wellingtons and closed the door and locked it.

"Anyone might come," he said.

"Not in this rain."

"Of course they might."

"I don't care." She drew the curtains.

"Have you any letters for me?" he said.

"No; you're not still worrying about that girl, are you?"

"How absurd!"

She seemed to accept this, and came across to him.

"No," he said. "You must go."

"I wouldn't care if we were discovered—I might even be glad. If you had to leave the school I'd go away with you —anywhere."

He laughed at that. He would take a retinue with him to Barbados, and to the Scala in Milan.

"Why are you laughing?" she said.

He almost told her about Silvia, but stopped himself in time.

"I'm going, anyhow," he said.

The light in her face died. "What do you mean?"

"I'm leaving the school at the end of this term."

"I thought you'd decided to stay."

"I haven't."

"No, Douglas," she said. "No. You can't do that. You

can't go. You can't leave me here. I couldn't stand it without you."

She pressed herself against him, letting her tears and her passion do the rest of her pleading. The rain thrashed down on the jungle outside and pounded on the roof. He couldn't hear her panting for the din, he could only see the quick rise and fall of her breasts. Then the rain ceased quite suddenly, leaving the sound of dripping trees and gutters still running. At the same time there was the sound of dogs scratching and whining at the door.

"You'd better take them away quickly," he said.

"Douglas, that was beautiful." She sighed. "That was beautiful."

"You mustn't come again," he said. "It was the last time."

"You're not leaving, after all? You've changed your mind?"

"I'm leaving," he said.

"You're taking me with you?" She still seemed to believe that he might.

"I can't take you. What about your husband? What about the school? Anyhow, I don't want to."

"But after this?" she said. "After this?" She thrust her body against him again to remind him what she meant. He drew himself away and got up. The dogs were still whining outside on the verandah.

"You don't love me," she said, lying there.

"Perhaps not."

"You do really, but you're afraid."

"Perhaps," he said.

"I shan't go unless you promise to let me come again."

"All right," he said. "You can come again. There are only four more days."

She took ages tidying her hair and making herself up. He walked about impatiently, thinking he might leave the school tomorrow. There would be little teaching in the last few days and they could easily manage without him. By the time she was ready he had made up his mind quite definitely to do this.

"I shall come tomorrow night," she said.

"Very well," he said. It was safer not to tell her what he had decided.

"Remember how much I need you, Douglas."

"I'll try."

The dogs leapt on to her with their wet paws as she went

215

out on to the verandah. She scolded them, "Down, Rex! Down, Queenie!" and then smiled back at him and went off down the muddy path with her slacks tucked into her Wellington boots. It sounded as though it was still raining, but it was only the drip from the trees. The air was very fresh and clear, and Kingston never looked closer. As he turned back into the bungalow he noticed that Mrs. Pawley had left her umbrella on the verandah. It was still wet. He opened it to shake it before he took it inside; and while he was doing this his attention was caught by some movement in the bushes by the path, and he looked up and saw Silvia.

He was uncertain, for a moment, whether she had been standing in the bushes or had just come down the path from the Great House. Then he saw that she was soaked to the skin. Her dress clung to her skinny body and her hair hung lankly. Her face was quite white. She stood still and stared at him, and there was an expression in her eyes that he had only seen once before, when he had sent her back to the school from the expedition.

He was still holding Mrs. Pawley's umbrella.

"Hullo, Silvia," he said.

She didn't move. Her arms were skinny and white and taut at her sides.

"I hate you," she said. "You're just the same as my father. I hate you."

She spat savagely in his direction. Then she suddenly turned and dashed swiftly away through the mud.

She was not in the Great House. The other children were having tea, and had not seen her for an hour. She had told them she was going down to have tea with Douglas. He left them and went down through the garden to the garage, to find out if Joe had seen her leave the grounds. The garage was open and the station-wagon was inside, but Joe had disappeared. He walked on through the gates as far as the corner. There was no sign of her on the road, so he returned to the grounds and followed the path round to Duffield's bungalow. Duffield was on his verandah, but hadn't seen her either.

"Probably gone off for good this time," he said cheerfully. "What's she got? Another boy-friend?"

"I don't know."

"Well, I'm not the sort of chap to say 'I told you so.' But

you don't knock sense into children with bars of chocolate. I reckon you're beginning to see that now. You'll keep a yard of stick handy, like me, next term. You've heard what I caught Alan doing, haven't you?"

"No."

"Showing off his bruises to the other boys. There were a couple of girls at the keyhole—that's what made me go in. Doesn't do any harm, mark you. It shows it made an impression." He smiled. "In more ways than one." That was too much to resist.

Douglas walked round the grounds, then went up to the Great House, and then walked round the grounds again. After that he made a longer circuit, below the farm and through the jungle. It was six o'clock, and the rain had gone and it was quite a clear evening. He returned to the Great House, but Silvia had still not turned up. At half-past six he went down to Pawley and told him that she was missing. He did not explain why. Pawley hugged his head, and said that he had known they were not going to get through the term without some terrible disaster. Douglas left him and walked round the grounds again, and as he was returning towards the main gate he suddenly became aware of an extraordinary stillness, so intense and in some indefinable way so unlike any stillness he had known up in the mountains before that he was compelled to stop and listen.

There was no sound whatever—not the stirring of a leaf. He had stood there for almost a minute when a tree suddenly creaked, and at the same time he heard an unfamiliar noise in the distance, a kind of hum that at first he could only think was some car on the hill. Then it became too loud and too close for this, it was like the roar made by a waterfall of tremendous volume, and all at once he realized it was the approaching storm.

He looked round him. The two tall eucalyptus trees on either side of the gate were still perfectly motionless. He turned towards the farm. At that moment the wind hit the farm slope. It moved swiftly across the slope, throwing the fruit-trees into incredible tumult, snapping some of the banana plants with the first impact, and snatching the broad, flat fronds from others and juggling with them in the air. A few seconds later it reached the eucalyptus trees. They became on the instant a frenzy of motion, epileptically writhing and tossing like wild animals surprised by sudden bullets.

217

Douglas had crouched as it came, but when he braced himself against it he could stand and keep his balance. He saw that the gate had been left open. It was being flung back violently against the post. He went down towards it to make it secure. As he did so he caught sight of Silvia.

She was on the road just below the Great House, making her way up in the shelter of the bank. She saw him and came on. She was in a filthy state and her dress was torn. She reached the gate before him, and waited there, holding on to the post for support. He could see that she was laughing hysterically and shouting, but he could hear nothing for the noise of the wind. Then as he drew closer he realized that she was shouting, over and over again, the word that she had written on his bungalow wall. He stopped in front of her. She went on shouting, but now she was laughing and crying all at once, and the tears that streamed from her eyes were being torn from her cheeks by the wind. He took her arm to lead her up to the Great House, but as he touched her she started to yell. He slapped her face and she gasped and was silent. She stared at him.

"I'll tell everyone what I've done," she said. "It'll ruin the school."

"What do you mean?"

"I've been with Joe," she said. "It serves you right."

CHAPTER SIXTEEN

THE scene in the library reminded Douglas of an air-raid shelter in wartime; and for that matter the noise outside sounded something like an unending series of near-misses. The electric lights had gone—they had gone out in the first half-hour—and the room was now lit by four or five paraffin lamps standing on the tables. The children were lying on their mattresses in lines on the floor, the boys at one end and the girls at the other. The removal from the dormitories had been organized by Duffield, and had been carried out in an orderly fashion.

Duffield was now sitting on a chair near the blackboard. He had wiped a space on the board right across Morgan's map and filled it with the injunction, "NO RAGGING ABOUT." He had used the red chalk with which Morgan had drawn his menacing zigzags.

Morgan was sitting in another part of the library, pretending to read a book by one of the lamps. He was sulking. He had regarded the storm as his domain, if not actually his invention, and had visualized everybody turning to him, when it came, as the natural leader. Now that Duffield had usurped his leadership and destroyed his map into the bargain, there was nothing left but to pretend that there was no storm at all. He might have been deaf to the tumultuous fury raging outside. When something crashed against a shutter, sending a spasm of alarm through the room, he only raised his eyebrows in puzzlement for a moment, as if wondering why everyone had suddenly sat up.

Only a few of the children were really frightened : amongst them Rosemary, who had always gone into a trance of terror during even minor storms of thunder and lightning. Now she had turned deathly pale, and was sitting bolt upright on her mattress. The others were still in a state of pleasurable excitement. They had looked forward to the storm, and at last it had come, and only Duffield's tyrannical presence kept them from the larks that were a potential of this sort of upset in the general routine.

Douglas was sitting at his desk at the end of the room, impatiently smoking cigarettes while he waited for Pawley to finish interviewing Joe. He had now been waiting over half an hour—ever since Joe had turned up at the Great House from his small hut below the farm, with his whole family linked together on a rope. Pawley had insisted on carrying out the interrogation single-handed—he thought he had a better chance of finding out the truth. So far it had been impossible to verify what had happened by other means. Mrs. Morgan had hardly been in a state to bandage a cut finger, never mind to handle Silvia. She had been fortifying herself with thimblefuls all day, as a result of her husband's forecast, but nevertheless the storm had scared her out of her wits. Now Mrs. Pawley had gone in to see Silvia. She was not likely to have much more success.

Douglas couldn't make up his mind whether anything serious had happened or not. At first he had doubted it— he had supposed that once Silvia got over her hysteria, they would find out that it had all been sheer invention. But Silvia's hysteria had passed off, only to leave her practically dumb with fright. She could say nothing except that now she would have a baby. The fear was genuine enough— it was right there in her eyes. And then Douglas had remembered disturbingly that Joe had not been at the garage when he had gone there to look. He had not been up at the Great House, or at the lighting-plant either—and it was most unlike Joe to absent himself when he was supposed to be on duty. But for that matter it was unlike Joe to go running off into the jungle with little girls. . . .

Joe was happily married. He was only in his middle twenties, but he had a wife and six or seven children, and his wife was his real wife—which was more than could be said of most of the so-called wives of Jamaican peasants. He had been married to her, after the third or fourth child, by a real minister in a real church. He never got tired of describing the ceremony. Douglas had always like him, and he would have laughed at anyone who had suggested that Joe was the sort of person to go running after children. He remembered that he had, in fact, laughed at Mrs. Pawley at the staff meeting when she had spoken of Joe lifting girls up the clay bank. It had been during the period of Mrs. Pawley's hostility. He had supposed that she was inventing or exaggerating the story to annoy him. Afterwards he had followed Pawley's instructions and warned Joe not to touch any of the girls; but he hadn't taken the matter seriously— and nor had he thought anything of Silvia's recent visits to the garage to learn unofficially how to drive a car. Quite obviously the initiative for whatever had happened this evening had come from Silvia. But that was not going to excuse Joe in a courtroom. And nor was it going to relieve Douglas himself of the ultimate responsibility. . . .

He lit another cigarette, glancing uneasily at the door. Outside the wind screamed and thundered, battering at the shutters and then retiring, and then returning with fresh fury to batter them again. Sometimes a rumble went through the Great House, like the rumble in a house where trains pass below; and once the whole building seemed to rock. All the children sat up.

John said, "Mr. Lockwood, do you think my tree-house will be all right?" He had placed his mattress close to Douglas's desk.

"It's probably getting badly knocked about."

"Might it blow away altogether?"

"It might," Douglas said. "But that will give you something to do next term—you can build a new one."

"You don't think the Great House could blow down, do you?"

"No, I don't. It must have stood up to hundreds of hurricanes since it was built."

John was silent for a while. Then he said :

"Mr. Lockwood—you're not frightened, are you?"

"Of course not."

"You look it rather. Or are you just thinking?"

"I'm just thinking."

"What about?"

"About what would happen if the wind blew us all away in the Great House, and we had to spend the rest of our lives together whirling round in space."

"I wouldn't mind if I had to spend the rest of my life with you," John said. "There's nobody else I'd like to spend it with, though—not all of it."

"You'd grow extremely tired of me," Douglas said.

"I wouldn't." He was kneeling on the mattress and resting his chin on his hands on the desk. His brown eyes regarded Douglas unwaveringly. "Do you know what I decided the other day? Even though this is a special school, where we can do almost what we want, I'd hate it if you weren't here."

"Nonsense," Douglas said, looking away. It was the first time that he had ever had to avoid a child's eyes.

"It isn't nonsense. And do you remember when I thought I had leprosy? I felt like killing myself. I probably should have done if it hadn't been for you."

Douglas didn't know what to say except to go on repeating "Nonsense." He had been intending to tell John that he was leaving the school, but now he couldn't bring himself to do it. Fortunately at that moment Pawley's beard appeared round the door. He was holding a paraffin lamp, and the light caught his spectacles and they goggled at Douglas. Douglas went over to him.

Outside the door Pawley said :

"You'd better bring Morgan and Duffield. I'll talk to you all." His voice sounded rather weak, and he was looking haggard.

"What did Joe say?" Douglas asked.

"I'd rather you fetched the others first," Pawley said. "You can come into the dining-room."

Morgan came along in sulky silence, but Duffield was quite enjoying the occasion, with its opportunities for sarcasm.

"Well, Pawley's been asking for it," he said, as they

crossed the corridor. "I suppose he's now going to pat the girl on the back and congratulate her for getting rid of her inhibitions."

"We don't know what happened yet," Douglas said.

"It's pretty obvious, isn't it?"

Pawley was waiting for them in the dining-room.

"Well, is everything all right in the library?" he asked. "We mustn't forget that we've other responsibilities besides Silvia."

"It's all right now," Duffield said. "But I'll give no guarantee that they won't all bolt off and start having fun and games in the bushes the moment my back's turned."

"I'm sure that won't happen, Duffield," Pawley said. He had been particularly nice to Duffield ever since the incident of Alan and the slipper. "You've been doing a splendid job of work this evening—splendid."

He put his lamp on the table and sat down, motioning them to arrange themselves round him. When they were settled, he let his hands fall on the desk with a gesture of resigned despair, looking at them each in turn. Then he said :

"Well, gentlemen, prepare for the worst. I'm sorry to tell you that Joe has admitted it."

Joe had not admitted it—not, at any rate, to anything like the extent that Pawley made out. Pawley regarded Joe's evident alarm as an admission in itself. But it wasn't surprising that he should have looked pretty scared in view of the crime of which he was suspected.

He had begun by denying that he had seen Silvia that afternoon at all, but Pawley's skilful interrogation (so Pawley had implied) had finally broken him down. He had then explained that while he was working in the garage Silvia had come running in to tell him that she had just discovered a rare orchid in the jungle. It was a tree-orchid, growing out of her reach. She wanted him to pick it for her, so that she could present it as a surprise to Mr. Pawley. Joe told her that he was too busy, and anyhow he was not supposed to leave the garage; but Silvia went on wheedling, and at length resorted to threats. She said that unless he came with her, she would tell Pawley some dreadful story about him that would get him the sack. After that Joe reluctantly agreed to go. He had already noticed something peculiar in Silvia's manner; and when they had gone about a quarter of a mile from the road, she suddenly stopped and admitted that there wasn't an orchid after all. She had brought him there to tell him a secret : that she was in love with him. She told him to kiss her. When Joe laughingly refused, she began to threaten him again : if he didn't do what she wanted, she would run back to the school screaming, and report that he had forced her to go into the jungle and had kissed her against her will. Joe was already feeling frightened—she had deceived him about the distance she was taking him into the jungle, and by now his absence might have been noticed at the garage—and he kissed her perfunctorily to avoid further trouble. Silvia then sat down, looking quite satisfied but more peculiar than ever. She seemed to have forgotten that he was there. He turned away thankfully, and hurried back by himself to the school. It was ten to six when he reached the garage again. At six o'clock, when his duty finished, he went off to his hut down the hill.

When Pawley arrived at the end of this account, he sat back in his chair and said :

"Well, gentlemen, there you have Joe's story. I'm sure you'll all have drawn the same conclusion as myself."

Duffield said, "It's a wonder he didn't make a bolt for it. Still, you never can tell how these blacks are going to behave. I suppose he didn't have the gumption to know he was going to be found out."

"Of course it's happened at the worst possible time, when we can't get hold of a doctor," Pawley said. "I don't know whether my wife will be able to do anything. She's in there now. But I'm afraid Silvia gave her rather a cold reception —she's taken a dislike to her ever since that little incident in the dining-room." He smiled painfully at Douglas. "Well, Lockwood, it was you that persuaded me to let Silvia stay at the school—you remember, after that petrol business, when I was all for getting rid of her. I hope you're not beginning to feel you made a mistake."

He might have expected something like that from Pawley but it wasn't worth arguing about now.

"It might have been a mistake," he said. "But not because she's been raped. I don't think she has. I think Joe's story is substantially true."

"I only wish you could convince me of it," Pawley said, managing a strained grin.

"In the first place, I doubt if Joe could have invented that story," Douglas said. "Silvia must have persuaded him to go

223

into the jungle, and she probably hit on the idea of the orchid because we were discussing orchids in class the other day."

"We needn't bother our heads about who was responsible for organizing the expedition," Pawley said. "We're only concerned with its outcome."

"I think the whole of Joe's story rings true," Douglas said. "Silvia is perfectly capable of behaving like that. The threats she made were typical."

"I've no doubt of it, Lockwood," Pawley said. "But I take it Silvia knew the facts of life?"

"She did in theory."

"Then if Joe's story was true, she could hardly believe she was in a position to have a baby."

"Nevertheless I think she does believe it."

"Well then . . ." He spread out his hands as if there was nothing more to be said.

Douglas said, "Even when she was in a normal state she was capable of believing all kinds of things that weren't true. In a state of hysteria like that, I'm only surprised she needed a kiss to convince herself she was pregnant. Personally I'm very relieved to hear Joe's story. I was terrified that she'd persuaded him to go the whole hog. Now I don't think she did."

There was no need to argue that point any further, or go into the details of why Silvia had run off to Joe in the first place, because just then Mrs. Pawley came into the dining-room. Pawley looked up at her and said :

"Ah, Joan . . . !"

"I suppose Rex still hasn't turned up?" Mrs. Pawley said. Rex had been missing since the beginning of the storm. She had been more upset about him than about Silvia. "You haven't heard him trying to get in, have you?"

Pawley said, "Joan, I think that perhaps the matter we have just been discussing is of more immediate importance. . . ."

"You're not still worrying over Silvia?" Mrs. Pawley said impatiently. "There's nothing in the least wrong with the girl."

Pawley goggled. "You mean . . . ?"

"I've had dreadful difficulty with her, but she's settled down at last. Obviously she's made up the whole story. I suppose she's just doing it to cause trouble again."

"She doesn't still think she's going to have a baby?"

"She says she does. But don't take any notice of that. It's not the first time she's told a lie and it's not likely to be the last."

Pawley turned back to Douglas.

"Well, Lockwood, it looks as though you were right. There's no need for me to say I'm not at all sorry. We can all breathe again." He beamed, feeling for his pipe. While he was stuffing the tobacco into the pipe, he looked round at them all and said, "I didn't like to tell you before, gentlemen, but if the worst had been true it would have meant disaster for us all. I should have had to give up the school."

Nobody looked quite so distressed about that as Pawley had obviously expected. Douglas was feeling too relieved about Silvia to register any other emotion, and Morgan was still lost in silent gloom, and Duffield just said :

"I suppose a blighted kissing party in the jungle isn't going to hurt anyone. We could have them on the time-table next term. What about every Wednesday afternoon?"

A bed had been made up for Silvia on the table in the common-room. It was next to the library. There was no point in knocking on the door with the noise of the wind, so Douglas went straight in.

Silvia was lying under a blanket, perfectly still. Mrs. Morgan was sitting with her back to the door on an upright wooden chair, which looked absurdly small under her bulging figure. Her fingers were pressed into her ears. She had not heard Douglas enter, and as she caught sight of him she gave a startled shriek and clutched her breasts and closed her eyes. He thought for a moment that she had passed out altogether, but presently she began to recover.

"It's this storm," she said. "It's terrible. Oh dear, it's really terrible."

"I came in to see Silvia," he said. He noticed her breath smelt of rum. Her hair was untidy, and her face red and distraught.

"The noise is so terrible," she said. "It sounds as if the house is blowing down. My husband says it couldn't, but it's what it sounds like."

"It's quite safe," he said.

"I'm glad you've come, anyhow," she said. "I'd like to go upstairs for a minute."

She waddled off, probably to reinforce herself with another thimbleful. Douglas went across to the table. Silvia was wide awake. Her face was white and her eyes staring, but he could see that it was not the storm that was frightening her.

"You're all right now, Silvia," he said.

She stared at him as if at a stranger, without friendship or hate, with nothing in her eyes but the inward terror.

"I'm going to have a baby," she said. She might have been talking to herself.

"No, you're not," he said. "You don't have babies as easily as all that—not just by being kissed."

"I know how you have them," she said. "I know what you have to do. I did it on purpose."

"You only imagined it," he said. "You remember what a good imagination you always had?"

She shook her head faintly, the expression in her eyes unchanged. She was very small and frightened, and she was only a child. He had never seen her look such a child; and now he saw her like this he realized all at once that his attitude towards her had often presupposed an awareness beyond her years. He had seen her as she wanted to be seen, almost as a woman; but she had only been a child dressing-up. She had been a child that played at being an adult until it tripped over and bumped its head, when in pain and fright it forgot the pretence. The dressing-up had taken him in. He had never begun to understand her.

"You've nothing to worry about," he said. "We shall look after you."

The wind exploded again outside, and there was another crash against the shutter, probably the branch of a tree. Silvia didn't seem to hear it.

"It'll be a black baby," she said. "It'll be a nigger."

Shortly before midnight the wind stopped. It stopped as suddenly as it had begun, and there was silence—silence that muffled them in the luxury of velvet.

Some of the children had gone to sleep, and at the sound of the silence they woke up and stared round the room with bewildered, suspicious eyes. At first this was almost as frightening as the noise: it was as if the house had been blown away and was floating in space, for there was nothing but the silence of space outside.

The silence was broken by Morgan, who said sullenly:

"We're probably in the centre now. It'll start again within half an hour."

Douglas went across to Pawley, who was sitting on a mattress with his wife, leaning against a bookcase.

"I'm going down to look at my bungalow."

"All right, Lockwood."

He took a lantern from one of the tables and left the library. Outside, he was surprised to find the sky was clear and he could see the stars. He turned down towards the grass slope. Before he was out of the garden, he heard the door of the Great House open and close.

"Douglas."

It was Mrs. Pawley. She hurried down to him.

"That's rather obvious, isn't it?" he said.

"I told them I was coming out to look for Rex."

"What do you want?"

"Douglas—I'm sorry about this afternoon."

"About Silvia?"

"No; I didn't mean that. I'm sorry I behaved so emotionally at your bungalow."

"It doesn't matter." He began to turn away, but she held him with her hand on his arm.

"You're not leaving the school, are you?"

"I don't know."

"You'd only leave because of me—because we can't go on like this."

"We can't," he said.

"I know. I didn't realize it this afternoon, but I do now. I was expecting too much of you. That's what I wanted to tell you : if you'll stay, I shan't ask anything more. I don't care what happens so long as you're here. We need only be friends."

She had always talked like a bad novelette. He moved impatiently away.

"I'll see."

"I promise, Douglas. I shan't ask anything."

He went down the grass slope, following the track with his lantern. The yellow circle of light fell on a juniper that had been uprooted. He walked round it. Should he stay . . . ? He was indecisive again. John had said pretty things to him, and Silvia hadn't been raped, after all. Why shouldn't he stay? Why should he go off with his bag into space and exist in relation to nothing? It was better to exist in relation to this place : better the failure he knew than the failure he didn't know. . . . Or should he leave? If only he had someone to tell him—someone to stand over him and say "Do this."

He could hardly recognize the track to his bungalow. The undergrowth sprawled across it, entangled with fallen branches. He made his way down slowly, wondering if the bungalow had been damaged by the storm. It was in a sheltered position, because the wind had been coming from behind the hill; but he hadn't been back to it since setting out to look for Silvia—not since the beginning of the storm —and the windows hadn't been closed or the shutters fastened. If the wind had caught it in the right way, it might have blown the roof off. He wouldn't mind much if it had. He had only used the bungalow as an excuse to come out for air, and to try and make up his mind. . . .

As he stepped through the wet and tangled vegetation, he suddenly decided how he would do this. He would make up his mind in the way that he had often made it up as a child, telling himself, "If there's a slug under the orange skin when I reach home. . . ." Now he would leave it to the elephant : if the elephant stood as he had left it, facing the window, he would remain at the school. If the storm had shifted it, he would leave. . . . Anything was better than indecision.

The lantern shone on the verandah steps. He kicked away the stuff that littered them. The verandah was covered with debris, and the wicker chairs had been overturned, but they were all there. The windows were unbroken. He opened the door and went in, holding up the lantern. The curtains were still drawn—they had never been drawn back since Mrs. Pawley's visit. Some papers were scattered on the floor, but otherwise nothing seemed disturbed. He went across to the table. The elephant stood there exactly as he had left it.

So I'm staying, he thought.

He went to the cupboard and took out the bottle of rum. There was only half an inch in the bottom. He poured it into a glass and began to sip it neat, wondering where he would go for the holidays. He might go up to Montego Bay : look at the coral reefs through glass-bottomed boats and study the British plutocracy buying sunshine for sterling. Make a few resolutions for next term. Presumably Silvia would no longer be with them next term, but there would be Rosemary and John. He might be wise to discourage John's attachment to him—there was danger in that kind of thing. What was the best way to do it, though? Not the way he'd done it with Silvia—he would have to find a gentler method. Disillusionment without tears. . . . Unless of course he tried more sincerely to live up to the illusion.

When he had finished the rum he replenished his pocket with cigarettes, fastened the shutters of the bungalow, and started back to the Great House with the lantern. There was still no sign of the storm starting up again. All the lights on the airport were out, but he could see the lights of Kingston spreading fanwise from the harbour, looking very clear and close. The door of the Great House was standing open. He slammed it behind him, and went back to the library and sat down in the chair by his desk.

"Did you go and look at my tree-house?" John asked.

"No, I didn't."

"I wish you had. I'm dying to know if it's all right."

"You can see it first thing in the morning."

Five minutes later they heard the rumble of the wind. They felt its impact against the Great House, and the stone walls began to tremble again. Outside there was pandemonium. It was as if they were in a ship that had been launched, all at once, into a tumultuous sea.

"I can go to sleep now," John said. "I was only waiting for it to begin."

Douglas lit a cigarette. Most of the children were tired out after so much excitement and were trying to sleep, but Rosemary still lay with her eyes open, her face white. Duffield was dozing in his chair, and Morgan was asleep with his face buried in his arms on the table in front of him. Pawley was leaning his head against a bookcase, his beard stuck out, goggling at the ceiling. Mrs. Pawley sat beside him, occasionally opening her eyes to give Douglas a look of mute appeal, faintly smiling. He had not told her yet that he was staying—he would leave it until morning.

He lit another cigarette from the butt of the last, thinking of Silvia. What would become of her? She would find out that she was not going to have a baby, as John had found out that he was not leprous—but that was only the physical side. For the rest, she was back where she had started; back where he had pushed her, and all the good was lost and he had forfeited his right to help her again. He was no more use to her now than her father; for you couldn't turn over a new leaf and start again when you were dealing with a child. . . .

John said, "What's the matter with Silvia, Mr. Lockwood?"

"I thought you were asleep, John."

"I was nearly. Is she very ill?"

"She is rather."

"I hope she gets better. I hated her at first, but she turned out very nice in the end. I let her come into my tree-house whenever she wanted. She's not ill enough to die, is she?"

"Oh, no," Douglas said. "She won't die."

"She looked so frightened when Mrs. Morgan was taking her into the common-room."

"It was probably the storm."

"I don't see why the storm should frighten her. She's quite brave, for a girl. She can climb up the rope to my tree-house better than any of the others." He looked at Douglas's ash-tray. "I say, you've smoked an awful lot of cigarettes."

"I must do something."

He had smoked through most of another cigarette, with Silvia's terror still in mind, when something made him remember that on his return from his bungalow an hour ago the door of the Great House had been standing open.

"John," he said, "did anyone leave here during the lull?"

"Some people went to the lavatory."

"Nobody else?"

"Oh, yes, Mrs. Pawley did."

He knew Mrs. Pawley hadn't left the door open—he had heard it slam behind her as he went down the hill. He got up.

"Where are you going, Mr. Lockwood?"

"I want to see if Silvia's all right."

"Say I hope she gets better from me."

He stepped into the gangway between the mattresses and left the library. The hall was in darkness, and he felt his way along the wall, aware that his alarm was probably quite absurd. . . . Someone during the lull must have gone outside for air. Nevertheless, groping for the handle of the common-room door, he was almost choked with dread. At last he found the handle and went in.

There was a lantern in the room, standing on the bookcase, but the flame was burning low from lack of oil. In the dim light he could see Mrs. Morgan's bulky shape on the

230

chair. At first he thought that Silvia was lying on the mattress on the table. He went across. There was nothing there but a rumpled blanket. He picked up the blanket as though she might have been underneath it, and stood looking at the white, empty sheets.

While he was standing there the wind fell for a moment, and he heard a noise in the room—a noise of deep and fruity content. It was Mrs. Morgan snoring. He dropped the blanket and went across and shook her. Her chin sank deeper into the comfort of her breasts; and as he shook harder, an empty medicine bottle fell from her lap to the floor.

Finally the wind went with the dawn. The shutters shook feebly for the last time, and silence lapped mercifully against the walls of the Great House.

"That's all," Morgan said. "We were lucky. I wouldn't call it a real hurricane."

The children stirred and stretched. They looked round with bleary eyes, waiting for something to happen.

"You'd all better stay in the library for a minute," Pawley said. Then he came over to Douglas and whispered nervously, "You'll remember what I told you, won't you, Lockwood?"

"I don't care what you tell people," Douglas said.

"We must all say the same thing."

"Why not find out what's really happened first?"

"I'm afraid we can take that for granted," Pawley said.

They probably could take it for granted by now. Douglas had been out with Morgan and Duffield during the storm, but of course the search had proved quite hopeless. It had been impossible to stand in the wind. They had crawled on their hands and knees. The torches, which they had borrowed from the children, had only penetrated a yard or two through the darkness and the terrible metallic whip-thongs of rain. Douglas had gone in the direction of the gate. It had taken him over half an hour to reach it; and then just beyond the gate he had suddenly been lifted right off the ground by the wind and hurled across the road. He had come to rest against a tree, with a fierce pain in his back. The torch had fallen somewhere and smashed. He had lain groaning in the darkness, but unable to hear his own groans for the noise of the wind. He had thought at first that he would have to remain there until the storm was over, but presently the pain had subsided, and he had made his way back to the Great House, guided by nothing but the slope of the hill. Both Duffield and Morgan had lost their torches, and had already returned without news of Silvia.

Before Douglas had recovered his breath in the hall, Pawley had come out of the library to discuss what line they were to take if Silvia had been killed. The truth was too unsavoury, even though she hadn't actually been raped —the school would never survive the scandal. They would have to explain her exit from the Great House in the middle of the storm as some childish prank—make it look as though her death was due to mischievousness and disobedience, for which the school couldn't reasonably be indicted.

Douglas had felt too disgusted to discuss it; and he felt too disgusted still. But Pawley was anxious to have everything clear before they went out to search again. He accompanied Douglas outside the library door.

"I'm not thinking of ourselves. I'm thinking of the other children. We must spare them all the unpleasantness we can."

"If a tree's fallen on top of her it might be rather unpleasant, anyway," Douglas said bitterly.

"You know what I mean. . . . But we can talk about it afterwards. The important thing to remember is not to discuss it with anyone—not until we've decided what line we're going to take."

"We might take the line that she went out to look for your wife's dog," Douglas said. "Let her pass down in history as the Heroine of Blue Mountain School."

"I know you didn't mean that seriously," Pawley said. "But as a matter of fact——"

"I don't mind telling people that," Douglas said. "I don't care a damn what we tell them. We can try to get her canonized, if you like."

He left Pawley and went outside. The sun had not yet risen over the mountains, but it was quite light, and the sky was cloudless—an immaculate sweep of pale blue that innocently disclaimed the storm. Beneath it, in the clear, still air, lay the turbulent scene of disorder. The garden was hardly to be recognized. All the green had been stripped away as if by locusts, or as if a northern winter had descended all at once on this Caribbean isle. The trees had taken on new shapes and bore fresh white wounds where branches had been wrenched from their trunks, and the ground was strewn desultorily with all the flotsam of the gale. He stood gazing about him, bewildered, unable to distinguish the familiar landmarks. It was like the aftermath of some fabulous drunken orgy.

Presently Duffield came out of the Great House with two or three boys that he had picked to help in the search. He despatched them in different directions. Douglas set off down the slope towards the gate. Only one or two of the junipers on the slope had been uprooted, but the others looked strange to him, bereft of the Old Man's Beard that had dripped from their branches like tinsel. The two eucalyptus trees by the gate stood denuded and stark.

He turned off the path towards Pawley's bungalow, poking amongst the debris and the undergrowth with a stick as he passed. Pawley's garden was in confusion, but the bungalow itself had been sheltered and bore no signs of damage. He walked round the garden and followed the path back to the gate. Once, lifting up some leaves with the stick, he saw a patch of white. Instantly everything inside him froze : he had seen the whiteness of Silvia's skin. He looked again, and it was Mrs. Pawley's dog. Its hindquarters were flat, crushed by the trunk of a tree, and its eyes bulged out of their sockets, glassy and sightless. He let the branch fall again.

Suddenly he thought, I shall support Pawley's story, I shall say that she had always loved dogs, and had run off —against orders, but heroically—to look for Rex.

Until this moment he had not brought himself to believe that she was dead. She had fled, perhaps, in the hope of being killed, even trying to kill herself, but there were few cliffs in these mountains, and only by remote chance could a falling tree have struck her. She might have been injured or stunned—but not killed. It had been impossible to think of her dead. But now, vividly and horribly, he had seen her body crushed. . . . He would say she had loved dogs, not to save the school, but to avoid perpetuating the horror with useless inquiry and research. In time he might come to believe it himself.

He reached the gate. The garage was intact, but the adjacent shed, that had contained the lighting-plant, had lost its door and corrugated-iron roof. He searched inside, and then went out through the gate and down the road, climbing over a tree that had fallen across it. At the corner

233

he stopped, looking out across the valley at the other mountains. From this distance there was no sign of devastation. They stood in perfect calm, with the appearance in this early-morning light of being a fresh creation—a new inspiration of God. The sky was brilliant behind them, and he waited for the sun to appear—waited for its warmth.

He was still standing there when he heard someone on the road behind him, and he turned and saw John scrambling over the tree. He came dashing down towards Douglas, stumbling in his haste. He stopped a few yards away, panting and speechless.

"What's the matter?" Douglas asked. "Has your house gone?"

John stood there, looking at him dumbly with large, brown, terrified eyes.

"Have you found her?" Douglas said.

John said at last, in a tiny, tremulous voice, "It was my fault, Mr. Lockwood. I once told her how to do it, just for fun."

Douglas climbed back over the fallen trunk. He went up between the eucalyptus trees and through the gate and past the garage, and as he climbed the path round the side of the hill he saw the dazzling liquid light spilling over the Blue Mountains from the tip of the sun. The naked wintry trees were touched with gold. He went on, and the branches of John's mango tree came into view, leafless and sinewy like upturned roots. The house had gone, all except for a few pieces of sturdy wood; but as he advanced he saw that the rope was still attached to the branch, and was hanging taut. He went on a few more paces, and then stopped.

For a moment it meant nothing; he had been more affected by the sight of the dog. Then, as he stood there, he saw that it was still turning—turning slowly round towards him in the golden light, a tiny, lifeless hanging sack.

Behind the mango tree, on Blue Mountain Peak, the blue shadows dwindled in the sun. He suddenly felt extraordinarily cold. He waited. It would only be a moment now before he saw her face.

CHAPTER SEVENTEEN

PAWLEY was the last to give evidence. He had been shaking his head tragically all week-end, and saying that he didn't know how he was going to bring himself to face the inquest; but now in some curious way he seemed to be enjoying it. He started off by saying that as headmaster he felt himself entirely responsible for what had happened, and then went on to demonstrate that neither he nor the school was responsible at all. His speech lasted about twenty minutes. This seemed an unnecessarily long time to point out that seductions in the jungle and suicide were not strictly part of the curriculum at Blue Mountain School, but the anxious little coroner listened with patience. Afterwards he asked Pawley about Silvia's character. Pawley said, "She was a most hysterical and abnormal child. I identify myself with all that Mr. Lockwood said. We realized the hopelessness of our task very early on. Her response to our treatment was never more than superficial."

Douglas had said none of the things that Pawley implied —but it didn't matter now. He was hardly listening. He was only longing for Pawley to stop speechifying so that they could get the inquest over. It had already been dragging on for an hour and a half in the hot, congested library. The term was ending today, two days before schedule, and most of the parents had come to the inquest before taking their children home. There were also half a dozen newspaper reporters there, five of them coloured.

He looked across the room at Mrs. Pawley. She caught his eye and smiled at him faintly. Before he had given his evidence her face had been a sickly mask, but now the colour was tinting her cheeks again. Her eyes had softened with gratitude and utter relief. It was amusing to think of her passionate protestations in his bungalow a bare three days ago—her indifference to discovery. There had been no indifference about her this morning. She had come to him an hour before the inquest, shuddering with nerves as once she had shuddered with passion, begging him not to reveal why Silvia had gone off with Joe. Her husband still didn't know —there had been enough to distress him without that. She wanted to spare him the public exposure of her shame, which would bring inevitable ruin to the school. No one else knew the truth—if Silvia had dropped any hints, Mrs. Morgan had been too scared by the storm, or too drunk, to pay any attention. Everything hung on Douglas. . . . He had sent her away, promising nothing. He couldn't invent lies for the inquest. But he had too much on his conscience already without delivering the death-blow to the school. He could leave his evidence incomplete. . . .

He had been up at the witness table for half an hour. It had seemed ironical to him, while he was standing there, that the inquest should have been in the library—that the coroner should have addressed him from behind his own desk. It was poetical justice : like the trial of a king in his own throne-room or a judge in his own court. Yet it had not been his trial, after all. He had come out of it with his character untarnished, with something like honour. He had listened to his own voice as though to the voice of a stranger —listened to himself spinning words, turning the coroner's questions away from the danger point. He had been doing this to save the school, and the saving of his own skin had only been incidental; but nevertheless, as he looked round the packed library at the faces of the parents, watching him without reproach, he had felt a guilty relief that there had been an excuse to withhold the truth—to get everything over in the quickest, easiest way. . . .

It had all been shamefully easy; and when he had finished giving his evidence the coroner had said, "Thank you, Mr. Lockwood, you seem to have had a remarkable understanding of Silvia's mentality. . . . I'm sure you have the sympathy of us all that your efforts were in vain." And he had half expected, after that, to hear clapping break out in the room. He had turned away from the witness table; and as he made his way through the congested room a pathetic little figure had risen nervously and clasped his hand. . . . Silvia's father. Silvia's father who had once told him, "I've a great deal of confidence in you, Mr. Lockwood. I know I can count on you. . . ." He had freed his hand and taken his seat again, wiping the perspiration from his face. Well, he had saved his own skin—but only his skin, nothing else. The memory hadn't been effaced. It didn't matter what words were poured out into the library, what verdict was given—when he closed his eyes the horrible image would still be there waiting for him, nailed into his mind. . . .

Pawley was still making speeches at the witness table.

He was trying to prove now that it had all been for the best.

"In one respect—and I hope I shan't be misunderstood —we should feel glad that this occurred sooner rather than later. I'm afraid it would have been beyond the power of any institution to turn her into a responsible citizen. Frankly, we only admitted her here as an act of charity. . . ."

The coroner listened with patient interest, no longer writing. He was a small man with thin grey hair, and the worried, earnest look of a bank clerk superannuated after fifty years of faultless calculations. A young Jamaican called Bennett sat behind him and sometimes whispered into his ear. Bennett looked capable and college-educated, and he seemed to know more than the coroner about inquest procedure.

When Pawley had finished talking, Bennett said something to the corner, and the coroner said :

"Thank you very much, Mr. Pawley. There's only one other thing. About Wilson's previous behaviour . . ." Wilson was Joe's surname.

"As far as I know he's always been quite well behaved," Pawley said, without bothering to sound very sure about it. He had lost interest now that he had said his piece about the school.

"You've never suspected him of any other relationships of that sort . . . ?"

"It's never come to my notice," Pawley said.

"Thank you then, Mr. Pawley. . . ."

Pawley went back to his seat, and it was all practically over. The coroner read in a worried way through his notes, and consulted with Bennett, and then began to speak haltingly. He said that obviously Silvia had been an unusual and troublesome child, but there was no reason to suppose that she would have taken her own life without great provocation. . . . The provocation in this case, since all evidence pointed to suicide, was her belief that she was pregnant. Her suicide showed that she didn't want to have a baby, and it was therefore not very probable that she had proposed the act which had given rise to her belief. Unfortunately there was only Wilson's evidence about what had actually happened in the jungle.

"Wilson has told us that Silvia wanted him to pick a flower for her, and that after he had followed her into the jungle she told him to kiss her. In other words, she was telling him to do the very thing that sent her running back to the school in such a terrible state a short while later. I must say"—he looked round as though searching faces for agreement—"I must say, this doesn't strike me as being very likely. . . ."

Douglas heard this with dismay: he had thought that his own evidence about Silvia's nature had removed all suspicion from Joe. He looked across the room and saw Joe straining forward, uncertain whether he had understood, his mouth half open in bewilderment. Pawley was sitting just in front of him, looking satisfied and nodding his beard. He was probably hoping to please the coroner by showing his agreement—and Joe's shoulders were broad enough, after all, to carry the blame.

"Of course, we have the doctor's evidence that actual rape was not committed," the coroner went on. "But we know that Silvia was quite well informed on these matters —and if she believed she was going to have a baby, something quite violent must have taken place. . . ."

The damn, blasted fool, Douglas thought, and he stood up.

"May I say another word?" he said.

The coroner broke off, and said pleasantly, "I think we've found out all we need, Mr. Lockwood. . . ."

"This may effect your findings."

The coroner turned to Bennett for advice, and then said discouragingly:

"Very well, if you really feel it's necessary . . . but I'm sure there's nothing you need add to the extraordinarily interesting evidence you've already given us."

"I didn't realize this was relevant before." He made his way over to the table.

"Well?" the coroner said.

"I don't think there's any reason to doubt Wilson's story," Douglas said. "Silvia was perfectly capable of behaving like that. I've already explained how she used to go off and meet a man who only existed in her imagination, and how she smashed up my bungalow."

"Yes, you explained that very clearly," the coroner said, and waited expectantly.

"I'm positive that Silvia made Wilson take her into the jungle because she wanted to commit some sort of outrage. It would be unfair to Joe to suggest he was lying."

Bennett spoke in the coroner's ear, and the coroner said,

"Yes, Mr. Lockwood, but I'm afraid that unless you've actually got some new evidence . . ."

"I have," Douglas said. "She'd threatened to do something like that. She'd threatened to cause trouble."

"For any particular reason?"

He hesitated for a moment, and then said, "I believe she did it for my benefit. During the term she'd grown rather attached to me. She expected me to return her affection. She was hurt and angry because I didn't."

There was silence in the library for a moment, and he saw the movement of the reporters' hands as they scribbled away at their pads, and then amongst the blurred faces he saw Pawley quite clearly, goggling at him in surprise and dismay. That idiot Lockwood! Why on earth hadn't he left well alone?

The coroner had become rather agitated. Bennett spoke to him.

"Yes, I rather agree," the coroner said, nodding. He looked at Douglas. "I don't quite understand why you shouldn't have thought this relevant before. . . . However, will you go on?"

"That's all," Douglas said. "I believe Silvia went off with Joe because she wanted to hurt me. Afterwards she took fright at what she'd done."

"I think you'd better tell us more about this attachment, if you don't mind," the coroner said. "How did it come to your notice?"

"She told me. She'd got hold of the idea that she was in love with me. I didn't take it at all seriously, because I knew it wouldn't last."

"You'd told the headmaster, of course?" the coroner asked.

"No, Mr. Pawley knew nothing about it."

"Wouldn't it have been wiser . . . ?"

"I thought I was quite capable of handling Silvia myself."

The coroner tapped his pencil on the desk for a minute, and then cast an anxious glance about the room, as if wondering what was expected of him. Then he said diffidently :

"I hope you don't mind me asking you, Mr. Lockwood . . . It may sound an unnecessary question . . . but what were your own feelings for Silvia?"

"I took more interest in her than in most of the children, because she was more in need of help. But I certainly wasn't in love with her."

"And you gave her no reason . . . ?"

"I'd always made it perfectly clear that I wasn't."

Bennett prompted the coroner again. While he was speaking in the coroner's ear he kept his eyes on Douglas. He had hard, penetrating eyes and a hard, ambitious face. He looked as though he was confident that despite the colour of his skin and his crinkled hair, he would finish his career as a High Court Judge. He was now about twenty-five.

The coroner said, "You're married, are you, Mr. Lockwood?"

"I have been married."

"You're a widower?"

"No, I'm divorced."

There was another silence, and the heat of the library seemed to grow more intense. He felt the perspiration trickling from his face on to his chin and down his neck, and it was in the corners of his eyes. He took out his handkerchief to wipe them. Presently the coroner said rather uncomfortably:

"Well, we can't necessarily blame you for that. . . . I expect you've had a good deal of experience with children?"

"Not very much."

"But you've been teaching for some time?" He was genuinely trying to be helpful.

"Not before I came to Blue Mountain School this term."

"But you felt quite confident—that is to say, with a young girl who told you . . . ?"

"Yes, I felt fairly confident."

"I suppose you'd realized there might be some dangers?"

"It had never occurred to me there was a danger of suicide."

The coroner looked anxiously at his notes, and then asked diffidently, "But you're prepared to say now that she committed suicide because of you?"

"Not directly," Douglas said. "She committed suicide because she believed she was going to have a baby. She went off with Joe—with Wilson—because of me."

It was impossible to hear what Bennett was saying, but it was something forthright. He was emphasizing it by slapping two fingers of one hand on the palm of the other. The coroner shuffled with his papers, and said presently:

"Yes, I think we must try to get this a little clearer. In what particular circumstances did Silvia threaten to do something desperate, Mr. Lockwood?"

"If she found I wasn't in love with her."

"Didn't you tell us just now that you'd always made it quite clear to her?"

"I'd tried to, but she didn't believe it."

"But evidently on Saturday afternoon . . . ?"

"She evidently did believe it then. I suppose she'd been thinking about it, and realized it was true."

Bennett spoke to the coroner with his eyes still fixed on Douglas, and Douglas waited, feeling the heat pricking him on his shoulder-blades and round his belt. Then the coroner said, trying to make it sound like a question he had thought of himself :

"You didn't see Silvia at all on Saturday afternoon, did you, Mr. Lockwood? I mean before all this happened?"

He hesitated. For a moment he thought he might say he had seen her, and invent an interview that had taken place; but he could think of nothing on the spur of the moment that would stand up to the test.

"No," he said.

He heard the false ring of his voice in the silence of the library. The silence went on for a great length of time, emphasizing the lie, and through the silence Bennett's eyes still came at him. The coroner turned vaguely in the direction of Pawley, and said in his worried way :

"I must say, it seems awfully strange to put an abnormal girl in the care of an inexperienced master . . . though Mr. Lockwood certainly gave me the impression before of considerable competence. . . . However, I'm not here to——" He leant back to catch what Bennett was saying. It was one of those questions of Bennett's that he felt awkward about asking, and he thought about it for a minute, and then discussed it with Bennett again. Then he said :

"I'm wondering if you can help me, Mr. Lockwood. . . . You've no idea if anything could have happened on Saturday afternoon—anything particular, you know—that could have made her suddenly behave like that? I asked you just now if you'd seen her yourself at all. I suppose you're quite sure . . . ?"

He turned his eyes away from Bennett's; but he knew he couldn't tell the lie again. He saw the blurred faces of the parents and the reporters waiting with hovering pencils.

"I did see her," he said. "She came down to my bungalow."

"She didn't seem to be upset . . . ?"

"Yes," he said. "I hadn't been expecting her, and I wasn't alone. She was upset because of that."

The coroner said earnestly, "I don't quite understand. . . ."

He caught a fleeting impression of the ghastly paleness of Mrs. Pawley's face. She seemed to have shrunk, as people do in death.

"There was a coloured woman with me," he said.

There was only the scratching of pencils to break the silence. He thought they would probably suspect Ivy now, so he added :

"A woman from down the hill."

The coroner was looking sorry he had ever asked. He waited for Bennett's advice. Bennett gave it—he was going to be a judge before he was forty.

"Yes, I rather agree," the coroner said presently, nodding. "It would have saved us a great deal of time if Mr. Lockwood had told us this before."

It didn't take him long to pack. He had only the one suitcase that he'd flown out with. The labels on it still looked quite fresh. He closed it up, and then had another look round for anything he'd missed. There were a few stamps in a jar that he had collected for John and forgotten to give him. He dropped them amongst the torn-up letters and paper in the wastepaper-basket. Then he carried the case over to Pawley's.

Pawley was at his desk. He got up, smiling in an embarrassed way.

"I suppose you're off now?" He picked up the piece of paper on which he had just been writing, and said awkwardly, "I'd been hoping to finish this before you left. I felt it was only fair to let you see it."

He held it out apologetically. It was a letter. The niceties of expression had evidently given him some trouble, and it was full of crossings-out. It began :

Dear Parents,
  Although the recent unhappy occurrence at this school was held at the inquest to be the individual responsibility of a member of the staff, who has now resigned, you may be glad of the reassurance that it has been decided in future to modify our policy and maintain a

242

*closer supervision of the children. This does not mean
that we no longer have confidence in modern progressive
methods, and we shall continue to apply them as and
when we think desirable. . . .*

Douglas didn't bother to read any more. He put the draft
down on the desk.

"I like the *as and when*," he said.

Pawley took this in good part. Then his smile faded and
he began to shake his head with infinite regret and
puzzlement.

"I can't think why you never came down and told me
how Silvia was behaving, Lockwood. You knew I was
always ready to talk things over with you. If only we'd put
our heads together, this could all have been avoided."

"I'm sorry," Douglas said. "I ought to have told you
about the native woman too."

Pawley looked uncomfortable about that.

"As you know, I've never liked to interfere with the
private affairs of my staff." He played nervously with his
pencil for a minute and then brightened. "By the way,
you'll be sorry to hear that John's leaving us this term.
His mother was up here this afternoon. Her husband's
gone off with that woman. She can't afford to keep John
at a good school any longer."

"Never mind," Douglas said. "Close supervision might
not have suited John. He was always an independent little
chap."

"We're not making any radical changes, you know,"
Pawley said reassuringly. "It's only that I feel we've been
a little too lax. . . ."

"Of course," Douglas said. "You must definitely draw
the line at suicide."

"Well, I expect you'd like to say good-bye to my wife,
wouldn't you?" He came round the side of the desk and
held out his hand, grinning fatuously. He could think of
nothing to say, and Douglas could think of nothing either.
Then Pawley said, "I'm sure you're doing right to give up
teaching, Lockwood. It isn't as though it's what you were
really cut out for." He smiled more easily after these feli-
citous parting words, and went off.

After a minute Mrs. Pawley came in. She had no make-
up on, and looked very middle-aged and dark round the
eyes. She pulled a cable out of the pocket of her slacks.

"This has just come for you, Douglas."
He opened it. It said :

All over. Returning Jamaica fifteenth. Judy.

He tore it up.

"I didn't read it this time," Mrs. Pawley said, attempting to smile.

"It wasn't awfully interesting." He picked up his suitcase.

"Douglas, I hope you'll be able to think of me sometimes without—without hating me."

"Why should I hate you?"

"I feel it was all my responsibility."

He laughed. "You too? Mrs. Morgan feels it was all hers for passing out, and Joe for kissing Silvia—and John for showing her how to tie slip-knots. That doesn't seem to leave me with any responsibility at all. Isn't that good?"

Duffield drove him down in the station-wagon. He was being damned kind. He came into the hotel for a drink.

"It was ruddy bad luck on you," he said. "You were doing your best. But it's no use letting children run away with the idea that they can do what they want. The only way to knock sense into them—however, there's no point in going into that again." He was looking rather melancholy, and presently he said, "Can't say I don't envy you in some ways. I'd like to be leaving that blighted place myself."

"You could leave if you wanted."

"I've got other things to consider." He said this mysteriously. Perhaps he was thinking of Mrs. Morgan. His feud with Morgan had survived all cataclysms, and even fed on them; but yesterday Douglas had surprised him with Mrs. Morgan in the surgery. Duffield had explained that she was bandaging a cut on his finger, but they had evidently been getting on quite well, and they had both looked sheepish. However, this was not what Duffield had in mind now. He said, "I suppose Pawley didn't mention anything about me before he left, did he?"

"What sort of thing?"

"It's like this—I can't see Pawley sticking it out much longer up there. Not with that ruddy wife of his, he won't. I reckon I've a good chance of the headmastership.

244

Pawley's beginning to respect me, you know. I just wondered if he'd said anything."

"No, he didn't."

"Well, we'll have to see. Nobody in their right minds would give the headmastership to Morgan. The only thing Morgan's good for is digging potatoes—and, anyhow, he's a nigger."

The next morning a newspaper was brought into Douglas's room with his tea. There was a rubber-stamped message on it, saying that it came with the compliments of the manager and wishing him good morning. On the front page was an account of the inquest. There was also a photograph of himself. It was the same photograph that had appeared on his arrival in Jamaica, captioned *Welcome to Jamaica, Mr. Douglas Lockwood!* This time it was captioned *Mr. Douglas Lockwood.*

He shaved and began to dress. As he was looking for a clean shirt in his suitcase, he came across the wooden elephant. There was no wastepaper-basket in the room, so he threw it out of the window. After breakfast he walked into the town. He had no reason for walking into the town except to demonstrate to himself that he was not afraid to show his face. In Harbour Street he saw one of the boys' father. He crossed over to the opposite pavement to save the father the trouble of doing so. It was already getting hot. He turned up King Street and went into a soda-bar and ordered a chocolate soda. After a time he remembered Judy's cable. He wondered what she had meant by "All over." He had supposed at first that she had meant her affair with Louis. Now it occurred to him that she might have meant Louis was dead. In that case her first cable, saying that he was very ill, had probably been true. If it was true, you couldn't blame her for staying with him. She would have stayed with anyone who was ill and dying. She would have stayed with a dying dog.

He thought about this, and couldn't bring himself to mind if Louis was dead. It would have pleased him—it would have meant that Judy hadn't insulted him with a stupid lie after all. It was nice to find he could still feel pleased about something.

As he left the soda-bar, he nearly knocked into a seedy-looking chap in a filthy suit. It was the mulatto who called himself a poor nigger. Douglas said, "Hullo." The man touched his forehead sheepishly and muttered, "Good

245

morning, sir," and then made himself scarce. Douglas supposed he must have been reading the newspapers—or just listening to people talking. It would have been bad for business to be seen in the wrong company.

He felt rather shaken after this encounter. Then he remembered he had been feeling pleased about something. For a minute he could only recall the feeling, without being able to remember what it was. Then it came back to him. He thought about Judy's cable again. "Realize you'll never forgive or understand how much I wanted you." So she had meant it—she had only stayed in Buenos Aires because Louis was dying. Darling Judy.

Suddenly he remembered about Louis' address. She had told him she had burnt it. She couldn't have done. She wouldn't have known he was ill unless she had gone to see him. In that case he probably wasn't ill. He probably hadn't died. So she had deceived him after all.

He would have to decide what to do—where to go. He thought of going to Africa. Then he thought of Cyprus and Egypt and British Honduras and British Guiana, but they all seemed equally pointless. He thought he would go to the first place he saw written in print, and he started looking in shop windows. Presently he saw a label saying "Product of Jamaica." Jamaica didn't count. Then he saw a boy selling newspapers. The headline said something about Moscow. Well, Russia didn't count either.

He supposed he would have to go back to England. He could go on a banana-boat. He thought he might as well see about it now, and he turned back towards Harbour Street where the shipping companies had their offices. On the way he suddenly saw a picture of himself coming up Arlington Street towards Piccadilly and running into Caroline and Alec by the entrance of the Ritz. Caroline said, "Darling! You're not back? Look, Alec, it's my ex!" He stopped going towards Harbour Street and turned in somewhere for a cup of coffee.

In the afternoon he went to a cinema. He sat the film round twice. As he was going into the hotel again he noticed the elephant by the side of the path outside his window. He left it there and went in and had a drink. He lingered over the drink and then went out and picked it up. Someone had trodden on it. A tusk and a leg were broken.

That night he read for a long time in bed. He hoped that after he put the book down he would drop off to sleep at once; but when he eventually closed his eyes the picture was waiting for him behind his lids, in horrible detail and more vivid than ever. The brain was supposed to draw a dark curtain across disagreeable memories—but the mechanism of his brain had miserably failed him. It had not even drawn a veil. He tried for a time to displace the picture by forcing other memories into his mind, and by making mental inventories of the objects in rooms he had lived in; but all these images soon disintegrated and faded, whilst the mango tree remained, in its awful clarity, holding up its leafless branches, and the tiny lifeless body in bedraggled pyjamas still twisted slowly round in the early sun.

After half an hour he turned on the light and began to read again. He could still see the picture against the printed page, but much less vividly than in the dark. At one o'clock he made another attempt to sleep, with no more success; so he turned on the light again and smoked a cigarette. While he was smoking he thought of Judy, and he got out of bed and fetched the crumpled pieces of her cable from his pocket. He smoothed them out and put them together on the bedside table. The message read the same as before, and still didn't explain what she meant by "All over."

When he had finished playing jig-saws he turned off the light again and played consequences. The consequences of a mechanical defect in an aircraft was that he had met Judy, and the consequence of meeting Judy was that he had made love to Mrs. Pawley, and the consequence of making love to Mrs. Pawley was that Silvia had hung herself from the mango tree. Therefore Silvia's death was the consequence of a mechanical defect in an aircraft. To-morrow he would have to write a letter to the *Gleaner* about it, demanding more thorough inspections before take-off. . . . He only woke once more that night, and it was because his face was being stroked by the poor mulatto who called himself a nigger. A cactus instead of a hand grew out of the mulatto's wrist.

In the morning there was a photograph of Pawley on the third page of the *Gleaner* and a statement about the school going on. Douglas only read the first sentence. The date on the newspaper was the eleventh.

At breakfast he asked the waiter which island in the Caribbean was the nicest. The waiter said he would ask the cook. He came back and said the cook said Tobago. He pronounced it to rhyme with cargo. After breakfast Douglas looked for it on the map in the hall. It was a tiny island near Trinidad. He asked the clerk about it, and the clerk said it had nutmegs and pimento and cool breezes and beautiful beaches. He pronounced it to rhyme with sago.

He went down to the cable office. He didn't know Judy's address in Buenos Aires, so sent the cable care of the airline. He said he would meet her in Trinidad. The aircraft stopped there *en route* for Jamaica.

Then he went to the air-line office and bought a ticket to Trinidad and two tickets from Trinidad to Tobago. The clerk was extremely polite and said :

"I hope you enjoyed your stay in Jamaica, Mr. Lockwood?"

He sat down in a seat next to a window in the aircraft, and then a man leant over and said, "I wonder if you'd mind if I took the window-seat, I want to get some photographs?" and he looked up and saw the expensive-looking camera and saw it was Burroughs.

Luckily Burroughs was only going to Trinidad. He was going to do Trinidad as thoroughly as he had done Jamaica, and he said incredulously, apropos of an English couple he had met, "D'you know they'd been in Trinidad a week and hadn't been to see the pitch lake. It didn't interest them. Imagine coming all the way out here, and not wanting to see the pitch lake." Douglas didn't bother to say that he had no interest in the pitch lake either.

Burroughs kept a watch out of the window and took a photograph of everything they passed over, even if it was only a rock sticking out of the sea. When they landed at Antigua he snapped the crew and all the passengers and the fuel-truck, and then they took off again and he put away the camera and started to write the shorthand account of his trip to send to his sister to type for his daughter.

At Trinidad they put up at the same hotel. The next morning when Douglas met him at breakfast, he had already been out. He described early-morning life in Port of Spain, and then said :

"I've decided to go on to Tobago with you today. It's a place I've always wanted to see. It's the original Robinson Crusoe Island, you know."

"What about the pitch lake?"

"I'll do that on my way back."

"A friend of mine may be coming along," Douglas said. He hadn't mentioned it before.

"The same one you were meeting last time? Perhaps she won't turn up again. Anyhow, don't worry about me. I shan't be in your way."

He insisted on sharing a taxi out to the airport, and while they were waiting at the barrier he took a photograph of Douglas to pass the time. Douglas wondered how he would look. He was probably wearing the look of forced indifference with which a gambler lays his last pound on the roulette table.

The aircraft was three minutes early. It taxied up and he stood quite still and Burroughs went on talking, and he remembered standing like this before with Burroughs talking, and it seemed as if they had gone back in time. And then the passengers began to descend and he turned away while Burroughs went on describing the burial of his wife, and then he turned back and saw Judy coming down the steps. She waved.

She came up to the barrier, smiling, and she looked happy and unchanged and quite excited.

"I got your cable," she said. "What on earth are you doing? Passing through, or something?"

"I'm on my way to Tobago."

"How marvellous!"

Burroughs was hanging around. Douglas said, "This is Mr. Burroughs. We met in Jamaica."

"How's the Argentine looking these days?" Burroughs said. "I was down there before the last war. I expect it's changed a bit since then."

"I expect it has." She smiled at him quickly, and then said, "Douglas, I have to go on in this plane because the company's given me a special passage. Can we talk somewhere? I've only an hour."

"You've only half an hour," Douglas said.

"The plane leaves again at twelve."

"It leaves at half-past eleven for Tobago," he said. "I've got you a ticket."

"For Tobago?"

"Of course."

She stared at him.

"Are you sure?"

"I have it here."

"I mean that you want me to come?"

"If you haven't any other plans."

"I've no plans at all."

"That's the way to travel," Burroughs said. "Without any plans. The only way to enjoy yourself."

"Have you any bags?" Douglas said.

"Yes, one—it's in the plane."

"You'd better get them to unload it."

"All right." She went off.

"I'm glad she's coming," Burroughs said. "She looks a decent sort. I must say it's sporting of her to decide on the spur of the moment like that."

"We'd better fetch our own bags," Douglas said.

The seats were in pairs on the aircraft. Burroughs sat just behind, but the engines made too much noise for him to hear their conversation. After they had taken off, Douglas said:

"What about Louis?"

"Oh, he's gone." She laughed rather artificially, looking out of the window. "You know. Dead."

"I'm sorry," he said.

"It was his own fault. He should have stayed in Switzerland."

"Was it dreadful for you?"

"Oh, yes, frightful." She said it brightly, still looking away from him. "You know how people die like that. He just coughed all his insides on to the floor. A lovely sight."

After a time he asked her, "How did you find him in Buenos Aires?"

"He was waiting at the airport. He'd been meeting all the arrivals from Jamaica. He was sure I'd turn up." She looked at him. "I suppose you thought I'd kept his address and gone after him? You must have been furious."

"I was rather."

It was a clear day. The sea was dark blue and crinkled and motionless, and there was a motionless cargo boat like a scale model with a motionless wake.

"How long are your holidays?" Judy asked.

"I've left the school."

"Left?"

"I hadn't much of a bent for teaching."

"I never thought you'd give it up," she said. "I thought you were too fond of your pupils."

"They'll manage all right without me."

"What about Silvia?"

He decided to leave that until later. "She doesn't need me now," he said.

"What are you going to do?"

"I haven't thought," he said. "I haven't any plans after Tobago."

When they reached the Tobago airport they tried to give Burroughs the slip, but it didn't work. Burroughs must have known they were trying to give him the slip, and he still hung on. The first two or three hotels they went to in the taxi were full up. At another the woman said she had only two rooms.

"That's all right," Burroughs said. "You and I can share."

"I think we'll look for something else," Douglas said.

"It's a bit late to go on hunting around. This'll do for tonight. I don't mind sharing at all."

Finally they stayed. The rooms were adjoining and opened on to the same balcony. There were two beds in the room that Douglas shared with Burroughs. Burroughs locked his camera in the bedside cupboard and undressed. He wore blue-striped cotton pants. He put on his dressing-gown and went off to have a bath. Douglas went along the balcony to Judy's room. She was unpacking.

"Do you like my new shoes?" she said. "They're rather smart, aren't they? Louis gave them to me."

"Good for Louis."

"I had to ask for the money," she said. "He never gave me anything unless I asked. Except the benefit of his culture."

"Be careful," Douglas said. "His duppy might be around somewhere."

"I don't believe in duppies," she said. "He's dead. Honestly, you ought to have seen him dying. He enjoyed it."

"I can imagine."

"He insisted on going into a public ward so that every-one could see him. He kept saying he was dying in case anyone misunderstood. It was rotten there weren't any newsreels."

"Didn't he have any last words?"

"Oh, yes. He said I was to forget him. I wasn't to let him ruin my life. I said I wouldn't. That's probably what killed him."

"I can hear Burroughs coming back," Douglas said. "I'd better go and have a bath."

"Damn Burroughs," she said. "Why didn't you tell him to go to hell?"

"I'm no good at telling people to go to hell. I'm too progressive."

"Well, you are," she said. "But, anyhow, I don't care about Burroughs. Nothing can spoil this."

"Only duppies," he said.

"I told you, I don't believe in them," she said. "I'm not hauntable any more."

It was a huge bath. He filled it almost up to the waste-pipe. There was a toy boat on the side and he played with it for a while. As he was washing he thought of Burroughs's striped pants and began to laugh. He was feeling rather light-headed after the flight. He thought they ought to ask Burroughs to bathe with them in his striped pants to scare away the barracudas. That seemed worth remembering to tell Judy. He got out of the bath and pulled up the plug. As he dried, he could hear the water running out of the pipe and splashing into the drain outside. It sounded like the rain splashing out of the gutter from the roof of his bunga-low. Then the noise of the waste-pipe stopped, and he remembered that when the rain had stopped the dogs had been scratching at the door, and he had watched Mrs. Pawley go off in her Wellington boots, and as he picked up her umbrella he had seen Silvia's little white face and her skinny white arms hanging at her sides and her wet lank hair, and then he had seen her eyes and she had said . . . It didn't matter now what she had said—if Judy could get rid of ghosts, why couldn't he? He put on his dressing-gown and slippers, and he thought of Judy's smiling eyes, and he began to feel light-headed again as he went back down the passage to the room. Burroughs was already dressed, and was standing waiting for him, looking upset. He came over to Douglas and said in a hushed voice:

"I say, old man, there's something up with your friend. She's been crying."

"Crying?"

"Sobbing her heart out. I heard it from the balcony. I couldn't make out what was going on, so I peeped in. She was lying on the bed with her face in the pillow. I thought I'd better not disturb her. It's funny. She looked so happy this afternoon."

"She lost someone recently," Douglas said.

He nodded sympathetically. "As you know, I've been

through the same thing. You don't think you ought to go in? I was always grateful for the comfort of friends."

"I'll see her later."

Burroughs seemed genuinely upset. The bounce had gone out of him. He said he would just go out and get his bearings—he would be quite happy nosing around by himself for a while. He went off, and Douglas dressed slowly. While he was doing his hair Judy knocked on the balcony door and came in.

"Heavens! Aren't you ready yet?"

"Very nearly."

"I've been waiting for ages."

He wouldn't have known she had been crying, but she kept her head turned away, looking round the room, in case there was some trace left in her eyes. She noticed the elephant on the dressing-table.

"What on earth's this? Something Burroughs takes round with him?"

"No, it's something of mine."

"It's broken," she said. "Why do you keep it?"

"It's supposed to bring good luck and fulfilment of dreams and all that sort of nonsense. But it's not awfully good at it."

"You keep it, all the same," she said.

"You must have something to hang on to. I used to think you could make do with a decent hobby, but photography hasn't helped Burroughs much."

"I never had anything," Judy said. "I have good luck, all the same."

"Do you?"

"I'm here in Tobago with you."

"You were crying just now," he said.

"Oh, Lord," she said. "Does it show?"

"Burroughs heard you."

She laughed. "Isn't it stupid. I found one of Louis' buttons in my case. I'd promised to sew it on for him. I can think of him coughing his innards out without turning a hair, and then I get upset over a button."

"Isn't it funny?"

"It doesn't mean anything," she said. "You know what I'm like."

They took a taxi to another hotel for dinner, to avoid Burroughs, and ate outside on a terrace. There was an evening breeze rustling the palms. Sometimes when the palms stopped rustling they could hear the rustle of the sea, and there was the clean smell of the sea in the soft, warm air. All the stage-props of happiness, he thought; and he pretended to himself that he was happy.

Presently Judy said, "Douglas, why arent you going back to the school? Something happened, didn't it?"

"How do you know?"

"You don't laugh properly," she said. "Your eyes haven't laughed once."

He shrugged. "I'll tell you if you like."

While he was telling her she sat in perfect silence. He saw the happiness melting from her face. By the time he had finished she had turned quite pale.

She gazed at him without speaking for a minute. Then burst out all at once, in a kind of fury of unhappiness, "Oh, Douglas, you are a fool! I always said you were, didn't I? You are, honestly, darling—a perfect fool."

"You don't have to tell me," he said.

"Not because of what happened in Jamaica. I mean for this. Why did you want to see me again? Why on earth were you such an idiot?"

"I wanted to be with you before," he said. "I do still."

She was shaking her head, almost in tears. "It won't work. You know damned well it won't. Not after all that."

"Why not?" he said. "We're grown up now. We no longer expect perfection."

"No," she said. "No, it wouldn't be any use. You'd never laugh again properly. You'd never be able to look at me. You don't think I want you like that, do you?" Her eyes had become blurred, and a tear fell as suddenly as a falling star and stopped abruptly on her cheekbone. She brushed it away quickly and smiled. "I don't know why I'm crying. I never cry, except over cigarette-ends and buttons and that sort of thing. Couldn't we go and talk somewhere else?"

All at once he felt quite flat.

"Perhaps we'd better go back," he said.

They took a taxi outside. It was a huge open car with battered mudguards. The driver had to bang the door several times to make it close. He was grinning happily as if he enjoyed it. They started off, and a moment later the door flew open again, and the driver stopped and got out and finally fixed it with wire. As the car moved forward again, Judy said brightly:

"You needn't feel awkward because you've brought me

here. I could easily go off somewhere. I could go to Haiti. There was an Argentine chap on the plane from Buenos Aires who was going there for the cock-fights. He invited me to go with him."

"Do you want to see a cock-fight?"

"I believe they're much more gruelling than bull-fights, but it might be quite a thrill to go once. He'd send me an air-ticket if I cabled."

"Did he want to marry you?"

"Oh, I don't think so. He has a wife already. Right up my street, you see. And bags of money."

"You always cared so much about money," he said. "Look at Louis."

"Well, it's not too late to start caring now," she said. "And I'd honestly like to see a cock-fight. It wouldn't be half so gruelling as watching you despising yourself. And before long you'd be despising me, too. We should be a rotten couple."

"That wasn't how I'd thought of it," he said.

"You'd thought of it without Silvia," she said. "Without any ghosts."

"Yes," he said wretchedly. "I was never much good at laying ghosts. I wish I'd taken more lessons from you."

"It isn't something you learn. It's something you are. It's just being shallow."

"Or just having courage," he said.

They were going uphill. Two Negro girls in pink cotton dresses moved off the road into the grass in front of the car. Their eyes were caught in the headlamps for a moment, and looked big and guilty and startled. They vanished in the darkness behind. It was two miles back to the hotel. They went the rest of the way in silence. When they reached the hotel, Douglas paid off the driver and they went upstairs.

In Judy's room, he said to her, "I suppose you really want to go to Haiti?"

She shrugged, and turned away, and said lightly, "Oh, he's a jolly attractive chap. I might get quite a kick out of it."

"Are you crying again?" he said.

She laughed. "Only a bit. But if you ask me like that, I probably shall. I'm rotten at farewells. It doesn't matter who they're with."

"You can't send a cable until the morning," he said.

"I know. But I'd better send it then, hadn't I?"

"We could decide tomorrow," he said.

"All right," she said. "Tomorrow. In the cold light of dawn."

"I'm at my best in the cold light of dawn," he said. "It's the nights that are the worst."

"Oh, darling, I'm sorry," she said, looking miserable again. "I'm terribly sorry. You can stay tonight, if you want—if you really think it would help."

"No," he said. "It probably wouldn't. It would hurt too much to think how different it all might have been."

When he was back in his own room, he undressed quickly and climbed into bed. Burroughs had not yet returned. The balcony door stood open, and the air was soft and full of tropical smells. He could see the light from Judy's room falling across the balustrade on to the dry tattered fronds of the palms.

Presently he heard the door open.

"I haven't woken you, have I?" Burroughs said. "I've been writing downstairs—telling my daughter all about you. Did you have a good evening?"

"Yes—splendid."

He saw Judy's light go off; but down below were the lights of the little town and the reflections of the lights in the water. Burroughs undressed and sat on the edge of his bed in his pyjamas. He was writing again. After a while he said:

"You're not asleep yet, are you?"

"Not yet."

"I meant to ask you. What did you teach at that school of yours?"

Douglas smiled wearily and closed his eyes. Behind his lids the Peak awaited him, standing serenely amongst its dwindling shadows. Slowly, beneath the naked branches, the tiny lifeless sack began to turn.

"Innocence," he said.